BARE SKIN

BOOK 1 IN THE DS JAMIE JOHANSSON PREQUEL TRILOGY

MORGAN GREENE

ALSO BY MORGAN GREENE

BARE SKIN

1

He didn't know how he got in the box.

Everything was foggy and numb like the bad end of a heavy dose.

He tried to blink himself clear, but couldn't focus his mind.

This wasn't heroin.

He knew the difference.

His throat folded over on itself as he tried to swallow. When was the last time he drank something? When was the last time he remembered doing *anything?* And why the hell was he in a box?

His hands were bound and he could feel the roughly cut end of a zip-tie digging into the skin on his leg where his wrists had been resting.

It felt like wood under his fingernails in the dark and he could feel the corners around him — he was hunched over, his knees to his chest. There were air holes the size of his fingers drilled through the plywood. He remembered the feeling of the layers from that time he'd been made to help his dad build that bookcase that fit in the nook under the stairs.

Mum had wanted to have one made, but dad had said it was way too expensive, and that he would build one — with Ollie's help.

Why the hell was he in this box?

His arm was itching, the track marks enraged and fresh.

Ollie kicked out, his bare heels catching splinters as he thumped against the sides, listening to the noise ring in the room around him.

He couldn't see anything, couldn't hear anything except his own heart in his ears. He could smell fresh sawdust, damp earth, something sharp and synthetic, like bleach, and his own breath, hot against his cheeks as he pressed his eye to the hole above him.

He tried to calm himself, replaying the last things he remembered over and over in his head. It was all fog. There were streets, people he knew but whose faces he couldn't see, then there was someone he didn't recognise, someone alien to him, and then nothing.

His fingers traced the seams, looking for a gap. There wasn't one.

Tears burned hot on his face, his eyes stinging in the dust.

He kept searching, the rough skin under his chewed nails discovering the hard protrusion of an angled nail. The tip was sticking out through the wood on his right side — hammered through the lid at an odd angle. God, how couldn't he remember being nailed inside a damn coffin?

He pulled at it, hands still bound, and felt his fingernails pull back.

He wept more, digging into the wood around it, focused solely on it. The only weak point in the box. His only chance.

There was no one else around and he had to escape. That was all he knew.

He kept digging, kept scratching — every finger, both hands, until he could feel the wood scraping on raw flesh.

His wrists throbbed, the plastic cutting into them.

He called out as one of his nails peeled back off the bed, screaming with a voice barely his own.

But he couldn't give up.

And after who knows how long, he could get his fingers around the tip. Now he needed to get it out.

He didn't really wear man-jewellery, but he had a ring he wore around his index finger. A ring she'd given him — stolen for him. For them. Grace. He had to get back to her. Tell her he was okay.

He got the flat side against the point and pushed, wedging himself under it.

Whether it took an hour or five, he didn't know.

He could feel blood in his palms as the steel stabbed at his skin with every slip.

But slowly he made progress, a millimetre at a time, forcing it upwards.

And then it landed softly in the dirt next to the box.

He managed to fold himself up under the new hole and shove his heel against it.

With what little strength he had left he pushed upwards, feeling the wood bow in the absence of the nail.

He kicked at it, then kicked at it again. And again. And again. Until the pain in his foot was unbearable.

And then he kept kicking, not feeling it moving, but knowing that staying inside meant death.

People didn't get nailed into boxes if they were going to survive.

The fuzz of whatever was in his system was still lingering. He didn't seem to be able to concentrate on more than one thing at a time — but Grace was always there. Thin, brown hair, pretty in all the right ways. She was all he had now. He had to get back to her.

The lid came loose, nails creaking in the wood, and in a blur he was out. Sweat-soaked, filthy, crying, he flopped out and into the dirt.

The room smelled like a swimming pool and polythene sheets hung from the ceiling.

He didn't wait to see what else there was.

At the far side of the room, he could make out a door, outlined in the dim red glow of a tiny bulb above the frame. Next to it there was a crowbar, rusted and rough, silhouetted in the half-light.

He limped over, his legs numb from the box and the drugs, and pulled it open, grabbing the bar.

The light blinked off, the little plastic control unit next to it clicking, but he didn't care. He had to get out.

The stairs beyond creaked under his weight as he dragged himself up on bloody fingers, the crowbar clanging against the mouldy stonework walls.

At the top there was another door — old and wooden, and locked from the other side. There was no handle.

Ollie ran his hands over the frame, looking for the bolt — trying to remember everything his father ever taught him about woodworking.

He felt the hinges, the paint flaking sharply over the rusted screws.

The wood was soft to his touch. He tried to dig his nails into it and found that the two on his middle and index finger were missing.

He stifled a whimper and pushed the tip of the crowbar into it instead, twisting awkwardly with his bound hands, hearing it crunch as the rotten wood broke apart under the steel.

A wave of joy rose up inside him and he forced it down. He had to focus. Had to make his mind focus.

He managed to get the tip down behind the middle hinge and pulled hard, feeling the screws rake out of the wood, the threads churning through the dry rot.

The bottom one came away too and the door sagged, clunking into the frame as it held on by the last hinge and the bolt on the other side.

He exhaled hard, tasting blood in his mouth, feeling his heart pound against his ribs, smelling the sweat on his own skin, ripe and thick.

The last hinge came free and he stumbled, the door swinging away from him, twisting into the room beyond.

He scrambled over the threshold, the pieces of loose wood sticking into his naked feet.

He didn't even feel them.

Doors flashed by, and then the cold sting of the night air hit his face, stung his nostrils, made his yellow teeth ache.

A car door slammed over his shoulder as he drew in a sharp breath, turning to see someone coming down the street after him, walking quickly, searching the alleys and side streets for any sign of witnesses.

He recognised them from some forgotten dream, knew that if he waited a moment longer he'd see the inside of the box again, and whatever lay beyond.

Ollie's feet slapped at the road as he took off in the other direction, the sky a bloody shade of violet beyond the glow of the streetlights, the dawn not more than a few hours off.

He didn't know where he was going, his brain was a mess — foggy and twisted and layered up with who knows what. His arms itched. He needed a fix. That would make everything better. That would save him.

Ollie kept running.

He'd not eaten in days and his muscles were weak.

But he didn't stop.

Couldn't stop.

The buildings began to thin, and then there was open space in front of him.

He didn't see the chain before he hit it and flipped over, landing hard.

It clanked against the metal posts and he groaned, rolling over, feeling the side of his face grazed and throbbing from the fall.

He made out a sign to his right that said *keep off the grass,* and started crawling, dragging himself forward, feeling it under his skeletal body, feeling it rub against his ribs and his knees, both sticking out under the skin like tent poles.

The floor seemed to fall away underneath him and the sound of running water echoed in his head.

A river.

He could feel the cold coming off it, his skin prickling in the frigid November air.

His fingers curled in the dirt, the pain searing, and he got to his feet, staring into the black liquid. Could he swim it? He couldn't even make out the far bank, and it would be freezing.

He shivered and turned, seeing the figure there, just beyond the chain.

They stepped over it, held their hands up, approaching slowly.

A plane rumbled into the distant sky out of Luton airport over Ollie's left shoulder and he wrapped his arms around his sunken stomach, the air biting at his cracked lips. He looked at the river again.

The figure drew closer, only five steps away now.

Ollie's thumb found the ring on his index finger and turned it around, the metal smooth to the touch.

He looked from the figure to the river and back again, thinking of Grace.

He could feel the bank under his heels, knew that he could jump the rushes and make the open water.

The current was slow.

He could make it, even with bound hands.

The figure's eyes flashed in the darkness as they moved within lunging distance.

Ollie made the decision.

His thumb left the ring and his arms swung in a circle as he turned, throwing himself forward into the water.

It swallowed him whole and punched all the air out of his lungs.

He coughed, spluttered, took three cyclical strokes, and then sank below the surface, the blood frozen in his veins.

Water gushed into his mouth and choked him, his ragged clothes dragging him deeper.

The surface faded away, out of reach, and the ripples washed away on the current.

Above, the sky continued to lighten, the fast-approaching dawn casting a dim and silent light over the empty river banks.

Another plane rumbled into the early morning cloud.

And the city began to stir.

2

The crescent kick is one of the most difficult kicks to master in Tae Kwon Do, but when executed properly, it is one of the most dangerous.

Detective Sergeant Jamie Johansson had been practising it for nearly six years, and despite being only five-foot-six, she could comfortably slam her heel into the ear of someone that was over six feet.

And now she had it down to a science.

She knew she couldn't do enough damage with a punch to put someone down if she had to, but a well-executed crescent kick would do the job. Especially from her lightweight trail boots. Her partner made fun of her for wearing them — said that detectives shouldn't be wearing hiking boots, especially not in the city, but they were tough and she was as fast in them as she was in her trainers.

Which she thought made them a lot more suited to tracking down scumbags than Roper's black leather Chelsea boots.

He disagreed.

She didn't really care.

Smoking thirty a day meant that he wasn't going to be doing much running anyway.

'Come on,' Cake said, jerking the pad. 'Again. Like you mean it.'

She flicked her head, throwing sweat onto the matt, wound up, lifted her leg, snapped her knee back, and then lashed out.

Her shin smashed into the training pad with a dull thwap and she sank into her knees, panting.

Cake clapped them together and grinned with wide, crooked teeth. 'Good job,' he said. 'You're really getting some power into those, now. But make sure to ice that foot, yeah?'

She caught her breath quickly and stood up, nodding, strands of ash-blonde hair sticking to her forehead, the thick plait running between her lithe shoulders coming loose. 'Sure,' she said, measuring her trainer.

Cake was six-two and twice her weight. He was Windrush, in his fifties, and ran a mixed martial arts gym just near Duckett's Green. He was a retired boxer turned trainer that scored his nickname after winning a fight in the late nineties on his birthday. When the commentator asked what he was going to do to celebrate, he said that he was going to eat a birthday cake. Everyone thought that was funny, and it stuck. He had a pretty bad concussion at the time, which probably contributed to the answer. But there was no getting away from it now.

He pulled the pads off his forearms and rubbed his eyes. 'Coffee?' he asked, looking over at the clock on the wall. It was just before seven.

He yawned and stretched, cracking his spine.

The gym wouldn't open until midday to the public, but he lived upstairs in a tiny studio, and he and Jamie had an arrangement. It kept him fit and active, and she could train one-on-one. Just how she liked it. She paid her dues of course, slid him extra on top of the monthly for his time. But he said that having a friend in the Met was enough of a payment. That, and he kept nagging her to start competing — said she kicked like a horse, and that once she had her grapple game on point, she could probably go pro.

Jamie knew having a pro fighter coming out of a gym was a great way to bring in new business, as well as get another taste of the big time. But she wasn't interested in that. She just needed to know how to handle herself. And she did. Though it didn't hurt to stay sharp, and Cake was one of the few people she could stand to be around for prolonged periods.

'We've still got six minutes,' she said, looking at the clock on the wall herself. Her accent had all but gone now, but anyone with a keen ear would know she wasn't a British native.

And the blonde hair and blue eyes, along with her second name, would be enough to tip off anyone with any sense to her Scandinavian heritage.

'You earned it,' Cake said, heading for the office. 'And plus, I don't think my arms could take anymore.' He chuckled, his broad shoulders bouncing as he stepped off the raised matt and onto the rubber-tiled floor.

Jamie cast a glance over at the heavy-bag in the corner, thought maybe she could get some more hits in. But her shin was starting to throb. Maybe she should ice it. Probably a good idea.

She pulled the sparring gloves off and unstrapped the kick-guards, wincing a little as they came away from her ankle.

Yeah, she'd definitely need to ice it.

The smell of coffee beckoned her towards the office and she followed her nose, entering to see Cake standing over a hotplate, a stove-top coffee maker steaming away on it.

He was a simple man, easy to talk to. Everyone wanted something. Except Cake. All he wanted was for people to treat him with respect. And Jamie did. He would always go on about it. People don't have respect for this, people don't have respect for that. No manners these days.

She watched as the steam shot out of the spout and Cake lifted it gently off the heat, pouring the dark liquid into a cup that read *Sweat is just your fat crying.* She smiled a little and took it.

'You know,' he said, 'no pressure or anything, but there's an open competition coming up and—'

Her phone started buzzing in her rucksack on the chair just inside the door, cutting him off.

She put her coffee down, a little glad they didn't have to have this conversation again. 'Hold that thought,' she said, unzipping it and fishing around under the hydration bladder.

She pulled it out, held up a finger to signify that she'd just be a minute, and then took the call, stepping back into the gym.

Behind her, Cake slurped on his coffee.

'Roper,' she said, lifting it to her ear, drawing in a lungful of stale sweat. 'What is it?'

'Got a body,' he said bluntly, the heavy night of drinking apparent in his gruff voice. No doubt he'd been woken up by a call from DCI Smith a few minutes before. He was grunting like he was trying to pull on a pair of trousers. 'Washed up in the Lea this morning. Fresh one. Hour or two in the water at the most, supposedly.'

She pressed her lips together, rolling it over in her mind. 'A body? Bit above our pay grade, isn't it?'

Roper grumbled. He'd been a detective for years, but a few bad cases had him working larceny and assaults mostly. A body was usually reserved for the more senior investigators. 'Maybe we're moving up. Maybe it's because Henley's finally come to his senses and seen that we're shining examples of what detectives should be in this goddamn city.'

'What's the real reason?'

He sighed and she could almost smell the beer and whiskey on his breath. 'It's a homeless kid. Arms all tracked out. Drowned by the look of it.'

'So why's this being kicked up to us and not being logged as accidental or—'

'Kid's hands were zip-tied together and his fingernails have been ripped off.'

'Jesus.'

'Yeah.' Roper sighed again. 'We'd better get over there. Don't think this is going to be a pretty one, but Smith wants us on it. Take what we can get, I suppose.' The phone crackled as he put it down, the hiss of deodorant being sprayed in the background humming in her ear. He picked it up again, breathing into the mouthpiece. 'I'm heading out now. I'll send you the case link and meet you there? Or do you want me to pick you up?'

'No,' she said, 'I'm good.' She didn't like him being behind the wheel after a night like he'd had. At least not with her in the car. Though she never said it. 'I'll see you there.'

'Probably take me an hour,' he grumbled. 'Traffic'll be a bitch at this time.'

'I'll see you when I see you.'

He didn't say anything else before he hung up.

She exhaled slowly and rubbed her head. Henley Smith was the DCI and the unit he ran had a couple of cases going on just then. A homeless heroin addict turning up in a river wasn't at the top of the priorities list.

Roper may have seen it as a win — a way to get back in good with Smith and claw his way back into the meat of things. But all she could think about was some poor homeless kid getting his fingernails ripped off.

She didn't know why it had happened, but she knew that this city could be brutal. And that it rarely gave an inch. In fact, if you let it, it would eat you alive.

She turned back to the office, ready to tell Cake that she couldn't stick around, and found him holding out her coffee cup.

'I put milk in — skimmed, don't worry   should be cool enough to drink.'

'Thanks,' she said, taking it. 'Sorry, I've gotta go.'

He nodded. 'I get it. Same time tomorrow?'

She slugged the coffee. 'Can I let you know?'

'Of course.'

Jamie tapped a button on her watch to start tracking her run, and turned for the door. She still needed to get her daily quota in.

'I can give you a lift if you want?' Cake offered.

'No, it's fine. Probably be faster if I run.'

'Probably.'

She nodded to him and then dipped through the door, shaking out her legs as she walked, the sweat on her neck and collarbones already cool in the early-morning air.

Outside the sun was barely up, but the city was churning to life.

Smog was already hanging in the air and the echo of a thousand engines buzzed in the streets like a wasp nest.

She took a few breaths, oxygenating her muscles, and then took off, clenching her fists against the cold.

With each stagnant, belching car she passed, she confirmed that she was right. It was quicker to run. And better, too. It gave her time to think. To think about the homeless boy with bound hands and no fingernails washing up in a river.

And about how the hell he got there.

3

Jamie got back to her apartment in nineteen minutes and forty-nine seconds.

It wasn't a personal best for a five-kilometre run, but it was still fast.

She showered and dressed, pulled on her boots, and was out the door in seventeen minutes flat. Which probably was close to a personal best.

She was wearing jeans she picked up from a supermarket. She liked them because they had a three percent lycra content woven into the denim, which stretched a little and meant that she could more easily crouch, walk, and kick someone in the side of the head if the situation called for it.

It hadn't yet, but she had a long career ahead of herself, she hoped.

She jumped into her car — a small and economical hybrid hatch-back which squeezed around the city easily — and headed north towards the Lea.

It took nearly forty minutes to get there in rush hour traffic, and by the time she pulled up, Roper was leaning against the bonnet of his ten-year-old Volvo saloon, smoking a cigarette.

He was tall with thinning, short hair, and a face that looked like he was always squinting into a stiff wind.

His long black coat was pinned to his right leg in the breeze and his shirt looked like it'd been pulled out of the laundry hamper rather than a clean drawer.

He was perpetually single, and it showed. There was no one to hold him accountable when he decided it was okay to skip a morning shower for an extra ten minutes sleeping off his hangover.

What she hated most about him, beyond the cigarette stink and the pissed-at-life attitude, was that she always had to look twice to make sure he wasn't her father.

Her mother had dragged her away from him in Sweden, and now, she'd been thrown together with a guy who seemingly had inherited all his bad habits. Her mum said it was because all detectives were like it if they did the job long enough. They saw too much and didn't talk about it enough. Which led inevitably to drink, and drugs, and other women.

She'd spoken from experience of course. And Jamie knew she hadn't exaggerated.

Though moving them both to Britain seemed like a bit of a dramatic reaction. But then again, her father had given her mother gonorrhoea and couldn't say which woman he'd gotten it from. So Jamie figured it was reasonable.

He would have turned sixty-one this year.

Roper pushed off the Volvo and ground out his cigarette under the heel of his battered Chelsea boot.

Jamie looked at it, stopping short of his odour-radius. 'You gonna just leave that there?'

He looked between his feet, rolling onto the outsides of them as he inspected the flattened butt. 'It'll wash away in the rain.'

'Into the ocean, yeah, where some poor fish is going to eat it,' Jamie growled, coming to a stop in front of him. She folded her arms against the cold, her suede jacket keeping the worst of it out.

Roper shrugged, cleared his throat and then swallowed the phlegm. 'Never liked fish anyway.'

'Just pick it up,' she muttered. 'Throw it in a damn bin.'

He looked at her for a few seconds, licked his bottom lip, and then turned towards the river and walked away, leaving it there.

Jamie stared at it, weighing up whether to pick it up and prove Roper right, or to leave it and admit to herself that it wasn't that important. She didn't like the idea of touching something that had been in his mouth, so she left it and followed him. This morning, they did have bigger fish to fry. Whether Roper liked them or not.

There was a police cordon set up around the area and three squad cars and an ambulance parked at odd angles on the street. It ran parallel to the water, with a pavement separating the road from the grassy bank that led down to the body.

A bridge stretched overhead and iron grates spanned the space between the support struts, stopping debris from washing into the Thames. It looked like the body had got caught on one and then dragged to shore.

Some bystanders had gathered on the bridge and were looking down, at a loss for anything else to do than hang around, hoping for a look at a corpse.

Jamie dragged her eyes away from them and looked around. The buildings lining the river were mostly residential. Blocks of apartments. No wonder the body had been seen quickly.

There were six uniformed officers on scene, two of whom were standing guard in front of the privacy tent that had been set up on the bank. It looked like they'd fished the body out onto the grass. Jamie was a little glad she didn't have to wade into the water.

To the right, a man in his sixties was being interviewed by one of the officers. He was wrapped in a foil blanket and his khaki trousers were still soaked through. Had he been the one to pull the body out? It took a certain kind of person to jump into a river to help someone rather than call it in. Especially in November.

That made three officers. She continued to search. She could see another two in the distance, checking the river and talking to pedestrians. The conversations were mostly comprised of them saying the words, 'I can't tell you that, sorry,' to people who kept asking what had happened in a hundred different ways. Jamie was glad her days of crowd control were over. She'd been a uniformed officer for seven years. The day she'd graduated to plainclothes was one of the happiest of her life. For all the shit her father did, he was one hell of a detective, and she'd always wanted to be one — minus the liver cirrhosis and gonorrhoea, of course. She was teetotal.

The sixth officer was filling out a report and talking to the paramedics. If the victim had washed up in the river in November then there would have been nothing they could do. But they had to be called. It was the way things worked.

She sighed and sniffed the air. The smell of dirty water hung thickly in it. They were supposed to be running a clean-up initiative. Whether they had and failed, or they'd succeeded and it had grown filthy again she wasn't sure. Either way, she wasn't fancying a swim.

'Johansson,' Roper called from the tent, beckoning her over, the report from the uniformed officer already in his hand. 'Come on.'

She approached and he held the edge of the door-flap open for her so she could pass inside.

It was eight feet by eight feet, and the translucent material made everything bright with daylight.

The kid in front of them could have been no more than eighteen or nineteen. He was skinny and had thick curly brown hair. His skin was blued from the cold and had the distinctly greyish look of someone who did more drugs than ate food. He was lying on his back on the bank, eyes closed, hands bound together on his stomach. His clothes were enough to tell them that he was homeless. It was charity shop mix and match. A pair of jeans that were two sizes too big, tied tight around pronounced hip bones with a shoelace. He was wearing a t-shirt with the cookie monster on it that looked as old as he was. But that was it. He had no jacket despite the time of year and no socks or shoes.

Jamie crouched down, pulling a pair of latex gloves from her jacket pocket. She had a box of them in the car. 'We got an ID?' she asked, not looking up. She knew Roper wouldn't get down next to her. He didn't have the stamina for it for one, and with his hangover the smell would make him puke.

He'd leave the close inspection to her.

'Uh, yeah. He matches the description of a missing person's — Oliver Hammond. Eighteen years old. No positive ID yet though. No picture on file.'

'Eighteen,' Jamie mumbled, looking over him more closely. 'Jesus.'

'Yup.' Roper sighed. 'Probably scored, got high, took a little stroll, fell in the river… And here we are.'

'Did he zip-tie his hands together before or after shooting up?' She side-eyed him as he scrolled through something on his phone. She hoped it was the missing person's report, but thought it was more likely to be one of the daily news items his phone prepared for him.

'I'm just testing you,' he said absently. 'What else d'you see?'

Jamie pursed her lips. No one seemed to care when homeless people turned up dead. There'd been eight this month alone in the city — two of which had been floaters like this. She'd checked it out waiting at some traffic lights. There were more than a hundred and forty homeless missing persons reported in the last six months in London. Most cases were never closed. She grimaced at the thought and went back to her inspection.

Oliver's wrists were rubbed raw from the zip-tie, but that looked self-inflicted. She craned her neck to see his arms. His elbows were grazed and rubbed raw, and the insides were tracked out, like Roper had said. He wasn't new to the needle. She didn't need to check his ankles and toes to know that they'd be the same.

She lingered on his fingers, honing in on the ones with missing nails.

'Ripped out,' Roper said, watching as she lifted and straightened his fingers, careful not to disturb anything before the SOCOs showed up to take their photographs.

In a perfect world the body would have stayed in situ in the water, but these things couldn't be helped.

She inspected the middle and the index fingers on the right hand — the nails were completely gone.

'Torture,' Roper added to the silence. 'Probably over the heroin.

You know, *where's my money?* Whack.' He made a pulling motion as if he had pliers in his hand.

Usually, she just let him talk.

Jamie found it was better not to say anything unless you needed to.

But this time, she did need to. Because Roper was wrong.

'I don't think so,' she said. 'Look at this.'

Roper screwed up his face and peered down, not leaning in. 'Looks like ripped out fingernails to me.'

'If they were ripped out there'd be less damage here, to the cuticle.'

'The skin?'

'Yeah, Roper, the skin. See the way it's split? Pushed back and flattened? Means the nails were lifted off from the tip, not pulled.'

He raised an eyebrow incredulously. 'Your dad teach you that one?'

She gritted her teeth and let the annoyance welling in her dissipate. Every time she spotted something he didn't he made a crack like that. She expected it considering who her father was — but it was getting old now. She'd been with the Met nearly ten years, and her father had been dead for fourteen. But she still couldn't get away from it. Jörgen Johansson was one of the most decorated detectives in Swedish history, with more convictions than any other police officer, and she didn't know if she'd ever outlive it.

The worst part of all was that he *did* teach her that. Along with most of the other things she knew about detective work.

Jamie didn't have a conventional upbringing. It was case files and crime scene photos, not dolls and bicycles.

She released Oliver's fingers, her eyes settling on the ring — scratched and scored — and stood up. 'We'll wait for the forensics report.'

'Not going to tell us anything we don't already know. Heroin in the bloodstream, river-water in the lungs.'

She could hear her dad's voice in her head. *Establish a timeline*, he would say. *Draw your circles. What do you know? What information do you already have?*

'Who reported him missing?'

Roper took a few seconds to navigate back to the report from whatever app he was in, making an *err* sound as he did, exhaling whiskey breath and cigarettes all over her.

She ducked out into the city air and waited for him to follow.

'Grace Melver,' he said, squinting at the name.

'Melver?' she confirmed.

'What the report says.'

'Address?'

He shook his head. 'No permanent address. No contact information. Nothing.'

'Homeless, too?'

'Looks like. There's a local shelter listed as a contact. But that's it.'

Jamie digested it. 'Alright. Let's go.'

'You want to park your car and I'll drive?' Roper asked.

'No, you park yours. I'll drive.'

'But I can't smoke in your car.'

She was already walking. 'That's the point.'

4

The shelter was on a quiet street that t-boned a residential road in a decent part of north-east London. About two kilometres north-east of where the body was dredged out of the water.

Jamie pulled up outside the building and cranked the handbrake.

Roper was shivering in the seat next to her and quickly pulled back on the switch to raise the window. 'You could have at least had the bloody heating on,' he moaned.

Jamie grew up north of Stockholm. Roper didn't know the meaning of the word cold. 'Not with the windows open.'

'Well if you'd let me wind them up—'

'If you wanted the windows up you should have showered and brushed your teeth.'

He blew out a long exhale of stale coffee and cigarettes and she turned her head to the open window. 'If this is your way of getting me to quit, it's not going to work.'

She could almost see her dad standing on the pavement next to the car, taking inhumanly long drags on a cigarette. He shrugged at her, like, what're you gonna do?

She rolled her own window up and killed the engine, getting out of the car to look at the shelter.

The building was sixties brutalist. A slab of concrete that looked like it would have been a chic and modern looking community centre six decades ago. Now it just looked like a pebble-dashed breeze block with wire-meshed vertical windows that ran the length of the outside.

Wide steps with rusty white rails led up to the main doors, dark brown stained wooden things with square aluminium handles, the word 'pull' etched into each one.

There was a piece of paper taped to the right-hand one that said 'All welcome, hot food inside' written in hand-printed caps.

There were five homeless people on the steps — three of them smoking rolled cigarettes. Two of those were drinking something out of polystyrene cups. The fourth was hunched forward, reading the tattiest looking novel Jamie had ever seen cling to a spine. His eyes stared at it blankly, not moving, his pupils wide. He wasn't even registering the words.

The last one was curled up into a ball inside a bright blue sleeping bag, his arms and legs folding the polyester into his body, just a pockmarked forehead peeking out into the November morning. Had they slept there all night on that step waiting for the shelter to open? She couldn't say.

Jamie and Roper crossed the road and the folks on the steps looked up. They were of varying ages, in varying states of malnutrition and addiction.

The smell of old booze and urine hung in the alcove.

Jamie wasn't sure if you could tell they were police by the way they looked or walked, but the homeless seemed to have a sixth sense about it.

Two of the three who were smoking clocked them, lowered their heads, and turned to face the wall. The third kept looking and held his hand out. The one with the novel didn't even register them.

Jamie knew that if they searched the two that turned away, they would have something on them they shouldn't — drugs, needles, a knife, something stolen. That's why they'd done it — to become invisible. The one who held out a hand would be clean. Wouldn't risk chancing it with a police officer otherwise. She'd worked enough uniformed time on the streets of London to know how their minds worked.

She took a deep breath of semi-clean air and mounted the steps, looking down at the mid-thirties guy with the stretched-out beanie and out-stretched hand.

'We're on duty,' Roper said coldly, breezing past.

Jamie gave him a weak smile, knowing that opening her pockets in a place like this would get them mobbed. If they needed to question anyone after they interviewed the owner, then she'd need the change in the cupholder in her car to loosen their lips. Giving it away now would only throw that chance away later.

Roper paused at the door and proffered it to her. 'After you,' he said.

She knew he just didn't want to touch the handle.

She took hold of it and pulled back, wondering for a second if she should open it just enough to slip through so that Roper would have to grab it to let himself in.

She decided that was too petty for the morning of a murder investigation.

Inside, the interior was cool.

A short reception area led into the main hall — a double-height function room with a hard rubberised floor filled with sleeping bags and other homeless people. There were at least twenty, maybe thirty. It was difficult to tell at a glance.

At the back of the room, a woman in her fifties with a long fleece vest on, the pockets heavy and sagging with keys and who knows what else, was filling cups of coffee from a big stainless steel dispenser, handing them to a line of people queuing silently, their heads bowed.

The air was humid inside and the low murmurings of the people talking around them created a soft background din that swallowed their footsteps.

Roper looked around, not hiding his disdain very well.

But with the nights getting colder, these people deserved somewhere warm to hole up. The winter was vicious and it was closing in fast this year, bearing down on the city in waves of rain and frost.

The woman serving coffee leaned around the line and looked at them, squinting a little to make them out. Her cheeks were rosy from the cold and her reddish hair was curled back up over her head, spilling around her ears. Big and cheap gold earrings clung to her stretched lobes and shook a little as she looked them up and down, her face a mixture of trepidation and worry. Police turning up at a homeless shelter never meant anything good.

She smiled warmly at the person at the front of the line, told him to help himself to coffee, and then walked around the table towards Roper and Jamie.

She held her hands wide and then clasped them together, raising her eyebrows and shaking her head. Her earlobes wobbled and her heavy earrings caught the halogen strip lights overhead, glinting. 'Can I, uh, help you?' she asked.

Jamie and Roper flashed their badges to get it out of the way.

'My name is Detective Sergeant Paul Roper, and this is my associate, Detective Sergeant Jamie Johansson.'

'Mary Cartwright,' she answered diligently.

'Are you the owner of this — er — establishment, Mary?' Roper asked less than tactfully.

Jamie guessed he wasn't sure if calling it a homeless shelter when it was filled with homeless people was somehow offensive. He'd had two complaints lodged against him in the last twelve months alone for the use of 'inappropriate' language.

Roper was a fossil, stuck in a by-gone age, struggling to stay afloat.

He of course wouldn't have this problem if he bothered to read any of the sensitivity emails HR pinged out.

But he didn't. And now he was on his final warning.

Jamie left him to flounder and scanned the crowd and the room for anything amiss.

People were watching them. But not maliciously. Mostly out of a lack of anything else to do. They'd been there overnight by the look of it. Places like this popped up all over the city to let them stay inside on cold nights. The problem was finding a space that would house them.

'No, not the owner,' Mary said, sighing. 'I just rent the space from the council. The ceiling is asbestos, and they can't use it for anything, won't get it replaced.' She shrugged her shoulders so high that they touched the earrings. 'But these people don't mind. We're not eating the stuff, so...' She laughed a little.

Jamie thought it sounded sad. It sort of was.

The council wouldn't let children play in there, wouldn't let groups rent it, but they were happy to take payment and let the homeless in. It was safe enough for them.

She pushed her teeth together and started studying the faded posters on the walls that encouraged conversations about domestic abuse, about drug addiction. From when this place was used. They looked like they were at least a decade old, maybe two.

Bits of tape clung to the paint around them, scraps of coloured paper frozen in time, preserving images of long-past birthday parties. There was a meagre stage behind the coffee dispenser, and to the right, a door led into another room.

'Do you know this boy?' Roper asked, holding up his phone, showing Mary a photo of Oliver Hammond taken that morning. The officers who arrived on scene had taken it and attached it to the central case file. Roper was just accessing it from there. It showed Oliver's face at an angle, greyed and bloated from the water.

'My God,' Mary said, throwing a weathered hand to her mouth. It wasn't easy for people who weren't exposed to death regularly to stomach seeing something like that.

'Ms Cartwright,' Roper said, leaning a little to his left to look in her eyes as she turned away. 'Can you identify this person? I know it's hard—'

'Oliver — Ollie, he preferred. Hammond, I think. I can check my files...' She turned and pointed towards the back room Jamie had spotted. 'If you want—'

Roper put the phone away. 'Not necessary. That's great, thanks. Jamie,' he said, turning to her and nodding towards the back room.

Jamie nodded back. 'Ms Cartwright—'

'It's Mrs,' she said automatically, the colour still drained from her cheeks. Her hand had moved from her mouth to her collarbones now as she processed it.

'Would you mind if I took a look at those files?'

She shook her head, her eyes vacant. 'No, no — there's nothing much to see, but… Of course—' She cut off, squeezing her face into a frown. 'He's… dead? But how? What happened? My God,' she muttered. 'He was… My God.'

Jamie stepped around her, leaving Roper to the interview. He was better at that sort of thing anyway. She rarely found interviewees easy to deal with. They always got emotional, blathered.

'Do you mind if I record this conversation?' Roper asked behind her as she walked towards the back room.

'No,' Mary said quietly.

'Great, thanks.' He exhaled slowly, fiddling with the buttons, adding the audio file to the case. 'What can you tell me about Ollie?'

The voices faded away as she reached the door and pushed on the handle.

Inside looked to be a rehearsal room. On the left there were two steps leading up to a red door that opened onto the side of the stage, and the floor was bare concrete painted red. The paint had been chipped from years of use and the blue paint job underneath was showing through.

Mary had a desk set up with two chairs in front of it, but no computer. In fact there was nothing of *any* value in the room.

On the right there was an old filing cabinet, and laid against it were rusted music stands as well as a mop and bucket and a couple of bottles of bargain cleaning supplies that had the word 'Value' written across them.

At the back of the room there was an old bookcase filled with second-hand literature — mostly children's books and charity shop novels. Next to that an old plastic covered doctor's examination bed was pushed against the wall. Sponge and felt were showing through the ripped brown covering.

Stood on the floor was a trifold cotton privacy screen that looked new, if not cheap. On the cracked beige walls, there was also a brand new hand-sanitiser dispenser and wide paper roll holder. She approached and checked the screws. They were still shiny. Brass. They had been put up recently. At least more recently than anything else in there.

The dispenser looked like it had come straight out of a doctor's office, the roll holder too. Paper could be pulled out and laid over the bed so patients didn't have to sit on the bare covering.

Jamie stared at them for a second and then reached out, squirting sanitiser onto her hands.

She massaged it in before moving on.

A door in the corner was painted the same colour as the walls. Beige. An old padlock kept it closed. She checked the seams and saw that they'd been painted over. It didn't look like the door had been opened in years. An old storage cupboard. She made a mental note of it and headed for the filing cabinet.

The bottom two drawers were empty, but the top one had a number of hanging files. She walked her fingers over them, reading the names as she went. When she reached Hammond, she stopped and pulled it out. Pausing only when she spotted another name. Grace Melver. The person who had reported him missing. She pulled that one too and pinned them under her arm as she closed the top drawer.

She took one more look around and then headed for the desk, putting the files down.

Roper would keep Mary busy for a few more minutes, which meant she could dig into the cold hard facts.

Her father was at the back of her chair, looking over her head, his big hands resting on her shoulders.

Information is your friend, he'd say. *Acquire it ruthlessly.*

She rubbed her eyes, ignoring the sting from the alcohol-based sanitiser, and dove in.

If there was anything to find, she'd find it.

5

The information was far from comprehensive.

Inside the file was a polaroid that looked like it had been taken exactly from where Jamie was sitting. She held it up and matched the outline of the door in front of her to the picture in her hand. In the middle of it was Oliver Hammond. He looked dishevelled and gaunt. Hungry was the word that came to mind.

His skin looked colourless and there were grazes and scabs hanging from his cheeks. The heroin scratch. That's what her dad used to call it. When addicts pawed at their faces. His hair was matted and his eyes sunken, but there was no mistaking him.

Jamie pulled the photo out from under the paperclip and went through the rest of the file.

There was a roughly photocopied form that looked like it had been put together in a spreadsheet. It had been filled in by hand.

Jamie closed her eyes and recalled the handwriting on the sign outside. It was different. Oliver must have filled it in himself.

It gave his name, date of birth, emergency contact, and blood type. Though there was nothing filled in under address. It also had two check-boxes under the words 'Naloxone Allergy?', and he'd checked 'no'. Naloxone was used to treat heroin overdoses.

There were also questions — 'How long has it been since you maintained a permanent residence?', 'Do your family know where you are?'. He'd written 'A year' and 'No' for those two. Then came the personal questions. 'What is your sexual orientation?', 'Are you sexually active?', 'How many sexual partners have you had in the last 12 months?', 'Have you been recently checked for sexually transmitted diseases?', 'Have you been diagnosed with any transmittable diseases?', 'Are they bloodborne?'. He'd written 'Straight', 'Yes', '1', 'No', 'No', and 'No'.

So he'd only been with one girl, and he hadn't caught anything. At least not as far as he knew. The girl had to be Grace Melver. Below those questions, it was more medical stuff.

'Do you feel well in yourself currently?'. He answered 'No'.

'Are you using any substances regularly. If so, what?'. 'Yes' was written, though it looked shaky. She could imagine him sitting there in front of Mary, reaching that question, and then looking up, afraid to admit it. She'd seen it before. Too many times. The word 'Heroin' was written quickly, as if admitting it was hard and he needed to get it over with.

'Do you want to receive support with the aim to become a non-user?'

The word 'Yes' was written there.

Jamie looked over the questions again. Non-permanent residence. Non-user. Those were terms that people who knew how to deal with the homeless used so that they didn't embarrass them. It was giving the answers without saying *I've been homeless for this long,* or *yes, I want help getting clean.* Mary knew what she was doing.

At the bottom of the page, there was one final question. 'Would you like to have a free health check-up by a qualified medical practitioner at this shelter?'

He had written 'Yes', and then signed the declaration underneath that said he understood that if he was carrying drugs or under the influence when he arrived that he would be turned away, and that if he appeared to be a danger to himself or others the proper authorities would be called and this information could be provided to them with his permission.

She wondered if he'd read that before he signed. No one ever read the terms and conditions.

Jamie sat back and tried to picture Oliver sitting there, and the circumstances that led him to the shelter. She opened Grace's file quickly and scanned down the same form to her answers for diseases and sexual partners. She's written the same answers as Oliver. Maybe they'd come in together, sat side by side filling the form in.

She held up the photo and matched it with the wall, a tired, thin-looking girl looking out at her. It was set to the right of Oliver's. They could have had them taken at the same time. She'd ask Mary.

Grace had said she had only been with Oliver — or at least that's what the answers suggested. She'd have to ask her to make sure. It wasn't unknown for homeless people to get into disagreements over love. When you've got nothing much to lose, the law doesn't come into play when you're asking yourself if you're prepared to kill for someone.

Grace also admitted to being a regular heroin user and agreed to have an examination. She also said she didn't have any diseases as far as she knew. She was the same age, too. Eighteen. Had they known each other before they'd become homeless? She'd have to find Grace to know the truth.

She went back to Oliver's file and checked the date next to his signature. It said the seventh of September. Just under two months ago.

Jamie leafed to the next and only other page in the file. It was another shabbily photocopied sheet. Mary must have been doing them on her printer-scanner at home, creating them on her computer. She really did care.

The sheet displayed a pixelated outline of the human body — no doubt an image pulled off the web and then stretched out to fill a page. The resolution was too low to keep any sort of detail, but the shape still came through okay. It was a human with their arms out, feet apart. At the top of the page, in Comic Sans, 'Examination Sheet' was written as the title.

In appropriately illegible handwriting for a doctor, notes had been jotted around the body. Parts had been circled with lines being drawn to the corresponding note. She read words like 'graze' and 'lesion'. 'Rash' cropped up a few times. But there didn't look to be anything sinister going on. The crooks of the elbows, as well as the ankles, were all circled several times but nothing was written at the sides. Those areas didn't need explaining, though underneath, as if encapsulating the entire exam were the words 'No signs of infection'. So he'd been relatively careful, then. Clean needles, at least. Under that, there was a little paragraph recommending a general blood panel, but overall, Oliver seemed to be in decent health. Nothing had been prescribed, it seemed.

She checked Grace's and found it to be much the same, complete with triple circles around the elbows and ankles. Though her genital area had also been circled and the word 'Rash' had been written. At the bottom, a prescription had been written for azithromycin.

Jamie clicked her teeth together, rummaging in her brain for the name. Was it a gonorrhoea medication or chlamydia? She knew it was for an STD, she just couldn't remember which. But that meant that where she'd put down '1' for number of sexual partners, she was either lying, or she'd had it for over a year. But Oliver's chart didn't show any symptoms and he hadn't been prescribed.

Jamie mulled it over in her head then acted on a hunch, pulling open the top right-hand drawer. Inside was a wholesale box of condoms. She stared at it for a second. At least they were using protection. She wondered how many Mary gave out a week.

Maybe there had been a third person in their relationship. A scorned ex-boyfriend who didn't like Oliver? He obviously didn't know about the rash — or hadn't noticed. Grace was keeping it from him.

Had he found out, confronted Grace's other boyfriend? Or maybe the other way around. Surprised by the guy? Taken? Tied up and threatened? She had a feeling that the person hadn't meant to kill him.

If you're going to kill someone, you don't take their shoes and then dump them in a river. He'd either fallen in accidentally, or he'd jumped. Either way, if there wasn't an ex — or *not* ex boyfriend — he was going to be someone Jamie wanted to speak to.

She held Grace's picture up, looking past the matted hair and sunken eyes. She was young, pretty. She'd have a lot of attention out there on the streets.

Jamie closed the drawer and looked at the file again, searching for a name. She wanted to speak to the doctor. The signature just looked like a wavy line. She'd ask Mary.

The chair squeaked as she pushed back from the desk and stood up, keeping the files in hand. Her watch told her it was nearly nine-thirty. Her stomach told her it was time for breakfast.

Back in the main room, some of the people had cleared out, venturing back into the city. Looking for some way to get by.

Roper was still talking to Mary, who appeared to be in the middle of a speech about how these people needed more help than anyone was prepared to give, and that Oliver wouldn't been the last.

Jamie stepped around her, piqued. 'Why do you say that?'

'Oh,' she said, seeing Jamie. 'Because people don't want to help them and they let them hurt themselves and each other without paying them any mind.'

She narrowed her eyes. 'Each other? Did someone have a problem with Oliver?'

'What?' Mary looked sheepish all of a sudden, as if she'd dropped someone in something. 'No, no — nothing like that. Not as far as I know, anyway,' she added quickly. 'Look, I just want you to find who did this — but for you to know that things are different with them. They don't act the same — don't believe in the same things, you know?' She kept her voice low now.

Jamie nodded. She'd worked the streets long enough to know what Mary meant. She'd seen more than she could have ever imagined. Seen people do crazy things. Things that people with something to lose would never think to do.

'Mrs Cartwright,' she said after a second. 'Grace Melver. She was friends with Oliver?'

'Grace?' Mary's eyes lit up a little and then tilted down in sadness. 'What a sweet girl. She'll be devastated. She's been back every day to check whether Oliver has turned up. She's been going out of her mind. Poor girl.'

'What was the nature of their relationship?'

Roper held his phone a little higher so the microphone could pick them up more easily.

Mary thought for a second, aware of the recording. She chose her words carefully. 'They were together, I suppose. As much as two people in their situation could be. They looked out for each other. Loved each other.'

'Did Grace have any other boyfriends?'

'No, no. She was sweet. She loved Oliver.'

'She was a heroin user, right?'

Mary looked like her face was about to droop and slip right off her head. 'Horrible stuff. Though they wanted to get off it. Together.'

Roper cleared his throat. 'Can you confirm that it was a *yes* to the question, just for the file?' He held the phone up a touch.

Mary sighed. 'Yes, they were both using heroin.'

'Did you speak to her much?' Jamie asked, softening her voice. 'Did she ever mention where they got it, or how they paid for it? How *she* paid for it?'

Mary narrowed her eyes a little, glancing at the file under Jamie's arm and then meeting her eye again. 'If you're asking if she was selling herself, then the answer is no. Not to the best of my knowledge. Oliver was always the one who got it for them. He wouldn't tell her where from. He cared about her.'

'Did he ever tell you?'

'No.'

Jamie nodded, letting the tension ease slightly. 'She was prescribed an antibiotic used to treat sexually transmitted diseases.'

'That was between her and Dr Day.'

Roper glanced at Jamie, who was trying to ease into it. 'Who is Dr Day?'

Mary sighed, knowing that Jamie had been through the files already. 'Dr Day comes down every week and gives free health checks to those who need them. When we first met Oliver and Grace — they both came in for a check up. Grace... I don't know. She and Oliver seemed happy, but — you know how it is out there. For someone like her...'

'Are you saying you think she may have been assaulted?'

Mary raised her shoulders, opening her hands. 'I don't know. She never said anything, but maybe. They often don't. But I know that the world isn't kind to people like her. But Oliver was different. He treated her well.' She paused for a second. 'As well as he could.'

'Do you know where Grace is? Is there some way we can contact her, or—'

'She usually comes in around lunchtime. Has been every day since Oliver went missing. Come back around one — I'll ask her to wait for you.'

Jamie nodded. 'Thank you. We will. And what about this doctor? Will he be in today, too?'

'He comes in on Wednesday afternoons for check-ups, unless he's on call. So he'll be here tomorrow if you need to speak to him.'

'Do you have his information to hand?' Jamie asked hopefully.

'I don't keep his number here. That back room isn't very secure — and I didn't want anyone finding him. Sometimes, when they meet someone like him, some of these people... they latch on, you know? They're not used to people being kind to them. It can be difficult, so we try to minimise the risk, where we can.'

'But you have his number?' Jamie pressed.

'Yes,' Mary said, barely above a whisper, looking around. She was nervous about admitting it, Jamie noted. This Dr Day had obviously had quite an effect on the people there if Mary was *that* worried about people forming this attachment she'd mentioned.

Jamie had heard of it before though — mistaking kindness for friendship, or even more.

Mary pulled her phone out and scanned through her contacts until she found what she was looking for, and then handed the phone to Jamie.

A contact was opened up, the name written merely as 'Elliot'. Dr Elliot Day.

Jamie pulled her own phone out and copied the number, hitting the call button and then immediately hanging up to save it to her call log.

She handed the phone back and nodded a thanks. She'd follow up once her and Roper had debriefed.

'You mind if I keep these?' Jamie asked, dropping the files from under her arm into her hand and holding them up. 'Once the investigation is over, you can have them back.'

Mary eyed them, and then eventually said, 'Of course, whatever I can do to help.' Jamie could see it in her eyes that she felt it was betraying the trust of these people, but the disclaimer had said that the authorities could take them, and they'd signed it, so Mary didn't really have any reason to deny Jamie unless she had something to hide. Mary didn't strike her as the sort, but sometimes you couldn't tell. Jamie made a living being able to read people. But then some people dedicated their lives to not being able to be read.

'Thanks,' she said.

'If there's anything else I can do for you...' Mary said, looking longingly at the coffee still.

Roper cleared his throat and put his phone away, curtailing the recording. 'I think that's everything for now. We'll review, and come back to you if there's anything else. Though if you can give us a call when Grace shows up—' he offered her one of the business cards he kept loose inside the breast pocket of his coat '—that would be great.'

'Sure,' Mary said, putting on a smile. 'I have to get back. But please, feel free to look around as much as you'd like.'

Roper gave her a look that said, *we don't need your permission for that,* but Jamie thanked her anyway and let her walk off.

He sucked on his teeth the way he did when he wanted a cigarette, and watched Mary go out of earshot. 'Find anything?' he asked, turning to Jamie.

She let out a long breath. 'Don't know yet. Looks like Grace wasn't as faithful to Ollie as she made out.'

'Lover's tiff?'

'Could be.' Jamie thought about it. 'Spurned ex, maybe. Maybe it's the drugs. Maybe something else entirely.' She rubbed her eyes. It'd been a long morning and she needed to eat. 'Come on. Let's head back to HQ, get this written up. We'll come back when Grace shows her face.'

Roper nodded without a word and headed for the door, already reaching for his cigarettes.

6

Jamie zipped up her jacket and dug her hands into her pockets, following Roper out the door.

He'd sped on ahead so that he could light up before Jamie told him not to. She didn't like that fresh stink in her car, and she definitely wouldn't let him smoke in there anyway. And he definitely wasn't above running out and doing it before she had time to protest.

Her effort to make him quit by forcing him to stand in the cold obviously wasn't working. He was a seasoned smoker and spent most nights standing outside pubs, come rain or shine, sucking down smoke.

That and the fact that he was far too stubborn to give in to such a weak ploy.

It was like those goats that stand on the side of dams to lick the salt off. One missed step and it was guaranteed death. But they were single minded.

And so was Roper.

If she cared more she might have tried harder, but she knew from experience that when guys like Roper made a decision, they'd stick to it forever. As far as he was concerned, the drinking and the smoking was as much a part of him as his belly button was. It couldn't be changed, and trying would only invite self-loathing. Guys like him had to hit rock bottom. Only then could they start coming back up.

But sometimes they just stayed there, scraping the ground until they gouged a hole deep enough to die in.

She should call her mum. It had been a while.

Outside, Roper was already two drags in by the time she reached the steps.

A couple of the people outside had moved on and the guy in the sleeping bag had woken up and headed inside, though the urine stain that had seeped into the stone under him still remained.

Jamie tried not to breathe through her nose as she hopped down the steps, her shin still throbbing from the morning's bout with Cake.

She opened her mouth to tell Roper to hurry up when she almost got knocked over.

A guy in his forties with an expensive suit and a long lambswool coat was rushing by, his head turned towards the steps.

'Filthy fucking cretins,' he almost yelled at the three homeless people still perched on the steps, before colliding with Jamie.

He stumbled sideways, down into the roadway, shoving Jamie backwards.

'Get off!' he shouted, flapping his arms.

Jamie steadied herself and stared at him. Roper even stopped smoking his cigarette and came forward. 'Hey!' he called.

'You're not having any!' the man yelled again, striding forward away from the shelter. 'You should all be drowned. Wash this goddamn city clean!'

Jamie arched an eyebrow, deconstructing the situation.

He was headed to work by the look of him, and judging from the direction he came from, he lived on the upmarket residential street that this one intersected. Homeless shelters often drove house prices down, and someone dressed like him would be a prime target for begging. And he'd obviously experienced enough of it to not even want to look at them as he passed.

Roper wasn't so understanding and inhaled hard to shout after him, coughing hoarsely as he did, unable to catch his breath.

'Roper,' Jamie said quickly, moving towards him, shaking her head. 'Don't.'

Roper leaned forward, reddening, then hawked and spat a chunk of brown phlegm onto the tarmac. He stood up then, hands on his hips, forehead creased, a vein bulging in his temple. 'Why not?' he squeezed out. 'You heard what he said. You think that's a coincidence?'

Jamie looked after him. He was already fifty feet away and walking hard. 'Don't know. But I'd say we'd be better off catching him at a more opportune time. He didn't even see me — didn't even look. Just bumped straight into me — thought I was about to put my hands in his pockets.'

Roper squinted down the street. 'Looks like this place has rubbed some people up the wrong way. Not surprised, though. I wouldn't like a shelter popping up on my doorstep.'

Jamie hummed her agreement with the first statement. Not with the second. 'We'll ask Mary when we come back later.' Roper's cigarette had burned down to the butt now between his third and fourth finger. 'Let's go.'

He sucked on the bare filter and then tossed it into a drain.

Jamie watched it but didn't say anything, and then circled her car, getting in.

By the time Roper sighed into the seat, she already had the windows open.

The coffee made by the six-year-old drip filter machine in the break room was as black as tar.

The DI who made it every morning had the tolerance of a bull and the neck of one too. His name was James Graham, and Jamie had seen him take a cup of coffee out of the jug when it was made by someone else, and then add a spoon full of instant coffee to it. More than once.

When that happened, he did nothing but complain about how weak it was.

It just so happened that Graham bought good coffee as well as making it strong, so it was easier — and tastier — for everyone to just let him make a pot, half fill a cup, and then top it up with water and milk until it was the right shade.

That morning Jamie didn't add any water, and took a russet-brown cup back to her desk.

She sat down and Roper eyed her, flicking through the files from the shelter. She'd laid it all out for him and he'd regaled her with the particulars of the conversation he'd had with Mary. She was listening back to the audio-clip anyway, and put her headphones straight in. She was in even less of a mood for small-talk than normal.

As Roper's voice spoke in her ears, asking Mary if she'd seen or heard anyone arguing with or threatening Oliver Hammond, she took a bite out a bagel she'd topped with light cream cheese. Someone had taken and eaten the two slices of smoked salmon she'd left in the fridge.

She didn't have energy to find out who.

Jamie chewed thoughtfully, glad of the noise in her ears to drown the world out. She'd become good at tuning out Roper's east-London rasp by now. It was practically white noise.

She was thinking about Oliver Hammond. His parents' number was written down in front of her. She was working up to calling them to follow-up.

It was nearly midday and they'd already been informed of his death and told that a detective would be calling to speak to them. She'd listened to the recording of the conversation. His father had said, 'I don't know what she expects to find out — we haven't seen him in ten months.'

The word *haven't* stuck out to her. As if they would again. It was always difficult to wrap your head around news like that. He'd sounded calm on the phone, as though he'd come to terms with this eventuality already, even before the news came in. Though when the reality of it all hit home the emotion couldn't be denied.

She knew from personal experience. She'd felt indifferent when her mum told her that her dad was dead. It was only three days later that the realisation set in, when she came downstairs and the birthday decorations were still up. Her mother was slumped on the sofa, an empty bottle of red wine lying on its side next to her, the contents soaked into the fabric.

She remembered pausing at the bottom of the stairs and looking at her mother, passed out drunk. She'd always hated her father for looking like that.

Jamie held it all back, headed to school, and then broke down during her first class and ran out of the room.

At the time, she'd despised her father for killing himself on her eighteenth birthday. Now, she saw it with more clarity. Her mum had denied him the chance to talk to her, to see her, to be a part of her life during those last months. And he couldn't take it.

The post-mortem report said that his blood-alcohol level was high enough to give an average male alcohol poisoning and possibly brain damage, and ruled that an investigation be launched to determine whether he had shot himself, or whether it had been staged, as they weren't sure that anyone could even stay conscious, let alone lift a gun with any conviction, after drinking that much.

Several character reports testified that he wasn't an average male, and he was very well-practised at both while being shit-faced drunk.

It was deemed suicide and never contested.

Her mother found out just after they'd finished her birthday meal — just two hours after she'd told him that he couldn't speak to Jamie. Not even to wish her a happy birthday.

It wasn't that Jamie blamed either of them for anything. They weren't happy people — apart or together.

She looked up, Mary's voice echoing back to her as she let the recording in.

Roper was snapping his fingers and waving at her.

She pulled the headphones down around her neck and sat up. 'What is it?'

'You called the parents yet to follow-up?'

'Not yet.' Her voice cracked a little and she coughed to cover it.

'Good. It's after twelve—' he checked his watch '—we should get going if we're going to catch Grace at the shelter.'

'Has Mary called?' Jamie asked, taking a sizeable bite out of her bagel. She'd already eaten a bowl of granola and an apple.

'No,' Roper said, standing up and taking his pea coat off the back of his chair, 'but I want to get there before she does and see her come in. Don't want her to know we're coming and come up with a story we can never disprove. Heroin, secrets, dead-boyfriend — there's a lot she's not going to want to say and I don't need her getting any prep in before we arrive.'

Jamie inhaled deeply, letting the oxygen seep into her muscles. 'Okay.'

'You call that doctor yet?' Roper asked, throwing his coat around his shoulders.

'No,' Jamie said, shaking her head.

'What the hell have you been doing all morning?'

She looked at her computer screen, at the twenty-eight windows she had open. All active reports of missing homeless people in the city. All under the age of twenty-one. She'd done some digging when she got back. It was estimated that there were more than eight thousand people sleeping rough on the streets of London. And last year more than six hundred deaths of homeless people were recording across the country. More than a hundred of those were in London alone. And those were just the ones who were found. She wondered how many died and never got recorded — how many slipped through the cracks and weren't added to the statistics.

More than a quarter of a million people were reported missing every year in the UK, and these numbers were growing.

Twenty-eight missing kids, though. She looked at the files. They had nothing in common other than that they were young, and someone, somewhere, was wondering where they were.

How many were dead already?

'Johansson,' Roper said, his voice hard.

'Hmm?' She looked up, still in her chair.

'I asked what you'd been doing all morning?' They may have been the same rank, but he was still technically her senior — in both age and experience — and sometimes he liked to flex. Make himself look like he gave a damn.

She leaned forward, hit the keyboard shortcut to minimise the windows, and got up. 'Nothing,' she said, pulling her jacket on.

'That's helpful.'

She ignored the comment, downed half her now-tepid coffee and bit lightly into her bagel, holding it between straight white teeth as she powered off her monitor and tucked her chair in.

'I don't know why you bother,' Roper said, flicking a hand at the now-black screen. 'Not while all this is burning.' He gestured around the room at the other desks and detectives working away. Dozens of screens were lit, the photocopier was buzzing, the lights were humming, and phones and devices were charging on every surface.

She shrugged. 'If you leave a monitor on standby overnight it wastes enough energy to—'

'Yeah, yeah,' he said, dismissing her with his hand. 'And the polar ice caps are melting and penguins are getting sunburn. Come on, we've got a murder to solve.'

He walked forward, draining what was left in his coffee cup, and put it down on a random desk — much to the disgust of the guy sitting behind it.

Roper swaggered towards the lifts, finally shrugging off the hangover, his caffeine quota for the next hour filled.

Once his nicotine level had been topped off, he might actually be capable of some decent police work.

Jamie fell in behind him, trying to get her mind off the other missing kids and back on Grace Melver.

Whatever the hell was going on, Jamie had a feeling that Grace Melver knew something about it.

Whether she realised or not.

7

She walked with Roper without thinking about it.

Jamie had dropped him back at the crime scene after the shelter so he could pick his car up. The medical examiner was there and the scene of the crime officers, or SOCOs, were crawling all over in their plastic-covered boots, snapping photos and putting things in evidence bags.

They hadn't stuck around.

It was best to leave the SOCOs do their jobs, and anyway Jamie and Roper had paperwork that needed to be done.

Her fingers typed on autopilot now. She'd had her prelim licked before she'd finished her first cup of coffee.

Roper headed for his Volvo without asking and got into the driver's seat.

Jamie pulled the door open and got in, closing the door only when he'd cranked the ignition so she could crack the window. The seats were covered with dust and ash, a fast-food coffee cup was sitting in the centre console with eight cigarette buts dropped in it, and the passenger footwell was littered with burger wrappers and cigarette packets.

She could comment, but it wouldn't make a difference.

He wheeled backwards into the middle of the underground car park and accelerated up the ramp. The scanner clocked his number plate and the barrier lifted.

The engine whined and the Volvo thrust itself into the mild midday sun, the sounds of the city engulfing them.

They didn't speak on the way over — both too engrossed in their own thoughts. Roper was no doubt planning his line of questioning for Grace. Jamie was thinking about Ollie. About how an eighteen-year-old kid goes from sixth-form to heroin in one fell swoop.

She still hadn't spoken to his parents. Or to the doctor. She really needed to.

Hopefully, once they'd spoken to Grace, she'd have more to ask and the calls would necessitate themselves.

Roper turned into the street with the shelter on it and pulled the handbrake up without pressing the button. It clicked angrily and Jamie resisted the urge to tell him that it wasn't good for the car.

They got out and she breathed through her nose again.

The air was marginally fresher.

Her watch told her it was half past twelve and the smell of soup coming out of the shelter, as well as the growing line of homeless people, told her that it was nearly lunchtime.

The door was closed and another piece of paper had been stuck over the last one. It read 'Hot food for all. 1pm.'

The people outside were lined up neatly, hugging the right-hand rail and stretching down onto the pavement and along the street.

Jamie did a quick headcount down and got to twenty-two before Roper moved in front of her and she lost the number.

He looked back, dipped his head towards the door, and she went after him.

A guy with a shaggy beard and a lined face wearing two coats opened his mouth to tell them there was a line, and then had his sixth-sense tweaked and clammed up.

Roper gave him a glance and then pulled the door open and headed inside.

The room was much the same as it was before — except it was

now empty of bodies and a dozen or so folding chairs had been set out for people to sit and eat.

The camp table at the back that the coffee still had been on was now mostly filled by a big soup heater. It looked like it was older than Jamie was and the caked droplets of a thousand broths stained the side.

Mary was standing behind it, emptying minestrone out of tins into the vat.

An entire slab was resting on the stage behind her with half of the cans missing. They looked to be wholesale and cheap. But the folks outside wouldn't complain.

A stack of plastic bowls and spoons had been set on the table next to the heater.

Once it was full and hot, she'd call them in.

Jamie was surprised that they hadn't flooded in already. The door was open, after all.

That said something to her about Mary, and about the respect these people had for her.

'Detectives,' Mary said, a little surprised. 'Did I call you?' She seemed to be asking herself as much as Jamie and Roper.

'No,' Roper said. 'But we wanted to be here when Grace arrived.'

Mary took it in, stirring the soup with a ladle. 'Oh, well she's not here yet — as far as I know. I won't be serving lunch for another half an hour or so.'

'That's fine, we'll wait,' Roper said, smiling. He thought he was charming at times. But he never was.

Silence hung in the air while Mary popped and emptied in another tin with a dull slap.

Jamie looked at the slab and saw that the soup was best before August last year. It was out of date — probably salvaged from a food bank. Jamie thought about the phrase, *beggars can't be choosers,* and then immediately felt bad about it.

'There was a guy outside this morning,' Roper said, pushing his hands into his pockets. 'Smartly dressed, short black hair, glasses.'

'Oh, um,' Mary said, not sure where he was going with it.

'He bumped into Jamie, said some pretty nasty things — about the good people who rely on this shelter. Didn't seem too excited about them being there.'

Mary's face lit up and then drooped as she realised who he meant. 'Ah, yes — I don't know his name, but he lives around the corner.' Mary sighed. 'He works in a law firm — or a finance brokerage — or something like that—' she lifted her left hand and moved her wrist in circles '—on the next street over. Of course, when you walk past a shelter wearing a Rolex you're going to be asked if you can spare some change.' She shook her head. 'But yes, I know who you mean, and I've heard him say those things.'

'He mean anything by them you think?'

She studied Roper for a second. 'Are you asking if I think he could have murdered Ollie?'

Roper stayed quiet. He couldn't lead her into anything. After a second, he said, 'I'm not asking anything other than whether you think that he's worth speaking to.'

Diplomatic he wasn't.

'I don't know. I've never spoken to him — only heard his voice, had him described to me.'

Jamie cut in now. 'Has he ever assaulted any of the people who come here? Any violence, or direct threat?'

'Direct threat?'

Roper sucked his teeth. 'As in, *I'm going to drown you* versus *you should be drowned.*'

Mary's mouth crumped into a wrinkled line. 'I don't know that I can really say whether... I... I don't know is the simple answer. Lots of people take offence to the shelter being here. It wouldn't be out of the question for someone to act rashly — but him? I don't know.'

She was being careful not to say anything that would incriminate the possibly innocent man. She turned to Roper, trying to sound casual. There was no need to worry Mary. 'We'll get some uniformed officers to canvas the area — ask around to see whether the shelter has had an impact on anyone in particular.' She smiled at Mary now. 'But don't worry, it's just eliminating the most improbable suspects first, narrowing down the scope of the investigation, you know?'

'Am I a suspect?' Mary asked, stopping her stirring.

Jamie hated being asked that question, because there wasn't a good answer that didn't make it sound like they were. Roper looked at her, not wanting to tackle it either.

'We, uh,' Jamie started, looking around the room. 'We don't have a list of suspects, yet. We're just gathering information.'

Mary looked relived, nodding. 'Okay, good. Well, if there's anything I can do.'

Roper smiled, rocking back and forth on his heels. 'Just let us know when Grace arrives and we'll do the rest. You've been a great help already.'

He turned away and headed towards the far side of the room. Jamie followed, knowing it meant he wanted to talk.

They stood side on so they had a view of both Mary and the door, and then Roper said, 'I'll make the call, get the uniforms out here. You think it's worth looking around this place again?'

Jamie shook her head. 'We'd be swinging in the dark. Let's speak to Grace first, then go from there. If she gives us any names — the third person in the love triangle — then we can grab another file. But for now…' She inhaled, knowing they had twenty something minutes to kill and she had two phone calls to make.

They couldn't be put off any longer.

'Let's head outside,' Roper said. 'It smells like piss in here.'

She thought that was rich considering that there was about a fifty-fifty chance that smell was coming from Roper himself. But she didn't say anything.

Roper had a cigarette lit before his feet hit the pavement and he circled into the street to get a look at the thirty-strong line that had now formed.

The people were beginning to jostle.

They couldn't have all been local — which meant that they were making the trek over for a plastic bowl of soup.

Jamie looked away, focused her mind on the calls, and dug her phone out of her pocket.

She opened the case file and attached an audio clip, hitting the background record button. She still had the doctor's number in her call log and dialled it.

It rang for a while and then went to voicemail. 'You've reached Elliot Day, I can't get to the phone just now, but if you'd like to leave a message, I'll return your call as soon as I can. Thank you.' The voice told her he was well-brought-up. South-England native. But she couldn't place where.

'Hi,' she said after the beep. 'This is Detective Sergeant Jamie Johansson. I'd like to speak to you regarding your work at the homeless shelter in Enfield. It's in accordance with an active investigation. If you could call me back at your earliest convenience, that would be great. Thank you.' She hung up and sighed, stopped the recording, and then went back to the case file, finding the number for Oliver's parents.

She hit record again, copied it and called them immediately, not wanting to put it off any longer.

After three rings, a tired voice answered. 'Hello?'

'Mr Hammond?'

'Yes?'

'This is Detective Sergeant Jamie Johansson with the London Metropolitan Police. I understand that one of my colleagues informed you that I might be getting in touch?'

There was silence for a second and then she heard him swallow. 'That's right... But I don't know what I can tell you,' he said quietly. It sounded like he was moving from room to room, cupping the phone to his mouth. Maybe he didn't want Oliver's mum to hear.

'Any information you provide could be very useful. Do you mind if I ask you a few questions?'

'Sure,' he said, his voice small.

'Would it be okay if I recorded this conversation?'

'Yes,' he said, almost absently.

Jamie hated asking it — it never had a positive impact on the conversations that came after. Made them stunted, reserved. But she had to ask.

'Have you had any recent contact with Oliver?' She started quickly. 'Did he reach out to you, to tell you he was in trouble, or—'

'We hadn't heard from him in months…' He swallowed again, fighting the catch in his throat. 'The last time we… the last time *I* spoke to him, he asked me for… God… money.'

Jamie didn't press him. It was best to just to let people speak sometimes.

'He wouldn't tell me what for, but… but we knew that he was… you know… using that *stuff*…'

Acceptance was hard.

He went on. 'We knew he was. We had a call from the hospital — he'd been admitted for an overdose. That was when we confronted him, and — since, he just… We didn't know where he was, or…'

His voice was barely a whisper, the words near incoherent. She thought he meant back when Oliver had first started using. But she didn't interrupt.

'That was why he left, you know? We thought that… *I* thought that giving him an ultimatum would… would… make him see, you know?'

She set her jaw, trying to keep perspective. She'd been through this herself. Felt this herself. 'I know.'

She felt like saying ultimatums don't work on addicts   they never do. But it's not your fault for trying. It's what everyone does. It makes sense to us. But addicts think differently. Their logic works differently.

'We barely heard from him after he left. Once he turned up at Maggie's work — you know? Asking for money. Thought that if I wasn't there… Of course she gave him some — told him to come home for dinner. But that night we had a call from you — the police, I mean — saying that he'd been found… And… Uh… I'm sorry —'

'Take your time,' Jamie said softly. 'It's okay.'

'So we said that we wouldn't, you know, help him any more — give him anything else. But that he could always come home? He wasn't himself, I don't think — the uh, the…'

He couldn't say the word.

Heroin.

'It changed him. We hadn't heard from him for a long time. We didn't know if he was alive, or... And now...' He pulled the phone from his ear and started sobbing in the background, the audio muffled as he put his hand over the mouthpiece.

'Mr Hammond?' she asked, forcing the words over the lump in her throat. 'Mr Hammond?'

He brought the phone back. 'I'm here, sorry. Sorry, it's... Sorry.'

'That's alright. Can you tell me when Oliver first started using? Who with, maybe? Did he have any friends, or?'

'No, I don't know. He was always independent, you know? Going to meet friends in the city, and... He had a girlfriend, but we didn't know who. He wouldn't tell us. Thought we wouldn't approve, or... or... I don't know.'

Grace came to mind. 'How long ago was this?'

'August last year, maybe? Before it all started to, uh...'

'That's great,' Jamie said, her free hand clenched tightly into a fist. 'I'm sorry to have bothered you. Would it be alright if I gave you a call tomorrow? Or if you'd prefer, I could come to—'

'No, no, that's fine. You can call... I'll be in work, but... I'll call you back when I can.'

Jesus. He was going back to work the next day? He didn't even think about it. Like missing a few days hadn't even entered the realm of the possible.

'Okay. Thank you,' she said. Apologising for it all was bad practice. Even though she wanted to.

'Goodbye,' he said.

She left it at that and hung up, letting him process. She had enough to start piecing together a timeline. And an idea of what had happened. At least at the start.

Jamie stared at the file open on her screen, at the names of his parents. Kevin and Margaret Hammond.

The address was in the good part of Brentwood. An expensive area.

You'd have to be well-off to live there.

A picture was forming in her head. Hard-working parents neglect their son for their careers. He rebels, lashes out, resents the private schooling, the luxury of his life. Starts mixing with the wrong crowd. Wouldn't mum and dad just hate it if I got a tattoo? If I went out with this girl? If I tried heroin.

She was gripping her phone hard, seeing it play out in her head.

She knew it was possible. Easy even. Her own father had been an addict her whole life and she'd not known until she was in her early teens. Until then, she thought her dad was superman. Catching bad guys by day, devoted father and husband by night.

Nothing could have been further from the truth.

'Johansson.'

She turned around to see Roper standing there, tapping the ash off his cigarette.

'Yeah?' she said, covering the tightness in her throat with a strategic cough.

'You good?' he asked, his eyes a little narrowed as he studied her.

She nodded and checked her watch. 'Yeah.' It was nearly one and the line was growing impatient.

'Good, then let's head inside. I don't want her to see us out here and bolt.'

'Okay.'

'You sure you're good?'

She exhaled, cracked her neck, and stuffed her phone back into her jeans pocket. 'Yeah, I'm good. Let's do this.'

8

Inside the shelter, the people came in quietly, as though if they rushed and demanded they'd be turned away.

Each accepted a bowl politely, not asking for more or for anything else. They all thanked Mary and then took seats, or stood and finished their lunch.

Most of them headed outside afterwards and then lined up again for seconds.

Mary served diligently, asking each how they were, whether they were okay, as well as an impossible number of personal things that Jamie couldn't believe she could remember.

But the whole time, while her and Roper leaned against the stage watching the door for Grace, she never showed.

Mary had said she was about five-four, slight, with mousy brown hair which was now cut into a sort of lop-sided pixie-cut. In the file-photo, it had been long, greasy, and pulled back into a low ponytail.

The words Mary had used were 'cute asymmetrical bob', and Jamie thought that probably meant she'd cut it for her.

Damn, she really did care.

No one that looked even remotely like Grace showed up, though. And after all the soup was finished, the crowd began to dissipate.

'I don't know what to say,' Mary said. 'She's usually here for lunch.'

Roper smacked his lips. 'Who knows. Word gets around sometimes. Maybe she heard about the vic—' He cut himself off. 'About Oliver.'

Mary nodded, like she concurred.

'Mrs Cartwright,' Jamie said, 'do you know where Grace sleeps? Does she have a usual spot, or do you know if anyone might know how we can get hold of her?'

Mary thought for a second. 'There's a bridge that runs across an old overground line — not far from here. I know that a lot of our patrons make themselves a space there. I don't know if that's where she sleeps, but…' She looked around, and seeing a guy in his late twenties with a tattered beanie hat pulled down to his eyebrows sitting on one of the chairs, polishing off a bowl of soup, lifted her hand and called out to him. 'Reggie?'

He looked up, the fur lining the hood of his jacket all clumped together and dirty. 'Hmm?' he said, looking scared all of a sudden.

Jamie smiled at him, but the fear of getting questioned by two police detectives couldn't be dispelled that easily.

Mary beckoned him over and he approached cautiously.

'Reggie — you've got a space down on the old overground line, right? Under the bridge?'

He looked at Roper and Jamie, as though admitting it was going to get him in trouble.

'You ever see Grace there? Maybe with Ollie?'

'Who?' he asked, his eyes still going from detective to detective.

'Ollie — the young boy with curly hair, came in here with a girl the same age — lopsided bob—' Mary moved her hands by her ears to demonstrate the cut '—slim, pretty, green eyes, and—'

He nodded once. 'Yeah, yeah, I know who you mean now, the ones on the needle, um…' He stopped talking, not wanting to say another word in front of Jamie and Roper.

'Go on,' Mary urged. 'You can tell them. Nothing's going to happen to you.'

He exhaled and a waft of tomato flowed out from under his scraggly moustache. 'They had a space down there. Nice tent, actually. Too nice, almost. New, like. She had it — brought it one day. They was in a tarp before, you know?'

Jamie nodded and Roper looked at her.

'Do you know if she's still there?' Mary asked.

'Tent was still there s'morning. The girl…' He shrugged and lifted the edge of his bowl, sipping the dregs out of the bottom. 'Who knows. With the boy, least she had some protection, you know. Now, well, I don't know who her friends are, you know?'

Jamie knew. 'Thank you. And how do we get there? Can you show us?'

'Me walk up with two coppers? Nah. I can't do that.'

'Listen, mate,' Roper said with the lack of finesse he was known for. 'This is an active murder investigation, alright? If you don't—'

Jamie squeezed his arm and he stopped talking. She thought about the old flies and vinegar adage.

'Reggie?' she said, trying to sound friendly. 'Could you just tell us where it is?'

He was staring at Roper, who was pretty much glaring back, but eventually he turned to her. 'Sure. Who am I to hold up a murder investigation?'

Back on the street with the directions etched in her mind, they headed for the bridge.

Roper was sulking. He didn't like this case and it was getting worse for him by the minute.

They had no solid leads and the one person they needed to speak to the most hadn't been seen since before Oliver's body was found. With what they knew so far, there was a good chance that someone else was involved in their relationship, and when you factored in the drugs, the azithromycin, and what Reggie had said about their supposedly new tent, things were starting to get muddy.

They needed to speak to Grace and find out exactly what was going on, and they needed to do it fast.

The longer time went on, the less likely they were to find a fresh lead. The longer there was for evidence to get destroyed or misplaced. The longer there was for people to shore up their stories. The longer there was for people to forget exactly what had happened.

Time was getting thin, and their investigation was hanging on the testimony of a heroin-addicted teenager who may or may not be missing herself.

It's what Jamie's father would have called a shit-clap.

The image was explanatory enough.

They kept a good pace through the streets, opting to walk rather than drive, retracing the route that Ollie and Grace would have taken every day to get to the shelter.

They caught up with and passed several nomads trekking back from lunch towards their nests, but none of them were Grace, or prepared to tell them whether Grace was there.

Maybe they didn't know, or maybe they just didn't want to help.

The homeless and the police had a frosty relationship to put it mildly.

Putting it more succinctly, neither liked the other.

Jamie considered herself outside that, but there was a definite feeling of distrust that underpinned every conversation, and a palpable sense of contempt that beat in the background.

She put it out of her mind and pressed on, hoping to hell that they weren't going to find Grace dead with a needle in her arm.

That would turn a shit-clap into a shit-pie.

Her dad had practically been a poet.

But she wasn't hungry.

A two-lane road swept across a bridge headed north out of the city. Below it, an old line ran perpendicular, the rails buried in stone chips grown over with brambles. It hadn't been used in years, and provided a sheltered area stretching across its width.

The banks on either side were fenced off and let down around twenty feet onto the flat at the bottom, and the space beneath the bridge was filled with tents and tarps, all huddled together out of the worst of the weather.

A section of fence had been pushed down, one of the posts dug out and shoved over.

It had been trampled flat and an old blanket had been laid over the crushed barbed wire at the top so that the denizens could make the traverse without getting nicked.

They'd walked the last stretch up a pretty much deserted street that had been blocked off at the bottom when the line had been put out of commission.

Jamie and Roper moved between the bollards and up the cracked pavement towards the gap in the fence in silence.

Three homeless people were sitting on the street — two by the makeshift entrance to the old line and one opposite.

He was wearing a bright green wind-cheater and had his arms folded under his armpits. He was doubled over and an old bobble-hat was hanging down between his knees.

Jamie took another look to see if he was okay, and spotted an empty vodka bottle between his heels against the kerb.

She sighed and dragged her eyes back to the man and woman sitting by the fence. They looked up at Roper and Jamie and stopped talking.

As they drew closer the pair got up and walked away quickly without another word, keen to avoid any questions that might have been directed at them.

Jamie and Roper didn't bother calling out, and neither were prepared to chase them down.

They were both in their forties, and neither of them were Grace.

Roper paused at the fence and put his foot on it, craning his neck to see under the bridge beyond.

Long green tendrils looped their way down the bank, the jagged bramble leaves twisting gently in the autumn air.

The sky overhead had turned turbulent and grey, bruised raw by the incoming winter.

Jamie shivered and stepped past Roper, who didn't seem inclined to make his way onto the loose bank in his old slick-bottom Chelsea boots.

Jamie didn't have that trepidation.

She looked back as she stepped over the stained blanket, her deeply-teased heel crunching in the loose stone.

Roper was grimacing, staring down at the bridge and the tents under it.

Jamie could see by the look on his face that he was hoping she'd not ask him to follow.

Sounds of conversation were echoing up and a thin blanket of smoke was clinging to the girders above. Someone was warming themselves.

Some faces had already appeared in the openings to the little makeshift huts and shelters, peering out at the two newcomers — at the two outsiders.

Some looked anxious, others scared. And some looked angry, baring their teeth in indignant snarls.

'You coming?' Jamie called back up, stepping sideways down the slope in a flood of pebbles.

Roper bit his lip, his fingers twitching at his sides as he decided. With an annoyed grunt he followed her, the stone dust caking his black Chelsea boots and turning them grey. 'Times like this I wished we were carrying,' he muttered as he got near. Jamie wasn't sure if it was to her or not.

Sure, sometimes it would pay to carry a gun. But she didn't think that going in there armed was going to yield any positive results. If they didn't like the police before, increasing the likelihood that they were going to have a pistol shoved in their face wasn't going to do anything for the relationship.

'Don't worry,' Jamie said back as they levelled out onto the bottom of the line, crushing syringes under their feet. 'If anything goes wrong I'll protect you.'

He wasn't amused and strode forward quickly, keen to get in and out as quickly as he could.

Jamie didn't share his blanket dislike for the homeless, but as they drew closer, she realised just how many people were packed into the little oasis under the bridge, and that among those half-hidden faces, peering out from darkened doorways and from under shadowing hoods, there might have been someone who wasn't afraid to kill.

Someone who might have done it already.

And someone who wouldn't think twice about doing it again.

They could be stepping into the front room of a murderer that didn't feel like getting caught today and would do whatever it took to make sure they didn't.

But as far as she could see, they didn't really have any other choice.

9

Eyes wide, Jamie. Don't give them an inch. Don't even let them think they can take one. Not even for a second.

That's what her dad would have said. What he had said to her. A hundred times.

He was no stranger to stepping into the wrong parts of the city. And he used to do it with the sort of attitude that scared most guys off. The kind of *try it and see what happens, shit-bag* stare that sent most people scampering.

She tried to carry that look. The look that conveyed that her crescent kick could crack a skull and they'd never see it coming. She didn't know if she could pull it off as well as her dad. He was six-three with the frame of a Scandinavian bison, after all, and about as intimidating. She, on the other hand, had her mum's frame. Though that did have its advantages. Mostly in part to the fact that if she did need to hit someone, they'd never expect it.

Roper pulled up short of the first tent and put his hands on his hips, looking around.

Narrow walkways wound around the little squats, making the thirty-by-sixty-foot space a veritable micro favela by all accounts.

There must have been fifty different shelters made up in there — of all varying sizes, shapes, and constructions.

'Jesus,' Roper grumbled. 'How the hell are we going to find Grace's tent in all this?'

Jamie surveyed the exteriors. All the heads seemed to shrink back inside as they got close. 'Reggie said that the tent was *too nice* to be here. So I guess we just look for the one that sticks out.'

He made a humming sound and pursed his lips, inhaling sharply. 'Grace Melver,' he called loudly, verging on yelling. 'Grace Melver!'

Nothing stirred.

'Smooth, Roper,' Jamie mumbled, sidestepping to look around the battered old four-man in front of them. Behind it a blue tarp had been hung from the girders overhead with what looked to be electrical wire. The sides were pinned down by rocks, making a shabby A-frame. There was no one inside.

'London Metropolitan Police,' Roper yelled again. 'We need to find Grace Melver, and any cooperation is greatly appreciated. If you could come out, and—'

'It's not going to work,' Jamie said, coming back. 'They know we can't just search their tents without cause.'

'How do you think they know that?'

'They're not stupid, Roper. They've been living on the streets — they know their rights when it comes to being searched, and they know that they can refuse — and they will because they don't want whatever they've got to be found.'

He hummed again, putting his hands on his hips. It had been a long time since he'd been in uniform and had to deal with them on a daily basis.

Things weren't like they used to be. There were rules now. And they had to be followed.

'None of them are going to invite us in to look around,' Jamie added. 'And demanding to be is only going to get their guard up. We need to be smart about this.'

He turned his back to the tents as if he couldn't bear to look at them anymore and stared into the sky. 'Then what do you suggest?'

Jamie thought for a second. 'I'd bet that most of them are holding drugs or a weapon of some kind. And they definitely don't want a team of uniformed officers and dogs down here.'

'So we offer them a choice?' Roper didn't seem enthused by the idea.

'Let me talk to them.' She wasn't really asking, and turned back before Roper could say anything else.

She cleared her throat, choosing the right tone. 'We know that Grace Melver sleeps down here. We just want to ask her a few questions. We don't know which tent is hers, so we're going to need you to help us out, alright?' She looked back and forth, but the shelters were unmoving, all the inhabitants waiting behind their doors, not daring to even breathe. 'This can go one of two ways — either someone tells us where Grace is and which tent is hers, or we're going to get a whole team of officers down here with sniffer dogs and vans and we're going to search every last one of these tents until we find what we're looking for.' She let that sink in. 'I don't want to spend my entire afternoon watching them confiscate your stuff and put you in handcuffs, so what's it going to be? You help us out, and we'll be out of here in minutes. If you don't…'

Roper came up behind her and planted his feet, folding his arms and sucking his teeth.

Jamie could feel her heart beating under her jacket, a sense of nervousness creeping up her spine, that from the impenetrable wall of tarps someone was just going to lurch out at them with a knife.

She had the unshakeable feeling that Oliver Hammond had escaped a cruel fate he was never meant to. That his body was never meant to be found. And a clue as to why that was lay somewhere just inside the fortress of tents.

No one replied from inside.

'Shit,' she muttered. They were calling her bluff.

They knew that getting a squad of officers out there with sniffer dogs to go through and dismantle fifty squats only for the inhabitants to be arrested and back out on the streets in a day — and for the tents to pop back up right after — was a huge waste of time and resources that DCI Smith would never approve.

It looked like they were on their own for this one.

Jamie set her jaw and inhaled.

'Now what?' Roper asked.

She knelt down and double-knotted her laces.

Eyes wide, Jamie.

'Now we do it the old-fashioned way.'

She stretched her shoulders and shook out her feet, shrugging off the tension building in her chest and stepped into the muddy passageway between two tents.

The pale November light died behind them. The low-hanging outer girders shielded the sky, the tarps strung up around them catching the rest.

It was darkness inside and the claustrophobic feel of rustling top sheets and rattling breath compounded the sense of unease coiled around Jamie's spine.

They stepped carefully, Jamie at the vanguard and Roper behind.

She didn't know where she was going, and moving methodically through this place wasn't possible. Every pathway led deeper into the labyrinth and most of the time dead-ended in a cul-de-sac of shelter entrances.

There was no way she could systematically cross off the wrong turns.

Roper was muttering and swearing behind her as he stepped in brown puddles and crunched syringes under his heels.

Yet another reason Jamie was willing to pay out for expensive, hard-capped boots. You never knew where you'd be stepping.

Right in the centre of the settlement a side-path led down a narrow little alley between the backs of two squats made out of shipping pallets, and opened into a little square where three tents all opened towards each other. Two of them looked ancient, propped up by sticks and other rigid objects, tied off and hanging from the bridge overhead with their support strings.

But the third tent looked pretty new.

It was a modest green and orange striped thing — big enough to fit no more than two people. But it matched the description that Reggie had given. He said that it looked too nice to be there, and this one did.

'Grace?' Jamie called softly.

Roper was right at her shoulder. She could smell the cigarettes on his breath.

There was no answer.

She stepped forward a little.

'Grace? Are you in there? Can you hear me?' There was an equal chance that the tent was empty, or that Grace was strung out and unresponsive. Either way, she needed to take a look.

Jamie glanced at Roper, whose face she couldn't read. His nose was wrinkled in disgust, but his flushed cheeks told her that he was as nervous as she was.

As much as she hated to generalise — confronting homeless people was never an easy thing to do. They could be unpredictable at best, and it was always smart to tread lightly.

She steadied her heart, took a breath and then clenched her hand to stop it from shaking.

The zipper toggle hung at the top of the entrance, shimmering gently in the half-light. Jamie couldn't tell if it was from movement inside, or from vibrations coming through the other squats around them.

She swallowed and reached for it, taking it lightly between her fingers, not wanting to startle whoever was inside.

Roper's breath was short and sharp in her ear.

'Grace?' she tried again, but there was no response.

She tugged left and the zipper began to unfurl, grinding its way along the teeth.

Roper exhaled behind her, filling the already ripe gap with hot air.

Jamie craned her neck to look through the widening gap as the flap began to fold down, but inside was shaded and dark.

The smell of urine wafted out and stung her nostrils.

She was aware of her boots in the mud, aware of the sounds around her, of the closeness of Roper as he looked over her head.

Everything was still, the zipper not seeming to move at all.

And then it tore itself down to the ground and out of her grasp.

Something flashed in the twilight and Jamie pulled her hand back just as the blade of a knife scythed through the air with a sharp hiss.

Roper caught her as she stumbled, the soft mud sucking on her heels and keeping her from stepping out of the way.

'Shit!' Roper called, nearly falling backwards himself.

The face of an older woman — in her late fifties and bedraggled, skin like creased leather, baring odd, broken and brown teeth — appeared in the gap, her hair tangled and grey around her head. She growled and then let out a guttural noise, swinging what looked to be a rusted paring knife.

She had one bony fist around the material of the tent door, and the other was brandishing the weapon. But she didn't seem to want to move from the threshold. She was there on her knees, mouth agape, wrapped in old blankets.

'Jesus,' Jamie, grunted, pulling herself upright and freeing her foot from the mud. She had her hands up, but they were out of arm's reach and the woman wasn't inclined to leave the safety of her tent.

'Put the knife down,' Roper ordered over her shoulder, pointing at her. 'We're police.'

'Fuuuuuck off!' the woman rasped, her eyes totally black, her pupils filling the entirety of her irises. Jamie could see a glass pipe on her blankets, the bottom charred black from a lighter flame.

The place stank and the woman looked like she hadn't eaten in months.

Roper was about to step around Jamie but she put her hand on his chest and turned away instead. 'Don't bother, we won't get anything from her.' That dead-eyed look was too familiar. 'She's not going to help us and that's not Grace's tent.'

'How can you tell?' Roper asked, locking eyes with the woman and staring her down.

'Because that woman's not left it for weeks, and we know Grace has been back and forth to the shelter.' She pulled on Roper's arm, pushing him back down the path.

'She didn't get you, did she?'

Jamie looked down at the mark on her suede jacket — the blade had slit into the top layer of material, but the thick hide had stopped it going through. There was just a thin line in the nap and nothing more. If she'd have been bare-armed or wearing something thinner, then it would have cut her. Her father had always worn a knee-length leather sherpa jacket for that exact reason. And she was glad she took his advice when it came to dressing for the job. 'No,' she said rubbing the mark and watching it disappear. 'She didn't get me.'

She was staring at her hands and watched as they hit Roper's back and folded up.

Jamie bumped into him, not realising he'd stopped, her chin hitting his coat between his shoulders.

She leaned sideways to look around him and saw why he'd stopped.

About ten feet ahead of them, where the passage between the squats met the next walkway, a man was standing.

He was tall — about six feet, and though he was skinny, his wide frame still made him look imposing. His bald head was silhouetted against the grey light bleeding in from beyond the lip of the bridge, the ruffled fur-lined hood of his oversized parka jagged around his ears.

His skin was marked and pulled tight against his cheeks, his dead eyes staring right at them, unblinking.

Roper's fists curled at his sides as he stared him down.

The guy was obviously homeless, but was wearing a pair of old boots and jeans that both looked like they fit.

Jamie narrowed her eyes, trying to figure out what was throwing her off about this guy — apart from the undead glare. It was the way his hands were in his pockets — like they were holding onto something. Like his fists were tightened around something, ready to be pulled out and used.

But he wasn't moving. Wasn't doing anything. He was just looking at them.

Roper didn't give an inch and Jamie breathed steadily, making sure her heart was even, her muscles well oxygenated. She measured the width of the walkway, the distance to this guy, how she'd get around Roper and how she'd take him out if he pulled something out of those pockets.

The space was too narrow for a roundhouse and the ground too slippery for a sidekick.

The guy turned from Roper to her and leaned his head sideways a few inches as if to get a better look at her.

Roper's left arm rose automatically and hung diagonally across the space in front of Jamie, as if barring the way.

She could hear her father's voice in her head. *Don't let them swing first. If you think they're going to do something, put them down before they get the chance. You never know what they're going to do or what they're going to have.*

She couldn't stop looking at his pockets. A knife? A gun? A dirty needle?

She tensed and pushed Roper's arm down, moving past him.

He tried to keep it up, but she wasn't about to let him go first. He wasn't exactly operating at full capacity and the only time he'd ever come sparring with her — the result of a lost bet that he could go an entire day without a cigarette — she'd laid him out with ease.

No, even if the guy in the parka was just a little bit handy — which Jamie wouldn't put past him — then Roper wouldn't come out of it okay. Especially not in these close quarters. Definitely not in his smooth-bottomed Chelsea boots.

At least if she got a clean shot at him, she was pretty confident she could put him down.

She stepped into the middle of the walkway now with Roper behind her.

The guy in the parka cocked his head a little further, curious maybe — a little intrigued.

Jamie pressed her right foot into the mud until she felt her footing was solid and then turned a quarter on, visualising the two steps, the hop, and the front kick that would stun the solar plexus and give her enough time to sweep his legs.

She narrowed her eyes, exhaling, letting her hands hang loose in front of her, waiting for a sign that he was about to do something. Striking first was key, but she was a detective, and assaulting someone without provocation was a great way to get suspended.

Her father would have hit first and asked questions later.

The guy would have been a bloody mess already.

But she wasn't her father, and that wasn't how she did things.

The guy in the parka met her eyes and righted his head.

His mouth curled sideways into a smirk, his pock-marked cheek folding up under his ringed eyes.

And then he slunk away.

He took one big step to the right and disappeared behind the corner before Jamie could do anything about it.

It took her a second to register that he wasn't attacking and she rewired her brain out of fight mode.

She moved into the junction and turned to follow him, seeing that he was moving fast — already fifteen feet away and slipping between two squats.

He cast a look over his right shoulder, his left hand hidden behind his head, his elbow up. Was he talking on a mobile?

She couldn't make it out in the shadow of the bridge.

It looked like he was.

She saw his eyes flash in the gloom, hanging still for an instant, and then he was gone, evaporated between two squats and into the maze of tarps and tents.

Jamie blew out a long breath, listening to her heart slow in her ears.

Roper came up on her shoulder and followed her gaze. 'What the hell was that all about?'

She ground her teeth. 'I don't know, but I don't like it.' She peered out from under the bridge at the darkening sky.

There was rain in the air and the light was already beginning to fade.

They didn't have much time left.

'Come on,' she said, pressing forward. 'We still need to find Grace and I don't want to be out here in the dark.'

Roper laughed sardonically and threw a cigarette between his lips. 'That makes two of us.'

10

Jamie tracked through the muddy walkway after Dead-Eyes. It was the only name that came to mind.

She could still feel his gaze on her skin, and she squirmed as she walked, needing a shower to wash it off.

The path zigzagged and she looked down each little off-shoot with more conviction than before, discarding the squats a handful at a time on the hunt for Grace's tent.

Every so often someone would poke their head out of their squat or walk around the corner, see Roper and Jamie coming, and then duck back inside.

None responded to their questions.

They were nearing the end of the bridge and the clouds were growing dark when they came to a fork in the path.

Jamie turned back to Roper, who was looking at her with the sort of expression that said, *this never goes well for the Scooby Doo gang.* He sighed. 'Fine.'

'You take left,' Jamie said, stepping right. 'Shout if you find anything.'

Roper nodded to her and went quickly, keen to get this over with.

Jamie was starting to get the feeling that either Grace had upped and left or that Reggie hadn't got his information quite right.

She sighed and plunged onwards, keeping her eyes peeled for anything out of place.

The path circled right and cut left, ending at the far side of the bridge.

Jamie had all but given up hope when she saw a streak of lime green in amongst the blue tarps.

She stepped lightly, navigating around a stagnant brown puddle and pulled back a tarp that had snapped its support strings.

It was hanging limply across the path and behind it Jamie saw what she could only have described as a 'tent that was too nice to be there'.

While most of the others appeared to be bargain-basement clearance sale items and second-hand rescues, this one was anything but. It was made by a high-end Scandinavian brand with a built-in top sheet and self-tightening support lines. She should know, it was the same brand that her dad bought to take her camping when she was a kid.

Even the three-man version, which this was, would set someone back hundreds of pounds. So why it was sitting down here, caked in human shit and bridge-runoff, she couldn't have guessed.

'Grace?' she asked, loud enough to permeate the waterproof membrane.

She thought about knocking, and then wondered how she would go about doing that on a tent door.

Jamie looked around, but the pathway was quiet.

She was about to reach out for the zipper again when her father's voice echoed in her head.

Eyes wide. She swallowed and retracted her hand, seeing the faint line of the cut in the suede on her forearm. Come on, you know that Grace was into heroin. Be smart. If she's in there, you don't know what sort of state she's going to be in. Hell, this could be a crime-scene…

The thought filled her with dread. What was she about to find?

She exhaled, tasting the rotten air on her breath, and dug in her pockets for a pair of latex gloves, pulling them on with a shiver.

This close to the edge of the bridge the tent was exposed to the elements and the temperature was noticeably colder.

Despite her boots being waterproof, her jeans were damp at the hems and the moisture was leeching heat from her body.

She shook her hands to get the blood flowing and wasted no time. She didn't want to get surprised again. She needed to be quicker.

In a quick movement she took hold of both zips, pulled them apart at the same time and then stepped back, giving the opening some space in case of any more attacks.

But there weren't any.

The flap folded over, curled onto the muddy ground, and a wash of warm, stale air flooded out.

It took a second for her eyes to adjust — inside she could just see a mess of blankets and sleeping bags.

'Shit,' she muttered, reaching into her inner-pocket for the multi-tool she kept there — a pliers and wire snip, a six-centimetre knife, a screwdriver, and most importantly, an LED flashlight. It came in handy surprisingly often. Her dad had always carried a light and a blade. He'd insisted on them. Except his was a five-inch stag horn hunting knife and a flashlight thick enough to bludgeon with.

She thumbed the light to life and stepped forward, crouching and sweeping the beam over the interior.

There were pillows and blankets stacked against the back and on top of the covers an electric lantern was lying on its side. Next to it, on what looked to be a snapped in half dinner tray, she could see a little plastic wrap crumpled into a ball, as well as a charred teaspoon.

'Shit.' She narrowed her eyes and leaned in further, taking hold of the bottom of the lumpy double sleeping bag that seemed to be filling the entire right side of the tent.

Jamie pulled on it, her heart beating hard, and watched as the far end flattened out and then dragged itself over a pale white face.

The lopsided bob came into view, the green eyes shuttered and fluttering slowly. Her skin was white and beaded with sweat under her bagged eyes, her breath shallow and raking.

'Roper!' Jamie yelled as loudly as she could from her crouched position. She climbed inside, stuffing the tool back into her pocket and pulling the sleeping bag down harder to expose Grace's body.

A syringe rolled out of the folds and settled somewhere among the blankets.

Jamie got in next to her and uncovered her arms, seeing a fresh bruise and smear of blood from where she'd slid the needle in what looked like just minutes before.

She took Grace in her arms and dragged her upright.

The girl grumbled a little, turning her head away. Jamie could smell the sweat on her skin.

'Grace?' she asked, striking that comforting yet assertive tone her mother had used a million times on her father. 'Can you hear me? Grace?'

She made a strange noise in her throat, but couldn't form any words.

Jamie swapped arms and brushed the hair from her cheeks to get at her pulse, shuffling around behind Grace, her knees protesting at the awkward angle and pressure. 'Jesus,' she muttered as Grace's neck became exposed. There were bruises around her throat and under her ears, like someone had been choking her.

Jamie cast an eye downwards, too, feeling for a pulse in her jugular without looking. Grace's wrists were red as well — like she'd been pinned down.

There was a pulse, but it was slow and weak. Jamie steadied her hand and moved it down Grace's midriff towards the hem of the loose hoodie she was wearing, pulling it up to expose her lower abdomen and the protrusions of her hips. She was thin.

But that wasn't what Jamie was looking for. There were bruises where the bones met the skin. 'Goddammit,' Jamie swore, supporting her head again. 'Roper!' she yelled for a second time.

She could hear cursing and squelching in the mud outside as he got closer.

Jamie fished in her pocket for her phone and slid her thumb over the screen, smearing it with whatever she'd got on her hands in the last thirty seconds. She dialled the emergency number and it connected instantly. 'This is Detective Sergeant Jamie Johansson with the Metropolitan Police — I need an ambulance immediately — possible drug overdose.'

'One moment,' a calm voice said as they tapped in the information. 'We've got a GPS lock on your location and paramedics have been dispatched. Estimated arrival time is three minutes. Please proceed to an unobstructed area so that you can be easily located.'

Roper appeared in the gap, eyes wide, panting. 'Everything okay? Jesus, Jamie,' he said, inhaling sharply as the situation became apparent.

'I'll stay with her, you get out into the open — flag the ambulance down,' she said, the phone still at her ear. It was standard protocol to stay on the line so that the operator could be updated if the situation changed or further assistance was needed.

Anything drug-related would automatically trigger a patrol car to be sent out, too.

Sirens had already punctuated the cold November air.

Roper nodded his compliance and backed out of the tent, moving out from under the bridge and into the open so that the ambulance would see him.

Jamie pinned the phone to her cheek with her shoulder, ignoring the feeling of whatever was on the screen. 'We're in a lime-green tent under the bridge,' she said carefully. 'Detective Roper will guide them in.'

'I'll relay that to the driver,' the operator said. 'Has the condition of the patient changed?'

Jamie counted the pulse beats. 'No, but her heart is slow.'

'Do you know if she has any other injuries, or any pre-existing conditions? Blood conditions or transmissible disease?'

Jamie thought back to the intake form. No hepatitis as far as she knew. No HIV. Just gonorrhoea. 'No, I don't think so.'

'Alright, the paramedics should be with you shortly.'

The sirens grew louder and Jamie continued to look at her wrists, at her throat. Someone had choked her, pinned her down.

The bruise on her arm looked raw, like the injection hadn't been gentle.

A question entered her mind.

Had she done this to herself?

The hip bruising was synonymous with someone straddling her, pinning her down.

Her mind went straight to Dead-Eyes. He'd come this way. He'd seen them — he'd rushed off. He'd made a call. And then suddenly, Grace was ODing in her tent less than a minute later?

She swallowed hard and kept her fingers tight against Grace's neck. The pulse was getting weaker.

Jamie could feel her head getting heavy against her hand as she fell limp, her breathing quietening down and becoming laboured.

'She's losing consciousness,' Jamie said, the words forming themselves on her lips.

There was tapping in the ether as the operator transmitted it to the paramedics.

Sirens wailed.

'Hurry.'

Roper's voice echoed around her. 'Down here! There's a gap — over there.'

Stones scrabbled and cascaded down the banks as bodies slid and stumbled onto the flat.

Footsteps echoed.

Grace's pulse weakened.

The light spilling in from the doorway disappeared and Jamie looked up to see two paramedics, a man and a woman, looking in.

They were both pulling on gloves, inspecting the scene.

'Alright?' the woman asked. She was in her forties with dark hair pulled into a ponytail and a full fringe. She had a northern accent. 'We're going t'have to come in there, okay? I'm goin'ta take her off you, okay? And Phil here will help her, alright?'

Jamie nodded and the woman smiled.

Phil pulled a dose of naloxone into a syringe expertly. He tapped the bubbles out and then nodded at the woman.

'Ready?' she asked Jamie.

She nodded back and in one movement there were three of them in the tent.

The paramedic took Grace's head and arm and pulled her upright out of Jamie's lap, standing with one foot between her knees, her back against the roof of the tent as Phil grabbed her left arm and raised it up squeezing with his fingers and thumb around her bicep to expose a vein.

It was a well-rehearsed dance that they'd done a thousand times by the look of it.

The paramedic moved her hips to the side so Jamie could climb out, and then Roper was pulling her upright by the elbows.

Inside, the plunger fell and Grace sucked in a deep breath, groaning as she did.

'Can y'hear me?' the paramedic said. 'What's yer name, love?'

Grace mumbled but didn't form words.

Jamie realised she was holding her breath and looked down to see Roper's hand still around her elbow, his face carved from stone.

Time seemed to lurch past in chunks as a truck surged by on the road overhead or as a horn blasted in the distance.

Roper was barely breathing himself, his eyes narrowed, focused on the mouth of the tent.

In the time it took for them to bring Grace around, a patrol car arrived and two uniformed officers came down onto the tracks.

A crowd of the denizens of the under-bridge settlement had also crawled into the light to see what was going on. It seemed that the spectacle of an overdose was too good to miss, and was worth being sighted by Jamie and Roper.

Jamie scanned the gathering crowd, dotted on the walkways between the tents, but there was no sign of the bald guy in the parka. He was gone. Fled the scene of the crime.

The northern paramedic whose name they caught as Bethany — Bet for short — came out of the tent, smiling. 'She's going to be okay. Have a sore head, I'm sure, but she'll be alright. We'll take her up t'the van, get her all checked over. Was a good thing y'called when y'did, though. Few more minutes and it would have been touch and go.'

Jamie nodded, sighing with relief. 'Do you think she'll be up to answering some questions?' she asked.

'I would think so, but don't expect too much. She'll still be coming round for a few hours yet.'

'Thank you,' Roper said, his arms folded against the cold.

It was getting late in the afternoon now and dusk was closing in.

He turned away and walked into the open, away from the uniformed officers who were talking to the other people living there, and away from the tents.

When they were in open ground, drowning in the noise of the rush-hour traffic building around them, he sighed. 'Jesus, what a day.'

'Yeah,' Jamie said, looking back at the tent. 'What a day.'

'You see Grace's wrists?'

She nodded. 'Yeah, throat and hips too.'

Roper pursed his lips. 'What do you think?'

'Best case?' She let out a long sigh. 'I don't know — her and Oliver were into that sort of thing... It's all consensual, and she ODed by accident.' Jamie paused and looked back at the mess of tents and tarps. 'Worst case?' She shook her head. 'Attempted murder? Long-term abuse? None of the options are any less horrifying.'

'I know what you mean. The drugs, the tent, Oliver, the bald guy with the—'

'Dead eyes?'

Roper stared at her for a second. 'Not just me then.'

'Hard to miss them.'

He scratched his head, taking his top teeth over his bottom lip. 'Shit. Stinks like someone's trying to clean up a mess.' He'd smoked three cigarettes in the last forty minutes. And she could tell he was scratching for another one. He checked his watch and then looked up into the cloudy sky.

Jamie's stomach was rumbling. She was hungry. But they weren't even close to being done yet.

Neither of them said it, but they both knew that the day was far from over, and that depending on what Grace was going to tell them, it may just have been getting started.

11

Thirty minutes later Grace was sitting on the rear tailgate of the ambulance four-by-four — a nimble SUV-crossover better suited for the city than a bulky box-truck.

Jamie was standing across the street, watching between the passing cars.

Phil and Bet were still tending to her. Phil was taking her blood pressure again and Bet was going through some forms and giving her a physical. She had a heart rate monitor hooked up and seemed to be doing better — though she was still doubled over a little with her head on her chest.

Jamie turned at the sound of footsteps. 'Finally,' she said with a relieved sigh, lifting her hands to catch the sandwich tossed to her.

The label read *Plain Ham* and it had a reduced sticker stuck on the front.

'Springing for the expensive stuff,' she joked, looking up at Roper, who was already halfway through his own wafer-thin on white.

'All they had,' he grumbled, choking it down. 'Believe it or not petrol stations don't carry a wide selection. Especially not at this time.' He took another bite and chewed like it was made of cement.

Jamie split the carton open and jammed the sharp end of a triangle into her mouth. The bread was all but stale, the ham slimy. But she guessed it had been sitting out since the morning. And she'd had worse.

'How's she doing?' Roper asked, proffering a bottle of water that the label said was bottled in Iran.

'Okay, I think.' Jamie didn't really know. 'She's sitting up on her own now, which is better than she was doing five minutes ago.'

Roper nodded. 'Alright, well let's head over,' he said, shoving the last of his sandwich into his mouth.

Jamie chewed hard, the bread soaking up what little saliva there was on her tongue. She didn't think she could finish the other half, so she carried it across the road with her and tossed it into the bin a few feet from the ambulance.

'Hi,' Roper said, stepping up onto the kerb.

Bet looked up from her clipboard.

'Is she okay to be asked some questions?'

'I suppose,' she said in her northern twang. 'But not too much, alright? She's been through it.'

The two uniformed officers still lingered in the background. They'd have to take a statement once Roper and Jamie had gotten what they wanted to know.

Roper moved in first, standing in front of her with his hands on his hips. 'Miss Melver,' he said assertively. 'Can you hear me?'

Grace picked her head up slowly, looking like a puppy who'd just been caught shitting on the carpet. She nodded, her head barely moving.

Her skin looked yellow in the orange glow of the streetlights.

Jamie hung back, inspecting her face as Roper talked.

He was the senior officer and the interrogation was his lead.

And as usual, he went in with the stick, not the carrot.

'You're lucky, Grace,' he said almost derisively. She was a lot less than half his age, but Jamie knew that speaking to her like a child wouldn't get him anywhere. Things had changed since he'd been in uniform. The city was different, and the people were too. 'If we didn't get to you when we did, well, you'd be dead right now.'

She lowered her head again and Jamie looked at Roper's back, wondering how hard she'd have to sock him in the kidney for him to shut up.

Grace said nothing in reply.

'So how about you answer some questions for me, huh?'

She lowered her head even further.

'Where'd you get the heroin?'

She couldn't control it. Jamie jabbed him hard with her knuckles and he buckled sideways, turning around. He looked fierce for a second — but then softened.

'What the hell was that for?' he hissed.

She had a long list of reasons why that was a stupid question and an even stupider one to ask first.

Jamie ignored him and stepped forward, crouching down so she was level with Grace. 'It's Grace, right?'

Grace looked up a touch, staring at her through her badly-cut fringe.

Jamie measured her gaze weighing up what to say first. And then it dawned on her. She probably didn't even know.

Jamie cleared her throat. 'I'm Detective Johansson — Jamie. I was the one who found you.' She paused, meeting the girl's stare. 'We were looking for you actually.'

She could feel Roper standing over her with his arms folded, and watched as Grace looked up at him, her eyes wide with fear.

'It's about Ollie.'

Her eyes snapped back to Jamie now. 'You found him?' she sounded hopeful.

Jamie nodded slowly. 'Yeah, we did.'

'Is he okay?' The hope waned a little.

Jamie sighed and looked away. 'I'm sorry, Grace, he's… dead.'

Grace's hands flew to her mouth, her eyes filling with tears.

'I'm sorry,' Jamie said quietly. 'There was nothing that could have been done.'

'Oh God,' she sobbed.

'We think someone did it,' Jamie said, putting her hand on Grace's knee, deciding what to say and what not to. 'Do you know who might have wanted to hurt Ollie? Was he arguing with anyone, or did he owe anyone any money, or—'

'No, no!' Grace said almost sharply. 'He never owed anyone anything. He wouldn't — some guys do,' she said, looking from Jamie to Roper and back, 'but not Ollie. He wouldn't!'

'Okay, it's okay.' Jamie nodded. 'That's great. But the way that he was, uh…' She cleared her throat again. 'It looks like someone wanted to hurt him. We don't think they meant for him to, you know — like it was an accident. But someone was holding him — keeping him. Do you know what I'm saying?' It was difficult to not use the words *die, prisoner,* or *victim.*

Grace looked at her for a few seconds, and then nodded. 'I understand, but I don't know…'

'That's okay.' Jamie bit her lip, looked up at Roper, who gave her a nod to keep going, and then took a breath. For all his faults, Roper knew when he was the right man for the job and when someone else was better suited. 'We spoke to Mary today, at the shelter.'

Grace's interest piqued.

'She told us where to find you,' Jamie said, leaving Reggie out of it. 'That's why we came. We wanted to speak to you about Ollie. She said that you two were trying to get clean together.'

Grace's face seemed to crease and sadden. She nodded. 'Yeah. We wanted to go somewhere.'

'I understand. I know what it's like to feel trapped.'

Grace looked at her and saw that it was the truth.

Jamie smiled a little and the girl returned it. 'It's hard to deal with the idea of losing someone.'

'Yeah.'

'Is that why you did what you did today?'

Grace seemed to pale a few shades, shrinking back into the hood of her jumper. Not sheepish, though. Scared, maybe. Scared to comment on it.

'You're not in trouble,' Jamie said, trying to sound warm. 'We just need to know about Ollie. About who his friends were, whether he was involved with anything he shouldn't have been.'

Grace had gone catatonic now. Jamie had seen it before. The barriers had come down. She wasn't going to say anything more about it.

This was going to be tricky.

She reached out and took Grace's hand, turning it upwards so that the dark bruises on her wrists shone in the lamplight. 'What are these?'

Grace pulled her hand back and shoved it into the pouch pocket of her hoodie.

Jamie had to take a leap. It wasn't protocol, and she needed to be careful not to put words in the girl's mouth, but they needed more than they were getting.

'I don't think you did this to yourself.'

Grace was still, like a statue.

'I think someone did this to you.' Jamie leaned down to try and catch her eye. 'To keep you quiet, maybe? To stop you from talking to us.'

'No,' Grace said quickly.

'We met someone else today. He was tall, with a shaved head and a big fur-hooded coat.' Jamie was focused intently on Grace as she reeled off the description casually. Over her head the heart monitor climbed into triple digits. She couldn't hide the physiological reaction.

Jamie glanced at Roper and then to the monitor and he followed her gaze.

She carried on. 'He ran from us, towards your tent, and then we found you. And you know what I think?'

Grace's eyes fell on hers, but she didn't move her head.

'I think you've been using long enough to know your limits. To know when too much is too much.' She'd tried the carrot. Now she'd have to go with the stick too. 'So how about this? You tell me who the man is, and we'll make sure that the two officers over there don't ask you about the heroin, alright?'

Grace's jaw flexed, her nostrils flaring.

'You've got to give me something, Grace. This is a murder investigation, and we need your help. Someone killed Ollie, and someone tried to kill you—'

Roper cleared his throat behind her. Putting words in a victim's mouth was wrong, but telling them what had been done to them was even worse.

Jamie ignored him. '—and I need your help to find out what happened.'

Grace looked up after a while and scanned the street, looking for any sign of someone watching them. 'I don't know who he is,' she said after a few seconds, barely above a whisper. 'Ollie knew him. He would... It's who he got it from. He wouldn't let me get it anymore.' She shivered. 'He said that he didn't want me to get it, and that he would get it for us so that we could...' She began to cry. Heavy tears rolled down her cheeks. 'He was serious, about us getting off it, you know? He was. We were getting help.'

'Help?' Jamie looked at Roper again. He was leaning in to hear better. 'From who?'

'From a doctor at the shelter,' she said, shaking her head. 'He was helping us. But... I don't know... Ollie and that guy with the fur... They would... He would... He said he was doing something that would help us, you know to get enough money so that we could...' She broke down into uncontrollable sobbing, the realisation that she was now alone setting in.

Jamie sighed, holding it together. 'Okay, Grace. That's enough.' She wouldn't get any more out of her tonight. Jamie stood up. 'Was Ollie sleeping in the tent with you?' she asked more firmly.

Grace didn't stop crying, but nodded, her sleeved hands pressed to her face.

'Is his stuff still there?'

She nodded again.

Jamie turned and waved to the uniformed officers, beckoning them over.

They came quickly.

Jamie swallowed the lump in her throat and nodded to Grace. 'Take her into custody.'

Grace's head snapped up. 'What? You said—' She looked pale with shock.

'Charge her with possession, hold her overnight. We'll question her in the morning.'

The officers nodded and then turned to Grace. 'Grace Melver, on the charge of possession of a class A substance, we're arresting you—'

Jamie pulled Roper away, shaking off the feeling of anger bubbling inside her. She didn't want to do that, but she didn't want Grace out on the streets. At least in a holding cell she'd be secure, and maybe tomorrow they could question her with more clarity. It was the best thing for her, whether she knew it or not.

'What do you think?' she asked him. She had her own ideas, but wanted to know his thoughts.

'I think it's a damn mess,' he said, rubbing his head. 'But I'm starting to see a picture forming. Boy meets girl, girl gets boy into heroin, boy wants to get girl off heroin, makes a shady deal with some bad people, gets in over his head. Kidnapping turns sour, gets out of hand. And they send a junkie to clean up the mess. Sound about right?'

'I don't think it sounds wrong,' Jamie muttered, staring back down onto the tracks.

Grace was still crying behind her as the officers got to the part about the right to silence.

She checked her watch. It was nearly six thirty. They'd been at it for nearly twelve hours.

'I want to search that tent before it gets any darker.' Jamie thought about all the unanswered questions — where it had come from and who paid for it. The STD. What Ollie was doing and how he was doing it. But they couldn't get all their answers tonight. It was late in the day and they needed to process. Needed to let Grace settle down before they questioned her. Needed more information.

Roper groaned, knowing she was right. 'Okay,' he said. 'But after that we're going to the pub.'

'I don't drink,' Jamie said for the thousandth time.

'Then you can bloody well watch me.'

12

They waited for the officers to put Grace in the patrol car and then headed back towards the ambulance.

'Bet,' Jamie said, touching her elbow.

She withdrew from the crossover and stood up, cracking her back. They were pretty much packed and ready to head out.

'Do you have a pair of sharps gloves we could borrow?' Jamie asked, smiling.

Bet looked as tired as she felt. 'Borrow? You going to drop them off later?'

She laughed nervously. 'Have.'

Bet made an 'mmm' sound and turned to her bag, fishing inside it.

She pulled out a pair of hard rubber gloves and handed them over. 'Here.'

Jamie took them thankfully. They were bright red.

She was going to be careful whatever happened, but she was tired and didn't want to get pricked. Gloves were the smart choice.

'Thanks,' she said, pushing them into her jacket pocket.

'Anything else?' Bet asked.

Phil turned from the cockpit. 'Come on — we've got another call,' he shouted, cranking the engine and powering up the lights.

Bet held her finger up. 'Hold that thought. Duty calls.'

Jamie didn't have anything else to say, but she held her hands up and let Bet get around the car anyway. 'Don't let me stop you.'

Bet was in the ambulance and it was speeding away through the traffic in seconds.

After a minute the sirens were swallowed by the city, just a distant echo bouncing through the streets.

Rush hour was fading and the road was growing quieter.

Most people had retreated to their homes. The only pedestrians on the streets now were wrapped up in scarves and thick coats, their shapes and faces obscured. They shuffled quickly along keen to get where they were going.

'Ready?' Roper asked anxiously, sucking on a cigarette. He must have smoked an entire pack today. That was why he offered to go and get them some food. He'd gotten a fresh one.

She nodded, feeling her eyes heavy. 'Let's do it.'

They stepped back over the fence and down towards the squats.

The colour that had seemed almost vibrant earlier now looked cold. The tarps sagged and flapped ominously in the wind, and Grace's lime-green tent was empty and devoid of life.

A shiver ran up Jamie's spine and her and Roper paused just short of it, both feeling the same sense of trepidation.

'After you,' Roper said, offering her the entrance.

'A true gentleman.'

'You're the one with the gloves.'

'You can have them if you want.'

He held his hand up, fingers spread. 'My hands are too big.'

'They're one size.'

He just stared at her, lips pressed into a line.

'Fine,' she muttered, pulling them on, knowing he would have stayed there all night looking at her if it meant not doing something he didn't want to. And she wanted to get this done and get home for a shower as soon as she could.

The tent beckoned.

She crouched down and pulled out her flashlight again, flicking the beam on.

It made everything except what was under the harsh beam look even darker.

She took hold of the bottom of the sleeping bag she'd grabbed earlier and pulled it out, handing the edge to Roper. 'Take this and pull it taut,' she said.

He obliged, roughly.

'Gently! Jesus, Roper — there's a needle in here.'

'Sorry.'

'Slowly, please.'

He did as was told and pulled inch by inch as Jamie flattened it out and moved the light back and forth, looking for the syringe.

She found it and picked it up, trusting the gloves. 'Roper,' she said, turning. 'Catch.'

She feigned throwing it at him and he dropped the bag and jumped back, realising a second after that she was joking. 'That's not funny, Johansson,' he grumbled.

'Yeah it was.'

He wiped his hands off on his jeans — which were probably less clean than the sleeping bag — and stood up, looking around. 'Place is a ghost town.'

Jamie knew that everyone would be inside sleeping by now. When the sun went down it was easy to lose heat fast. And if they lit a fire, some local would call the police. No, there was an art to turning in early and conserving the warmth of the day. And the homeless had that down to a tee.

Jamie kept looking, turning out the folds and pushing everything to the side as she discarded it as unimportant.

The dinner tray with Ollie and Grace's kit had been taken as evidence by the officers, but Jamie expected there to be something hidden inside that was designed to be passed over by hurried hands.

But she wouldn't miss anything. She never did.

Under the sleeping bag there were four pillows — all odd, two of them with covers, two without. Jamie shook and pressed on them to see if anything was concealed inside. There wasn't.

She put them with the sleeping bag in the corner.

The floor was lined with an old duvet, some picnic blankets, and a few padded coats that looked older than Jamie was. She went through the pockets, ran her hands over the liners, and then put them aside too. All she found were some old chocolate wrappers and a receipt from seven years previous. She expected they fit Ollie and Grace but didn't check the sizes.

The floor underneath was a bare bottom-sheet and a little muddy. Stones and leaves had found their way in and been pressed flat into the material, pushed into the soft dirt underneath.

There were three rucksacks there as well. The first two had some spare clothes in them — extra jumpers, a few pairs of soiled and dirty underpants. Socks with holes in them. There were also empty bottles of water.

She put them aside too, the pile to her right growing.

The third and final rucksack didn't have old clothes in it, but had more than two dozen used syringes. Some were wrapped in tissue and dropped in. Others were tossed in loose. But this was obviously their trash-bag. A lot of users just tossed them outside. It said a lot about Ollie and Grace's morals. She wondered if they took them to a needle exchange that swapped new for old — it was becoming more common now. A trend that was thankfully catching on.

Otherwise, though, the bag was empty.

'Shit,' she muttered.

'What is it?' Roper asked.

'Nothing.'

'What?'

'There's nothing here.' She swept the flashlight around again, seeing if she'd missed anything. 'They didn't have anything between them except dirty underwear and used needles.'

'I supposed you were hoping for an envelope with a big question mark on it?'

'There was always hope,' Jamie said with a sigh.

She gave the tent one last sweep and turned to leave when a gust of wind shook the sheets around her.

'Bugger.' Roper swore from outside, shuddering. 'That's cold.'

Jamie stopped and snickered a little and then paused, hearing something flap behind her.

She turned and looked into the gloom.

'Something wrong?' Roper asked.

'I don't know,' Jamie said, stepping back in and combing the back of the tent more thoroughly. 'I heard something.'

'Probably my bones rattling together. It's bloody freezing out here.'

Jamie ignored him and looked for the source of the noise.

In the back at the corner of the tent she could see that a slit had been cut into the groundsheet.

She thought it may have been a tear, but she knew that the material was a Gore-Tex reinforced ripstop. It couldn't just be torn. It would have to have been cut.

She approached, homing in with the flashlight, and reached out.

The cut was clean, done with a sharp blade. Though what kind she didn't know.

She spread the edges carefully with her left hand, squinting into the gap and moving the light around to see what was underneath.

The ground looked pressed flat — like under most tents, but disturbed.

She was about to put the flashlight between her teeth when she thought twice. She'd been handling stuff in the tent, and while she wasn't a germaphobe by any means, there was good sense. She reminded herself to disinfect it later.

'Roper,' she called.

He ducked his head into the gap. 'Yeah?'

'Hold this,' she commanded, giving him the light. 'Come in and shine it over here.' She pointed to the cut.

He took it like it was radioactive and squeezed himself in, either struggling to bend or making it seem like he was. But either way Jamie wasn't buying it. She was holding the edges of the cut open and nodded to it.

'Here.'

He obliged, hanging over her and shining the light down from above.

Now that she had both hands on it she could see the telltale lump of something buried in the dirt.

She dug her fingers in carefully, pulling out chunks of clotted earth rather than scraping away. She had no idea what was in there.

Jamie moved slowly, not wanting to get caught out, and pretended that she didn't hear Roper's pained grunts.

It wasn't that he was decrepit, just hungover and tired.

She shared the sentiment — at least the tired part.

The mud began to come away, and she saw the corner of something white push itself out.

Roper made a little 'Oh,' sound.

Jamie plucked at it but her fingers slipped off. It was slick with muddy clay.

Roper smacked his lips overhead.

'Keep the light steady,' she said, having another go.

'Sorry,' he muttered, swapping hands.

She got a firmer grip this time and pulled it back and forth to work it loose.

The ground split around it and then pulled itself apart and she took more of what now seemed to be the edge of some cloth.

Jamie could feel Roper's breath on the back of her neck as she dragged the thing free.

It came through the cut and flopped onto the groundsheet.

They could see that it was a filthy sock, and that there was something inside.

Grace and Ollie — or one of them — had gone to the trouble of cutting through the bottom of the tent — sacrificing the water tightness — just to bury this. Whatever it was, they didn't want it to be found.

Jamie and Roper were both holding their breath.

She swallowed and reached down, taking the sock by the toe.

She lifted it and shook gently, watching as the lump moved downwards, catching on the threads.

And then it fell out, landing heavily on the ground.

'Well shit,' Roper said, the surprise in his voice apparent.

Jamie stared at it, confused, processing. 'Well shit is right.'

There, lying on the dirty groundsheet of a homeless couple's tent was a gold watch.

And not a cheap one, either. It was a Swiss brand, pearl faced with a gold link bracelet. It must have been at least five hundred pounds worth. Maybe a thousand. She didn't know. But she would soon.

The question of value was secondary to her, though.

What mattered the most was why it was there.

Either Grace knew about it and had kept it quiet, hoping it would stay a secret, or she didn't know, and Ollie was keeping it a secret from her.

She was a hundred percent sure that whoever had put it there hadn't come by it legally, and as far as she was concerned, if Ollie had stolen a watch like this, then that meant someone out there was missing it.

And if they found out who had taken it, well then that constituted motive.

She turned to Roper and he looked at her.

'Looks like things just got interesting,' he said.

'What,' she laughed, 'you were bored before?'

13

The door closed behind her and Jamie slumped back against it, the clean smell of her apartment enveloping her like an old friend.

She slid downwards onto the hardwood floor and reached down, pulling on the laces of her boots with both hands.

Jamie kicked them off, her feet throbbing, and watched as they came to rest in the hallway of her modest apartment, flecked with mud.

She didn't even want to think about that right now.

From the hallway, she could see the living room and kitchen on the right — with a window that let out over the street — and on the left her bedroom door.

At the end of the hallway — which was only twelve feet long in total — there was a bathroom.

She lived alone, without pets, and didn't need any more space than that.

The sound of the clock above the stove in the kitchen ticked away.

It was after nine now and she was dog-tired. After the watch, they'd swung back to the station, logged it as evidence, checked whether Grace had said anything — she hadn't — finished their paperwork, and then headed out.

Roper had insisted that they go to the pub.

She refused, saying she'd prefer to shower and go to bed.

He said that sounded pretty tantalising, too, and she'd nearly shoved him over right there in the parking garage.

'Jeez, I was just joking,' he said, rubbing his ribs.

And he wasn't totally lying. It was a half joke. She'd never go there with him — or anyone from work. But especially not Roper. He reminded her so much of her father; if she stared at him too long it would send a shiver up her spine. Going to bed with him would be wrong in every sense of the word. Biblical included.

'Good night, Roper,' she said, longing for home. And then she got in her car and drove there.

She checked her watch now. Roper would no doubt be on pint number three and whisky number four. He liked to alternate. Said that it was efficient.

Jamie felt dirty. She could smell the sweat on her skin, feel the dirt in her hair.

Her stomach was empty and aching and her mouth was dry. She didn't think she'd drank a litre of water the entire day. And that was saying something compared to her normal three-plus.

She groaned, her shin still throbbing from the morning's workout — what seemed like weeks ago — and heaved herself to her feet, stepping over her dirty boots.

She'd clean up in the morning.

With every step she shrugged off a piece of clothing.

She took her jacket off and dragged it behind her, pulling her socks off one at a time, hopping to keep her balance as she made her way towards the kitchen.

She opened the washing machine door and shoved her clothes in, putting her phone and keys on the counter. She peeled her jeans and shirt off and pushed them in on top along with a washer tab, glancing only momentarily at the purple welt on her shin. No wonder it was throbbing.

The door clicked shut and she cranked the setting to sports-intensive and hit go.

It started filling and spinning and she shuddered, realising now how cold the air was on her bare skin.

She needed a shower.

Jamie got halfway across the living room before her phone started buzzing.

She stopped, let her shoulders fall, and considered stamping her feet in anger. She sufficed for a string of under-her-breath swear words and a strange noise halfway between a growl and a shout.

For a second the idea of screening the call came to mind, just letting it ring. But it might have been about Grace. And she couldn't afford to let anything slip by. They were already on the back foot with this one and any lead was a good one.

She padded back, her feet heavy under her, and picked it up, looking at the screen.

Jamie didn't recognise the number.

'Hello?' she said, her voice hoarse, pulling the phone to her ear. She grimaced, realising that whatever was on the screen from earlier was still on her cheek and at this point she was just massaging it into her skin.

'Is this Detective Johansson?'

'It is,' Jamie said cautiously. 'Who is this?'

'This is Elliot Day, returning your call.' The voice was familiar now. The well brought up twang. It was the doctor from the shelter.

'Ah, Doctor Day,' Jamie said, forcing brightness into her voice. 'Thanks for getting back to me.'

She spun in a circle, feeling exposed suddenly. She was in nothing but her underwear. Though he'd have no way of knowing, it wasn't exactly how she liked to talk to potential witnesses in active investigations.

'Of course. Sorry I couldn't come back to you earlier — I've been in surgery all day.'

'That's fine,' she said, going into the hallway to look for her dressing gown. It was hanging on the back of the bathroom door. 'Thanks for getting back to me.' She threaded one arm through, juggled the phone, and pressed it to the other cheek, smearing the unknown substance for the second time.

'You already said that,' he answered, a little bit of caution in his voice. 'Is everything alright? You sound, uh—'

She didn't know how it sounded when someone was trying to get a dressing gown on, but she expected there was some panting involved. 'No, no, I'm fine. Sorry. It's just been a long day.'

He laughed warmly and Jamie felt a wave of prickly heat in the back of her head. 'I know the feeling. If I'm honest, I don't know that I've ever experienced any other kind.'

'You and me both.'

He chuckled, the sound muted, like his lips were pressed together. 'What can I do for you?'

She looked around, wondering if she could muster the energy to go into the living room and open her laptop to take notes. She decided that she couldn't and with a long sigh, committed to actually finishing for the night. 'Look, Doctor Day—'

'Call me Elliot,' he said, his voice soft, dulcet in her tired ears.

'Elliot,' she said, finding herself smiling. She cleared her throat and then wiped it off her face with the back of her hand. 'I really appreciate you calling so late, but if you're not working tomorrow, would you mind if I called you then?'

'Sure,' he said. In the background, a muffled screech of rubber on poured concrete echoed through the line and she pictured him sitting in his car in the hospital parking structure, another doctor or nurse coming off the back of a twelve-hour shift whirling out of the place, heading for home behind him. 'I'm off all day so you can give me a call in the morning, or if you'd like to come by the shelter, I'll be there from around two.'

It was Wednesday tomorrow. Jamie sighed with relief. 'That would be great. I'll give you a call tomorrow and we can talk then.'

'Okay. But, sorry — just before you go — can I ask what this is about? Your message just said that it was to do with an active investigation. I've got all of my permits and—'

Jamie bit her lip. 'No, no, it's nothing to do with your work at the shelter. It's to do with a murder investigation.'

'Oh,' he said, his voice a mixture of shock and immediate sadness. 'Can I ask whose?'

'Oliver Hammond. You were treating him, correct? And his girl-friend, Grace Melver?'

Elliot was silent for a few seconds. 'I knew Oliver and Grace, yes. They were both trying to get clean…' He thought on his words. 'Murder? Do you think it was someone else from the shelter?'

'We don't know yet,' she said truthfully. 'We just don't know. But if we could talk more tomorrow — go over what we know, see if you can fill in any of the blanks for us, that would be great.'

'Whatever I can do to help. I keep records of all the patients and—'

'Yeah, I saw the files,' Jamie said, maybe a little more curtly than she'd intended. Shit, she was tired.

He cleared his throat. 'Right, well, it's getting late,' he said, reading the tone in her voice.

She felt like apologising, but didn't.

'I'll speak to you tomorrow, then. Detective.'

'Doctor.'

He chuckled again, the same closed-lips muted laugh. Just one sweet note, as if amused by the titular formality. She smiled as well. And then the line went dead.

Jamie dropped the phone onto the sink edge, realising she'd never moved out of the bathroom, and looked at herself in the mirror. Her eyes were bagged, lined with dark circles, and her lips looked pale. She could almost hear her mother's voice in her head, telling her that if she made something of herself she could find a man. *A little bit of lipstick never hurt.*

Jamie's fingers curled around the edge of the sink and she closed her eyes, breathing hard. She was aching all over.

Before she forgot again she ran the hot tap, spat a lump of anti-bacterial handwash onto her phone screen and rubbed it clean with her fingers.

Waterproof smartphones. What a time to be alive.

She powered up the now-spotless screen and unlocked it, still thinking of her mum. She opened her messages, scanned down the list for her mum — who despite only being three from the top, behind Roper, Cake, and her dentist saying that it was time for her bi-annual checkup again, had sent the last message over seven weeks ago. She opened the thread and looked at the humdrum exchange on the screen which had ended with a simple, 'got to go, talk soon x' sent by her mum. But they hadn't.

She started typing out a new message. 'Hey mum, hope you're okay and the cruise went well.' She'd seen photos of it on Facebook. 'Let's catch up.'

She put a kiss, then deleted it, and then hit send and put the phone face down on the counter, ready to finally be clean again.

The shower creaked to life and steam began to fill the room. Jamie kicked the door closed behind her to lock it in, and then stepped into the cubicle and under the water.

She was in there for over thirty minutes, and once she was done wrapped herself in her robe, grabbed her phone, and then went into the living room.

She'd had a notification that a fitness and martial arts vlogger she followed had posted a new video, and she figured that she could probably stream it before she went to bed. This week was all about feinting from a front into a side-kick. Sounded useful.

But she only managed to get five minutes in before she fell asleep, an unopened bottle of water on one side of the laptop, and an empty bowl of granola on the other.

She'd eaten half of it on the walk from the kitchen to the sofa, polished the rest off before the video had even buffered, and then laid her head back, draping her wet hair over the back of the cushion.

The next thing she knew, it was getting light and her phone was buzzing.

It was morning, day two of the investigation, and things were about to get complicated.

14

Jamie jolted out of the darkness.

She wasn't dreaming at all. She was just switched off for the night. She couldn't remember if that had ever happened before.

It was disconcerting for her — like a long blink that hurled her forward in time.

Her phone was in her hand instinctively and she pulled it to her ear. 'Johansson,' she croaked.

'Jamie.' It was Cake, his gruff voice heavy on her ears. 'You okay?'

'Yeah,' she said, sitting up and squinting in the glare from the streetlight coming through the blinds to let left. The sun wouldn't be up for a while yet. The TV had gone into standby mode sometime in the night. She clicked the remote and saw that it had gone through a dozen videos automatically before deciding she wasn't watching anymore. 'What's up?'

'What's up is that it's six-fifteen and you're not here. You've never missed a session before.'

Jamie slumped backwards, exhaling loudly. 'Shit, I'm sorry. I'm just — it's this case. Yesterday was—'

'No need to explain. I know how things get.' She could hear him smiling. He was about the closest thing to a real friend — outside of Roper, of course — that she had. 'I could probably do with a morning off myself.'

'Thanks, Cake.'

'You sure you're okay, Jamie?'

She thought about it for a second. It was only the third murder she'd worked, and both times they'd been the second pair of detectives on it, not the leads. Doing groundwork and combing CCTV footage mostly. This was the first time she'd had the lead on an investigation like this, and it was getting darker by the minute.

She wasn't out of her depth, but she was being pushed. 'Yeah, I'm okay. Big case, is all.'

'Well, you know where to find me if you need anything.'

'That means a lot.' It did.

'Let me know if you want to do tomorrow as normal, or—'

Jamie bit her lip, wondering if today would be as hard as yesterday. 'Let's say raincheck for now, and if anything changes…'

'Sounds good to me. Just don't shirk on your training!' He laughed.

Jamie returned it, running her hand through her knotted hair and looking at the spin-bike in the corner. 'I won't.'

He hung up and she put the coffee machine on and went to brush her hair. When it was loose it came halfway down her back. She'd always liked it long, regardless of whether she wore it down or not. She didn't. She'd perfected the three-strand plait long ago and could do it without thinking. Just like she did this morning while the coffee machine dripped its liquid goodness into the pot.

She took the half-a-cup's-worth out of the maker mid-brew and poured it into a cup, returning the pot with a hiss of steam from the machine. It was about as close to a cry of protest at the bad coffee etiquette as it could muster.

Jamie topped it up with milk, drained it, then took a half-litre bottle of water out of the fridge and slugged that too. She was dehydrated and jumping on the bike like that was begging for a migraine.

Within five minutes she was dripping with sweat, pumping hard on the spin-bike, the video she'd missed the night before playing on her TV in front of her.

A fifty-five-year-old woman with abs that looked like a six-pack of white bread rolls was holding up a bunch of kale and talking about the benefits of Quercetin.

Behind, on the counter, the drip-machine filled her flat with the bitter-sweet smell of coffee.

Her stomach growled and she checked her watch. It was still early and she had another fifteen kilometres to go yet before breakfast.

She picked up the pace and felt her heart hammer in her chest. Almost loud enough to drown out the noise of the case banging around in her head.

Almost.

Another cup of coffee and a shower later and she was ready to face the day. Her calorie burn before eight was more than most people did all day.

She headed into HQ without incident. No one had called her to let her know something was wrong. Which somehow felt wrong in itself.

When she got there she headed straight to holding. She wanted to check in on Grace, build a rapport.

Her dad had always believed in making suspects sweat, scaring them into submission. She thought that was antiquated and brutal.

She was wearing another pair of stretchable jeans and slipped her keycard out of the back pocket, flashing it at the scanner to let herself into holding.

The block was on the ground floor, past the elevators, and through two secure doors, the first of which opened with a card, the second controlled by a human. It was one of the few things in the building that still was.

'Hey George,' Jamie said, smiling at the older guy in a white shirt with thick-framed glasses behind the reinforced glass.

'Detective Johansson,' he said, nodding. 'Morning. In early, as always.'

'Birds and worms, George.'

'Any sign of Roper?'

She laughed. 'This side of noon? You're hoping.'

'Surprised you haven't whipped him into shape yet. Get him out on those morning runs of yours.'

She laughed again. Seeing George always brightened her mornings. 'Hell will need to freeze over first.'

He chuckled. 'I've seen stranger things from behind this glass. Never say never.'

'Never.' She grinned at him and he returned it. He was the only other person in the building as far as she knew who liked the mornings as much as she did. Maybe that's why they got on.

'So who are you here to see?' he asked, looking at his screen, the information reflecting in his thick lenses.

'Grace Melver,' she said, lifting one of the cups of take-away coffee she had in her hands. She took a punt and went with a double-shot full-fat latte for Grace. She got a tall Americano with skimmed milk for herself.

'Who?' He looked up.

'Grace Melver. Young girl — skinny, dark hair, green eyes.'

He looked up at her, his brow crumpling. 'Oh, didn't you get a call? Was she your arrest?'

'No — and she wasn't being formally charged, no evidence had been logged. She was arrested on suspicion of possession. Just an overnight hold. The booking officers were—'

'Sorry, Jamie,' he said with a sigh. 'She was transferred this morning.'

'Transferred? What do you mean? To where? On whose authority?'

'At around three-thirty, she started saying she was feeling ill. By four she was throwing up. Then there was the diarrhoea, the fever.' He rolled his hand through the air.

'Withdrawal,' Jamie said darkly. 'Set in fast.'

George pressed his lips into a line. 'Mm, we called the para-medics — they treated her, the officer on duty signed the release.' He was reading off the screen now. 'She was transferred to St.

Mary's and the charges were dropped. She was never formally processed.'

Jamie leaned down, her head between her elbows. 'Goddammit.' She balled her fist and smacked it on the counter. 'Goddammit!'

'I'm sorry, Jamie,' he said, genuinely sorry. 'I wasn't on duty. If I was…'

'It's fine, George,' she said through gritted teeth. 'It's not your fault.' She pushed herself upright and pressed the few loose strands of hair that had come out of her plait back against her scalp. She could feel the vein in her temple pulsing softly.

'I really am sorry.' He looked it.

She nodded to him and turned away, letting herself back through the security door towards the parking garage.

Her phone came out of her pocket reflexively and she found Roper's number in her recent contacts, moving on autopilot as she dialled and waited for him to answer.

It went to voicemail and she called again, gripping the phone hard in her hand.

He picked up, coughed, cleared his throat loudly, and then said, 'Yeah?'

'Roper,' she said, taking the stairs down to the garage two at a time. 'Get your ass out of bed. We're in trouble.'

'Shit,' he said, sighing and groaning like he was sitting up. His headboard clacked against the wall as he slouched back against it. 'What now?'

'Grace is gone. She went into withdrawal in the night, they released her to St. Mary's without charges.'

'Shit.' He strung the middle vowel out and started hunting for clothes. 'You want me to meet you over there?'

'I'll pick you up on the way — be ready in five.'

He groaned. 'Fine.' The word was mumbled. He had his lips around a cigarette. 'See you then.' The snap of a lighter came down the line.

'Be ready, Roper.' She opened the door into the garage and broke into a jog. 'And for God's sake, take a shower.'

.   .   .

She got there in seven minutes, and waited four more for Roper to appear.

He jogged out of his building, the water running out of his hair making the collar of his shirt damp. He was wearing a white button-up, open at the top, with a hardy wool jacket over it. He was pre-empting another day outside.

The weather was brighter than the day before, but long white streaks like lazy brushstrokes cut across the sky, letting the cold air wash down from above.

The word *crisp* came to mind.

He slotted into the car, smelling fresh-ish, and slapped the dashboard. 'Well, go then.'

Jamie didn't say anything about the smell or the handprint on the dash and pushed the car into gear, pulling smoothly into traffic.

Neither said anything on the drive over. They were both thinking about the implications of Grace's transfer, and neither wanted to say anything in case they jinxed it.

Jamie was doing everything she could not to open her mouth because the only thing that was going to come out of it was going to be something nasty about the officers who had been dumb enough to release her to the paramedics.

For the sake of some vomit and shit, they may have just lost Roper and Jamie their best chance at uncovering a real suspect in this thing.

The wheel groaned under her grip as they picked their way through morning traffic.

When they reached St. Mary's it was busy as always.

They swung around the side and parked in the multi-story, then got out and walked briskly to reception, their badges in their hands.

Jamie and Roper lifted them in unison.

'Detective Sergeant Roper.'

'Detective Sergeant Johansson.'

'We need to see a patient who was admitted this morning.'

'Grace Melver.' They spoke alternately like a well rehearsed dance.

The woman behind the counter — mid-forties, dark skin, black hair — looked from each to the other and then said, 'One moment,' before she started tapping on the keyboard in front of her. The glare coming off her screen cast shadows along the bags on her cheeks.

Her eyes moved back and forth above them, her mouth twisting into a frown.

She paused and then looked up at them. 'Grace Melver you said?'

They both nodded.

Jamie's throat tightened, her blood pressure rising, squeezing against her skull.

'She was checked out of the hospital at seven forty-six this morning.'

Roper's hands hit the desk. 'What?' he asked, his voice hard and low.

The woman pushed back from the desk so that she was out of arm's reach. Roper wasn't going to do anything, but she'd obviously learned her lesson when breaking bad news before. 'I'm sorry, Detectives, but I don't know what to say.' She squinted at the screen from her position back from the desk. 'It says here that she was administered with fluids and anti-withdrawal medication, prescribed with stomach liners and anti-nausea tablets, and then against the recommendation of the attending consultant, checked herself out.'

'How could you let this happen?' Roper demanded.

Jamie was grinding her teeth behind him, pinching the bridge of her nose, arms tightly folded around her ribs.

'How could we let *what* happen?' the receptionist asked calmly.

'She is a witness in a *murder* investigation. And you just let her go?'

'There was nothing on file to that effect, and nor was she accompanied by officers when she was admitted. She was brought in with acute heroin withdrawal and we treated her. When she felt well enough, she left.' The receptionist sighed, her voice becoming more human. 'Look, we've got people on gurneys in the hallways, people lying in the back of ambulances, people sat in wheelchairs in waiting rooms. They're all holding on for beds — all waiting for a space. Hundreds of them. So when we've got someone taking one up who doesn't want it anymore — you can be damn sure there's someone else who does — and needs it.' She seemed to harden, her eyes narrowing at Roper, who was glaring at her. 'So I'm sorry if your shoddy paperwork and lacklustre policing meant that a witness was allowed to walk out the front door. But honestly, that's not our problem. We treat patients, and we did that, okay?' She arched an eyebrow and if Jamie was in any less of a foul mood, she might have been amused at her doing it to Roper. But she was in a foul mood, and she didn't think there was anything that could make her crack a smile.

'Now,' she said, 'if you'd like to take your hands off the counter, there are other people waiting to be seen.'

Roper was seething.

Jamie inhaled slowly, coming forward. 'What room was she in?'

The receptionist took a few seconds to pull her eyes from Roper, but eventually did. 'Open ward. Ward G.'

Jamie processed, thinking about the circumstances as to why Grace would have checked out so suddenly. No doubt she would have been feeling like shit. And homeless people usually liked to string out a hospital visit as long as they could. Free medicine, heating, a shower, food, clean sheets, a roof over their heads. Especially in November. It made no sense that she'd check herself out. Unless she was trying to avoid them.

She'd seemed scared the day before. Jamie took a chance, her dad's voice ringing in her head. *A leap is only one letter from a lead.* And one can change to the other pretty quickly.

'Did she have any visitors?'

'I don't know. We don't log visitors — you'd have to check the security tapes.'

Jamie nodded. 'Alright, then we'll do that.'

Roper was looking at her, but didn't say anything. By now he knew to trust her hunches. They'd paid off enough times before.

'Which way to security?'

The receptionist pointed left. 'Down the hall, take a right.'

'Thanks.' Jamie and Roper took off.

'What're you thinking?' he asked as they covered ground quickly.

'I don't know,' she said. 'But I've got a bad feeling we're not going to like what we see.'

15

R oper came back into the room, putting his phone away.
'They're dispatching two uniforms to see whether Grace
has headed back to her tent under the bridge.' He bit his lip, itching for
a cigarette.

'Doubt it,' Jamie said, scrubbing through the security footage from
Ward G. She was watching it for the tenth time. Grace was lying there
in the bed, and then, she calls over the nurse, speaks to her, and then
she leaves. Two minutes later, another nurse appears, takes the cannula
out of her hand, and leaves too. Grace then gets out of bed, dresses,
and walks out the door.

And that's it.

The security guard to her left was slurping a coffee loudly, annoyed
that they were still in his office.

His mouse was sticky under Jamie's fingers, and the noise was
annoying, but she couldn't leave yet.

Roper sighed behind her. 'We should go,' he said. 'There's nothing
here. No one visits her, no one—'

'Wait,' Jamie said. 'I'm not finished.' She reeled it back earlier than
before and hit play.

She squinted, leaning in, trying to make out the finer details from the ancient security camera positioned right at the end of the ward. It gave no clear view of any one bed particularly, as the privacy curtains all had to be able to block its sight. As such, it was near-useless for trying to make any specific patient out in any sort of useful detail. Just a row of pixelated beds on each side of the screen stretching into the distance.

'Jamie,' Roper said, the defeat clear in his voice. 'Come on. We screwed up. It happens. Let's go, regroup, figure out our next move, and then go from there.' He paused, watching the back of her head. 'Are you even listening to me?'

'No.'

He sighed. 'I'm going out for a cigarette. I'll meet you at the car.' He checked his watch. 'You've got ten minutes.' He was technically her superior officer, and though he rarely cracked the whip, she couldn't disobey a direct order.

She found herself smirking. 'I don't need ten minutes.' She lifted her finger to the screen and pointed at the grey bed-bound blob that was Grace Melver. 'There.'

'I don't see anything,' Roper said, leaning in.

'Watch it again.' Jamie wound it back five seconds and let it play.

'I still don't see what you're looking at.'

She made a sort of *grr* sound and did it again. 'Look at her head.'

'She turns it. So what?' Roper wasn't impressed.

'She's looking around aimlessly, see — turning, turning, turning, and then boom.' She hit pause. 'She stops. Right there. Looks in that direction for ten seconds, and then immediately calls the nurse over.'

Roper stood up, cracked his back, and then scratched his head. 'So what?'

'She sees something, Roper. And then immediately wants to get out of there. You don't think that's weird?'

'No. The thirty seconds I was on the phone in the corridor I saw a dozen things that made me want to get out of here. It's a hospital, Jamie. People don't want to be here.'

The security guard scowled at them but said nothing.

'You're reaching, Jamie,' Roper continued. 'And plus — we can't

even see what she's looking *at*. For all we know someone shit themselves just out of frame and she thought, *you know what, I want to
leave this place.'*

Jamie set her jaw and turned to the security guard, the screen
frozen on Grace's head-turn. 'What's over this side of the room?'

'Hmm?' he asked absently, as though he hadn't been listening to
every word they'd been saying.

'Where she's looking. Over here,' Jamie said, pointing to the
corner.

'Don't touch the screen,' he said, taking another sip of coffee.

'Mate,' Roper cut in, 'don't be a dick.'

The guard raised an eyebrow, sucked at the rim of his cup, and then
leaned forward, on his chair, staring at Roper.

Jamie had to give it to him, he had a knack for rubbing people up
the wrong way.

After a few seconds, the guard relented and put his coffee down,
looking at the screen with a sigh. 'Right. Where?'

'This corner,' Jamie said, trying to keep her cool.

The guard stuck his bottom lip out. 'Where's this? Ward G?'

Jamie resisted saying, *that's what the label in the corner of the
screen says*. She nodded. 'Mhm.'

'Oh,' he said, picking up his coffee again. 'There's another door.
Ward G has two doors — the main door at the end of the ward, and one
in the corner, where the girl is looking.'

Jamie looked at Roper who was still chewing his lip. 'Okay, so
there's a door. That doesn't prove anything.'

'Want to bet on it? If there's something there that spooks her you
buy the next coffee?'

Roper deliberated for a second. 'See, now that's not fair. If I say
yes and I'm wrong, then I've gotta admit I'm wrong *and* spend ten
quid.'

'Coffee's not that expensive.'

'I'm hungry too.'

'Of course.'

'Or do I not take the bet, admit that I think your hunches are worth pursuing, and then have you say *remember that time at the hospital* every time I challenge you?'

Jamie smiled, lacing her hands across her stomach. 'You know that's the best bit of deduction you've done in weeks.'

'Shut up.'

'It's your call, Roper.'

'Shit.' He hung his head and turned to the security guard. 'Is there a camera that covers that door?'

He scratched his chin, drawing it out.

Jamie said, 'So does that mean you're not taking the bet?'

Roper didn't answer.

The security guard finally made up his mind. 'Yeah, I think so. Do you mind?' he asked, a little condescendingly.

Jamie opened her hands and scooted out of the way of the keyboard on her wheeled chair so he could get at the screen.

As he slid into place he shook his head and Jamie looked at Roper, who sort of laughed, making a face that she understood intrinsically. What the hell was this guy's problem?

Jamie stayed seated with Roper standing behind the guard, who was skipping through feeds. 'Here it is,' he said. 'The door is at the top on the right. This camera covers the length of the corridor.'

'Thanks,' Jamie said, leaning a little closer.

The guard looked at her, groaned, and then pushed himself back out of the way so she could get at the computer.

She used a keyboard attachment that was like a spring-loaded dial used to scrub through video faster. Turning it one way or the other would allow you to scan forward or back, and pressing on it would play at normal speed.

She pushed it all the way left and watched as the live feed paused and switched over to the recorded footage, reeling back to Grace's check out.

People leapt backwards down the corridors as the timestamp jumped in ten-second intervals.

She wheeled it back at full speed until she hit the minutes before Grace left, and then hit the button, letting it play.

The three of them crowded closer to the screen to watch.

They waited in silence for almost a full minute before something out of place appeared on the screen.

A figure walked into frame at the bottom, headed up the corridor. He was swaggering a little, wearing a dark hoodie, the hood pulled up. He had his hands in the pockets and he was walking quickly.

When he got to the doorway he stopped and lingered at the frame, looking in.

He was only there for around fifteen seconds or so, and then turned around and walked back down towards the camera.

They all leaned in, squinting at the poor resolution.

The guy came closer to the camera, keeping his head down.

'Come on,' Jamie urged. 'Come on.'

Roper was breathing harder behind her.

'Come on.' She willed him to pick his head up.

He was walking fast, closing in.

Thirty feet.

Then twenty.

Come on.

Then ten.

They all held their breath.

And then, at the last second, he did.

In the final frames before he slipped out of view, he glanced up at the camera.

'Gotcha,' Jamie said, restraining a grin.

She slapped the dial to pause it — a little harder than necessary, which made the guard make a stern *hmm* noise. But she couldn't have cared less in those moments. She pulled the wheel back and rewound frame by frame until the guy in the hoodie popped into view, his face blurred and grainy, but large at the bottom of the screen.

And unmistakeable.

Jamie nodded in triumph. 'Recognise him?'

Roper swore under his breath. 'Don't think I could forget that face.'

'Or those dead-goddamn-eyes.'

'Shit,' Roper said, shaking his head. 'When you're right, you're right.'

Jamie folded her arms, looking at the screen. 'I don't think it's quite time to celebrate yet.' She pursed her lips, thinking aloud. 'If he came here to find Grace, gave her one look, and that was enough to get her out of bed and checking out — then she knows more than she's letting on.'

'No shit.'

'How'd he even know she was here?'

Roper shrugged. 'Add it to the list.'

'List?'

'Of questions we don't have an answer for.'

'Mhm.'

The security guard finished his coffee, seemingly uncaring about the investigation. 'Is there anything else?'

'Can we see the feed from outside the main entrance?'

The guard stared at the bottom of his cup, as if deciding whether to refuse and get more coffee, or oblige the detectives investigating a murder.

Roper shook his head. 'If it's not too much trouble, of course.'

They went back into a staring match, but Jamie couldn't take her eyes off the screen.

'Who are you?' she muttered, staring at the dead-eyed man.

From the screen he stared back, those awful eyes seeming to say, *why don't you come and find out?*

16

The camera over the main entrance showed Dead-Eyes exiting with his hood up, then hanging a left out of frame.

No more than ten minutes later Grace came outside and stood at the kerb-side, looking left and right. She stood there for a few seconds, and then a black Range Rover with oversized wheels — a model that was about ten years old — roared up the street and braked hard.

Grace looked at the front window, then hurriedly got into the back.

It pulled away equally as hard and disappeared down the street.

That was all they had. No clear view of the driver. No clear view of the license plate. Just a make and model, of which there were nearly eight thousand registered in the greater London area alone.

Armed with a copy of the footage they'd headed back to HQ to see what they could dig up.

Jamie sat in her chair with a squeak and flicked her monitor on.

A cup of coffee sat steaming in front of her as her screen came to life.

She maximised the windows and the missing persons reports she'd been looking at the day before popped up.

It was nearly eleven by then and it had begun to rain.

Drizzling. Cold. Grey.

Jamie longed for the biting, clean, frigid air of her youth, and the peace that came with it.

The room was abuzz with noise as the other detectives all scrambled around. A big case was breaking that DCI Smith had put nearly everyone else on. Roper had updated him on the way back from the hospital and he'd told them to stay on this.

Jamie didn't know if that was better or worse. Their case had ground to a halt and everyone else around them was in a whirlwind. It was like being a ghost while the world rushed by.

She rubbed her eyes, halved her coffee, and leaned forward.

The uniforms that Roper had sent to the bridge said that Grace's tent was empty and that no one had seen her — or at least that's what they said. Whether it was the truth was another matter.

They didn't have much chance of finding her if she wasn't already in the places they were looking, and there was no way the DCI was going to let them commandeer a fleet of uniforms to canvas the streets. Not for a homeless girl who may or may not know something about the murder they were investigating.

She was as good as gone until they got a solid lead on where she might have disappeared to after the hospital.

Roper had headed down to see an old buddy of his who'd been working drugs cases for years. Between the Range Rover and Dead-Eyes, along with the circumstances of the case, this whole thing stank of a drug-debt gone sideways. And Roper said that if anyone could identify the car and the dealer, or at least point them in the right direction, it would be him.

Which made it so that Jamie had very little to do, at least until she could speak to the shelter doctor, and see whether he could shed any light on the situation.

Jamie plugged her thumb drive into her computer and downloaded the footage from the hospital, logging and attaching it to the case file, typing up the notes so that the file was up to date. She sighed, staring at a still of Dead-Eyes from the corridor. She wished life was like the movies where you could clean up an image until it became crystal clear. But not even the supposedly 'smart-enhance' feature built into the app they used to playback and edit footage could find more pixels. It softened and sharpened, muddled with the contrast and brightness, and even tried adding shadows where it thought the facial features were.

The end result made the guy's face look like the underside of a toe.

Totally goddamn useless.

She groaned and pulled out her phone. Nothing from Roper. But he'd call when he had something.

Jamie drummed her phone on her other palm and exhaled, leaning back on her chair, trying to unpack it all in her head.

What did they know? Oliver and Grace had been together for longer than a year — supposedly monogamously. They were both using heroin — together — but Grace said that Oliver had told her that she wasn't allowed to get it any more, that he was going to handle it from now on. She said that he was getting it from Dead-Eyes, but she didn't know who he was. But if he was the one who attacked her, who pumped her full of heroin to cover his tracks... Would you do that to a stranger? If she couldn't ID him then what risk did she really pose? Which meant that Grace was lying about not knowing who he was. That was doubly confirmed by him visiting her in the hospital and then getting picked up straight after. And then there was the gonorrhoea. Either Grace was cheating on Ollie, or... She thought back to the bruises on Grace's wrists.

It wouldn't be the first instance of that kind of attack that she'd seen in the homeless community. Was that why Ollie had told her not to go and get the heroin any more? Was that how she was paying for it? They didn't have any money between them, but they were still using regularly.

Jamie kept drumming her phone on her palm, sinking her straight white teeth into her bottom lip as she processed.

It would have explained the gonorrhoea — as well as why Ollie wanted to take over pick-up duties. But there was still the matter of the gold watch to attend to. Where had Ollie gotten it? Where had he stolen it from? Did Grace know about it? Was it just pick-pocketed off the street? If so, why didn't he pawn it straight away? Why didn't he trade it for drugs?

She drummed harder, the plastic slapping on the heel of her hand.

Jamie knew the pieces all fit together somehow, but she couldn't make it work. Not yet, at least. And any guesses she made right now would be just that. There were theories forming, but half-baked ones could be more dangerous to a case than anything else. *You can't operate on assumptions, Jamie.*

She growled under her breath, hating that she thought in her dad's voice.

They needed more information. They needed to find out who Dead-Eyes was, and what Ollie and Grace were doing with — or for — him. That was a new thought. Dealer gets homeless kids hooked, tells them they can pay in other ways than cash…

It was another question to add to Roper's list. And another unfounded theory to pin up on her mental corkboard. Nothing was worth writing down yet.

Her phone started vibrating and she turned it over, pulling it up to her ear. 'Roper, tell me you've got something?'

He sighed. 'No. Seems that every drug dealer from here to goddamn Glasgow owns a black Range Rover, and most of them are bald, too. We're going through mugs now, seeing if anything jumps out. Thompson says that these guys usually get picked up every few weeks for possession. If he's active, he's probably been nicked in the last month or two. It's not a long list — few hundred faces. Shouldn't take too long.' Thompson was about as close as Roper had to an old friend. Roper and him had been uniforms together back when. Partners.

'Okay, keep me posted.'

'Listen, Jamie, Thompson's had a couple run-ins with guys that mess with the homeless — thinks it's worth maybe showing Grace's face around, shaking a few trees, seeing what falls out.'

'You want me to head down?'

'No, you go to the shelter, follow up with Mary and the doctor. Thompson's got some leads to chase down himself on another case, so I'll tag along and meet up with you later.'

'Compare notes.'

'Yeah, something like that.' She could hear wind in Roper's mouth-piece, his words mumbled like he had his lips around a cigarette. Looks like he was already on the way out.

'Keep me posted.'

'Same. And watch your back, alright?'

'Sure. You too.'

He hung up and she finished her coffee off.

If she left now she'd be early, but she didn't like sitting around in the office and the windows were beginning to steam up, the hot bodies making everything humid and thick.

Jamie printed the best frame she had of Dead-Eyes, grabbed her waterproof jacket off the back of her chair and headed for the door.

She'd stop for a bite on the way, then hit the shelter, see if Mary could identify him. If not, maybe she'd work some of her magic on the people there, show the picture around. Grace may have been too scared to give his name, but she hoped not everyone would be.

That was all she needed. A name.

If she got that, then she had a feeling the whole thing would come unravelled.

She took the stairs, smiling at the thought.

If only things were that simple.

17

By the time Jamie arrived at the shelter, there were thin streams of water running down the sides of the road and the drizzle had intensified.

The sounds of horns hung in the air and drifted out of the innards of the city. People always seemed to be more impatient when it was raining.

She killed the engine and got out, pulling her hood up against the sideways droplets. It pattered on her hood as she jogged up the steps and into the shelter.

Lunch and the drive over had taken her past one o'clock now. There was a little Thai place that she liked which served Pad Thai in cartons. And while she wasn't a fan of eating in her car, the situation called for it.

She unzipped her jacket halfway as she got inside, squeezing past the dining patrons. Today's serving looked like bean-stew.

Everyone was crowded in on account of the rain — but even among the melee she could see two distinct lines — one for the food. And the other for the door to the right of the stage.

Jamie shouldered her way towards Mary, whose hair was slicked to her forehead with sweat. 'Grab a spoon!' she laughed, filling bowls at breakneck speed to keep up with demand.

She smiled politely, wondering if she could get away with saying that she wasn't allowed. Instead, she just asked, 'Is Dr Day in yet?'

'Oh,' Mary laughed. 'Of course — knock first, though. Been caught out by that myself!' She seemed to be in a good mood despite the weather and the hungry customers.

Jamie stepped behind her and headed for the side door.

The homeless people in the line for the door looked at her, readying themselves to say something as she went right to the head of the line, but then their sixth sense was tripped and they all fell quiet and still.

From the corner of her eye she saw one woman about to say something, but a guy grabbed her arm and shook his head. She stopped, understood, and scowled instead.

Swarm intelligence.

Humans were more like animals than they would ever admit.

Jamie cleared her throat and knocked on the door.

'You'll have to wait,' came a muffled reply. 'There's a line.'

'This is Detective Johansson,' Jamie said, her voice a little raised to carry through the wood. 'We spoke on the phone.'

'Oh,' he said with a little laugh. 'Right. Give me a moment.'

It was actually more like ninety seconds, and when the door opened, Jamie was confronted with someone she didn't expect to see.

The guy was in his forties, with a big grizzly beard, a tattered knitted beanie hat, and a pair of cargo trousers tied around his waist with string. He was just doing it into a knot.

Jamie didn't want to imagine what he'd been showing the doctor.

He stood right in the doorway, staring at Jamie.

She saw a hand rest on his right shoulder and he looked back.

'If anything changes, you come back, alright?' said the well-spoken doctor.

The guy with the beard nodded, grunted in thanks, and then headed off into the room to queue up for stew.

Jamie turned back to see the man who had to be Dr Elliot Day. He was tall — just over six feet, and lean. But not thin. He looked fit.

Jamie could tell. She could tell just from the way someone stood if they ran or exercised. She was comparing him to Roper in her head — who most certainly didn't exercise. And held himself like a man who didn't.

Dr Day had good posture — straight backed. He was smiling warmly at her, wiping his hands with an anti-bacterial cloth. His jaw was sharp, features fine. His almost amber-coloured eyes were narrow-set, his cheeks darkened with the stubble of someone who shaves every day except for their day off. And this was his.

He had sandy coloured hair, short, but fashionable, and he was wearing grey, slim-cut jeans, brown wingtips, a white shirt with rolled up sleeves, a black banded watch with silver face, and no wedding ring.

He caught her looking at his hand and offered it, as though that's what she was hoping for. 'Elliot Francis Day,' he said formally. 'Elliot is fine.'

'Jamie Johansson,' she replied, taking it and shaking. 'Jamie.'

'A pleasure,' he said, grasping firmly but not squeezing. His hand was soft but strong. 'Please, come in.' He opened himself out so that she could walk past and into the office, but stayed by the door. 'Is this an official interview, or would you mind if I continued to see patients while we speak? There are quite a few today.' He looked apologetic about asking. It wasn't ideal, but the line for his office stretched to the far wall.

'That's fine,' Jamie said, finding herself smiling. She didn't know why she'd said it. It really wasn't and she shouldn't have agreed. Now she'd have to watch what she said. But she supposed she could talk, see how it went, and then once the patient left ask the pressing questions.

'Do you mind if Detective Johansson is present during your examination or do you need to be seen in private?' he asked the next waiting patient.

The man in a faded blue raincoat looked in through the door at Jamie, and then back at the doctor, unsure whether he wanted to be in a closed room with a police officer.

'I'll go if you don't want to!' came a voice from behind the guy in the coat.

He shuffled in quickly, fearing to lose his place in line. 'I don't mind,' he muttered, heading for the table at the back of the room.

The chair that was behind the desk had been turned around to face the examination table and the privacy curtain had been folded up and leaned against the cupboard door.

Elliot nodded to the chairs behind the desk for Jamie to sit on and she did, watching as he proffered the table to the patient.

The guy hopped up on it and it rocked back and forth.

Elliot went to the file cabinet and opened the second drawer down, spidering over the labels until he found the one he wanted.

He pulled it out, flipped open the cover, and approached the man, his back to Jamie.

'So,' he said brightly. 'How's the toe?'

'S'hurtin,' came the finite reply.

'Come on then,' Elliot said, sitting down in the chair so that he was at a better level. 'Boot off. Did you take the course of antibiotics?'

He nodded vigorously. 'Din't work though.'

'Did you keep it clean, as I said?'

''Ow the hell you e'spect me to get 'old of salt water on the streets, aye?'

Elliot closed the folder. He sighed. 'Look, Gareth, you can fight me on this or you can do what I suggest. It's your toenail at the end of the day — so it's either we treat it like this, or we take the whole thing off. But then that means a higher risk of infection—'

'Yeah, yeah,' Gareth said, kicking his boot off. His foot was bare under it, and dirty.

Elliot pulled on a pair of gloves and leaned in, elbows on his knees, turning his head to look at Jamie. 'Did you have any questions, Detective?' he asked, seemingly happy with the idea of treating Gareth's grossly ingrown toenail, around which several pustules had begun to bulge, and answering her questions simultaneously.

Jamie cleared her throat. 'Of course. Sorry, I just didn't want to interrupt.' She gathered herself and then looked at Gareth, trying to think what she could ask or say that wouldn't be against policy or jeopardise the investigation. For all she knew, this Gareth person might have had something to do with it.

'Detective?' Elliot asked, still looking at her.

'You know what, it's okay, I'll wait until we have the room.' She gave a quick smile, but Elliot looked a little confused.

'Oh, I thought you said—' He cut himself off and shook his head lightly. 'Never mind. I shouldn't be a minute.'

She didn't know if she'd ever met someone quite so mild-mannered.

He checked the foot over and then went over to a case of some kind, about three feet by two, like an oversized briefcase. It was laying on the floor in the corner of the room for lack of a better place to put it. He unlatched it and lifted the top, running his hands over the contents — a meticulously organised mobile pharmacy by the look of it.

As the top lifted, the innards spread themselves out on hinged shelves.

Jamie craned her neck and made out all different types of over-the-counter medication and pills, creams, ointments, pastes, and washes. He made a little, 'Ah,' sound and pulled out a small tube.

He took it over and gave it to Gareth. 'This is anti-septic cream — about as strong as it gets. Keep the foot dry and apply this three to four times a day.'

Gareth reached out to take it.

Elliot held firm. 'This isn't going to solve the issue, Gareth,' he said gently. 'It's only going to—'

Gareth pulled it out of his hand and shoved it into his coat pocket. ''S'fine.'

He pushed himself off the bed and shoved his bare foot into his boot.

He didn't say another word before he headed for the door, scowling at Jamie as he passed.

She didn't even look at him. She just watched as Elliot stared after him, his brow crumpled, shaking his head slowly.

The door snapped shut and Jamie rose out of the seat so that they were both standing.

'He's going to have to have it off,' Elliot said after a second, pulling off his gloves and tossing them into a bio-waste bin that he'd seemingly brought with him.

'The nail?'

'The whole toe if he's not careful. But they won't be told. They just say *fix it, fix it!* And when you tell them that it's their responsibility — well then you can imagine how they take that.' He chuckled softly and her mind cast back to their phone-call. 'Not well.'

She put herself back in detective mode. She was here to interview a potential witness, not make small talk. 'Is that how Oliver Hammond and Grace Melver reacted?'

His face changed slightly. A look of mild shock took him, and then he just looked sad. 'No. They were unique, I'd say. They both wanted to get clean, and they both wanted to lead better lives.'

Jamie looked at him for a moment, calculating how to approach it. 'They trusted you.'

He went back to the case and closed it carefully. 'Yes, I believe they did,' he said.

'Then I'm hoping you can fill in some blanks for me.'

He stood up and walked over to the sanitiser, taking some in his hands and massaging it in. 'I'll do my best.'

'Both Grace and Oliver put down on their charts that they'd only had one sexual partner each in the last twelve months — presumably each other.'

He stayed with her eyes, not looking away or blinking.

'But you wrote a prescription for azithromycin for Grace. To treat gonorrhoea. But not for Oliver.'

'That's correct.'

'So how did she have it, but not him?' That's what Jamie couldn't figure out. If they were sleeping together, how didn't he contract it?

He exhaled slowly. 'Grace was smart. Smarter than Oliver gave her credit for. She's been living on the streets since she was fourteen. And they can often be *unkind* to young girls. She learned to survive, and sometimes, that means using what is available to you. Though some-times the alternative to death is not much better. Protection, food, shel-ter… drugs… they can be hard to come by without something to trade.'

Jamie set her jaw. 'She was prostituting herself?'

'She never said so in such certain terms, but I would say so, yes.'

'Did Oliver know?'

'I think he suspected. She would take condoms every week — make Oliver wear them. She said she didn't want to get pregnant. But I'd also written her a prescription for birth control pills — though she begged me not to tell him.'

'And you didn't?'

'Morality aside, I still can't break a patient's confidence.'

'Unless they sign a waiver saying you can talk to the police.'

He smiled, amused by her sharpness. 'Unless they sign a waiver.'

'So she made Oliver wear condoms, but not the others?' Jamie asked grimly, determined to get back on, and stay on topic.

'I'm not sure. But I know that she had gonorrhoea, so you'll have to make that call for yourself. Perhaps the decision wasn't up to her.'

Jamie swallowed and started pacing in a circle. She didn't like any connotation that came with that remark. 'Grace said that Oliver told her that he was going to get the heroin. That she wasn't allowed to any more.'

Elliot leaned back against the examination table. 'Then it seems that he did know.'

Jamie thought for a second. 'Was Grace taking heroin before she met Oliver?'

'Her body showed signs of more prolonged use.'

He wasn't saying anything definitive where he didn't know, but he could still speak in biological terms when he didn't have the answers verbatim. She respected the directness of that. Conjecture was rarely useful from witnesses.

'So she got him into it?'

'That's a fair assumption. I believe that she was his first for several things.'

She remembered what Oliver's father had said. That they'd

received calls from the hospital about Oliver. And they were obviously together — and felt deeply for each other. Or at least Oliver did. He falls for her, then gets hooked on heroin, finds out how she is getting hold of it — how she is paying — flips out, tells her he's going to get it from now on. Then he confronts Dead-Eyes, says he's no longer allowed to see Grace. He doesn't like that — kidnaps Oliver to get at Grace again — maybe he holds him hostage, demands that Grace *pay* for his release. Then he gets loose, makes a run for it, gets chased to the river, and then… He was pushed? He fell? It was a stretch, but it felt like a working theory. But then if Dead-Eyes was a lowly pusher would he have the gall or the ambition to kidnap someone? And was it his Range Rover? That was all presuming that it was the dealer who was using Grace — that it was him who gave her gonorrhoea. Or was he just a puppet in a larger game?

'Detective?' Elliot asked from the examination table.

'Hmm?' she said, looking up.

He folded his arms. 'Are you alright? You've been quiet for about thirty seconds.'

'Oh.' She smiled and pushed a few loose strands of hair off her forehead. 'Sorry, just putting it together in my head.'

'I have more information on Grace and Oliver — notes I took after our consultations.'

'Really?' Jamie said. Things were finally coming together. 'That would be great.'

He laughed a little. 'Well, not here. Sorry if I made it seem like I had them on me. They're at home. I try to limit the amount of information I leave here.'

'That's no problem,' Jamie said quickly. 'I can send someone to pick it up.'

'Aha.' He chuckled nervously. 'That's just the thing — I can't release those notes. I'm bound by doctor-patient confidentiality. They may have signed the waiver, but those are my personal notes, and aren't included under the loose agreement in place here.'

'This is a murder investigation,' Jamie said stiffly.

'Do you believe that there's an immediate and imminent risk to someone's life if I don't release these notes to you?' He knew the law. She had to admire that.

'It depends what's in them.'

'Therein lies our quandary.' He smiled disarmingly again and Jamie looked away. 'But what I can do is go home, review them and then make that call. I don't remember what's in them exactly, but I can let you know if I find anything?'

Jamie ground her teeth. It seemed like the long way around but she didn't know if she had another choice. While it was of no concern to her, Elliot obviously took his job seriously, and the ethics of it even more so.

'Fine,' she said. She had enough to work off so far.

'Look, why don't you come around eight — that will give me enough time to look over them, and then I can let you know if I've found anything. You can also quiz me about anything else that comes to mind. While Grace and Oliver are the focus of this investigation, I see a lot of people who knew them. A lot of whom are standing outside that door.' He pointed over her shoulder. 'I can ask to see if anyone knows anything — if anyone saw anything?'

Jamie bit her lip. 'That would be great.' She didn't want to seem too enthused. And she wasn't sure about going over there. Though it seemed like he did just want to help, and she couldn't refuse extra information. Still, she didn't want to give him any sort of impression. But then again, she didn't want to deny him on that basis and then find out that wasn't his intention, and thereby embarrass herself. It was, what did he call it? A quandary.

She swallowed and took the plunge. 'Eight o'clock?'

'I'll text you the address.'

Jamie nodded and exhaled. 'Just so we're clear, this is an active murder investigation. Right?'

He smiled again, as though amused. 'Of course. Why, what did you think?'

She returned the smile, hoping her cheeks weren't flushing. But she could feel they were. 'Nothing.'

'Good. Then I'll see you at eight.'

She was torn. One half of her wanted to tell him she didn't mean anything by the comment — and the other wanted to turn and run out of there. She didn't know which would be more telling.

Luckily, her phone started buzzing.

She held a finger up. 'One sec,' she said, digging it out of her pocket. She looked at the screen and then back at Elliot. 'Sorry, it's my partner. I've got to take this.'

'And I've got a queue of patients to see.' He pushed off the table and walked her to the door, opening it for her. 'But we'll continue this tonight?'

She nodded. 'Thank you, Elliot.'

'If you need anything else, you know where to find me.'

She gave him a quick wave and then slipped into the crowd of bodies outside the examination room.

When she heard the door close behind her she lifted her phone and stared at the screen, wishing it was Roper.

But it wasn't.

It was someone much worse.

It was her mum.

18

'Mum,' Jamie said, answering, forcing brightness into her voice as she muscled her way towards the door.

'Jamie,' she nearly yelled, seemingly overjoyed to be on the phone. 'You're alive!' She laughed shrilly.

Jamie echoed it with closed lips. 'Just about.' Her mum was just as capable of picking up the phone as she was.

'I'm so sorry I missed your birthday,' she said quickly. 'I was away, and, well, you know how things get around this time of year.' She trailed off and then added one word. 'Difficult.' It was about as loaded as words got. 'I meant to call, but then time went on, and I didn't want it to seem like I'd forgotten and then called after the fact, so... You know how it is.'

Jamie felt like saying, *no one wishes Dad didn't kill himself on my birthday more than me, Mum,* but she didn't. Her mum had been away for the last six of her birthdays — not that she celebrated them, anyway. It was hard to.

'How was the cruise?' Jamie asked.

'Oh, the Caribbean. Such a beautiful place. The beaches. The food!' She laughed again, seemingly having forgotten that she'd missed her birthday and spent it drunk on some beach somewhere.

'The people. And the men…' She chuckled lasciviously to herself. 'You would have loved it.'

Jamie was standing in the middle of the road outside without her coat on. It was over her forearm, and she could feel the rain sinking into her hair. 'If you say so,' she said, deflecting the comment. 'Hey, look, mum, this is a bit of a weird time — can I call you back later?'

'Oh, sorry, I'm away with the girls at the moment — I just had a spare second to call. I wanted to make sure there were no hard feelings. But you're right — you've got important things to do. Bad guys to catch and all that.' She was always dismissive of Jamie's job, just like she was of Jamie's dad's. Her mum always hated it, but seemed to have found a way around the fear of her father never coming home — met with some grisly end instead while on the job — by exchanging it for simply not caring. And it had obviously carried generationally. When her dad died it seemed that all the baggage he carried transferred to her and her mum. Jamie got the cold-shoulder, the derision, and the secrecy that her mum had always reserved for her dad, and her mum seemed to inherit his drinking habit and desire to be at home as little as possible.

Jamie cleared her throat. 'What *girls?* I didn't know you had girls.'

'Oh, just some people I met — on one of my jaunts. You know.'

She didn't know. And she didn't know why every sentence started with an emphatic *oh* as if Jamie was still ten years old and fit to be condescended to.

'When are you back?' Jamie asked. 'We should get together — I could come over, and—'

'Oh, there's a new cocktail bar opened in SoHo that you just *have* to try! We'll go there and—'

'You know I don't drink,' Jamie said, for perhaps the thousandth time.

'What? You're *still* doing that? When will you grow up, Jamie?' She could hear her mum shaking her head. 'You know, just because *he* couldn't control himself, doesn't mean that you won't be able to.'

'That's not why I…' She trailed off, clenching her teeth. Jamie felt her head go down, her blood pressure rising. 'Never mind.' Her mum had a way of pushing her buttons. Maybe it was a good thing she missed her birthday every year. She didn't know if she could endure how she might behave.

It wasn't a criminal offence to be so mean to someone that they kill themselves. But it was certainly a moral one. Her mother had refused her father the chance to be a part of Jamie's life out of spite, and then he'd shot himself. Right through the temple. Movie style, with his phone in front of him, the last calls to Jamie's mum — unanswered — and a bottle of whisky drunk to the bottom.

Her mother still carried that with her.

If she'd answered, it could have been different. But she didn't.

Jamie had long-since let it go.

She just hated that the thing that stuck in her mind the most was the image of her mother crying at his funeral. Or pretending to cry. Or was that too harsh? Was she feeling the sadness of his death? Mourning a loss? Or was she crying because of the guilt?

Could Jamie really hold her responsible? She was responsible for a lot of things — for taking Jamie away and moving them to England. For not letting him visit her. For not letting her visit him. For not being there after. But could she really say that her mother was responsible for her father's death?

And now, to be as much of an alcoholic carouser as her father was — which was the very reason she left him.

Jamie didn't think she'd ever understand her.

She wondered what her life would have been like if she'd have gone back to Sweden and lived with her father.

Her mother had said that if she went to see him, she wouldn't be welcome back.

And she'd not gone before that. She hadn't seen him for nearly two years before he died. Not spoken a word to him. She wasn't allowed. And for that her mother *was* responsible. His death couldn't be put on anyone, because it was on all of them.

'I've got to get back,' her mum said quickly. 'But call again soon, okay?'

'You called me—' Jamie started saying before the line went dead. She got more of a goodbye from Roper.

Jamie let the phone drop from her ear, not sure what to do with that or how to process it.

She turned to face the shelter and stared up at it, brutalist and nearly black with the rain.

Her phone began to ring again, and for a second she thought it might be her mum coming to her senses, calling to apologise, to actually give a damn.

But it wasn't. This time it really was Roper.

She answered. 'Yeah?'

'We've got something.'

She sighed, grinning that she had something to take her mind off her and her mum's paper-thin relationship. 'Thank God.'

'I'll text you the address.'

'I'm already on the way.'

Jamie pulled up beside Thompson's car — a Five-Series BMW from the early millennium — and killed the engine.

They were in a little open air car park that overlooked a communal green in front of a high-rise apartment building.

There was no one on the green on account of the rain, but a group of teenagers were stationed under the concrete awning attached to the block of flats.

The car-park they were in serviced the green and the playground, but apart from a camper-van that looked like it hadn't been moved since the year before — it was empty.

Jamie got out, zipped up her coat, and then slipped into the back of the Five-Series.

The air inside was thick with smoke. It seemed both Roper and Thompson were smokers, and neither minded the smell.

She left the door open as long as she dared before pulling it closed.

They were sitting in the front, and Roper was picking chips out of a fast-food bag. Thompson was chewing on a straw. She could see the cups between Roper's feet, lying on their side.

These two were kindred spirits.

Roper turned to face her. 'You good?' he asked casually.

She nodded. On the ride over she'd reckoned with herself that her mum was the one who was missing out, not her. Though she didn't know how long it would hold up. For now, she had to focus on her work.

'Good.' Roper turned round and got comfortable in the seat, returning his gaze to the front of the high-rise.

Parked in front of it, in a space that had been blocked out with a big *NO PARKING* paint-job, a black Range Rover was parked. It looked to be a match for the one in the video.

'Recognise the car?' Roper asked.

'The match confirmed?' she replied.

Thompson spoke up, his East London accent thick. 'We ain't seen your girl or your dealer. But I'd say it's a match. Been tracking this geezer for a few months, now. He's pushing heroin, operates in the same area as your lad went missing, and is known to target the homeless and trade favours after their hooked. Nasty piece of work all things considered.'

'Sounds like a charmer,' Jamie muttered.

'He is,' Roper chimed in.

'Bloke was inside for aggravated assault, larceny, possession with intent. You name it. Got out six months ago — and now he's got himself a top-floor flat and a Ranger. He's a bloke who's been around the law. Knows to keep himself clean. Doesn't touch anything himself — all prepaid phones, uses dead-drops for his pickups, never meets in person with the dealers. It's done in a blind chain — you know I got it from someone who got it from someone who's friend got it who don't know who got it. You get the picture.'

'So what's the plan?'

'The plan is to nail him to the post for murder,' Thompson said, his thick mop of black and grey hair poking over his long ears.

'Murder?' Jamie kept the shock out of her voice. 'You think he killed Oliver Hammond?'

Thompson shrugged. 'I think if there's anyone who's capable it's Donnie Bats.'

'Donnie Bats?' This time she was shocked. 'That can't be his real name.'

'Donald McCarthy,' Roper said. 'Donny for short.'

'Bats because the aggravated assault charge was filed on account of him breaking a guy's spine with a baseball bat.'

'Baseball bat,' Roper practically scoffed, shaking his head. 'When did people stop using cricket bats, aye? Reverse colonialism is what that is.'

No one laughed.

'So you think he's good for Oliver's murder? Doesn't make sense for him to get his hands dirty like that if he's been so far removed from everything else,' Jamie said, interrogating the point.

Thompson shrugged. 'Did it himself, ordered someone to do it. What's the difference?'

'I'd say there's a pretty big one.'

Thompson shrugged again. 'If we go in there, acting like we got proof—'

'But we don't have proof.'

'S'why I said *acting*.' He looked at Roper, gave him eyes like *sheesh, get a load of this one,* and then carried on. 'Tell him that unless he gives us the name of who did the dirty, that we're going to come down on him for every charge we can. I think he'll roll pretty quick.'

'That's a lot of supposition,' Jamie said, folding her arms and sitting back. She could barely see them for the smoke and the windows had fogged so much she could barely see her own car five feet away. 'And anyway, what the hell would he want with a homeless kid? You think Oliver what, broke out of his cage, ran down forty flights of stairs and then ran the two straight kilometres to the Lea, just to be thrown in?'

Thompson pulled out a pack of cigarettes. 'No. They got a lift.'

Roper chuckled at that one.

Thompson jammed one between his lips and offered the pack to Roper. 'Look, if there's one thing I know about these pushers and homeless kids its that they get them hooked, and then get them on the hook for payment-owed. Tell them they gotta pay some other way.'

She scowled. 'At least you've got that much right,' she muttered.

Thompson eyed her in the rear-view. 'So what you got here is a classic case of example making. Oliver gets taken, knocked around a bit — fingernails pulled—' he looked at Roper, who nodded to confirm '—gets tossed back out on the street as a message to anyone else who owes that now's the time to pay up. They scramble to find the money — with interest. Beg, steal, borrow, whatever. And the whole greasy machine keeps on turning.' Thompson sucked hard on his cigarette.

Jamie scowled from the back seat, cracking the window. 'Except there's two problems with that theory. Firstly, his fingernails were ripped upwards, not pulled out — and secondly, if you didn't notice, he's dead, not out on the streets spreading the message of repayment.'

'Yeah, yeah, same thing,' Thompson said, waving her off. 'I've been doing this long enough to know when it's a drug-hit gone sideways. Hell, maybe they *wanted* to kill him. Maybe they tossed him in the river? Ever think of that. Hands bound, fingernails ripped off — clear signs of torture—'

'There weren't any—'

'He washes up — all prints and forensics wiped away by the water — clean kill. His buddies all still get the message. Bing bang boom. Case solved.' Thompson sucked on his cigarette and then jammed it into the cupholder. Which was being used as an ashtray.

'Case not solved,' Jamie growled. 'What about Grace, huh? How does she figure into it?'

Thompson put his hand on the wheel and drummed on it with his thumb. 'Well, dead or not, the kid still had a debt to be paid. And Roper showed me a picture of the girl — a bit dirty for my tastes, but she's not half bad — if you're into that sort of thing.'

Jamie grimaced. He was more than twice her age. Closer to three.

'And let me tell you,' he carried on, locking eyes with her in the mirror. 'These guys probably are. Young, nubile, and willing to do anything to pay off her boyfriend's debt… That's how these assholes get off.' He smirked grimly like it was a mark of pride to be so in touch with this calibre of street scum. 'So what we're gonna do is march up there, walk in and say *Donnie, you goddamn piece of shit — we know you did it. So hand over the scumbag who held the pliers, and we'll let you off.*'

Roper grinned, turning to face Jamie over his shoulder. 'And then we flip the guy he gives up, get him to turn evidence on Donnie. And boom, straight back to jail.'

They looked at each other, sharing that shit-eating grin, and the word *circle-jerk* popped into Jamie's head. In all the time she'd been partnered with Roper, she didn't think she'd ever heard him say *boom* anything. But she knew that him and Thompson went way back — apparently back to a time where personal vendettas and lying about evidence in a criminal investigation meant more than good police work.

'That good with you?' Thompson asked, still eyeing her in the mirror.

'Do I have a choice?' Jamie asked glibly.

'No. Now be a good girl and get the umbrella out of the boot. It's bloody pissing down.'

19

They moved down off the slope carefully.

Thompson was at the front with the umbrella tight around his shoulders, Roper was at his side, his peacoat pulled up around his ears, and Jamie trailed behind, begrudgingly.

If this Donnie Bats — as much of a bastard as he seemed to be — was the one who was holding the gun, or the pliers, or the zip ties, or whatever implement you wanted to use — then she would be surprised.

But then again, nothing had been as it seemed so far.

This one just stank of jealousy rather than a straight drug-related kidnapping-gone-wrong.

It didn't feel like that to her.

If she could speak to Grace, then she could get this ironed out. She knew that, but she couldn't convince either Roper or Thompson of it without her.

And that was about the only thing she was sure of.

And if the Range Rover was a match, then this was as good a place as any to look for her.

Which annoyed her.

She checked her watch and made the calculation to eight that evening before she could stop herself. Five hours and twenty-two minutes.

Plenty of time to go home, get showered and changed, and then head to Elliot's house.

Or apartment.

She wasn't sure which it was.

She checked her phone reflexively but he hadn't text.

Did it even matter?

She shook it off and pocketed it as they got onto the tarmac in front of the building.

The teens looked up from under the concrete awning.

'Aye, boss, you got any fags?' one of them called.

The others laughed.

The kid couldn't have been more than fifteen.

Thompson and Roper were both smoking as they walked but barely looked up.

In a synchronised move, they both pulled their badges from inside their pockets like they were on some ancient episode of X-Files. 'Piss off,' Thompson grunted.

'Before we search your pockets,' Roper added, barely above a growl.

Jamie restrained a smile at the tough-guy act. The old camaraderie was obviously inspiring a spike in testosterone production.

The kids dispersed, running into the rain with their hands over their heads to keep the water off their spiked haircuts.

Roper and Thompson both pulled up under the awning and stared after them.

'Goddamn thugs,' Thompson muttered.

'Future Goddamn criminals,' Roper added.

'Gosh-dang beatniks,' Jamie chimed in with an American accent, punching the air for emphasis.

They both looked around at her.

She wasn't sure if they got that she was mocking them.

Or maybe they were just so invested in their own bravado it didn't even enter their minds.

Thompson dropped his umbrella to his side and put his free hand in his pocket, sucking a piece of burger out of his yellowed teeth.

Roper raised an eyebrow and folded his arms.

She looked at the both of them, dinosaurs in their own right — and saw her father. He could have been right there with them, ready to tell her that this was how *real* police work was done. That you had to crack skulls and raise your fist without a second's hesitation.

But those days were as gone as he was.

Dead, buried, and best to be left in his grave. Undisturbed.

And yet, no matter how much she reminded herself he was gone, he always seemed to come back to her.

She stared at Roper and Thompson, and wondered if their way of doing things would ever die. If they were a necessary evil. If police work was always going to be part mind, part body. Part intelligence and part fist.

Her dad was standing there, between them, giving her that same patronising look. Like she didn't know what it meant to be a detective.

It was crazy to her how quickly Roper seemed to forget that she could plant her heel in the side of his head. That she could wind up and crack his skull before he could even sling an antiquated punch. And yet just because she thought twice before doing it, she wasn't in the club?

Thompson sucked on his cigarette, staring at her. Measuring her. Weighing her up.

After a few seconds, he decided he didn't like what he saw, and rolled his eyes instead. 'There's no room for passengers on this ride.'

She held her hands up. 'I'll just observe. I won't say a word, I promise.'

'Humph,' he said, scoffing. 'We'll see. Never met a woman who could hold her tongue.'

Jamie did just that. It was one of those un-winnable social situations. Prove him right by telling him to shove it up his ass, or let the insult land and prove that women weren't strong enough to hit back.

She watched her dad break into a grin in the background. As much of a hit-first-ask-questions-later guy he was, he always lived by a saying. *People talk a lot. It's what they do that makes them.*

And that's what she saw Thompson as. A talker. He was happy to throw his weight around, hide behind the badge. But if she took that away, what was left? Would he still be ready to raise his fists?

Maybe she'd invite him to the gym when this was all over.

Lay him out.

See whether she could kick that chip right off his shoulder.

'We going?' she asked coldly.

He curled a smirk, shook the drips off his big black golf umbrella, and tossed it to her. 'Here,' he said, turning away.

She caught it, his back already to her, and she looked at Roper, who just sort of looked away sheepishly and followed Thompson into the building.

Jamie pulled up behind them at the elevator with her hands empty. She'd dropped the umbrella as quickly as she'd caught it, right there on the tarmac.

Thompson jabbed the elevator button, still smoking his cigarette, and waited, tapping the toe of his boot.

When he was down to the butt he dropped it on the tiled floor and ground it in.

The place was a dump, sure, but it was home for hundreds of people. And despite the mess and trash in the lobby already, she thought adding to it was just an asshole-move.

She kept quiet, though. She doubted saying anything would help.

When the elevator arrived, they all got in.

She could feel her heart beginning to beat pretty hard.

Dropping in on known felons and accusing them of murder — especially when they were named Donnie Bats because they nearly beat someone to death with a baseball bat — wasn't her idea of a good day out.

She could handle herself, sure, but she didn't think that it was going to achieve anything.

Still, she was there.

Thompson and Roper seemed calm. Or maybe that was the testosterone talking.

She looked at Roper, finding the pulse under his jawline. One. Two. Three. Four. Five. Six.

She counted, bringing her watch up casually to check against the second hand.

He was doing at least a hundred beats a minute.

And regardless of whether he was doing his weekly cardio input or not, that was well above resting.

Looks like he wasn't as cool as he was playing it.

The elevator topped out on the nineteenth floor.

Jamie could see that the button for the twentieth had been pried out with a screwdriver. There was just a dark hole there now instead.

'We walk from here,' Thompson said, turning to Roper. He cast a side-eye at Jamie. 'Don't mind some stairs, do you?' he laughed, looking down. 'At least you're not wearing high heels.'

Jamie smiled a little. It was like he was right out of a noir crime show. Right down to the knee-length black coat.

She wondered if he was moonlighting as a grave-digger. He definitely had the charm for it.

His seemingly lazy demeanour had gone now and he strode out of the elevator with sudden purpose, his chest out, shoulders back.

They headed for the stairs without another word, and Jamie noticed Roper was swaggering like his testicles were the size of cricket balls.

She wondered just what they were walking into. She'd not really stopped to consider the gravity of the situation. She was too focused on the double-act in front of her.

Who exactly was this guy to pry the elevator button for his floor out of the wall? How many apartments were up there — at least six — maybe eight? He couldn't have all of them, surely. But then again — was it so far out of the question?

Thompson crested the top step of the top floor, exhaled, and then reached out for the handle, pulling it open.

Sitting in the corridor opposite the door was a kid no older than sixteen. He was sat on a chair and was wearing a thick black winter jacket, a permanent sneer etched on his face. He had a close-cropped head with the sides shaved down to the bone. His eyebrows were a mess of razor-cut lines and he had a black eye.

He looked them up and down, spreading his tracksuit-clad knees in some sort of dominance display, sinking lower into the steel chair like he couldn't give two shits who they were. Jamie believed it.

He bared teeth that looked like they hadn't been brushed in a month and pushed his filthy Adidas trainers into the marked tiles, holding his ground, taking a strong base.

I won't be moved, his face said.

Jamie was more interested in the rope that was hanging next to him.

Brass rings had been screwed right into the breeze-block walls, two rising up next to him, and then running parallel with the ceiling to the far end of the hallway. She couldn't see where it went, but she knew an alarm bell when she saw one.

This kid was a lookout — obviously trying to rise through whatever back-alley ranks they had. He looked like he was no stranger to a fight, either. So maybe she'd get to see what Thompson could do after all. If he wasn't above punching a kid. Which she doubted he was.

'Where's Donnie?' Thompson asked, putting his hands on his hips and standing over the boy.

Thompson's stomach pushed out over his belt no more than sixteen inches from the boy's face. He was practically on his toes.

'Dunno no Donnie,' was the reply.

'Bet you don't know anything, you little runt,' Thompson spat. 'And why aren't you in school, aye?'

'Don't need school,' the kid grunted. 'Got all the education I need right here.'

'Sitting on that chair staring at the wall all day, waiting for some rival dealer to come up here and blow your balls off with a shotgun?' Thompson scanned the hallway. It looked empty, but there was a faint throb of music coming from down the way.

'Don't gotta talk to you,' the kid said, looking away. 'Now piss off before I sort you out, old man.'

Thompson smiled almost sadistically and slowly reached into his coat.

The kid watched his hand go in and tensed up, shuffling back on the chair a little, not sure what was about to fly out.

Thompson dragged his badge into the air and hovered it in front of the kid's nose. 'You see this? It means I can go wherever I want. So either you tell me where Donnie is, or I'll march down there, find him myself, and tell him you're the sorriest excuse for a lookout I've ever seen.'

At that the kid seemed to go a few shades paler. But he wasn't backing down so easy.

'You go down there,' he said, 'and you'll get clapped, old man. Copper or not.'

'Yeah, you think Donnie wants to go back to jail? Back to drinking fermented piss out of the toilet?' Thompson lifted his head and looked around. 'Though it'd be a damn-sight better than this shit-hole. So maybe I'll just go ask him.' Thompson pocketed his badge and started walking.

'No! Wait,' the kid said, jumping up, eyeing the rope, unsure whether to pull it or not. 'You can't.'

'I can do whatever the hell I want, kid. This hallway belongs to the city, and I can smell the heroin in the air. So this is going to go one of two ways.' He came back to the kid now, hands on hips still, coat pushed back around his wrists, widening him in a display not unlike a pufferfish. 'Either you're going to pull that phone out of your pocket, call Donnie and tell him to get his ass out here to talk to us, or I'm going to put you in cuffs for obstruction, kick down his goddamn door, and tell him you had exactly fifty chances to pull on that alarm bell, and instead all you did was shit your pants. So what'll it be, huh?'

The kid glanced at the rope again.

'Just try it,' Thompson growled. 'See what happens.'

Jamie suspected that the alarm bell would make Donnie and his buddies rush out with whatever arms they had. A baseball bat, she suspected. But that wasn't going to be good against three detectives from the Metropolitan police. It would have them in handcuffs quicker than if this went any other way.

And that was the dilemma that the kid faced. Go for the bell, risk whatever came after; let them go past and arrive at Donnie's door unannounced; or make a call that said three detectives were outside and waiting for him.

Jamie wouldn't have wanted to be in his position, and despite Thompson's obvious flaws as both a man and a detective, she had to hand it to him, he could have handled it worse.

The kid looked at Thompson, then at Roper, and then at Jamie.

His eyes lingered on her for a few seconds.

'If I was you, I'd make the call. That,' she said, 'or run.'

20

Afraid for his life, the kid pulled out his phone and dialled a number from memory.

He didn't have Donnie saved in his phone, but he'd memorised his number. Smart. On both their parts.

After a second, eyes locked on Thompson, he said, 'Cops are here, wanna talk to you.'

Jamie didn't know when they'd gone from *police* to *cops,* but she didn't think now was the time to bring it up as a discussion point. Too much American TV, no doubt.

The kid's eyes widened, and then he started nodding to himself. 'Yeah, okay, cool—'

The line obviously went dead as the kid pulled the phone from his face before he could finish.

He planted himself in the chair like he'd been told to go to the naughty step, and nodded them up the hall without another word. Jamie couldn't tell if he was about to burst into tears or defecate. Either way he looked to be straining in some fashion.

Thompson walked off up the corridor without stopping at any of the doors. They all looked nondescript, the numbers removed from them. Probably to make it harder for anyone to know which was which if they came looking for Donnie. Though for anyone with sense it wasn't hard. All you had to do was follow the line of rope pinned to the wall until it took a sharp turn right through the concrete and into the apartment on the end.

Jamie counted four doors on each side, eight apartments per floor total.

Normal apartment noise rang through some of the doors — TVs on too loud, music with heavy bass — nothing out of the ordinary. At least she didn't think so.

And yet her hands were sweating.

She'd been a detective for four years and had worked murder cases before, but it felt different when you were in charge. When it was your neck on the line. The same went for drug cases. She'd never been on the vanguard like this — first through the door with someone of Donnie Bats' calibre waiting on the other side.

And with Roper's demotion back to a DS, it'd been a long time since he had either.

He called it a string of bad luck. Jamie called it getting drunk seven nights a week and doing piss-poor police work. It was hard to solve anything with a perpetual hangover.

They halted outside the end door, Thompson at the front, Roper and Jamie behind.

Thompson reached out and banged on the wood with the heel of his fist.

He wasn't shy about it, but the door didn't move in the frame. Jamie could see from where she was that it was locked tight in there.

The confirmation came with the sounds of deadbolts sliding out. Two of them — one at the top and one at the bottom, and then the main lock. Bang. Bang. Clack.

The door swung inwards, a boy in his early twenties with a snarl carved into his pimpled cheeks staring out at them.

He looked them up and down and then moved aside for them to come in.

Thompson didn't even look at him, he was staring right at Donnie Bats.

Or at least the person Jamie assumed had to be him.

He was sitting on an armchair in the middle of the room, a wide-screen television playing pornography behind him. It was muted, thank God.

Though it didn't look like he'd been doing anything other than just sitting there, so why he wanted it on at all made no sense in her mind. Especially surrounded by other guys.

The male psyche would forever remain a mystery to her.

The man himself must have been six feet, maybe a touch over, and was heavy-set, but not well muscled. Or maybe he was and it was just being covered with a layer of post-prison flab.

He was wearing a white vest and tracksuit bottoms above unlaced classic honey-coloured JCB work-boots.

Donnie's head was wide, his face covered with thick, dark stubble that seemed to join seamlessly with his chest hair below and thick hair shorn down to a short fuzz above. It made his head look like a black toilet brush.

But if that — combined with the ugly grin he had for Thompson — wasn't enough to put a face to the name, the baseball bat he was holding was as good as having it written on his forehead.

The weapon was standing upright next to the chair, with Donnie's hand draped over the hilt.

He widened his knees like the kid had in the corridor, showing Thompson his crotch, and then peeled his lips apart even more to show off his crooked teeth.

Jamie looked around the apartment. It was run-down and hadn't been decorated since the mid-nineties, but that hadn't stopped Donnie from adding some drug-dealer-chic to it. There was an ungodly stereo with speakers that came up to her naval, a television big enough that you had to sit ten feet back just to see the whole thing at once, and a collection of random fur rugs to cover the filthy carpet.

The smell of cannabis smoke hung thickly in the air as he and Thompson stared each other down.

Jamie realised that the door to the right led into the bedroom — she could see the purple silk bedsheets if she craned her head — but there was also a door on their left that could only have led into the next apartment. This room shared a wall, and it looked like Donnie had installed a door to the next one along.

Somewhere in the corridor behind them another door snapped shut and hurried footsteps rang out.

Jamie back-pedalled and leaned around the frame to check out, seeing only the door to the stairwell swing closed, the kid gone from the steel seat.

At the noise, Donnie finally spoke. 'Detective,' he said, his voice coarse. 'What can I do for you?'

He'd waited until his cronies had got away before speaking — probably with whatever they didn't want them to find — or see — when they walked in.

Roper looked at her, his face like, *what was that?*

She just shook her head. There was no point pursuing it, they were already gone.

'What you can do for me, you piece of shit,' Thompson said, seemingly uncaring about the disappearing evidence, 'is save us all the time and effort of nailing you, and confess to the murder of Oliver Hammond.'

Damn, he really wasn't beating around the bush.

Donnie was unperturbed. 'Who?' he asked lightly.

'Look, you piece of shit—' Thompson went on, moving forward a step.

Jamie thought two *piece of shits* was a little redundant, but it got the point across.

'—we know you did it. We got your Range Rover dead-to-rights on CCTV removing a witness from St. Mary's hospital this morning. Got your boy on the hook already, ready to spill his guts. So what'll it be, huh? You want to make this easy?'

Donnie was perfectly at ease. He leaned back in the chair, holding the bat upright with one finger now. 'I don't know what you're talking about. I don't know any Oliver… *whoever,* and I've got at least twenty people who'll attest to the fact that I've not left this building for the last twenty-four hours. So I don't really think you've got *shit, detective.*'

Thompson drew a deep breath and planted his hands on his hips again. 'So maybe I just toss your apartment, put you in cuffs for possession of whatever drugs you've got hidden around here, and for possession of a deadly weapon. How about that?'

'This is sports equipment, and I'm perfectly within my rights to keep it in my home. And as for — what did you say — drugs? Well, be my guest, but if you're hoping to search my apartment without a warrant, then…' He turned his head to the pimpled kid, who already had his phone out, filming the entire exchange. 'I'll be sure to forward this footage to DCI Smith and then bill him for the damages, see if we can't get a few of those stripes stripped off your shoulders.'

Thompson's jaw flexed. 'Where's the girl?' he asked coldly.

'I don't know *shit* about no girl. Your move, *detective.*'

Donnie had obviously learned a few things since the last time.

And worst of all, he was perfectly right. He was well within his rights to have a baseball bat, he wasn't acting threateningly, either physically or verbally, and he'd invited them all inside. But that didn't mean they had the right to search his apartment. Not without probable cause. And while the smell of cannabis was ripe, Jamie knew they could open every seat-cushion and pull up the floorboards, and still not find a damn thing. He kept his nose clean, and what little he might have had — some weed, maybe a few pills — went straight through that side door, through the apartment — or apartments, depending on how many doors he'd put in, next door — and down the stairs.

Thompson was at a crossroads and he didn't know which way to turn. Maybe he was expecting Donnie to be less prepared. Maybe he expected him to be more scared. Either way, to Jamie it looked like his bravado had led them straight into a buzz-saw, and the torch blaring off the back of the kid's phone was doing nothing except get him more riled up.

She could see his fists curling, feel another *listen here, you piece of shit* coming. And if he was about to lose it, then they'd all be on the hook for whatever came after.

Sure, Donnie was a dirt-bag, there was no question there. But they were tasked with upholding the law, not with harassing alleged drug-dealers. As far as she could see, Donnie was doing nothing illegal, and they were on camera.

She was pretty sure a video of a detective pouncing on a former-convict for no reason was prime fodder for a viral internet sensation, and she didn't want to be in the background if that happened. Any way she spun it, that was a one-way ticket to an indefinite suspension. Just being in the same room as Thompson was making her nervous, and now throwing in the camera and Donnie's smirk? He was a time-bomb waiting to explode. And the fuse was getting short.

Before Roper could stop her, she stepped forward, dragging Donnie's attention from Thompson.

'You haven't lost a gold watch recently, have you?' she asked casually.

He looked at her, then narrowed his eyes, trying to figure her angle.

Thompson turned to stone next to her.

'Because we found one,' Jamie said, sticking out her bottom lip and shrugging. 'Expensive thing. Really nice. And we're looking for the owner so we can get it back to them.'

'No,' Donnie said flatly. 'I haven't.'

'It'd be a shame if we had to just leave it in evidence, you know? All that money going to waste—'

'I said I didn't lose one,' he practically snapped. 'What is this?' he asked, turning back to Thompson. 'Good cop, bad cop?' He laughed loudly. 'Seriously?'

Thompson set his teeth, glowered at Jamie, and then grabbed her arm, pulling her towards the door. 'Sorry to have bothered you,' he grunted over his shoulder at Donnie.

He laughed even louder as they left. 'Have a safe drive!'

The door shut behind them and Thompson dragged Jamie down the corridor, his fingers deep in the flesh of her bicep. She thought about planting her left leg in front of him, reaching around and hip-tossing him right there in the corridor — but then she thought better of it. He was her superior officer and she had just broken rank. Then she thought about doing it again. He was gripping hard.

When they got to the stairwell, he shoved her inside and pulled the door closed behind her. 'Move,' he ordered, and she obeyed.

Thompson had a temper, and when it came to professional pecking order, whether you were well-intentioned or not, there were rules to be followed. And she felt like she'd just broken one too many.

They rode down in the elevator in silence.

Outside the rain was still sheeting, and Thompson waited until they were under the awning. And then he exploded.

He was in her face close enough that she could make out the blocked pores on his nose. Dark and blotchy, the colour of beetroot.

'Just what in the *hell* do you think you're doing?' he snarled, spitting flecks of saliva over her. 'You do realise you just *blew up* every chance we had of getting that guy for this?'

Jamie stepped back out of the splash zone and counted to five before answering, ignoring her father over his shoulder, saying *kick him in the side of the head.*

She took a breath. 'I didn't blow up anything. And if you think that was going well then you've got another thing coming. You were stalled, with no way to turn. I stepped in to—'

'To what? Disobey a direct order from your superior?' He turned and span in a circle, throwing his head back and laughing. 'Jesus, Johansson. You had one thing to do. One thing. Keep your goddamn mouth shut, and you couldn't even do that!' He was nearly shouting now. 'I knew it was a mistake to bring you in on this.' He shook his head. 'But Roper said we should — that you knew your station. That you could be relied upon. But all I saw in there was an over-zealous girl trying to play detective.'

Jamie looked at him for a while, deciding what to do. Everything in her heart told her to take this smug son of a bitch apart. To call him out on every little thing that made him unfit to do the job. But her head was telling her different. That this wasn't a truthful reaction. That he knew the interview was screwed and now he was hiding behind it.

He'd underestimated Donnie, gone in there with one card to play, and had his bluff called the second he laid it down.

If she'd said nothing, they would have retreated anyway. The fact that she tried to ask a question gave Thompson an excuse. He didn't screw it up. She did. It was her fault. And he could play it off like that.

That's all this was. More bravado. More of a show. Passing the buck.

She nodded and took it. Whether she was right or not, she had spoken out of turn. And he could have let it slide or he couldn't have. And he wasn't.

Though he was being a prick about it, he was within his rights to.

So Jamie bit her tongue. 'You're right. I'm sorry,' she said, trying to sound sincere. 'I shouldn't have said anything. I just thought—'

'Well you thought wrong. And any chance we had of getting something out of him is *gone*. Thanks to you. Think about that.' He looked her up and down for good measure, and then sneered, digging in his pocket for his cigarettes. 'C'mon, Roper,' he grunted. 'Let's go. Nothing here for us.' He turned and lit his cigarette, walking back towards the car.

Roper looked at her, not sure what to say.

She felt like telling him to grow a spine. But she didn't. Maybe it was because she didn't want to put Roper in a position to choose between them. Maybe she didn't want to be that petty.

But in reality, she just didn't give enough of a shit to draw it out and involve herself in Thompson's orbit for any longer than she absolutely had to.

He'd said his bit, offloaded his own guilt. She hoped that would be it now. That he could just leave it to die, deluded and happy.

Ignorance is bliss after all.

'Go on,' Jamie said, nodding to Roper. 'You go. Go get a drink. He looks like he needs one,' she said, smiling.

'You good?' he asked, lingering for just a second.

'I'm good, Roper. Thanks.'

He narrowed his eyes a touch, trying to read into her words. But he wasn't a good enough detective to glean anything if there was something hidden there.

Roper nodded and then turned away, heading off after Thompson, who'd looked back no less than four times to see whether he was following.

She stayed there under the awning until they were both in the car, and watched as it peeled away into the rain.

Jamie hoped that to Thompson it looked like she was drowning in misery, feeling shitty about what she'd done.

But she wasn't. She stood by it, and she'd do it again. Because the answer she got from Donnie gave her a second piece of information that she knew Thompson had missed. That the gold watch in evidence, the one they found under Grace's tent, didn't belong to Donnie. She didn't think he was lying. He was too definite about it.

The first piece of information was just a slip of the tongue. An answer to a question not quite asked.

Thompson had said that they had his Range Rover on camera. That they had his man. But he never mentioned Donnie being in the car. Even though that's exactly what Donnie denied.

And while it might have been thin — a leap, even, like her dad said — a leap and lead were only one letter apart.

They hadn't really made any assertion that they thought Donnie himself was there. Just that his car was. That it was likely Dead-Eyes was driving.

But he'd gone straight there. *I wasn't in the car.* Unprompted. If they'd have asked, 'Who was driving?' and he'd said it, then it would have been fine. Perfectly understandable as an answer. But they didn't. And that made her think.

He said twenty people could give him an alibi. That was an awful lot. Too many, maybe. Sure, he was being hyperbolic. But still. It was niggling at her.

And the more she thought about it, the more it niggled.

Grace had gotten into the back seat, too. Why wouldn't she have gotten in the front if there was only Dead-Eyes in the car? Unless he was already in the passenger seat, Donnie driving.

She stared out into the rain and watched it hammer the empty green.

An empty Quavers packet blew across the grass, flipping and fluttering into the distance.

Donnie Bats was in the goddamn car.

Which meant that Thompson was going to have to thank Roper for insisting she came along.

Because she doubted either of them caught it.

And all she had to do now was prove it.

21

J amie got home soaked. It was late in the afternoon by the time
she'd picked her way back to HQ, keen to get her reports and
paperwork done for the day, but despite sitting in the stuffy
office, she hadn't dried off.

The downpour had soaked her in the short run from the awning to
her car, and she'd stayed like that, sodden, her clothes clinging to her
skin, until she headed home.

Everyone had crammed in on her street, too, so she couldn't get a
space near her building, and had to trudge almost a hundred and fifty
yards to her door.

She left trails of water up the stairs and into her kitchen.

Things had been so crazy she hadn't had time to empty the
machine and the clothes from the night before were still in there.

She sighed and rubbed her eyes, unable to comprehend how it had
only been thirty-six hours since the case had started, and yet she was
aching like she'd not slept in a week.

Her shoulders were sore, her feet throbbing, and not the sort of pain
she got from the bike or the bag either. This was the bad kind of rusty
ache that she was afraid would creep in with age.

And yet here it was now.

She grumbled and stripped off, leaving her clothes in a heap in front of the machine. Something she never did.

Jamie pulled a clean towel from the airing cupboard next to the shower and dried her hair, feeling the warmth creep into her bones with every passing second.

Her phone was low on charge, and it was almost six. She had a little time before she had to head to Elliot's. If she was even going. He still hadn't text her to let her know the address. She didn't know how she felt about that.

Before she realised, she was sitting on her bed.

She looked at Elliot's number, thought about calling him, then decided against it. He was probably just caught up at work.

She called Mary instead, hoping to catch her before she left for the night.

After three rings she answered tentatively. 'Hello?' She didn't recognise the number, but Jamie had hers on file.

'Mary,' she said, noting how tired her own voice sounded out loud. 'Detective Johansson. How are you?'

'Oh, detective!' she said a little more brightly. 'What can I do for you?'

'I just wanted to check whether you'd seen Grace Melver today?'

'No, no I haven't. Is everything alright?' She was concerned.

'Yeah, everything's fine. Just checking. Thanks.'

'Is there anything else I can do for you?'

'No, that's everything. I'll be in touch.' She hung up without waiting for a goodbye. Also something she never did.

She exhaled, staring at the blank screen. Still no sign of Grace. She'd just have to wait for her to surface, and hope that she was alive when she did.

Jamie grimaced. That was a dark thought.

She rolled onto her back, plugged her phone in to charge, and pressed her head into the pillow, relaxing finally.

The next thing she knew her phone was buzzing on the nightstand.

She jolted and grabbed it, her eyes bleary. She'd fallen asleep and now it was after seven.

Elliot had messaged her. It said, *Sorry for the late notice — hope you can still make it over.* His address followed. It was in a decent part of the city. Though she didn't know if she expected it not to be. London was expensive, but then again doctors were well paid. Especially if he was... well, she didn't know what sort of doctor he was. He'd said that he'd been in surgery when he called her back the first time, that it was the reason he missed her call. A surgeon then.

She'd have to be quick, but she could make it over there.

Jamie showered quickly and dressed. A pair of jeans, a pair of dune-coloured boots and a long-sleeve merino wool top. It was aubergine and her mum told her it made her look like one. Said the looseness of it made her look shapeless.

She wore it as much to spite her as she did because it was comfortable and she liked it.

That was what they called two birds, one stone.

The rain had eased some but Jamie donned her coat anyway.

She got there a little after eight and pushed the buzzer.

The building was an old Neo-Georgian style block that had as many apartments as it did floors. Six.

It wasn't huge, but it was definitely one of the pricier places to live in the city. Not that there was a cheap part these days.

She hit the buzzer for his apartment. Apartment two.

After a few seconds, his voice rang out of the intercom. 'Hello?'

'Elliot, it's Jamie — uh, Detective Johansson,' she added, not sure whether or not she needed to be formal.

He chuckled softly. 'I'll buzz you up and leave the door unlatched. Just let yourself in.'

'Oh, okay,' she said, pushing through the heavy wooden door and into the hallway. The floor was tiled with checkerboard black and white, and the staircase was painted a dark mahogany, the bannister posts and sidewalls of the stairs glossed with white.

The place was quiet. She had to admit that it was nice.

The door to apartment two was ajar, painted white too, the brass number polished to a shine.

She eased it open, conscious of her wet boots on the hardwood floor, and crept into the living room, closing it silently behind her.

There was a leather sofa and matching chair set up around a coffee table, but there was no television in sight. A pair of bookcases — one filled with fiction, and the other filled with medical texts — sat against the wall instead.

Music was playing from the kitchen, which Jamie could see through a doorless double frame. She didn't recognise the band, but it was catchy. Soft and jazz-influenced, but with a modern feel. The sound masked her footsteps as she moved forward, cautiously almost. She felt just as nervous coming up to this door as she did up to Donnie's.

A gentle knocking of steel hitting wood reached her ears between the thrums of jazz. He was chopping something — cooking. She could smell beef roasting, the mellowness of garlic underpinning it.

She found herself leaning on the frame before she could think about what she was doing.

Elliot was the other side of a work-island, the beautiful white and wood kitchen around him making him look like he was inside of a homeware catalogue.

He looked up, dressed in a white shirt rolled up to the elbows, and smiled.

She had the same burst of pins and needles in the back of her head as when they were on the phone. She wouldn't go so far as to say it sent a shiver up her spine. But it wasn't far off.

'Hey,' he said, cleaning the chopped garlic off the blade of his expensive chef's knife with his fingers.

'Hey,' she said back, suddenly shy.

'How was the drive?' He swept the garlic into a pile without looking and picked up a carrot, all the while keeping his eyes locked on Jamie.

He started chopping it expertly, his knuckles raised, the blade flashing up and down against them, his fingers deftly raking along the top of the vegetable until it neared the top, and then it stopped, pushing the orange end off the board. All without looking. She noted that he was left-handed.

'It was good,' she said. Even though it wasn't. She'd had to pick through traffic all the way.

'Good. Terrible weather.'

'Mhm,' she said. Trying to think of something to say.

'You're not a vegetarian, are you?' He said it half playfully, half genuinely asking.

She shook her head. 'No, I'm not. What's for dinner?'

Jamie hadn't thought that they'd eat together. Hadn't been banking on it. She'd even gone so far as to promise herself that if he offered, she'd decline. But now, with him already cooking, and a coldness that only came with rain holding onto her fingertips, she couldn't even reckon with turning it down.

'Beef — braised and stewed with garlic and carrots, shallots, some bay.' He shrugged. 'Winter food.'

'Sounds delicious.'

'It's easy,' he said, not a hint of cockiness in him. 'Hope you don't mind. I had planned something more extravagant, but I didn't get away from the hospital in time.'

'It's fine.' She felt herself grinning. She hadn't been cooked for since her mother did it. 'I mean, I wasn't expecting anything, so…'

'Good. It means I haven't had a chance to check those files out, though, either. But we can do that after dinner… Or if you'd prefer, I can do it now, and—'

'No,' she said, almost a little too quickly. 'No, it's fine. We can eat. I'm pretty hungry.'

That seemed to make him smile. 'Please, sit,' he said, proffering one of the stools on the island.

She sat opposite him, easing onto one, the wooden top between them.

They were no more than four feet apart now as he prepped on the surface she was resting on.

She could make out the finer details of his face, the individual strands of hair in his eyebrows, the stubble showing along his jaw.

She looked away and cleared her throat, feeling her eyes heavy.
She rarely napped. Rarely needed to. She felt out of sorts, out of her
depth.

'Do you want something to drink?' Elliot asked, dicing shallots.
'I've got a nice red that's—'

'I don't drink,' she said, wanting to get it out of the way before
anything else. Her eyes began to sting. He didn't seem phased by either
the onions or the comment.

He looked at her for a few seconds, then stuck his bottom lip out a
little and gave a quick shrug, going back to the onions. 'Me either.'

'You don't drink alcohol?' She was surprised.

'No. Never really saw the point.'

'Hmm.'

He looked up at her now. 'I just always felt it impairs judgment.
Diminishes inhibition.'

She laughed sardonically, thinking of her dad. 'Yeah, I know what
you mean.'

'And as far as the social element goes,' he said, shaking his head.
'Well, if you need alcohol to stimulate conversation, then maybe
you're not talking to the right people.' He looked at her intensely. 'I've
always found that if you're speaking to someone interesting, there's no
need. The conversation makes itself.'

'That it does.'

'What about you?' he asked casually, still dicing.

'What about me?'

'What's your reason for not drinking?'

'Do I need one?'

'No, but most people have one. Either for why they don't drink. Or
why they do.'

'My dad,' Jamie said, closing that line of questioning down.

He read the situation, the look on her face, and said, 'Okay.'
And that was it. He understood. At least enough not to keep
pressing her.

'What about a water? I have some juice. Milk?'

She laughed. 'Water would be great.'

He picked up the chopping board, turned, and tipped all the vegetables into a pan that was simmering away on the stove behind him.

She watched as he filled a glass of water from the filter on the fridge, noting the curve of his shoulders, the well-defined musculature in his back. The veins in his forearms. His strong hands.

Despite working sixty-hour weeks at the hospital and volunteering on the side, he still found time to keep active.

But then again, so did she. She *made* time.

Elliot put the glass down for her and she nodded, taking it.

He turned, stirring the stew gently.

They didn't speak for a minute or two, but there was no awkwardness there.

'Do you want to eat here, or in the living room?' he asked.

'I don't mind.'

Fifteen minutes later, after some more light conversation — a little about the music, a little about books, a little about why he didn't have a TV — because he found it too passive — and then Jamie asked if he followed any vloggers or channels, because they were a good source of active viewing. Learn and enjoy. And he said no, but asked her about it. And she explained. And he seemed interested — they ate.

He filled two bowls, asking her if *al dente* vegetables were okay. She said sure, not knowing if they were or not. She always did hers in the microwave. Cleaner and quicker.

They turned out to be flavourful and she made a mental note to try it herself. She thought only pasta could be *al dente*, and she didn't really like that. At least not when she'd tried it herself at home. Though looking back, she might have just eaten it undercooked.

The food was delicious, and as promised, it was true winter food. Warming and moreish. Though she resisted asking for a second bowl.

He gave her one anyway, spooning more in from the pan before she could object.

She thanked him and they ate facing each other. He pulled the second stool around and sat where he'd been preparing, cradling the bowl in his right hand while he spooned with his left.

'Just leave them,' he said about the dishes when they were done.

'I'll clean up after. We should take a look at these notes. It's getting late.'

It wasn't a hint for her to leave, just a statement of fact. And he was right. It was after nine-thirty already. With the food and the conversation, more than an hour had passed before she even realised.

Usually she'd be settled down for the night, ready to get to bed, prepping for an early start.

On the way to the living room she pulled out her phone, text Cake saying that she couldn't make the morning session. Not that she had any intention of staying there — but by the time she got home it would be even later. And she didn't know that she had the energy to get up at six and have the crap knocked out of her in the ring.

'Everything okay?' Elliot asked, seeing her texting.

'Yeah, everything's fine,' she said, stuffing it back in her pocket.

'Do you need to get back, or…'

'No, I'm good. I've got time.'

He looked at her for a while, smiling slowly. 'Good. That's good.'

She felt her head prickle again, and looked away.

'I'll get the notes. Sit.' He gestured to the sofa and she obliged.

There was a desk along the wall with a window either side, the blinds pulled shut, and he went to it.

It took him no time to find the notes. They were all perfectly arranged it seemed. He opened the bottom draw, pulled out a stack of files, and leafed through them, finding both Oliver's and Grace's immediately.

'You keep files on all the homeless people at the shelter?'

'Only the ones I think have a chance.'

She thought that was sweet. She knew some people were too far gone to help. Too set in their ways. Too tired to try. But some still had a chance. People like Oliver, and Grace. They were young. They still had parents they could turn to. They could still get their lives back on track.

'Why do you volunteer at the shelter?' Jamie asked as he walked back over, the files in his hands.

He looked up. 'I want to help people.'

'Sixty hours a week at the hospital not enough for you?' she said with a laugh.

'It's more like seventy — and no, I guess not.' He sat next to her, close enough that she could smell his skin. Despite being home from work late, he'd still showered and changed instead of getting food started or finding the notes. She tried not to read into it too much.

He laid the file on his knees and stared into space. 'These people have no one. No one who believes they're anything more than something to ignore as they walk past. But they're not. They're people — with lives. Lives that are worth something. That are worth doing something about.'

'So it's just nobility, then?' She looked at the side of his face, watching his pulse drum gently in his neck.

'No,' he said with a sigh. 'I'm not that benevolent. But I guess you could call it guilt.'

'Guilt? For what?'

'My sister.' His voice took on the same tone as hers when she said *my dad.*

She nodded, processing. 'Okay.'

He turned to her, his eyes soft. 'But that's a story for another time.' He put his hands on the folders. 'For now, let's see what we've got.'

'That'd be good,' Jamie said, not looking away.

'Yeah,' he said, not looking away either. 'It would.'

22

Jamie fell asleep happy.

Or as close to as she'd been in a long time.

She'd left Elliot's at just after eleven.

The files had been largely unhelpful, and shed little light on the inner workings of Grace and Oliver's lifestyle. Grace's only had sparse notes regarding sexual partners — who she wouldn't name, or talk about the circumstances under which they'd met — which explained her need for azithromycin, but not much else. It also contained the names and old address of her parents, though Elliot had written, *(not current)* next to it.

They'd moved, and she didn't know where.

Under the heading 'Medical History', the letters N/A were ascribed.

Either she didn't have any history, or she wouldn't say.

Oliver's was even more sparse. It had his parents address and names on one page, and on the next his medical history. All it had was his blood type and that he was allergic to penicillin.

Elliot had frowned looking at them and then said, 'Huh, I thought I'd written more.' She suspected that he knew there was nothing of use in the files.

And that was why she was feeling happy.

It was a great reason to ask her over, and a great reason for her to go.

And she was glad she did.

There'd been no pressure, no need for effort. It had been easy, and it had been nice.

Elliot was a genuinely good guy, and they had more in common than she thought she did with anyone else. Even if their viewing habits were polar opposites.

That didn't seem to matter in the slightest, though.

They clicked on all the things that mattered.

And after more conversation, right there on the sofa, he'd looked at his watch — the same silver faced, black-banded modest timepiece from before — and said, 'It's getting late.'

She'd looked at him for a second, wondering what would happen next.

'I had a good time,' she said.

'Me too,' he replied.

And then, he got up and walked towards the door.

That was all it took.

There was no hurry.

No need to rush.

Anything else wouldn't have been them. They were both too prag-matic, to fastidious and self-effacing to push it any further.

She stepped through the open door and into the hallway.

'Get home safe,' he said.

She nodded. 'I will.'

'Speak soon?'

She nodded again.

He smiled. 'Good night, Jamie.'

'Good night, Elliot.'

He waited for her to go down the stairs before he closed the door, and then she was alone in the hallway, feeling warm.

Tiredness crept in on the drive back, and by the time she got into bed, she was all but asleep, still smiling.

She sank into the darkness and languished there for a long time. But then, as the hours ticked by, she grew restless. The serenity that had found her dripped away. Her dreams became mobile and mercurial.

There was pounding. She was running. She was banging her fists on a door. She was kicking at a figure that wouldn't go down.

She was scrambling up a hill, her legs churning.

She was reaching out for something too high to grab.

She was yelling, her voice strangled in her throat.

She was — awake.

Jamie sat upright in bed, dragging in a breath like the hands around her neck had been real.

Her phone was buzzing angrily on the nightstand and she blinked herself clear, twisting to squint at it with one eye closed.

It was five twelve in the morning.

The number on the screen wasn't saved in her phone, but she'd stared at it enough over the last day to know who it was.

She answered quickly. 'Elliot?' She couldn't keep the concern out of her voice.

'Jamie,' he said, seemingly a little out of breath. 'I'm sorry to bother you—'

'It's fine, what's wrong?' she asked quickly, reading his tone.

'It's Grace,' he said.

'Is she alright?'

'She's here.'

Jamie was already on her feet. 'What? Where? At your apartment?'

'Yeah,' he said, his voice muffled as he pinned his phone against his shoulder. 'She's strung out, beat up — she's — she's — shit—' He sighed. 'I know it's late — or early — but do you—'

'I'm already on my way,' she said, shoving her heels into her boots and pulling the bedroom door open.

It wasn't uncommon for her to get calls like this in the middle of the night. Work calls. When something was happening, or something was wrong. Crime didn't keep regular hours.

She had two sets of clothes ready at all times. A long-sleeve thermal t-shirt — good for all weathers — her normal stretchy jeans, and her trusty boots.

Maybe she needed more variety in her wardrobe.

But then again, it wasn't like her routine changed much. And her choices were functional.

Who did she really have to show off for?

She was down the stairs and in the car in less than ninety seconds.

The route was still fresh in her mind, and the city was still sleeping for the most part. The dawn-treaders were up, going home from night shifts, or heading to whatever early-morning engagements they had. But it was mostly taxis, flashing past, their roof-signs illuminated, like the thoraxes of fireflies darting through the night-drenched city.

She made good time, skating through some questionable amber lights, and arrived at Elliot's in twelve minutes. Just over a third of the time it had taken the previous evening.

She parked the car on the double-yellow lines outside the building, threw her police permit onto the dash, and then headed up to the front door. She rang for Elliot, but he didn't come over the intercom, just hit the door buzzer.

She let herself in and took the stairs two at a time, an image from her dream flashing through her mind.

Jamie shook it off, along with the last dregs of tiredness, and swung around the balustrade post at the top of the stairs.

Elliot's door was left open for her and she pushed in without knocking.

She saw him first, half-hidden behind the sofa they'd been sitting on just hours before. Despite getting less than five hours sleep, she was wired.

'Elliot,' she said, coming up on the sofa quickly.

Grace came into view, lying on her back, right hand on her stomach. She was wearing the same clothes that she'd been in when they'd first found her.

She was asleep, her chest rising and falling under the worn coat.

There was a gentle wheeze ringing from her nose.

Her eyes were sunken, dark bags under them. But they weren't what Jamie was looking at.

Her lip was split, a purple welt around the corner of her mouth shining nearly black in the dim light. Elliot only had the desk-lamp on and the apartment was barely lit.

Another bruise covered her left cheek and disappeared behind the strands of hair matted to her face, and a final mark ran down the side of her right eye vertically. Her eyebrow was swollen and crusted with blood. The line looked strange though, too uniform to be from a fist or weapon.

She was sweating, her skin pale, her lips the colour of chalk.

'Jesus,' Jamie muttered, looking her over.

Elliot was on his knees, holding her left wrist, his first two fingers pressed gently on her radial pulse. 'She's been knocked around pretty hard. There's a cut and bruise on the back of her head, too.' He reached down with his free hand, and tilted her head to the side.

Jamie could see that the towel he'd folded up and put under her was spotted with blood.

'I gave her something to help her sleep, some naloxone to get the heroin out of her system, some anti-withdrawals to help with the fever, ease the nausea.' He never looked away, an expression of true concern on his face.

Jamie nodded. 'Who did this?'

Elliot looked at her gravely. 'She said his name is Simon Paxton.'

She took the name in, memorising it.

'He's known on the street as Sippy,' Elliot added, looking down at Grace. 'It's the person who… Who has always… I think…' His eyes moved down her body a little. He couldn't say it, but Jamie knew. The azithromycin, the drugs, the reason Oliver didn't want her to get them anymore.

'Sippy?' Simon Paxton. An image of Dead-Eyes burned itself behind her eyes. Sippy.

He nodded.

'What happened?'

He shook his head slowly. 'I don't know. She showed up here, crying, strung-out. I let her up, and she fell in, bleeding, cut up. Concussed.' He looked pensive for a second, inspecting her face. 'Looks like he'd hit her. She turned, tried to run—' he touched the back of her head delicately '—and he hit her, sent her sprawling into some-thing—' his fingers touched her eyebrow and the bruised line touching the corner of her eye '—a doorframe, or something else.' He turned her wrist out for Jamie to see now. It was black with finger marks. 'She barely got away.'

For all the horror lying in front of her, she couldn't help but think how smart he was. How he would make a great detective. It took a special kind of mind to look at a body and see its history.

He went on. 'When she got here she was hyperventilating, fighting whatever was in her system — she took something else — other than the heroin, I think — to bring her up, maybe, so she could move. So she could run.' He looked up at her, fear in his eyes. 'But it was too much — I had to give her something to get her down — her heart was racing — I couldn't even see the colour of her eyes.' He lowered his head and slouched backwards onto his heels.

Jamie let the silence ring for a second before she spoke. 'She say anything before…' Jamie nodded at the sleeping girl.

'I asked the same as you — who did this. What happened. She could barely speak — but she gave me his name, said where she'd come from. I couldn't wait any longer, I had to give her the sedatives. I couldn't wait. But I knew that calling you without anything would be…' He shook his head again, holding her hand. 'Goddammit, I should have given it to her faster. It wasn't fair.'

Jamie set her jaw. 'You made the right decision,' she said stiffly. 'A few seconds wouldn't have made a difference if she'd run here from—'

'A few seconds *always* makes a difference,' Elliot said sharply, looking up at her. 'A few seconds is the difference between life and death. You nick an artery, you run a red light, you step off the kerb without looking. Life and death are always just seconds apart. Some-times less.'

Jamie nodded. It had obviously struck a nerve.

He really did care about this girl.

'Thank you,' she said quietly, not wanting to press, but knowing she had to. 'You need to tell me where he is — where she came from.'

Elliot looked up at her.

'We can get this guy. I can get this guy.' Her eyes were hard. 'If not for Oliver, then for this. We can bring him in, we can squeeze him — we can question him. We can get him.'

He swallowed. 'If you don't, then she's dead. You know that, don't you?'

Jamie digested that, wondering what she could say. What choice did she have?

'Yeah,' she said after a few seconds. 'I know.'

Elliot measured her, and then finally relented. 'Okay,' he said, exhaling. 'I'll stay with her. You go and get this bastard.'

She smiled. 'You're a good man, Elliot.'

He laughed a little. That same prickle in the back of her head. 'I'm not,' he muttered. 'I'm just doing what I can.'

She reached for her phone, wanting all of this to be over. Wanting everything else except them to just disappear.

Jamie found Roper's number and called, chewing on her thumbnail as it rang out, eventually going to voicemail.

'Shit,' she muttered, dialling again.

Same thing.

'Come on, Roper. I need you.'

Again.

'Damn it.'

'What's wrong?' Elliot asked, narrowing his eyes, trying to read her expression.

She let out a long sigh. 'Is there a twenty-four-hour coffee place around here?'

'Why?' he asked, his brow crumpling.

'Because I'd bet everything I own that my partner is passed out shit-faced drunk and if I don't show up with a triple-shot-something, then he's going to be no use at all.'

In any other circumstance, that might have elicited a laugh. But

Elliot didn't seem to like the idea of her relying on a drunk for backup. 'Are you sure he's the right person for it?'

'For all his faults, Roper is one of the best men I know,' she said without faking it. 'And there's no one I'd rather have for backup.'

'I hope so,' Elliot said, looking back at Grace's face — at the bruises there. At the violence there — 'Because you're going to need it.'

23

Roper slumped down into the passenger seat with his eyes closed.

She'd switched to his home phone after the twentieth call, hoping that the ringer would rouse him.

Eventually, it did.

And despite having only gotten in three hours earlier from his pub-crawl with Thompson, he'd risen to the call.

She could smell the alcohol streaming out of his mouth and nose as he huffed, looking green. He'd barely slept and was still about as drunk as people got while they were conscious.

She handed him a large black coffee with two extra shots — which made five in total. Enough to invigorate a horse — along with a croissant that had been out on display since the morning before. He needed both, desperately.

Jamie pulled away cleanly, glancing left at Roper, who was sitting upright, still in the clothes from the night before, clutching the pastry and coffee in front of him, unable to lift either to his lips.

'You've got twenty minutes to sober up,' Jamie growled, gripping the steering wheel.

Roper groaned as she decelerated into a red light.

She was focused. Completely so. And totally wired.

Elliot had text her the address after she'd left and she'd memorised the route. It wasn't far and she knew the area.

It was in an older part of the city that had gone downhill in recent years. A lot of the buildings there were empty or under construction, left derelict and handed over to whoever had the gall to pull the boards off the windows and get inside.

They weren't fit for habitation, but users who'd do anything for a taste rarely needed more than privacy to get their fix.

And sometimes not even that.

Elliot had tagged the address with a *'Be careful, this guy is bad news.'* And Jamie would be, but she could feel the kevlar-enforced toe caps in her boots if she pushed her toes upwards, and she wasn't afraid to use them.

She glanced in the rear-view and saw her dad in the back seat. He was looking at her.

They locked eyes and he nodded. Go get him.

Jamie smirked for a second, and then caught herself, looking away.

When she checked again, he was gone.

Roper sucked on the coffee, but didn't touch the croissant until they were practically there.

When she pulled up and killed the engine at the corner of a street that speared off from another at ninety degrees, and ended in darkness, Roper opened his eyes.

Jamie was parked under a streetlight, looking out of the driver's side window.

The name of the street had been spray-painted over. A tired sign bolted to the side of the brick building, now stained black. But she knew that under it the words Mott Street were embossed.

Of the eight streetlights on it, only three were working.

The far end just seemed to end in darkness about sixty yards down.

Jamie knew that just beyond it, the road ended and there was an entrance to a building site that had been stagnant for a few years. They'd begun developing on the ground, but the site had lost funding and been sitting ever since.

The whole street was zoned to be redeveloped, but due to the state of the rest of the buildings, and the inhabitants who made their homes inside their rotten walls, no more investment could be found.

It was the perfect shit hole for someone like Simon Paxton to hold up. 'Sippy…' Jamie muttered, glaring down the street.

'What was that?' Roper asked groggily, spitting crumbs of pastry over his knees.

Jamie didn't have the spare mental capacity to even comment on it.

'Sippy,' she said, her head snapping around. 'The lump of junkie-shit we're about to arrest.'

Roper nodded, washing down the stale croissant with a big gulp of coffee.

He looked slightly clearer. But still not in any fit state.

Though Jamie didn't have any other choice.

By the time it would take to scramble back-up at this time, Sippy would probably be long gone. And there was no way she'd have a patrol car rolling up here. He'd be out the window the second he heard the sirens. No, they had the element of surprise, and they needed to use it.

Grace hadn't known the number of the house they were in, but she told Elliot that it had front steps leading up to the entrance, a white 'X' spray-painted on the door, and cardboard tacked up in the windows.

That was good enough for Jamie.

'Come on,' she said, getting out of the car.

Roper drained the last of his coffee and followed her out, swaying on his feet.

She stepped cautiously under the streetlight on the corner, staring into the darkness ahead.

It was just before six now but the street was empty.

In either direction, nothing stirred. In an hour, the place would be awash with cars. But for the moment, it was a graveyard.

Witching hour, her dad used to say. When all the scum come out to play.

On her left, Roper was taking a piss against the side of the first rundown ruin of a building, bent over, hand on the wall above his head, forehead against the bricks.

He zipped up after an age and came over, squinting in the glare of the streetlight.

'You done?'

''Til the coffee goes through me,' he replied, slurring a little.

She drew a breath, settled her heart, and started forward.

It was moments like this that being unarmed did make her feel naked.

She clenched her fists against the cold morning air, glad that she'd taken her clothes out of the machine and hung them to dry before she'd headed out to Elliot's. Her suede jacket would provide some protection, and it was one of the warmest things she had.

Her head bounced left and right, looking for the steps and the white 'X'.

It was hard to see in the gloom between the lights, and with every door they passed, she grew more and more anxious.

From what Elliot had said, they were headed into a heroin den. Sippy's home turf.

They'd have to tread lightly.

The denizens wouldn't take kindly to two detectives letting themselves in.

Some of the doorways had been boarded over, some chained up.

But none had a white 'X'.

'Shit,' Jamie mumbled, stepping into the street, measuring the distance to the end.

There weren't a lot of houses left.

And then, she saw it.

The last but one house — a tall, three-story brick affair. The windows were Georgian and broken for the most part, sealed shut with cardboard boxes, the white paint around the frames peeling and flaking in chunks.

Broken glass littered the pavement in front of the building and syringes were piled against the kerb.

The door looked like it had been kicked through more than a few

times, and sat askew in the frame, a white 'X' cutting across the faded
black paint.

'Here,' Jamie said, turning towards it. She patted her back pocket
reflexively, feeling the outline of the combination hinge handcuffs
there. She always kept a set in her car, along with a box of latex gloves.

She had a pair of those in her pocket, too.

Roper looked up at the house, his face a mixture of disgust and
disdain. 'Great. And what are we doing here?'

'Arresting Dead-Eyes,' she said, her voice as cold as steel.

Roper processed, then nodded. 'Okay.'

'After me, I suppose?' Jamie asked, already moving.

'Being a gentleman, and all,' Roper chuckled gruffly, careful to
keep his voice low.

Despite the humour, they were both distinctly aware of the danger
that lay ahead.

They took the steps slowly, listening for any sound coming from
within.

There wasn't any.

On the top step, Jamie was met with the thick stench of urine and
the glint of syringes left around the door.

She glanced at the ancient doorbell — at the needle that had been
snapped off and pushed into the rubber so that it stuck out like a barb,
ready to stab anyone who reached out to ring it.

Jamie nodded to Roper and he followed her eye, sticking out his
bottom lip in disapproval.

It was a common thing in squats like these. To discourage anyone
who wanted to come calling.

A lot of the time that unlucky person would get a nasty prick.
Sometimes it would be Hep. Every now and then HIV.

It was always better to knock with the toe of your boot than go for
a bell. Her dad had told her that when she was eight. And she'd never
forgotten it.

Luckily, they didn't need to knock at all.

The lock had been broken right out of the door, a hole where the
handle used to be.

It swung open as she pushed it with her foot, cautiously opening it into a bare hallway.

The walls had been stripped of all cables and wiring. Deep trenches through the plaster ran in a web around the house.

The floor was exposed, dusty boards, most of which were stained. Some were cracked.

The tacking strips for carpets still ran around the outsides. But there was no sign of them.

What few patches of unbroken wall there were had been drawn on, spray-painted, or smeared with human shit.

People were strange. They carried so much hatred at times that all they had in them was to destroy. To destroy their homes. To destroy their relationships. To destroy themselves.

Inside the building, the rasping sounds of laboured wheezing filled the air.

Jamie breathed slowly, pushing the rotten smell out of her mind.

Roper swore under his breath, then pulled his coat collar up around his face like a balaclava, holding it there with his hand as they investigated.

She couldn't imagine how sick he must already be feeling.

And the smell could only be making it worse.

She was surprised that he hadn't thrown up already.

Practice, she guessed.

The stairs ran up to the first floor directly opposite the door, with a corridor stretching down the side of it towards the kitchen. On their right a double-doorway led to a living room.

Jamie pointed to herself and then motioned to it. Roper nodded, gesturing down the corridor to the kitchen. They'd take one route each and circle back to meet each other, trapping Dead-Eyes if he was in there.

Roper's heavy steps creaked on the boards as he walked.

Jamie was more pragmatic, choosing to step where the boards met, where the nails went in. It was where they were affixed to the joists. Stepping on those wouldn't put pressure on the boards. Would let her move quietly.

She didn't want anyone to know she was there until it was too late.

Jamie stuck her head around the frame and scanned the room, seeing the first of the users.

He was slouched against the window, a rubber tube around his arm, a syringe in his lap, lying on his filthy tracksuit bottoms.

His chin was on his chest, his breathing shallow.

But he had hair — a mop of it roughly cut in a straight line across his forehead. He could have been thirty or sixty — Jamie couldn't tell. He was nothing but scabby skin stretched over bones.

Definitely not who they were looking for.

Across from the doorway was another guy. He was sitting with his knees against his chest, his head between them, shins exposed, a patchwork of needle marks shining above the tops of his ragged trainers held together with tape and string.

He was wearing a fur-hooded parka. Same as Sippy. Her heart kicked up a gear.

Jamie couldn't make the colour out in the semi-darkness of the room — lit only by the glow of the streetlight coming in through the section of the window out of reach to put cardboard over.

Everything in the room was drowned in a dirty shade of orange.

Jamie swallowed, tasting the stale smell of dying humans in the air, and reached into her pocket, pulling out the pair of latex gloves.

The floor creaked to her left and she looked up, seeing Roper appear in the doorway that led to the kitchen-diner. He shook his head.

No sign of Sippy.

On his right, slumped in the corner, was a woman in her forties, her hair a black tangle of matted strands. There was a puddle of urine under her, a low wheezing telling them that she was just about clinging to life.

Jamie tilted her head to the guy in the parka and Roper came forward slowly until he was close enough to smell. She could pick out his unique blend of booze and John Player Specials, even among the symphony of stench that permeated every inch of this hell hole.

Jamie crouched a little and reached out, taking a few strands of fur between her fingers as Roper lingered behind.

She could feel his breath washing over the back of her head.

Jamie exhaled, gripped, and then pulled the hood back in a smooth movement, standing up and stepping back all at the same time to give them space.

The head underneath was covered with thick black hair and both Jamie and Roper exhaled and looked at each other.

It wasn't him.

They both turned in unison and looked back into the hallway. At the stairs.

One floor down. Two to go.

24

They crept towards the stairs, both aware that with every second they spent in the house, the more chance there was of someone waking up.

Jamie went up first, careful not to touch the walls or bannisters. She didn't want to risk anything. By the look of this place, everything was set up to dissuade visitors.

Rusty nails had been pulled up and turned out, splinters poked through the veneer on the bannister, and razor blades had been pushed into the plasterboard. If you ran your hand up the former, or brushed your shoulder on the latter, you'd get stabbed or nicked. And in here, you definitely didn't want that to happen.

If this was Sippy's den — his personal heaven, and everyone else's personal hell, then it would be set up like a fortress. And it was.

Jamie scanned the steps in front of her, choosing her footing carefully.

Her dad had a jagged scar on his right knee and thigh from ascending a set of stairs just like these. A trick step had given out under his weight and he'd plunged straight through, shredding his leg on the screws and wooden teeth.

He'd only needed to learn that lesson once.

Jamie hoped to never learn it at all.

She stepped on either side of the steps — pushing her feet against the outsides as she moved upwards, letting the wooden struts underneath bear her weight.

Every time her foot came down, she ground her toes in, pressing slowly, putting weight onto them one at a time to test.

She hated being so cautious when time was running thin, but she was right to be.

The fourth step moved as she rested her foot on it, and as she twisted her heel out, the whole step slipped and rotated towards her.

Looked like Sippy or someone equally as cruel had removed the screws and filed down the angle so that anyone who put their weight on it would kick it out behind them and fall face-first into the stairs.

Her eyes moved upwards and sure enough, three steps up, right where your stomach and chest would hit, nails had been roughly hammered into the corners of the steps.

Anyone unlucky enough to lose their footing would plunge onto them and impale themselves. She didn't know if they were long enough to kill someone, but it would guarantee a trip to the emergency room, and delay whatever notice was being served.

She looked back at Roper and then pointed to the step, which was now twisted off the mounting struts.

Then she leaned sideways and pointed to the nails.

He shook his head in disgust and motioned her onwards.

'Careful,' she mouthed. 'Step where I do.'

He nodded, clenching his shaking hands.

It was gloomy in the hallway, the only light the pale pre-dawn and streetlight spilling in through the window over the front door.

She was perfectly sober and she was nervous going up there. She didn't like to think how horrible it would be doing it drunk.

But she couldn't think like that. If he wanted to take this as a wake-up call then that was his prerogative.

Jamie moved from left to right, picking her way up the booby-trapped stairs, and got to the top, inspecting the bare boards in front of her.

She didn't think that the traps would end.

The landing was shrouded in darkness.

There was a window directly above the front door at the end of the landing, but a thick black cloth had been draped over it and nailed to the wall. The two doors to her left led into bedrooms she guessed, and the one behind her offered entry into a toilet that stunk so badly she had to hold her breath.

'Shit,' Roper whispered, catching the smell as he got to the top behind her.

'That's what it is,' she whispered back. 'Lots of it, in a toilet that doesn't flush.'

Roper craned his head and looked around the door, the little window in the bathroom throwing a dim glow over the tiles. 'And in the bathtub.'

'Let's keep moving,' Jamie said, turning back to the landing. The two doors there beckoned.

The first was missing a knob and didn't move when she pushed it, laying her gloved hand flat on the wood. Though it wasn't locked it was blocked by something heavy and pushing on it could alert the whole house to their presence, and she wasn't ready to do that until they'd eliminated all other possibilities.

She moved on down the hallway, stepping on the seams of the boards, careful not to make them creak. She couldn't see anything untoward, but she wasn't letting her guard down.

The second door down was open and she approached with care, her heart thudding against her ribcage. She could feel it in her fingers, behind her eyes.

Roper's breath was hot and sharp behind her. He was panting almost. As nervous as her despite his years of experience.

There was no escaping the fear that crept in when you were in someone else's house. On someone else's home turf. And it was compounded by the fact that they knew he wouldn't come easy.

With every step she felt like they were backing him into a corner. And they both knew what happened when you cornered a dog.

Jamie reached the frame and peered through the gap. It was darkness inside.

She nodded him up the stairs and he agreed, both of them keen to get Sippy locked down as quickly as possible.

She could feel the handcuffs in her back pocket, tight against the fabric. She'd thought about reaching for them a hundred times in as many seconds — the route her hand would take, so she could do it as soon as she needed to without missing a beat.

Roper shuffled around the balustrade post, pushing his feet across the wood so he didn't skewer himself on anything.

When he reached the stairs he looked over at Jamie, who was waiting to see if he was sure about going up before she pushed inwards. If he wasn't, she would have taken the stairs.

She nodded to him reassuringly and he hung his head, drew a breath, and then took the first step. Following Jamie's method, slotting his feet against the sides as he moved up.

Jamie watched him until his head disappeared above the line of the ceiling, and then reached for her multi-tool, opening it up and resting her thumb on the LED torch switch.

She took a few breaths to settle herself, tasted the putrid air, and then blew it all back out, spreading her feet to get a better stance.

She'd have to be quick.

Jamie planned her actions — she'd step in, push the door open, plant her right foot wide to stop the door from rebounding into her shoulder, sweep the light around the room, and charge down Sippy if she saw him.

Now or never.

She pushed in, slid her right foot wide, clicked the torch to life, and then moved it in a wide arc, covering the whole room.

Her heart seized in her chest, her muscles all tensing at once.

But the beam hit nothing but gouged plaster and used needles.

And a big hole in the wall.

She paused, looking at the smashed edges, the beam hitting a swath of dark fabric pinned from the other side. They looked like old curtains.

Whoever had made the hole had done so in a vague attempt to knock the two bedrooms into one — or create a more secluded space in the second.

The perfect place to shoot up in peace.

Jamie stepped in, flicking the torch to her feet, finding her route.

Her eyes adjusted to the darkness and she searched the corners more thoroughly.

The front bedroom was practically empty. An old sleeping bag was crumpled in the corner, a few empty crisp packets around it. Other than that the room was bare boards.

She headed towards the hole — about five feet tall and four across.

Jamie stooped to get under the jagged top edge, held the nose of her torch against her hip to stub out the light, and stepped in through. She pulled the fabric aside, the stink of sweat and urine thick in the air.

She held her breath and tweaked her ears, halfway past the curtain, listening for breathing — any signal of another body in the room.

There was nothing.

Deathly silence.

The torch came off her hip and she covered the room.

A putrid, naked mattress was pushed against the back wall, an old bedsheet had been hung off the curtain-pole over the window. The privacy it afforded as a blind was more important than the comfort and cleanliness it would offer as a sheet.

Next to it was a backpack — a familiar-looking one. A soiled pair of women's pants were thrown on the floor next to it.

She let the light rest on the battered rucksack, something in her mind telling her that it was familiar.

It was Grace's.

She remembered it from the tent under the bridge.

This was where she'd been then.

Jamie picked out the used needles strewn around.

The empty soft drink bottles.

The used condoms.

Jamie grimaced and kept the torch moving, finding the source of the obstruction behind the first door.

Another mattress had been stood up and pushed against it.

A huge brown stain marked it right in the middle. Jamie could smell what it was.

Whoever had been lying on it hadn't been able to hold themselves.

It wasn't uncommon with heroin. It relaxed the muscles. And addicts weren't known to have fibre rich diets.

She was staring at it when something thudded overhead.

The beam shot upwards and she tilted her head back, staring at the ceiling.

A crash. Something falling — something thrown? Footsteps.

Roper was shouting. 'Hey! Hey!' The first was loud, the second hurried.

More footsteps. Fast now. Someone running.

'Johansson!' Roper roared.

It was all she needed.

There was a gap in the footsteps for a second, and then a loud bang coming through the wall.

Sippy clearing the last few steps and hitting the landing.

Jamie was through the curtain and charging for the door.

She skidded through the frame as Sippy flashed past wearing a yellowed vest, his parka nowhere to be seen.

He gripped the balustrade post as he reached the end of the hallway and flung himself around it.

Jamie's eyes met his for a fraction of a second — those same dead eyes — and then he was hammering towards the ground floor.

She went after him as Roper clattered down the stairs above her, swearing and slipping.

Jamie took the top four steps, watching as Sippy pulled the front door open, and then vaulted sideways, kicking off the wall, and into the space over the bannister.

She didn't have time to look for the nails and trick step — this was quicker.

Jamie landed like a cat, twisted, and then kicked forward towards the open front door.

Sippy was already down into the street.

Roper was panting at the top of the stairs, taking them one at a time, swearing continuously as he stared down at them.

She didn't have time to wait for him.

When she reached the stone steps outside she heard him fall, slipping on the movable stair, saving himself on the bannister, yowling as he caught a splinter.

Sippy was fast, out ahead, heading for the corner.

But he was a junkie.

And Jamie could sustain any pace he threw down.

She was built for this — built *herself* for this.

Her heart beat steadily in her chest as she pumped her arms, keeping her knees high, chest forward, shoulders down, powering up to a sprint.

By the time she'd reached the corner, she'd already pulled back thirty feet.

He hung a right, then ran across the road, around her car.

Traffic was beginning to build up now. It was after six and the early-birds were making their way into the heart of the city.

Jamie stepped up onto the kerb, took two steps, and then hurdled clean over her bonnet, the metal ringing like a gong as her palm smacked into it, helping her clear the last few inches.

The thick soles of her boots absorbed the impact and she took off, maintaining pace, reeling Sippy in. They were lighter than less than most trainers, and twice as supportive.

And she was as fast in them as she was in her running shoes.

Roper was somewhere behind, running as hard as he could. She could hear him calling between ragged breaths but she wasn't slowing down.

Sippy took a left and made down the pavement, drawing opposite with the street again, looking down the alleys between the houses and buildings as he did, searching for an out.

He glanced over his shoulder at her, stumbled, nearly fell, and then caught himself.

He was fifty feet ahead, swearing and sweating.

He had no idea where he was running to.

She could see the shine on the back of his head as he streaked under the streetlights.

'Police! Stop!' Jamie called between her own breaths. She knew it was pointless, but when she filled in the report she wanted to be able to say she tried to stop him without the use of force. And she wanted to be able to say it truthfully.

He didn't, and cut right at the end of a street, heading back towards the city.

He'd gone in a loop, moving right and then left again, before finding the route he was looking for.

Roper made up some ground heading in a straight line across the road and by the time Jamie hit the corner that Sippy had rounded, he wasn't that far behind. But every shortcut he took to make up the ground was countered by his slow, loping pace.

She could hear him wheezing from across the road, cursing his rusty lungs. He'd probably smoked eighty cigarettes yesterday with Thompson.

And he was paying for it.

Sippy had moved into the road again, weaving between the traffic.

Horns blared and people yelled from behind their steering wheels as he raked his grubby hands over their cars, pushing himself clear and back onto the kerb.

Jamie followed, yelling, 'Police!' at the drivers who didn't seem to care.

A space between two cars closed up as an annoyed driver squeezed right up to the bumper of the car in front and Jamie skidded to a halt, clattering into the front wing of a four-by-four with her hip.

The driver swore at her and gave her the finger.

She growled, peeled herself off his paintwork, and took a second to shove her badge against his window.

Jamie only saw the colour drain from his face for an instant before she swung around behind him and took off again, catching her breath as she did.

The car had damn near winded her.

Sippy had pulled out more of a lead now and Roper was hot on her heels.

A dull ache was ringing down her right leg — she'd really hit the car hard.

Her pace had slowed some, her leg numb under her.

But she wouldn't stop.

Sippy was heading for the city, the buildings rising in the distance.

But then he slowed, looking left and right, and changed direction.

Jamie followed his line and saw where he was heading.

A tube station entrance at the next corner was beginning to bustle with early morning commuters. If he made it inside, she didn't know if they'd be able to catch him.

She swore and pushed harder, feeling the sweat bead on her forehead, run down between her shoulder blades.

Sippy reached the railing, stopped for a second, looked back, and then plunged in, shoving between two women, sending them sprawling.

People clamoured around, the women screaming, passers-by jostled and shoved off balance.

It was immediate carnage, and Sippy had just dived right through the middle of it.

People thronged in an impenetrable wall as they helped each other up and pushed each other down in equal measure — some desperate for assistance, some loathing the touch of strangers.

She'd never get through.

Jamie measured the distance, sucked in a deep breath, chose her steps, neared, tensed, and then jumped.

She was only going to get one shot at it.

And she took it.

25

J amie sailed through the air, tucking her heels against her hamstrings, clearing the throng of people, and the entirety of the first stair-set.

She landed hard on the solid stone platform that separated the two flights, and rolled, pain lancing through her ankles and knees.

Her back went over the edge of the top step and the space under her allowed her to get back to her feet, skipping and jumping down the rest.

Jamie got onto solid ground and ploughed through the commuters, using every spare breath she had to yell, 'Police! Out of the way!'

People froze up and turned into trees, throwing their arms into the air, not knowing which way to go.

Up ahead, Sippy was scrabbling through the crowd, and behind, she could hear Roper's voice telling people to move or get trampled.

Jamie didn't dare turn around. Weaving through the bodies at this speed was dangerous facing forward, let alone back. And Sippy had a good lead now, his recklessness and disregard for the people giving him an edge as Jamie did her best to keep to a run, pulling herself past people like she was swimming.

Sippy reached the gates and turned back, looking for Jamie in the thickening crowd.

She caught his eye and froze, holding her hand up. 'Don't move!' she yelled, her voice barely carrying in the din.

The people Sippy had shoved out of the way were beginning to encircle him, grab for him, shout at him.

He fought them off.

'No!' Jamie yelled, fighting forward once more, the people around her all turning to look at the spectacle, making them an impenetrable bog of bodies. 'Don't! Give him space — Goddammit! Move! Get out of the—'

She was cut off by a woman's scream.

It was high pitched, shrill, and it sliced through the thick station air like a razor.

Everyone froze, reality lurching.

'Knife!' a man howled.

Everyone leapt back from Sippy as he slashed at them with what looked like a flick-knife; a four inch blade.

Jamie raked in a deep breath, seeing the fear in everyone's eyes, feeling the stampede building in the air.

Sippy's eyes found hers, the blade glinting in front of him for a split second.

And then he turned, and jumped over the gate.

Jamie felt her feet flex under her as the two bodies in front, still facing the same way she was, began to backpedal under their own steam.

She was about to lose him.

She exhaled, let herself sink backwards, and got low.

Roper was roaring behind her, elbowing and beating his way forward.

She didn't have the strength or size to pummel her way through. She had to think of something else.

The current kicked up, the wash of humans starting to surge.

She couldn't swim against it.

She knew that.

Jamie dipped right and threaded her way to the wall, her hands slapping against the tiles as she was crushed against it.

She kept her body tight to it and drove forwards, her shoulder impacting on every commuter as she made for the gate.

It loomed closer, her arms and legs screaming as they churned, propelling her along.

The crowd began to thin — everyone this side of the gate crushing towards the stairs — and Jamie cut inwards shunting past those who'd lagged behind, or decided not to run.

Roper was trapped in the swirl behind her.

He may have been stronger, but Jamie was fast, and the gate slipped under her like it was moving.

She was over it and running again, grabbing her breath as she did.

The station only had two platforms — north and south. At the bottom of a staircase, the corridor split.

Jamie was suddenly alone, her body aching, sweat running down her nose. Left and right were both empty, both swinging back towards the platforms.

She had a decision to make.

There was no sign of Sippy. He was already on one of them.

But which?

She looked around, tweaking her ears. Nothing. Shit.

Roper was clapping down the stairs behind her, huffing and panting.

She looked back, unable to keep the angst out of her face. At least this way they could take one side each.

Roper sank into his knees, resting his hands on his thighs. It looked like he was going to throw up. It wouldn't have been the first time.

'Which way?' Jamie asked.

Roper looked up, coughing, spitting, and then looking at the sign. 'Train comes in,' he wheezed, 'in two minutes on the northern — twelve on the southern.' He hawked, then gagged. 'He's gone north. If he went south, he'd be stuck on the platform for ten minutes.' He flicked a hand to their left.

'How do you know?' She sounded as unsure as she felt.

Roper looked up at her, then stood. 'I looked at the board. Didn't you?'

She growled. 'Come on.' She turned and headed right, towards the northern line, battling the hot wind sweeping up from the track.

He groaned and then jogged after her.

She took the stairs two at a time, ignoring the pain in her knees and hip, and flattened out on the platform ahead of Roper.

The platform, despite the approaching train, was empty.

Jamie shuddered, coming out in gooseflesh. The only reason that it would be empty was if the people had all left. And they'd only do that if there was something to run from.

Sippy was only a minute ahead, but seeing someone coming down the stairs with a knife would clear a platform like this in seconds.

Jamie slowed to a walk, collecting herself, slowing her breath.

Her heart wouldn't calm though.

Her hair fluttered in the wind, her skin tingling. The ceiling vaulted up overhead, the milk-white tiles grimy with age.

Ahead, on the platform, alone, pacing, twitchy, was Sippy.

He was at the far end, running back and forth, staring into the tunnel. Willing the train to arrive.

'Simon Paxton!' Jamie yelled, turning half on, holding her left hand out, her right finding the bulge of the handcuffs in her back pocket.

He looked up, his eyes landing on her, and then darting to the emergency exit to Jamie's right. She'd been sure to get past it before calling out. She didn't want to give Sippy an escape route.

Sippy stared at her, looked at the track, and then lifted his knife.

'Don't come any closer!' he yelled, his hand shaking.

'Put the knife down, Simon,' Jamie said, trying to calm herself. Her voice was lost in the wind, in the distant echo of the train rumbling down the tunnel.

She didn't have long. If the train arrived, the platform would flood with people, and Sippy would be gone.

Jamie walked slowly but steadily.

'Stay back!' he shrieked, waving the blade. 'I'll do it!'

Roper was at her side now, snatching for breath. 'Put it down! On the ground. Now!' He was shouting, his husky voice echoing through the station.

'Don't come any closer!'

Roper was out in front now, one hand up, one behind his back, on his own set of cuffs.

'Roper,' Jamie said, conscious of his pace.

He was closing up too quickly.

Sippy was getting spooked.

But he wasn't listening.

Roper kept going and Sippy walked backwards, nearing the wall.

When he hit it, he'd have nowhere to go.

'Drop the knife on the ground and kick it away,' Roper ordered.

Sippy looked from Roper to Jamie and back. The tunnel was dark and his exit was blocked by Jamie. She stepped sideways, twisting a little, readying to take him down if he ran. He'd get round Roper, but she'd take him down. Roundhouse — high arc, heel to the face. She didn't want to, but she wasn't letting him go.

Roper was close now. 'Simon Paxton, you're under arrest for the murder of Oliver Hammond—'

'I didn't! Stay back!' He was out of his mind — eyes wide and black, hand shaking violently.

'Get down on the—'

'I'm not going back! I'm not going...' He looked at Jamie, then at Roper. He had the knife in his hand and this was only going one of a few ways. Either he was going to kill them both with it and be on the hook for double-murder, looking over his shoulder for the rest of his life. Or, he was going to try, and fail, and get arrested for the attempted murder of a police officer. Or, he could give it up and throw the knife down. Surrender.

But Jamie knew he wouldn't do that. He'd already said. He wasn't going back. Not back to jail, not back—

But she couldn't finish the thought, because he did something she couldn't have anticipated.

The blade flashed.

'No!' Roper yelled.

Jamie plunged forward.

Sippy raked the knife across his wrist.

Blood spurted and then splattered on the flagstones.

He mewled, staggered backwards, and swung his arms, flicking blood all across the platform.

Roper surged forward.

'Don't come any closer,' Sippy shouted. 'I'm positive!' He raised his arm, a thick red stream of blood gushing from the wound, dripping from his elbow.

Roper froze. So did Jamie.

HIV positive.

But he was losing a lot of blood — too much. He wouldn't be able to stay upright for much longer.

He swayed on his feet.

'Get down on the ground!' Roper yelled again, his voice strained now. 'Hands above your head!'

Blood began to pool between Sippy's feet.

'Simon,' Jamie urged. 'Let us help you!'

'Ground!' Roper was rising to the limits of his voice. 'Now! I'm not going to ask again — son of a bitch!' Roper threw his hands up to protect his face, the bloodied knife whipping past his head, glancing off his arm as he dove sideways.

Sippy had thrown the knife with the little strength he had left.

Roper went to a knee, throwing his right hand to the underside of his left arm.

It came away bloody.

He swore, twisted, and then scrambled away.

Jamie didn't know if it was his or Sippy's. She didn't think he did either.

But he wasn't in danger of bleeding out, and Sippy was. And he was their only lead, one of their only suspects. If he died, then the case would go with him.

He stumbled sideways, gripping his bloodied wrist, and slumped against one of the tiled pillars.

She heard Roper's feet on the steps behind her. He was fleeing.

Jamie couldn't look away though, couldn't risk losing a second.

Sippy slid down, leaving a bloodied trail, and Jamie caught him, stepping over and around, pulling him onto her lap, her still-gloved hand clamping around his wrist.

'Shit,' she hissed, watching as the blood poured through her fingers, the slash at least three inches long and down to the tendons.

'I— I cut too deep,' Sippy said, barely above a whisper. 'I cut too deep.'

'You're okay,' Jamie found herself saying, nodding. She could feel his blood hot on her legs.

He tilted his head back, looked up at her, those dead eyes suddenly full and human.

Her throat closed to a pinhole as she looked down at the black puddle under her. At the blood pouring over her knees. She had both hands around his arm, holding it up. Her phone was in her pocket, wedged under him. If she went for it, she'd have to take a hand off his wrist, and if she called for an ambulance, it would be ten, maybe fifteen minutes before it arrived. And he'd be dead in two.

'Simon,' she said quickly, knowing this was only going one way. 'Why did you kill Oliver?'

He crumpled his brow and sucked in a shallow breath. 'I… didn't. We didn't… mean to… just to grab him—' he coughed, struggled to get another breath into his lungs '—to sell him to his… parents.' He smiled weakly. 'His idea…'

Jamie set her jaw. His idea? To ransom him back to his own parents? 'Who is we? Who is *we*, Simon?'

He shook his head. 'No… No, I can't. He'll…' Sippy looked at his wrist, at the solid sheet of red running over Jamie's fingers. And then he laughed.

Jamie knew what he was going to say. Knew *who* he was going to say. Donnie. Donnie Bats. 'Is it Donnie?'

Simon's eyes flashed and he looked up at her.

'Just nod, Simon. If it was Donnie — if Donnie and you grabbed him — and — and something went wrong? Simon?'

His eyes were beginning to close.

'Simon? Stay with me. Just nod. If it was Donnie — Simon — just nod…'

She gripped tighter on his arm, watching for any movement, and then, his chin sagged.

She held her breath.

And then he raised it.

And dipped it again.

A nod.

Donnie.

He was heavy in her arms.

'Simon?'

He was limp, eyes closed, pale.

'Simon?'

The blood stopped flowing so steadily, trickling now.

She couldn't feel it pulsing through her fingers.

'Simon?' Her voice grew thin.

The platform began to shake.

The rails shook.

The squeal of brakes cut through the roar, and the train rumbled into the station.

And while it did, Simon Paxton died in Jamie's arms.

26

W hen the train pulled in, the doors opened, and people started screaming.

Within five minutes, two uniformed officers arrived.

The station was closed and trains roared past, windows glued to faces, looking at the spectacle.

Ten minutes after that, the scene was cordoned off, and three more officers were there. Paramedics seemed to appear from thin air and prised Sippy out of Jamie's arms.

No one had moved her — no one dared to. She was doused in blood, and though she had no open wounds and the chances of contracting anything were very slim, none of the officers seemed intent on risking it.

'Here you are,' one of the paramedics said, his face no more than a blur to Jamie, as he took her arms, peeling her hands from Sippy's cold wrist.

She resisted, near-catatonic. Later, she couldn't even recall it. It was like a vague dream.

Then she was on her feet, being led away.

Someone else cradled Sippy's head and laid him down, the smell of rust sharp in the air.

She was steered away, her arms sticky with blood, legs soaked.

Roper was there, talking to Thompson, regaling him with the details of the chase.

Jamie was pushed to a seated position, and had a blood pressure cuff put around her bicep.

The paramedic asked her name and she said, 'Jamie Johansson,' with someone else's voice.

'Good, good,' he said, no more than a silhouette — like a child's drawing. A blank face with sketched eyes and a line for a mouth. She couldn't have picked him out of a line-up after. 'You're in shock,' he said and she felt her brow furrow.

He was pouring something over her arms then and sponging her off with gauze, leaving scarlet streaks across her skin.

'Any open cuts?' he asked.

She shook her head.

'Did any get in your mouth?'

She shook her head.

'Your eyes?'

She shook her head.

He nodded. 'Okay. The chances of contraction are very, very low, okay?'

She looked up at him.

'Okay?' he asked again.

It wasn't rhetorical then.

She nodded.

'But you should still get a blood test to confirm in a few days. Until then, don't engage in unprotected sex or sexual activity, and...' He trailed off a little, then dropped his voice. 'Don't participate in any intravenous drug administration with shared needles.'

She may have been off her game — barely cognisant — but she still found the energy to glare at him.

'Sorry,' he said, now coming into focus — middle-aged, short, greying hair — 'But I have to say. I know you're a police officer, but—'

'I'm fine,' she said, pushing herself to her feet. 'Thanks.'

She shook off the feeling of being underwater and sucked in a few deep breaths, the scene morphing into view.

They'd cordoned off the entire platform, and uniformed officers swarmed.

Roper saw her on her feet and came over. 'Jamie,' he said with something like warmth in his voice. 'Are you okay?'

'I wish people would stop asking that,' she growled. How could she be?

He looked over her shoulder, then sighed. 'You know, sorry that I — It's just—'

'Forget it,' she said, screwing up her face. She exhaled, feeling queasy. She'd not eaten or drank anything and her stomach was shrivelling.

'Did he give you anything? Paxton, I mean,' Roper said awkwardly.

Jamie stared at him for a minute, wondering whether to tell him or not. Whether she could be bothered to form the words. All she wanted to do was go home and curl up in a ball in the tray of her shower. 'Yeah,' she said. 'He did. They grabbed Oliver. Didn't mean to kill him.' She grit her teeth. 'But they grabbed him — with his consent.' She shrugged. 'Planned to ransom himself back to his parents to pay off his debt and get his and Grace's runaway cash.' That was the only thing that made sense.

He took it in. 'Shit.'

'Mhm.'

'And then something went wrong?'

She shrugged again, suddenly very tired of it all. 'Probably. Changed the figure, or decided to keep all the money, maybe Oliver got cold feet. Maybe he tried to run. Changed his mind even...' She let out a long breath, her hands shaking at her sides. 'Who knows. But something went sideways. And now he's dead.'

'Jesus.' Roper looked at her for a second. 'Smith is coming.'

She looked up. 'What?'

'Smith is on the way.' DCI Henley Smith. Their boss.

'Why?'

'Paxton was confirmed as a known affiliate — Smith wants to know whether we got anything off him before...' Roper cleared his throat. 'He's pissed we didn't get that positive ID until this morning.' He dropped to a whisper. 'And that we didn't call it in.' He cleared his throat now. 'If we had — with the positive ID from Grace, he would have put a hold on the arrest... Got Armed Response to take the house. We moved on Paxton too fast, and now...'

Jamie looked at her feet. 'He's dead.'

'It's a shit-sandwich. Taking Paxton in would have been the unit's ticket to nail Donnie Bats.'

'Deathbed confession.'

'What was that?'

'Deathbed confession,' Jamie said more decisively. 'Admissible in court.'

Roper bit his lip. 'Don't know that Smith will be as happy with that — not when we could have had Paxton in custody.'

Jamie felt anger well up in her. 'And if we'd have brought him in he may never have flipped on Donnie. And we would have had no way to tie him to Oliver or anything!' She was rising.

'Keep it down,' Roper urged her. 'Look — it's inconsequential now. Paxton is dead, and Smith is—'

'Here,' Jamie said, spotting Henley Smith coming down the steps onto the northern line platform.

Roper turned. 'Shit.'

Jamie looked down at her clothes soaked with blood. She was a mess.

Smith made a beeline for them and pulled up, standing tall. He was over six feet, bald, tanned with a strong jaw and small ears. 'Roper. Johansson,' he said stiffly, nodding to them. His long charcoal-grey wool coat billowed in the hot draft coming out of the tunnel. He looked Jamie up and down, staring at the blood. 'Go home, Johansson.'

'Sir?'

'Go home.' His voice was like iron. 'Get cleaned up. Come back in this afternoon to write up.'

'But—'

'No buts,' he said. 'Have one of the uniformed officers drive you.'

'My car is—'

'You're not hearing me,' he cut in. 'Go. Home. Give your keys to them, they'll take your car to HQ. I'll send someone for you later.'

'Sir?'

'Now, Johansson.'

She pressed her lips into a line, looked at Roper, maybe for support, maybe for confirmation that going quietly was the right thing to do.

He didn't want to meet her eye.

She could see by the look on Smith's face that he was pissed off. She could see by the sheepish look on Roper's that he thought it was warranted.

She'd screwed up. In everyone else's eyes, she'd screwed up.

Roper would go to bat for her — she hoped — say that she got the confession. But she didn't even want to think about how it was going to go down when she came clean to Smith and told him it wasn't so much of a confession as it was a vague nod. And one that she led him into as well. He'd not said a name, not said anything. She knew what she saw, but if she got up and testified under oath, any barrister worth their salt would argue that Jamie had coerced him, and that she'd put words in his mouth. That on the verge of death, he might have been trying to do *anything*... That a nod meant nothing, and certainly not enough to convict a man of kidnapping and murder.

And Jamie knew that.

Maybe Smith thought that they had a chance. A slim one, but a chance. A chance to put Donnie Bats away for this if they couldn't for something else.

When he found out, there wouldn't be any. And if she knew Smith — which she did — he wouldn't even want to make an arrest with such flimsy evidence.

Smith and Thompson had been looking for Paxton for questioning. Struggling to pin him down. And Jamie and Roper had been chasing him, not knowing who he was.

Their Dead-Eyes and Smith and Thompson's Simon Paxton were

one in the same. And if she'd taken the time to let them know what they were about to do, Smith would have stopped it.

Would have made sure it was done right.

Paxton was the only one who could tie these two cases together. Who could give them a chance to put Donnie away for this.

But Jamie didn't.

She'd purposely not called it in — knowing that more bodies would screw up her arrest. And yet, in her *capable* hands, he'd ended up dead on a tube station platform.

Roper had already said it was a shit-sandwich. But she was ready to upgrade it to her dad's famous *shit-pie.*

Her stomach twisted and she felt sick. If there was anything in her guts, she would have emptied it onto the flagstones right there.

Instead, she just grimaced, nodded, and then moved past Smith, heading for the stairs.

Roper stayed behind — presumably to answer the questions that Smith had.

She didn't have the whole story herself, didn't know how Roper stumbled upon Paxton, what happened upstairs. But she would. She just didn't have the energy right then.

She headed for the surface, sick of the stale air.

She heard Smith call over a uniform and order them after Jamie.

Boots clapped on the stairs behind her but she didn't look back.

Jamie pushed through the police blockade at the top of the stairs to the station and kept moving.

The officer, a woman in her late twenties, jogged to catch up, appearing at her shoulder. 'It's this one,' she said, pointing at a nearby patrol car.

People were clustered at the top of the station — annoyed that it was closed as they needed to travel, or just there for the spectacle. Both demographics gasped and pointed at her — the woman soaked with blood emerging from the underground.

She walked numbly towards the car.

'Wait a second,' the officer said as Jamie reached out for the handle.

Her hand paused in the air and she looked down at it, still caked with blood. It made her feel queasy.

The officer ran to the boot, opened it, and then slammed it, running back around the car.

She scooted past Jamie, careful not to touch her — she was as good as a leper covered in Sippy's blood. The door opened and Jamie watched, cracking a wry smile as the officer, a woman with sharp features and pinned back black hair, spread a waterproof plastic cover over the seat for her.

'There,' she said, standing up and presenting it like it was a prize from a nineties game show. 'Sorry,' she added quickly, seeing the semi-incredulous look on Jamie's face. 'It's just the seats — you know — the car's not ours, and if we get…' She sort of shook her head, reading Jamie's sour expression. 'You know what — never mind.' She laughed awkwardly and then walked around the bonnet and got in the drivers' side.

Jamie got in and leaned her head back, the plastic rustling under her.

'Where are we going?' the officer asked brightly.

Jamie gave her address automatically and they set off in silence.

The officer didn't try to make conversation.

Cars and buses roared and chugged around them, cyclists flying to work beside them.

Jamie felt like she'd been up for days. But it was still rush hour. Barely seven in the morning.

She knew she'd sleep when she got back. Her body was crying out for it.

It took a long time to get back to her building, and as they neared, she dug her keys out of her pocket and unhooked the car key from the others.

When the car came to a stop she held it out for the officer. 'Corner of Mott Street. Not far from the station.'

The steel shimmered in the weak morning light.

The officer stared at it, smeared with blood, unsure whether to accept it or not.

Jamie studied her. She was deciding whether to grab it. Whether to risk touching it.

Jamie didn't have the patience and dropped it into the cupholder between the seats. She sighed, and then pushed the door open.

'Hey,' the officer said, catching her as she got to her feet. She leaned across the centre console and looked up out of the door. 'Are you okay?'

Jamie laughed, shook her head, feeling her throat ache, her cheeks burn, eyes blurring with tears. 'What do you think?'

She didn't wait for an answer before she slammed the car door and headed for her building, dying for a shower. Dying to wash off the smell of death.

She wanted to sleep. To forget about it all.

But she knew she wouldn't.

And she didn't think she would for a long time.

At least not without Sippy invading her dreams.

And even though she could catch him, she knew that no matter how hard she tried, she couldn't outrun him.

27

T he blood curled off her in misty rings, spinning lazily towards the plughole as the boiling water clattered all around her.

Had she been in her own head, she would have felt the water burning her skin. But she wasn't, and she didn't.

She scrubbed at her arms at first, then at her legs, until they felt raw. But she still wasn't clean.

Her hands shook as she looked at them, her nails caked in dark blood that wouldn't seem to come off.

But when she'd decided that enough was enough when it came to scrubbing, she still couldn't get up, and tucked them under her thighs instead, pulling her knees to her chest, too weak to move.

And that's where she stayed.

Jamie sat in the shower for fifty-three minutes before her phone started ringing.

She picked her head up, hearing her phone buzz, and shivered. The water had run cold and she'd not even noticed. For a second she was completely disoriented, not sure if she'd been asleep or not.

She unclenched her jaw and felt it ache.

Her muscles were stiff and seized.

Jamie needed to eat. Her lizard brain told her that. Get food into your system. Drink water. Get the muscles working again.

She rose, steadying herself on the wall, and stepped out, her toes completely numb.

Her phone had stopped buzzing, but when she looked at it she saw a new message from Roper. It said, 'HQ in an hour.' and nothing more.

He rarely text. He was more a call sort of guy. On the rare occasions he did, it was never good. Usually because he wanted to avoid an awkward conversation. He knew she'd ask whether Smith was pissed or not, and he'd wanted to forgo that line of questioning specifically. So she guessed he was.

But honestly, at that moment, she didn't really give a damn.

She closed the message and pulled up Elliot's number, hitting it with her thumb.

It rang once and then he answered. 'Jamie?' he sounded surprised.

'Hey,' she said quietly, seeing that her hands were clean now. The blood must have dissolved during the shower.

She hadn't noticed.

'What's wrong?' he asked, reading her tone.

She sighed, not wanting to get into it. 'How's Grace?'

'She was asleep when I left,' he said, catching his breath halfway through the sentence. 'I'm in work,' he added. 'Just getting ready for surgery. Appendectomy.'

'Oh,' she said, immediately disappointed. All she wanted to do was talk.

'I'm sorry, Jamie.'

'It's okay.'

He exhaled. 'If you want to go over and check on her, then you can do. If you buzz for apartment one, the lady who lives there has a key. Her name is—'

'No, no,' she said. 'It's fine, let her sleep.' She nodded to herself. 'Can you let me know how she is later?'

'Of course. I get off at eight.'

'Okay.' She wanted to ask if she could go over. But didn't.

In the background, there was a muffled voice ringing over the tannoy. 'They're calling me,' he said hurriedly. He sounded as if he'd been moving the whole time.

'You go,' she said, holding back the cracking in her voice. 'Good luck.'

'Thanks.' He paused for a second and Jamie held the phone against her ear, hoping he'd say something else. 'I...' he started.

'Yeah?'

'I'll speak to you later.'

She thought he was going to say something else, but she didn't know what it was.

He hung up and she put the phone down next to the sink, looking at herself in the mirror. She was naked, and though she worked hard on her body — was proud of it — what she saw she hated. The athletic frame, the points of her collar bones sticking out just inside her shoulders. Her hips tight against her skin, the bruises on her knees and ankles from the bag work with Cake. And now another one on her right hip joining it from where she'd run into the car. Her shoulder was red too, her elbow grazed. From the landing and the roll.

She was a mess.

Jamie looked at her hands again. They were wrinkled and veined, her nails nearly white, fingers thin. They didn't look like hers.

She curled them into fists and looked up at her blonde hair, slicked to her head and neck, falling in wet strands over her. At the bags under her eyes. The pointed jaw. The blue eyes she'd always thought were bright now looking watery in the harsh light.

Jamie wrapped her arms around herself and turned away, shivering.

In the minutes following she moved from room to room like a ghost, drying herself off absently with a towel she couldn't recall picking up.

She felt like she was thinking intensely, but didn't have any thoughts in her head.

She dressed in a pair of jeans and black leather boots that her mother had once told her were "mannish". Whatever that meant.

When she got to the hallway, she saw the pile of soiled clothes. Her jeans, boots, and jacket. All bloodied.

She grimaced and went straight to the kitchen, pulled a black bag from under the sink, along with her washing up gloves.

Regaining herself with every step she marched out to the hall, pulled the gloves on, flapped open the bag, and then shoved everything inside. Her boots as well.

It was almost painful to do it — they were only a few months old and still had a year of life left. But she couldn't wear them again. Medically speaking, she could wash and disinfect them. But she'd know. And that would be enough.

She tied the bag off, sealing in the smell, and then went back to the kitchen.

Jamie double-bagged them and grabbed some bleach, carrying the bag and the bottle out to the hall again. There was a red stain where the pile had been, and she doused in enough bleach to cleanse an entire hospital, and opened the front door, dropping the bag outside.

By the time she'd mopped the blood off the floor, her phone was vibrating in her pocket.

It was HQ letting her know that a patrol car was outside ready to take her in.

She sighed and dropped the mop, leaning it against the wall, and then headed out, grabbing a leather jacket off the hook by the door.

The ride out was quiet.

The officer was different than before, but equally as happy to not make conversation.

Jamie leaned her elbow on the sill of the door and put her face on her palm, her hair still damp and pulled into a loose ponytail. She hadn't had the will to plait it.

On the way, she realised she still hadn't eaten. But now her appetite seemed to have abated.

It was just after ten by then.

And nearly half past by the time they arrived.

She was dropped off at the front door and then the patrol car peeled away.

Jamie looked up at the building and licked her lips. She wondered if she still knew how to talk. She had no inclination to. But maybe she'd just forgotten all together? She didn't feel like herself. She had to really think about moving her feet, and they didn't feel like they belonged to her. Her brain in someone else's body, piloting via remote control.

The interior was warm. She hadn't realised how cold it was outside until she'd come in.

People moved past in a blur and she was in the elevator on autopilot.

Bodies got on and got off, but nobody paid her any attention as she stood at the back leaning against the wall, her eyes closed.

When she felt the elevator level out on her floor, she squeezed through the wall of guys in front of her and stepped into the melee.

Desks buzzed and rang all around. Papers shuffled, and fingers tapped on keys. She'd always liked the noise. But today it was like having spikes jammed into her ears.

'Johansson,' Roper said, appearing in front of her, two cups of coffee in his hands. He rarely called her that anymore. He hadn't since they'd been first partnered up.

He offered her one.

It was strange to hear him say it.

She took it and held it between her fingers, warming them on the porcelain. 'Roper.'

'How you holding up?'

She sighed, sipped a little coffee, and then looked up. 'Been better.' She could barely taste it.

Roper looked forlorn. Like he knew something bad was coming.

He dipped his head over his shoulder towards Smith's office. 'We should get in there. He's waiting.'

It was glass-fronted and he was sitting in there behind the desk, talking to Thompson.

Jamie looked over indifferently. She was too tired to care. 'Mmm.'

Roper turned and led her over, knocking only cursorily before walking in.

Jamie followed.

Thompson got up and moved to the back of the room, leaning against the glass to leave the two chairs in front of the desk free.

'Close the door,' Smith said sternly.

She abided.

'Sit.'

They both did.

Smith looked from one to the other, not giving anything away. His mouth was carved into his face, his skin lined with age and stress.

Thompson behind them dragged air in through his nose and cleared his throat.

Smith glanced up at him, and then back and Roper and Jamie before sitting back. He picked up a pen and started tapping it on the top of the glass desk.

For a second he sucked his teeth, running his tongue over them as he chose his words. 'Well,' he said after an age. 'This is a goddamn mess. I don't really think there's any other way to put it.'

Roper shifted uncomfortably.

'Johansson — if it was any other day — any other suspect   I might be congratulating you.' He stared at her intensely. 'But it's not. And it wasn't. And you not only blew up your own investigation, but also managed to derail one that's been going on for six months. One that was going to get a truly dangerous son of a bitch off the streets for a long time. And to top it all off, not only did you destroy two investigations, you also chased an unstable drug addict into a crowded tube station — where he *slashed* at innocent people with a knife — before dying in view of no less than a thousand people.' He threw the pen down. 'Nothing short of a PR nightmare. And at a time when public opinion of us isn't at an all-time high. And if you'd thought just for a *second*—' he held up a finger '—for a single second. Long enough to call it in, which is what you *should* have done, I might add.' His voice was rising, despite his best effort to stay even. 'But you didn't. And you barrelled into a private residence with no warrant, no probable cause, and botched the arrest in the most monumental of ways.' He exhaled hard, the vein in his temple swelling. 'And to top it all off, you brought *this* fool with you.' He looked at Roper. 'Who should have had the sense to rein you in. But I'm not surprised he didn't, being drunk. Again.' He narrowed his eyes and stared fiercely at Roper. 'You smell like a brewery, Paul. How many times do we have to have this conversation? How many times do I have to pull you in here? Take you off investigations? Demote you?'

Roper looked at his knees.

Jamie looked over her shoulder at Thompson, who was standing stoically, like a statue of himself. He was saying nothing, and Smith seemed to have no problem with him being hungover. Hell, him and Roper had been out together the night before. He was just as drunk as Roper. And yet...

Smith turned around on his chair, stared out of his window at the city drowned in smog. The sky was an ocean of roiling grey, the air cool and moist.

It felt like rain.

'I don't know what to say,' he began quietly. 'But I don't think you could have made more of a mess if you'd been trying to. There's going to be an official inquest into Paxton's death, as well as a review of your investigation to date. But, until they are completed—' he spun back around and leaned forward onto his elbows, hands clasped in front of him '—your investigation is officially on hold and you're both suspended until further notice.'

'What?' Roper said, seemingly in disbelief.

Smith didn't repeat it.

'Sir,' he started. 'I think—'

'That's your problem,' Smith said, cutting him off. 'You don't ever think. And that's why you're where you are, riding your third suspension in as many years.' He met Roper's eye, a familiarity there allowing him to be more brutal than he would with Jamie. 'Think about your life, Paul. Is this the path you want to go down? Is this the example you want to set for Johansson?'

Roper had gone vacant. He didn't say anything. Jamie couldn't read his expression. Or at least she wouldn't have been able to if she was looking at him.

And she wasn't.

'And you,' Smith said, looking at her. 'Do you have anything to say for yourself?'

She swallowed, looked at her hands turned upwards on her thighs.

After a few seconds she curled them into fists, reached into her jacket pocket and pulled out her badge.

She slapped it down on the desk, looked up at Smith, only mustering the strength for one word. 'No,' she said, and got up, heading for the door.

She needed to eat, to sleep, and to recharge.

And nothing else mattered until she'd done those things.

Right now, she was no use to anyone.

On the way to the elevator, she saw her dad leaning against her desk, arms folded, smirking at her. *First suspension, eh? Maybe you're a little more like your dad than you thought.*

'Shut up,' she growled.

'What?' a detective asked as she passed, looking up from his screen.

'Nothing,' she said, rubbing her eyes.

She could feel them burning again.

Jamie didn't know who she was. But what she did know was that for the first time since she could remember, she couldn't wait to get out of there. And that made her feel worse than anything else.

28

J amie slumped down into the driver's seat of her car after picking up her keys at the security desk.

The first thing she noticed was that whoever had been driving her car had pushed her seat right back, and adjusted the angle of the rest. She grimaced and looked down between her knees, seeing crumbs.

She sniffed the air.

Despite there being no rubbish left there, she could detect the unmistakable smell of fast food. The odour of cheese that was more plastic than dairy, of chips so salty you just had to buy a litre of sugar-rich cola to wash them down.

Jamie reached out for the wheel, ready to throttle it and rip it out of the dashboard, and found her hands came up short, missed, and slapped her thighs instead.

She laughed abjectly, coughed, then felt tears form in the corners of her eyes.

Suspended.

Her.

Suspended.

She couldn't believe it. But she understood. How could she have let it happen? How couldn't she have seen that she was headed down that path?

She didn't know. But she wasn't going to put it on Roper or anyone else. It was her choice, and if anything, her fault. Roper had been asleep and she'd dragged him out of bed knowing he'd been drunk and borderline useless. He could blame her for his suspension. It was more her decisions than his which led them there. But she knew he wasn't like that. Didn't she?

She swallowed and looked at herself in the rear-view. She didn't feel like herself.

She'd been so caught up in the case — in Elliot, and Grace, and everything else — she'd lost her pragmatism. Looking back at it she never should have gone ahead. The second she'd found out about Simon she should have called it in. She should have reported it. And what was worse was that she didn't even report what he'd done to Grace. She'd been clouded, and out for blood.

And damn, didn't she just get it.

She had her phone in her hand, looking at the screen.

Her call logs had Elliot at the top of the screen.

Jamie's thumb hovered over his number, her teeth pressed into her bottom lip.

No, she couldn't call him. She wanted to, but she couldn't. Things were already too… She didn't know what. But he was a material witness in an active murder investigation on which she was the lead detective. Or at least she was before she was suspended. But it didn't matter. If he had to give testimony in court, she didn't want him to be compromised by a question from the defending barrister that was as simple as — what is the nature of your relationship with the lead detective?

That was a sure-fire way to derail a prosecution. No, as much as she wanted to talk to him, she couldn't. She had to distance herself. Until this was done at least. Then, if there was something between them beyond proximity they could explore it. For now, she had to keep her head down.

She scrolled down through the names on her call log and stopped at Cake.

Did she feel like working out? She'd definitely skipped a few days, and it wasn't like she had any work to do. She hit his name with her thumb and waited for it to ring out.

It went to voicemail.

She sighed and ran her hand through her hair. It was the middle of the day. He'd be training someone, or—

Her phone started ringing and she answered it almost a little to hurriedly. 'Cake?' she said.

'Hey, Jamie, everything okay?' he asked, sounding concerned. She never rang him during work hours.

'Yeah, I'm okay,' she lied. 'Got the afternoon off — don't suppose you can spare a bag, maybe some ring time?'

He laughed a little. 'Afternoon off? You? What'd you do, get suspended?'

Her silence was enough of an answer.

He cleared his throat. 'Uh, yeah. Of course. I've got a one to one coming up, but I can reschedule.'

'No, don't do that,' she said, running her nails along the textured plastic sill of her car window. It was beginning to mist in the cold garage air.

'Come on, Jamie,' he said, his voice warm. 'You and I both know that if you're calling me and asking for it then you need it. You wouldn't otherwise.'

She swallowed, feeling her grip tighten around the phone.

'Shall we say one-ish?'

'That sounds great,' she almost whispered, trying to keep her voice from cracking.

'Okay. I'll see you then.'

'Thanks, Cake.'

She could hear him smiling. 'Of course.'

She hung up and leaned her head back. Today wasn't going to get much better, but if there was anyone and anything that could cheer her up it would be Cake and a heavy bag.

．　．　．

Nearly two hours later Jamie pulled up outside Cake's gym and killed the engine.

There were a couple of cars parked outside, overshadowed by the plants growing through the worn brick exterior. Jamie knew it would be busier than she was used to.

Other people used the gym, of course. It was a boxing gym of sorts — not a serious one that competed, Cake wasn't in that world anymore — but those who wanted to work the bags, spar, or learn self-defence went to him. He trained a lot of women. There seemed to be a trend towards that in the last few years, he said. A reflection of the state of things in the city. Jamie had met that with a casual hum of agreement, but she knew he was right. She'd seen the crime stats. Violent attacks on women were rising. And she couldn't blame anyone for wanting to know how to handle themselves.

Jamie walked in in three-quarter length leggings, a sport bra, and an oversized hooded sweatshirt that looked more like it was drowning her than she was wearing it.

Inside, things were musty. It had the quintessential gym smell — stale sweat and heavy breath. She loved it.

In the corner, a guy in his sixties was jabbing at a heavy bag.

To the left, against the wall, a woman in her thirties was pulling on a rowing machine. She was bathed in sweat and was built like a gazelle. Jamie had passed her a couple times heading in when she was heading out. She was a hard worker. They'd never spoken, but Jamie respected that.

She'd thought about talking to her a few times. They'd exchanged nods of mutual respect, but Jamie had never made the first move. The woman had always had headphones in and she didn't know how awkward it would be.

Making friends in your thirties was hard. Jamie's circle consisted of Cake and Roper. The latter of which was a colleague and the former her trainer. She stopped keeping touch with her university friends, and she never followed through on plans with new ones. She was always just so busy. Or at least that was the excuse she always seemed to use when she cancelled on them.

She didn't know if that made her lonely or not.

She felt it sometimes.

'Jamie?' Cake sidled out of the office, beaming at her, his big frame dwarfing her as he neared.

He held out his fist for their customary bump and she punched it lightly. 'It's good to see you, Cake,' she said, a little more desperation in her voice than intended.

Cake chuckled heartily. 'You too. Was beginning to think you'd found another trainer.'

She shoved him playfully, feeling the stress draining away already. 'Come on, it's only been two days.'

'Jamie, since I've known you, you've never missed a day. Even when we had all that rain last year and the streets were flooded — you showed up in wellies.'

She flushed a little. 'We were right in the middle of learning to crescent. I couldn't afford to miss a day.'

'Hey, I'm not complaining. You're keeping me in business.'

She felt herself grinning. 'Speaking of which.'

'Sure,' he said, proffering her the empty ring. 'After you.'

She jumped up into the ring and started stretching.

He lifted a duffle bag he'd placed next to the ring and tossed it in, climbed up after her. 'You want to start with the pads?'

'Let's just spar.'

'Without a warmup?' He arched an eyebrow, letting go of the arm pads he'd picked up.

'I'll go easy on you — that'll be our warmup.'

He could see by the look on her face that she needed to get some energy out, and hitting a bag that wasn't going to hit back wouldn't cut it.

She appreciated that he didn't hold back — at least for the most part. He never stepped into his punches, but they still carried weight. Of course, it was offset by the protection they always wore when they sparred.

She needed to feel her fists hit flesh, but not to the point of forgetting how dangerous getting hit in the head was.

They strapped up with padded helmets, amateur gloves, and shin-pads.

Jamie mostly led with kicks and knees, and Cake came in for grapples and crosses, mimicking the fighting style of most men when they came up against women. He was a great trainer. She had to give him that.

Cake circled slowly, panting. Despite the helmet hugging his cheeks his right eye was still a little bruised. He'd moved into a side kick — his fault, really — and taken the sole of her shoe to the side of the head.

Now, he was tiring. As was Jamie. This was their third bout, and despite his advice that it was time to call it quits, she'd insisted. He'd only agreed on the proviso that they'd get pizza afterwards. Jamie hadn't ever gone out to eat with Cake. She'd never even seen him outside the gym in fact. But, he said he wanted to talk to her about something, and he wanted to do it over pizza.

She didn't really eat it — all cheese and dough. It didn't really fit into her diet. But she'd agreed. She could do with the company, and she hadn't thought about her suspension since she'd been with him.

She wasn't worried though. They were friends, neither interested in the other in any other way.

'Come on,' Cake said, beckoning her between breaths.

He had the sort of look that told her if he caught her, it was going to hurt.

She was already nursing her ribs. He'd socked her with a body-shot that had made her feet tingle. That was when he'd said they should stop.

She smiled a little, feeling her hair stuck to her forehead in thin strands.

Jamie moved in, leading with her left foot, telegraphing a crossing kick — shin impact to the flank or knee.

He dropped his elbow to block it.

She kept a straight face, watching his hands.

His right tensed up, wound up, and then shot out, aiming for her jaw.

She twisted right and struck low, catching him in the calf, stepping to his left.

He grunted, lifted his left arm and drove his elbow backwards.

Jamie threw her arms up in time and caught the brunt of the impact with her forearms.

The blow sent her reeling and she bounced off the ropes, regaining herself as Cake came forward. He wanted to put her down and fast. He was expending a lot of energy moving around like this and was closer to exhaustion than her. He wouldn't last much longer and wanted to put her on the mat before he got to that point.

But that meant he would be hasty. And when he got hasty, he got sloppy. And when he got sloppy, he left openings.

She danced left and stepped in, throwing her guard up, making it too tight to throw a decent right-jab through the middle. But the side of her head was exposed.

And Cake took the bait.

He swung lazily, too tired to get a swift punch in.

Jamie saw it coming and stepped back onto her right leg, watching the punch sail in front of her.

Cake's eyes widened as her knee rose up.

Her muscles tensed and pulled her into position, the mat groaning under the balls of her feet as she twisted.

Jamie's foot rose, her leg straightened, and then she snapped it down into a mix between a swing and a whip kick, sending the sole of her trainer thumping into Cake's helmet just behind his left ear.

Combined with the momentum from the punch he sprawled forward, making the whole ring quake as he landed on his knees and keeled sideways with a muffled grunt.

Jamie found her balance as the ring shuddered and lowered her leg, breathing hard.

She turned to see Cake on his back, his chest rising and falling quickly, his grey shirt soaked with sweat.

He pulled his gloves off with his teeth and then dragged the helmet free of his round head, tossing it on the mat.

'Okay,' he panted. 'Now we're definitely done.'

Jamie felt tired suddenly, her hands loosening in her gloves. 'That'd be good.' She'd worked out all her anger, and stress. She was too exhausted now to even think about it.

Cake put his arm over his face, shielding his eyes from the halogens overhead.

He mumbled something as Jamie tore her gloves and helmet off, stretching out her shoulders.

'What was that?' she asked, leaning in.

'Pizza,' he said, still trying to catch his breath.

Jamie laughed, feeling her stomach growl. She was starving.

'You know what, Cake?' she said, looking around the now-empty gym. The light was starting to wane and rain had begun to patter on the windows. 'That sounds great.'

29

J amie promised herself she'd only eat three slices.

It had been four years since she'd eaten pizza, and on that occasion, it was a party to celebrate Smith's promotion to DCI at work, and they'd put on a little buffet.

There'd been streamers and bunting, and a plastic table-cloth set up over camp tables.

People served themselves finger food on paper plates. Cocktail sausages. Mini sausage rolls and pasties. Samosas and little deep-fried balls that Jamie couldn't identify. And, of course, little triangles of pizza all stacked up on top of one another.

The sausages had looked withered and ancient, the pastries all flake and no filling, and the samosas greasy. She didn't even want to think about the unknown balls. They were red and crispy, but neither of those things appealed to her.

The least of the evils was the pizza.

Plain cheese, cold, and chewy. She'd choked down two slices having missed lunch, and since, hadn't touched the stuff.

They'd taken Cake's car and driven to a little restaurant simply called Naples. There was only enough space for sixteen people to sit down on four tables, with the bar and the pizza oven taking up most of the space inside.

From outside, the place looked nearly dilapidated, down one of those side streets that was more like an alley than anything else. Cake had assured her it was worth it.

She hadn't protested. Too hungry. And she trusted him.

Their entire menu was contained on a blackboard no bigger than an A4 sheet of paper. There were three types of pizza and one type of pasta that simply said 'Weekly Pasta'. But Cake said that she didn't want that — that it was made by the owner as an alternative, but that the only reason to come was the pizza.

He ordered two Neapolitans and took a seat in the window.

The owner-cum-waiter sidled over with two dark green plastic glasses and a jug of water, putting it down between them. He was wearing a check shirt strained around his stomach and had hair so thick it looked like a wig. Though Jamie was sure it wasn't.

They said thanks and he answered with, '*Prego*,' just for effect. Cake said he was a full-blooded Italian.

Jamie didn't doubt it.

They'd both grabbed a shower at the gym, but the ancient plumbing was only good for a lukewarm dousing, so the faint smell of sweat still clung to them. Still, they were both glad they were there, as was the owner.

The place was deserted except for them.

Jamie looked across the table at Cake, wearing a hooded sweatshirt that said 'YES PAIN' in bold letters on it. The thing was faded and worn, but looked comfortable. He didn't really go out for fashion. In fact, she didn't know if he went out at all.

They sat in silence, Cake looking through the window, her looking at him.

She didn't really know much about him. She knew his boxing history, how long he'd lived in the city and owned the gym — and that he was doing his best to stay fit and afloat as the years wore on. But other than that, she couldn't have answered a question about who he was.

She didn't know where he lived, if he was married, or what he did with his time.

He was obviously feeling that strangeness between them too. They'd known each other too long to just come right out and ask the things they should already know.

Jamie cleared her throat. 'So, how's the gym?' she asked, immediately annoyed she couldn't come up with anything better.

'Sorry?' Cake looked around. 'How's...? I was in a world of my own.'

'The gym.' She smiled. 'How are things?'

He shrugged a little. 'Okay, I guess. As well as could be expected. It's a double-edged sword. I don't want to be busy, don't want to get back into competitive training, but that means the gym stays quiet. I can run it on my own for now, and we have our regulars... But they come because it's quiet. Because it's cheap. If I try and appeal to a wider audience, bring in new members, then it gets busy, I have to bring on staff—' he started rolling his hand through the air '—which means more overheads, payroll, tax implications, insurances, yada yada. I like life to be simple and I'm getting by. The lease is cheap because of the asbestos—'

'Asbestos?' She raised an eyebrow. She spent almost as much time in there as he did.

He laughed. 'Don't worry. It's only in the ceiling.'

'What ceiling?' Jamie pictured the place — the ceiling was a mess of bare concrete, exposed wiring, and foil-covered piping.

He gave her a finger-gun and winked. 'Exactly. I took it down the second I moved in there. Lucky for me the owner lives overseas, so doesn't visit. I locked into a long lease on a lower deal, ripped the ceiling down and got rid of it, never told him. Works out okay. It's not pretty, but it's cheap.'

'Oh I don't know,' Jamie said. 'It's got some charm.'

'I suppose in the same way that snakes are cute.'

'Snakes aren't cute.'

'You obviously haven't seen the memes of them wearing top hats with the noodle arms.' He pulled his elbows into his body and hung his hands out next to his shoulders, wiggling them.

Jamie raised an eyebrow. 'The what?'

'The me—' He cut himself off, seeing that the word and his demonstration were both useless without context. 'Here, it's easier if I show you.' He scooted his chair around a little so they were more next to each other than facing, and pulled out his phone, typing into the search bar.

He seemed younger to her then. He'd always been fatherly, but now, outside the gym, free from the ring, he was more casual. Playful even. A little bit comical. She didn't know if she'd ever get the image of a six-foot-two eighteen-stone fridge-shaped black guy pretending to be a noodle-armed snake out of her head. It was nice though.

She could see the home-screen on his phone was a picture of a young boy. He was grinning, standing in a park in the winter. He must have been about six, wearing a pair of khaki trousers and a gilet and knitted scarf. He had gaps in his teeth.

'Yours?' Jamie asked, watching his huge thumbs bash the little keys, the boy's face swimming behind the predicted answers that swirled under the search bar as he typed in the words.

'Hmm? No, nephew,' he said with a little sigh. 'Great kid.'

'You don't sound too happy about it?'

'I don't get to see him much. That was… Damn… Must have been a year last winter now. He'll be nine in the spring.' He shook his head and stopped typing.

'Why don't you get to see him?' She didn't want to pry, but she thought this was a more genuine route towards friendship than noodle-armed snakes. Whatever the hell they were.

Cake laid his phone down and looked at her. They were about to cross the boundary of professional relationship into friendship. She would have considered them friends anyway, but they never spent time like this. So were they friends — were they really?

He let out a long breath and sat back. 'He's my brother's boy.'

'I didn't know you had a brother.'

'You never asked.'

He was right. 'Older?'

'Younger. He got married, had the boy — Trevor — then things went as things go these days. They split up.' He shrugged again. 'Things were okay for a while. They had joint custody — fifty-fifty, really. I used to look after him in the afternoons, pick him up from school and have him until his dad got home. It was nice.'

'I never knew.' Jamie had been going to Cake every morning while he was doing that every afternoon, and he'd not said anything about it. Not mentioned it once.

'But then his mum got a job up north with a big pay rise — moved there, took Sam — that's my brother — back to court for custody, said she'd be able to provide him a better life. Not living in an apartment anymore, more flexible working arrangement, better schools. Sam was struggling, you know? He was keeping a flat with two bedrooms in the city and Trevor was only there two or three days a week. It was killing him. And she knew that.' Cake sighed again, looking at the picture on his screen. 'So the judge ruled quickly, and that was it. Trevor was gone.'

'Shit,' Jamie said, wondering if his brother was anything like him. 'Does he see Trevor at all?'

'One weekend a month, if he's lucky. He makes the trip up, stays in a hotel, makes a go of it. They do theme parks, go for walks, that sort of thing. But it gets old, you know? Sam says that he'd rather sleep in his own bed than a hotel. Can't blame the kid. And he's at that age now. Got friends, wants to see them, not get stuck with his dad for two days straight. It's hard, you know?' He looked at her, his eyes like soft leather.

She nodded. 'Yeah, I know how hard that is on a kid.'

He measured the look on her face and knew that she understood. They were learning a lot about each other.

'So I don't get to see him at all,' Cake finished. 'It's been nearly twenty months, I think.' He held his hands up. 'I mean, I don't blame the kid. His mum is making serious money — got a great house, good school, everything he could want. Not surprised he doesn't like coming back here. It's not as if we live in Chelsea.'

She could see the kid was important to him. 'Never thought about having any of your own?'

He laughed at that one. It was a mixture of heartiness and sadness. 'Sure, and where am I going to meet a woman, huh?' There was nothing in it. Nothing between them. They may as well have been siblings.

'What about the gym? Women must come in there.'

'Yeah, because all women want to be seduced by the owner when they're mid-workout. Apart from being completely inappropriate and a little creepy, you think I could afford to scare off any of my members? Nah,' he said, waving a hand. 'I'll pass on hunting in my back garden.'

'Hunting in your back garden?'

'Well, it was either that one or *shitting where I eat*... The latter of which seemed a little more derogatory than the first.'

'Which compared women to animals?' She couldn't help but laugh.

'Better than calling them, er, toilets?' He started laughing too.

She couldn't ever remember laughing with him.

It felt good.

Jamie didn't know if he had any other friends, or if he was just spending time with her to cheer her up. Either way, she didn't mind. And she appreciated it.

'Ah, I don't get out enough to meet anyone,' he said when the laughter died down. 'All the guys I used to hang out with have shacked up, married, moved, or gotten so intolerable I wouldn't want to spend a second with them. Dry spell or not.'

'You know what, Cake,' Jamie said, 'I know exactly what you mean. The only people I meet are through work. But sometimes, it's worth putting yourself out there, you know?' She tried to keep the grin off her face as she thought of Elliot, but Cake was deciphering the strange face she was making. Like when you try to hold back a yawn.

'Sounds like you've got someone in mind,' he said, leaning back. 'A new suitor, eh?'

'Hardly,' she said, brushing it off. 'A witness, actually.' Saying it out loud made it ten times worse. 'We can't, you know — we can't do anything until the case is over, but…' She cleared her throat, realising that might be a while with her suspension.

'Hey,' he said, lacing his hands behind his head. 'You take what you can get. Unless you're out there trawling the streets, or you're looking for love on apps or the internet, it doesn't seem like there's much hope of finding anyone. So like I said,' he chuckled. 'Take what you can get.'

She understood what he meant, but she didn't think she was settling. It didn't feel like it. It just felt right. 'Yeah, don't think I'd ever go online. Sheesh, if you could see some of the stuff I have that's online. Did twelve months in cyber a while back.' She sucked air through her teeth. 'I want as little of myself online as possible.'

'Yeah, and I don't photograph well, so I guess we're both screwed!'

They laughed again.

'It'll happen,' Jamie said after a few seconds. 'You'll meet someone somewhere — out shopping, or on the street.'

'Yeah, maybe.' He didn't seem very hopeful. 'Working seven days a week and doing most of my grocery shopping at five-AM before our morning sessions at the twenty-four-hour around the corner from my flat doesn't exactly put me in the path of many eligible women. You know who's awake and shopping for pot-noodles at five-AM?'

'Enlighten me.' Her cheeks were hurting. She couldn't remember smiling this much since she didn't know when.

'Weirdos. And me.'

'I'd say you're included in the first category.'

Despite only the two of them being in the restaurant, they made it seem full with their laughter.

'Of course, I'd have much more chance of meeting people if I didn't work seven days a week.' He was trapped in the cycle. She could see it in him.

'I could always open up for you on my day off if you want some time to—'

'No,' he said, smiling at her. 'It's… That's not what I meant. But thanks.' He looked at her for a few seconds, choosing his words. 'You just live and breathe work, you know? And then what's left?'

'If you love your work—'

'Come off it, Jamie. I know you like chasing bad guys, but seriously, you want to do that 'til you're in your sixties?'

She hadn't really thought that far ahead.

'Or would you rather take a risk, make some real money now, and get out of the drudge?'

'The drudge?'

'You know what I mean.'

She couldn't read his face. 'Yeah, I mean sometimes work sucks — but it's work. No one likes work all the time. But it's life, right?'

'I dunno. I never took the opportunities I had. Never trained hard enough, never pushed hard enough. Retired early because I didn't think I could make it and my trainer never pushed me to try.'

She could see where this was going, could feel herself tensing up a little, the humour gone from between them. 'Right.'

'What I'm saying is that there's more than just solving crimes for you, Jamie. You have options. Real ones. You've got skills, got the focus, the fitness. And you can kick like a mule.' He put his hands on his chest. 'I can vouch for that, personally. My ears are still ringing.'

They laughed falsely to try and ease the tension.

'Cake...'

'Just listen for a second.' He held his hands out, his eyes intense now. 'There's a tournament coming up in just over a month — it's an open.'

'Cake...'

'Mixed disciplines, weighted, with a top prize of ten grand.' He was serious.

She pressed her lips into a line. 'We've been over this ...'

'Hear me out, okay?'

She didn't think she'd ever seen someone look so sincere. After a breath, she nodded. 'Sure.'

'I think you could win it. Easily, in fact. These women don't know how to fight like you. We put some more time into your ground-work — how to counter and reverse — and you'll walk it. There's another few tournaments in the early part of the year. A little travelling, but you could make what you do in twelve months for the Met in three days. Three days, Jamie.' He tried on a smile but it didn't seem to fit. 'And from there — hell, once you start to dominate we can line up some invitationals, start touring. Make some real money. And if you went pro, with sponsorships and—'

'Cake,' she said more sternly this time. 'I'm flattered, and in another life, maybe, but…' She lowered her head. She didn't really have a good reason other than that she didn't want to. She didn't like violence. Training was one thing — with pads and foam to dampen the blows. But competitive mixed martial arts? She didn't think she had the stomach for it. Not for a career in it anyway. Training for her was about the skill, about the technique. It was about the satisfaction she got from mastering a tough kick, or from seeing her fitness hit a new level. 'I can't,' she said after a while. 'I just can't, okay?'

Violence had plagued her childhood. Her father had always been a brutal man. She'd heard so many stories from his friends about his exploits. Like beating on junkies and suspects was some sort of macho rite of passage. And he'd stand in the background grinning with a painted-on smile because no one liked hearing about how much of a bastard they were. No matter how masochistic. And yet he couldn't stop. It wasn't in him to stop hurting people.

He'd never raised a hand to her mother, though that had never stopped her hitting him. He'd come home drunk, stinking of perfume, another woman's lipstick on his mouth. And she'd beat on his chest like an ape. Slap him. Claw at him until he caught her wrists and held her like a marionette without a word until she went limp and began to sob.

And then he'd release her, letting her collapse on the kitchen floor, or in the living room, or wherever they'd had their wordless argument, and go to bed.

He liked to hurt people, or at least couldn't help doing it, and she wanted to hurt him. There seemed to be no joy in it for either of them.

And Jamie didn't want to see which she had in her. The want to hurt people, or the inability to stop once she started.

'Will you just—'

'I said no, Cake,' Jamie almost snapped this time, her eyes hard.

His shoulders seemed to sag as the smell of hot, sweet bread filled the air.

The owner approached with two freshly baked pizzas and put them down on the red and white checkerboard-clothed table that matched his shirt. They were on wooden blanks.

'Enjoy,' he said, clapping and walking away.

Jamie stared down at the pizza — Neapolitan style, already cut by the owner. Thick crust with a thin base, a rich tomato sauce, and huge splotches of melted mozzarella perfectly dotted with brown heat-spots. 'Looks good,' she said, trying to bring back some of the happiness that had been between them just minutes ago.

'Yeah,' Cake replied, grabbing a slice. 'The best.'

Jamie promised herself she'd only eat three of the eight slices.

She ate the whole thing.

As did Cake.

And by the end of it, luckily, they were talking again as if nothing had ever happened.

They were an unlikely pairing, but they had a lot in common.

Most of all, Jamie thought, that they both just needed a friend.

30

Cake finished his pizza before Jamie was even halfway through, and eyed hers hungrily.

She lied about being full and offered him one of her last two slices, regretting it as she watched him sink his teeth into it.

While Cake may not have had good taste in hoodies — or after-shaves — he knew what good pizza was.

Her phone buzzed in her pocket as she pushed the last piece of crust into her mouth and she wiped her hands on the paper napkin next to her plastic cup of water before pulling it out.

It was HQ — an impersonally typed message from the central switchboard number that was trying to sound auto-generated. It was a reminder to get herself tested for HIV. She didn't know if she'd ever gotten a more horrifying text.

She exhaled hard and tried to remind herself that with no open wounds and having ingested no blood or got it in her eyes, the chances of her contracting it was very low. But the thought still terrified her.

'You good?' Cake asked, seeing her vacant stare.

'Hmm? Yeah, sorry, just full is all.'

'Sure,' he said, eyeing her. He didn't buy it but didn't pry either.

She appreciated that too.

She appreciated all of it. Cake had closed up the gym early to take her out. He shut at around six on a Friday anyway, and said that it was never busy, so he didn't mind. He'd weighed the loss of business against potentially convincing Jamie to enter the competition.

He'd lost that gamble, but didn't seem too downtrodden about the whole thing.

After a short deliberation about ordering another pizza between them, they decided to part ways.

As much as Jamie would have liked to have stayed there talking, she needed to get home and take stock of things. To rest.

This week had been one of the longest of her life. From the early morning call letting her know Oliver's body was found, right through to that morning, when she'd had the call from Elliot — it had been nothing but less-than-full night's sleep, and long, troubling days. Her body was flagging, but her mind was running on fumes.

As much as she hated being slapped with a suspension, she could do with the recuperation. And even just thinking that she knew that she *must* need it.

She was dead on her feet by the time they got back to the gym, and by the time she wound her way home through the early evening traffic she was verging on falling asleep at the wheel.

All topped off with dough, Jamie crashed out on the sofa, remembering that her gym bag was in the boot of her car only after she'd laid down.

She thought about getting up, but just couldn't find the energy.

The TV jabbered away in the background and she lay on her side, digesting the food, rolling the past events over in her head, trying to make sense of them. Of where she went wrong. The only thing she came up with was that she was too close to it all.

She'd learned that lesson when she was young. You get too close to things and you make mistakes. Distance means perspective. Her dad told her that. And for all his flaws, he was excellent at what he did. One of the best detectives Gothenburg ever had.

Becoming emotionally invested in the cases meant your judgement was compromised. Though his callousness got him in as much trouble as a bleeding heart ever would. But she thought that there was a middle ground to keep. His perspective with just a sprinkling of compassion.

She'd obviously not found it yet.

It was exactly nine forty when her phone started buzzing again.

She looked at the screen, having barely moved in the last three hours due to the sheer amount of bread in her stomach.

It was Elliot.

She thought twice about answering it.

Perspective.

Space.

She needed them. If she answered, the first words out of her mouth needed to be, 'I'm suspended, and can't talk to a witness while they're involved in an active investigation.' But she didn't feel like doing that.

In fact the idea of doing it plain made her feel like shit.

At least if she screened his call she could wait out the suspension, the investigation, or just muster the courage to tell him she'd screwed up. Either way, she decided not to answer.

The call clicked off and the screen went dark.

There. Finally. Peace.

A second later, it started ringing again.

Elliot.

She sighed. Persistent.

It was sweet. But she still wasn't answering.

It clicked off before it rung out and then a few seconds later a text came through that said, 'If you're there, answer.'

She looked at it for a few seconds, biting her lip. She shouldn't.

'PLEASE' appeared on screen and it vibrated in her hand as the texts began to stack.

A second later it began ringing again.

Something was wrong.

She answered this time. 'Elliot?'

'Jamie,' he said, sounding strained. 'It's Grace.'

'What?' She sat up, feeling the blood drain from her head. Stars swam in front of her eyes and a dull ache cut through her skull. 'Is she okay?'

'She's gone.'

'Shit,' Jamie muttered, getting up. 'Gone where?'

'I don't know,' Elliot said. He sounded worried. 'I worked over, got back just now. And she was gone. She left a note that just says "I'm sorry". Jesus, Jamie — I don't know if she would try and... but...'

'I'm on my w—' Jamie cut herself off, freezing as she got into the hallway, staring at the front door.

'Jamie? Are you there?'

She set her teeth, her free hand curling into a fist. 'Yeah, I'm here,' she said, her voice subdued. She let out a long breath, and then sank backwards into her heels. 'But I can't.'

'Can't what?'

'I can't help. I'm...' She gathered herself. 'I'm suspended.'

'Suspended? What does that mean? How? Why?' He knew what it meant in literal terms. He just couldn't understand how she could be.

'Paxton is dead.'

'Dead? Did you—'

'What? No!'

'Sorry — it's just the way you said it—'

'He killed himself. Slashed his wrists before we could make the arrest.'

'And they suspended you for that?'

'No. For not calling it in. It turns out he was a person of interest in a bigger case and...' She was sick of reliving it for the hundredth time. 'I just didn't follow protocol. And it was stupid, okay?'

'Alright,' he said, not seeming phased by the news. 'But I don't see what that has to do with Grace.'

'I can't get involved. You'll have to...' She hated saying it because she knew it wasn't an answer. 'You'll have to report her missing and get help—'

'Jamie, come on,' he said, almost incredulous. 'You know given her history they won't even bother to send a patrol car! And even if they did, you think officers are going to go searching the streets for someone like Grace? No. Your best chance is to go out quickly and—

'I know.'

'What?'

'I know! But I'm suspended, Elliot. If I'm seen involving myself with an investigation, then they could sack me altogether. I'm not prepared to risk everything for this.'

'For someone's life?' He sounded grave. 'If you can tell me you value your job over another human being's life, then you're not who I thought you were. Are you that person?' His voice was strange. A direct question there was no escaping. Who was she? How did she rate the value of one human's life against another? Elliot wanted to know. He was someone who took lives in his hands every day. He knew how he saw himself. Now he was asking her.

She stared at the door. 'You're right. There's no contest.'

He took a breath. 'Okay. Then I'll see you soon.'

When she got there, he was waiting outside his building in his car — a new German saloon. She wasn't surprised.

Jamie parked up, jumped out, and then slid into the passenger seat, suddenly aware that she still probably smelled like the gym and pizza, and that her hair was tied up roughly, not combed or washed since the workout.

Elliot didn't seem to notice. He was in a shirt rolled to the elbows, trousers, and what looked like running shoes. He must have slipped them on instead of his wingtips.

Despite the situation, he looked calm. She didn't think that he scared easily. He radiated pragmatism. Panic never helped anything. Her dad had said that too.

She shook him out of her head and buckled in.

Elliot set off, greeting her simultaneously as he pulled away from the kerb and accelerated towards the end of the street.

'She'll be okay,' Jamie said out loud.

'Maybe.' He sounded more angry than anything else.

'You know where she might be?'

'I have an idea.' He had a focus she hadn't seen until then. The word *surgical* came to mind. His mouth was set in a hard line, his brows tilted down into the bridge of his nose.

They drove quickly and he weaved through traffic, squeezing through amber lights, uncaring of the police officer in the passenger seat.

She said nothing, and neither did he until they got stuck behind a bus that belched thick clouds of black diesel smoke over the bonnet of the car.

The interior was tanned leather and completely clean. There was no debris, no rubbish. He could have picked the car up that day. But then again, his apartment was just as spotless.

His knuckles flexed around the wheel, the leather groaning under his grip. 'I told her to wait.'

'What was that?' Jamie asked. He'd practically whispered it.

'I told her to wait,' he said. 'Before I left. I said *Grace, stay here.*'

His grip tightened.

'She'll be okay.'

He met it with silence, the anger coming off him in waves, and then said, 'Why didn't she listen?'

Jamie set her teeth. 'Because she's an addict.'

She didn't mean it in a derogatory way. But she'd lived with one for the first sixteen years of her life. For them, there was no escaping it. When someone else was there, it was easier. But alone, there was no buffer. The thoughts burrowed in like an insect inserting itself under the skin. Scratching, clawing, eating at your self-control until you switch back to that baser version of yourself. One with a single directive. Get high.

She'd been left places — outside houses, on park benches, at her father's desk — for long enough to know that reasoning and promises like, 'I'll be right back, I promise,' weren't worth anything more than the air used to make them.

There was more silence from Elliot. He agreed.

They set off again and headed left, slowing as the buildings got lower, pulling around the back of a fenced-in cemetery. Inside, a few bare trees stood like skeletons of themselves. Opposite, old Neo-Victorian town-houses sprawled into the darkened sky. Dim streetlights burned at the corner, but this stretch of street was without light.

Jamie looked around. 'Where are we?'

Elliot stared out of the windscreen at the cemetery fence, unbuckling as he did. 'Grace and Oliver told me that before they set up at the bridge that they used to sleep here.'

'In a cemetery?' Jamie unbuckled too and the conversation transitioned from the warm interior to the cold November air. She shivered. She didn't have a jacket — only a zip-through hooded sweatshirt over a loose t-shirt. She'd run out so fast after Elliot had called her humanity into question she'd not even thought about getting a jacket.

'Yeah. There's a mausoleum with a broken stone at the back—' he moved to the back of the car and popped the boot, grabbing his medical hard-case '—and a good place to sleep is—'

'A good place to shoot up.'

'She wouldn't go back to the bridge.'

'No?' Jamie gave him a questioning look.

'No.' He strode past her towards the cemetery wall. 'Too many people. She wouldn't shoot up with so many people around. Wouldn't leave herself vulnerable like that. Especially since everyone else knows Oliver is gone. Come here.'

It was grim, but true. Jamie went to him.

He gave her the case, put the heel of his running shoe on the low wall, and pushed himself upwards.

The iron bars rose to chest height for him, and the tops were spiked. Though it didn't seem to bother him. Nor did the idea of trespassing.

He braced his weight on the cross-bar running below the spikes and hoisted himself up, wedging his foot between them.

In a swift movement, he vaulted over, landed cleanly on the grass, his feet crunching on the leaves. 'Case,' he said, holding his hands up.

Jamie threw it over and he caught it.

'Coming?' he asked.

Jamie swallowed, looking at the fence. Trespassing was only a misdemeanour at best, but the law was the law.

Her father appeared next to her, turned, and leaned back against the fence, sucking on a cigarette. *It's just a church, Jamie. You gonna let a girl die for the sake of the law? What's more important?*

'Shut up,' Jamie growled, moving towards the fence.

'What was that?' Elliot asked, starting to move backwards, keen to get moving.

'I'm coming,' Jamie said, taking the climb with a sigh. 'I'm coming.'

31

Jamie landed with a grunt, her legs aching. She'd felt okay on the way over, but now she could feel the workout sinking its teeth into her quads and calves.

'You okay?' Elliot asked, more trying to ascertain her capability than out of concern.

'Yeah,' she said, moving forward. 'I'm good.'

He nodded and turned back towards the cemetery, surveying it in a wide sweep.

It was fenced in on all sides, probably about thirty yards by thirty yards. The broad side of the church was exposed to the cemetery, throwing deep shadows over the headstones. From their position at the far side, they were looking into the interior. A row of mausoleums stood at the back, facing inwards in a single row. Jamie only picked out six roofs in the dim light coming from the lamp in the street behind. At least they wouldn't have many to search.

'Here,' Elliot said, offering her a small LED torch.

'Thanks,' she said, pushing her multitool back into her pocket. She was going to use that. But the one Elliot was offering was more powerful.

He didn't say anything back before moving forward, carrying the heavy case with ease.

He held it at his side as he swept between the tombstones, his long, purposeful strides taking him across the ground quickly.

Jamie weaved through the graves to catch up.

'You take the left three,' he commanded. 'I'll take the right. Work your way in from the outside and we'll meet in the middle. Got it?'

'Got it.'

He peeled off and she clicked the torch on, the middle of the cemetery nearly pitch black, the grass long and tendril-like underfoot, grabbing at her ankles as she moved through it.

The mausoleums loomed, ancient and algae streaked.

They all occupied the same footprint — ten feet by twelve by the looks of it. Jamie could gauge that sort of space well. A lot of cells were that size.

She grimaced at the thought and inspected the entrances. They all had bars over iron doors. The intricate metalwork — all roses and crucifixes — was sealed in, protected by padlocks. She jangled the first one. It was solid.

The stonework around was no less extravagant — Greek columns and lions — but it was worn and faded with age.

Jamie glanced right, saw that Elliot had already moved between them towards the back. There was no getting in at the front.

She followed suit and headed to the outside, moving the light over the exterior, looking for any cracks or means of ingress. She doubted it would be obvious, or they would have fixed it.

The side looked clear. It was solid blocks and ivy, but none of the stones were even loose.

She checked it off and moved to the back, sinking low, sweeping the torch along the bottom, pinched between the wall of the mausoleum and the cemetery wall.

There was no iron fence here, it was stone right up to about ten feet.

It looked as old as the mausoleums.

No doubt it was the original, built to keep people from grave-robbing back when people were buried inside them. Nineteenth-century? Older? They'd obviously taken down a section of the wall to extend the cemetery at some point, to accommodate more graves. That's where the fencing started.

Jamie sighed.

The first mausoleum was clear.

'Grace?' she said, almost afraid of her own voice. She called softly. Shouting in a cemetery felt as wrong as creeping around one.

She didn't know if Grace would answer even if she could hear her. Especially if she'd come here to escape, to… Shit. She didn't know if Grace would answer because she was lying in a strung-out heap. Or worse.

Jamie swallowed, steadied her hand, and pressed onto the second mausoleum.

Elliot was already on his.

This one was older, more beaten up. It was covered in ivy, its stonework riddled with cracks.

Jamie's heart sank. This was a contender.

She slipped between the two structures, pushing her back against the first to get the light in front of her.

It was blinding in such close-quarters, the wall of the second mausoleum no more than twelve inches from her face.

She could crouch — but her knees hit the stone. She shimmied instead, squinting and pulling chunks of ivy out of the way.

A spider's web wrapped itself around her face and she twisted in shock, throwing her head back, cracking it on the wall behind her.

Her skull sang and then throbbed and she felt herself lose balance, the sharp, uneven stone in front of her cutting into her palms as she dropped the light and threw her hands out.

'Shit,' she growled, raking her nails over her face to pull it off.

She didn't feel like she got it all and now her hair was stuck to her forehead, beads of sweat forming on her brow despite the cold air.

Steam curled off her head and into the bony trees above.

She managed to lean down and scoop the torch up off the ground, spotting an old needle glinting in the beam. Jamie froze and looked down.

Underfoot, the long grass had been trampled a little, and she could see the mud gleaming between her shoes.

Someone had walked here recently. Very recently.

Her throat tightened.

'Jamie?' Elliot's voice reached her ears from somewhere behind her.

'Here,' she said, barely above a whisper.

Elliot appeared in the gap, having seemingly finished his sweep. 'You find something?'

'I dunno,' Jamie said, flashing the torch over the wall of the dilapidated mausoleum.

Elliot muttered something under his breath and then disappeared from the gap over her left shoulder.

A few seconds later he appeared in front of her, looking down the narrow corridor from the front of the mausoleums. She couldn't see the corners of his shoulders past the two walls. It would be a tight fit for him.

'Jamie,' he said, moving his torch towards the ground.

Paving slabs had been slotted in and leaned against the wall in a stack that was four deep in front of Elliot. But on Jamie's side, there was one lone slab leaned at a different angle.

Elliot's torch fell on it and he looked at her.

She came forward and reached down, pulling it out to lean the other way.

Behind it was a crack in the stonework that ran vertically from the ground. Blocks had crumbled away and the hole looked like it had been kicked through and widened.

The gap was about eighteen inches wide and a little taller, tapering into a point around thigh height.

It would be snug, but two skinny homeless kids could squeeze through without too much trouble.

This had to be it.

'Jamie.'

She looked up to see Elliot, his eyes wide, a mixture of something she couldn't identify there — but she could feel the urgency in him. He needed her to go in.

Jamie nodded and stepped over the angled slab, slotting her feet into the hole and lowering herself down until her back hit the slope of the concrete.

Elliot was leaning forward to give her light as she manoeuvred herself downwards, sliding into the darkness.

It enveloped her completely, her breath echoing suddenly in her ears. She was on her butt and sat up, swinging the torch around.

It smelled like an old changing room and she choked on the dust, throwing her arm to her face to stop herself inhaling it.

To her right she could see the inside of the door — iron with rusted hinges and ornate handles.

On her left, she could feel the weight of the place looming over her.

Around the three walls were stone tombs stacked up four tall. The mausoleum held twelve bodies all in all.

Jamie kept the light moving, not letting it rest on the dead.

And then she froze as the beam swung lower, the torch catching something yellow.

She blinked herself clear, staring into the swirling dust. 'Jesus,' she muttered, scrambling forward.

'Jamie? What do you see?' It was Elliot.

'She's here!'

There was scrabbling as he clambered over the slabs to get to the hole.

Jamie didn't look back, instead closing the gap on Grace, who was lying on her side, her arm under her head, outstretched, a strip of yellowed tube circling her bicep.

She was unconscious, and blue.

Despite lying on an old sleeping bag, she was wearing the same clothes as she had been that morning at Elliot's. Just a vest. She was freezing.

A needle lay next to her hand and two tea-lights had burned themselves out just beyond her knuckles.

'Grace?' Jamie skidded next to her and kicked the needle away, putting her hands on the girl's face, and then pushing her fingers into Grace's throat to feel for a pulse. 'Can you hear me?' The movement of blood under her fingers was barely there.

'Shit! Goddammit,' came Elliot's voice, gruff and angry from behind her. She glanced back, seeing his legs poking through the hole. He was stuck. He couldn't fit. And if he couldn't get himself through, there was no way his case would fit. And Grace needed medical attention.

Elliot levered and hauled himself back out and disappeared.

Grace was barely breathing, her skin frozen to the touch. 'She's hypothermic,' Jamie called. 'I'm... I'm starting CPR. She's barely breathing.' Her voice sounded strained and echoed around her.

Jamie's eyes stung in the dust, but it didn't matter. She had to do something.

She rolled Grace onto her back and locked her hands over one the other, finding the right spot between her breastbones as Elliot stomped around outside. She couldn't tell where the noise was coming from. It was everywhere.

A loud clang cut the air as Jamie started pumping on Grace's chest. Her lips were the colour of ice and her skin chalky.

There was a loud bang and the chain rattled on the door outside and Elliot's muffled voice seeped in as she kept pumping on Grace's chest. He was trying to break the padlock with his hard case.

She let off, leaned in and pinched the bridge of her nose, exhaling into her mouth. The taste was old and stale, rotten nearly.

Jamie waited, tilting her head to Grace's lips to listen for her breath. It was tiny, choked. As well as hypothermic she was hypoxic too. If she didn't have brain damage already, she would soon.

Another loud crack rang from outside. Something hard breaking metal.

The chain slithered to the ground and the gate creaked beyond the door.

Jamie turned her head, now pumping on Grace's chest again, the torch on its side throwing a shadowy light around the filthy room.

Elliot was rattling the door handles. They were shaking. 'Jamie?'

he called. 'Open the door.'

She squinted at it, saw that it wasn't bolted — but there was a keyhole under the handles.

'You need a key,' Jamie called, feeling herself breathless already, her skin itching and grimy in the swirling dust.

There was silence for a second, and then a loud bang. The door shook on its hinges but didn't budge.

It happened again.

Elliot was trying to kick the thing through.

'It's no good,' he yelled, wrenching the handles up and down. 'It's solid. You have to do something. Jamie? What can you see?'

Jamie looked at the girl in front of her. She was completely unconscious. Jamie didn't know if what she was doing was saving her life, or if the sheer amount of heroin in her system combined with the hypothermia was going to kill her regardless.

Jamie could see the door — solid iron with a mortise lock. The frame was iron too, set right into the stone. The thing wasn't going to budge with brute force.

Did she leave Grace to find a way to let Elliot in? He had Naloxone, adrenaline — his kit could be the difference between life and death for her. She could give her CPR forever and it might make no difference.

She made the call, let off Grace's chest, and snatched up the torch, running to the door.

Jamie coughed, flashing the light all around it. There were no cracks, no weak spots, nothing. She could see Elliot's silhouette through the holes in the intricate ironwork. He was still, waiting on her to find a solution. If she couldn't, their only other chance would be to drag Grace to the hole and manhandle her out of it — and that would be nearly impossible with the space between the mausoleums being what it was.

No, it came down to her, and whether she could get Elliot through this door.

What could she see?

Handle. Solid.

Threshold. Stone.

Ironwork. It was goddamn ironwork! She'd never get through it.

Hinges.

Hinges?

Hinges! She looked at them. Two of them. Three flatheads in each.

Her heart skipped a beat and she plunged her hand into her pocket, fumbling out her multitool.

'Jamie?'

'Hang on.'

'What is it?'

'Hnnghnhnh.'

'What?'

She bit down on the torch with her teeth, ignoring the question. She couldn't make more than a noise with it in her mouth, and she needed her hands to get the right screwdriver out of her multi-tool.

Her eyes stung in the dust and she risked a glance at Grace. The light spilled over her, prostrate and laying awkwardly. Unmoving.

Jamie focused.

Damn flatheads. Why couldn't they be Phillips?

The screwdriver dug into the rusted metal and twisted. They wouldn't budge.

'Jamie?'

'Ngggold on,' she forced out, working the screwdriver into the screw, leaning into it with her weight so as not to slip.

It creaked, flaked, and then turned.

She knew that it was about even pressure and being methodical. It couldn't be rushed. She turned, moved her hands, turned, moved her hands, turned, moved her hands, turned. The nose of the multitool was a pliers and it was digging into her palm, cutting into the skin.

The first screw was out and she moved onto the next.

It tinged on the floor next to her foot.

Elliot was waiting on the other side, muttering, 'Come on, come on…'

Jamie's eyes flicked to him and back. She wasn't rushing, but she knew that if she did it would only cost more time. And she couldn't risk rounding one of the screws. Too much force would gouge the old metal. No, she had to keep it steady.

She ignored him and kept turning.

The second and third screws fell quickly.

Jamie crouched, seeing Elliot take hold of the handle, holding the door straight while Jamie worked on the other screws.

The top hinge had pulled itself away from the stone, twisting the whole thing in the frame.

She could feel the beads of sweat cutting lines in the dirt on her forehead.

The fourth screw came away, and Jamie's shoulders were aching from the angle. The way the door was leaning was putting pressure on them, making them hard to turn, the rusted hinge iron biting into the back of the screw.

She changed position, kicking one leg out, planting her heel on the door, pushing it straight in the frame.

Her knee sang on the flagstone floor.

Number five twisted loose.

She could feel the tension in Elliot's hands, ready to throw the door inwards the second the last screw fell. He was holding it in place. If he let go, it would twist and bend, fall on Jamie, make it impossible to get to the screw.

'Jamie,' he said.

'Nghhh!' she grunted.

'Listen to me,' he said, his voice oozing calmness, his eyes fixed on Grace's body.

She glanced up, letting number five fall.

'I'm going to go to her — make an assessment. Perform CPR. I need you to bring my case, open it, and do exactly as I say. Do you understand?'

'Nghh,' Jamie said, working the last screw out.

'Nod.'

Jamie nodded, losing sight of the screw for a second.

'Good.' He exhaled, never taking his eyes off Grace. 'On your mark.'

32

T he last screw popped off and Jamie pulled her heel away. Elliot dragged the door sideways and the bolt slid out of the wall, still protruding from the door.

It clanged to the ground and then fell against the wall as Jamie kicked herself backwards from it, rolling to her feet and then springing back through the doorway as Elliot surged towards Grace.

He fell to his knees and pressed his ear to her chest with the sort of precise speed that only years of practising as a surgeon could provide.

A second later he was upright and pumping on her chest like Jamie had been.

'Grace? Grace? Can you hear me? It's Elliot. Grace?' He grit his teeth and kept going.

Jamie had the case and carried it in as Elliot pinched her nose and filled her lungs, feeling for a pulse as the weight of her chest expelled the air.

Though she was trained to give CPR, Elliot was a doctor. His skills far outweighed hers and his ability to assess the situation was something she just didn't have.

Jamie hit the ground next to him and popped the case, staring at the contents. Phials and bottles were lined up neatly along with syringes, other first aid supplies, dressings, and everything else you could need to treat or save someone.

'Jamie,' Elliot said clearly, unhurried or flustered. 'Remove a syringe from the packaging and follow my instructions. Find naloxone and epinephrine. Pull fifteen millilitres of naloxone and ten of epinephrine into the same barrel. Hold it upright, flick the bubbles from the solution, release a droplet from the needle and hand it to me.'

His voice was hard and cool. Unphased by the pressure.

Jamie nodded. 'Naloxone and epinephrine — fifteen and ten.' She was just confirming as her hands moved towards the bottles.

Elliot nodded once and kept pushing on Grace's chest, pausing momentarily to check her pulse, give her mouth-to-mouth, or inspect her body.

He was like a spider, seemingly doing five things at once.

Jamie scanned the labels, using the torch in her left hand to illuminate the bottles under her right.

There were more than a dozen.

She worked her way left to right.

Azithromycin. That was the antibiotic prescribed for gonorrhoea.

Erythromycin. That was another antibiotic, she thought.

Triazolam. She didn't know that one.

Epinephrine. Good. Artificial adrenaline. That was one.

Chloramphenicol. An antibacterial, if she was remembering correctly.

Tetracycline. She didn't know that one either.

Naloxone. Yes. The anti-overdose medicine.

Jamie pulled out the naloxone and epinephrine and set them down on the floor, going for a syringe.

She pushed the torch between her teeth again, ignoring the taste of dirt and cobwebs, and took the needle in both hands, splitting the paper between her fingers.

Ten naloxone, fifteen epinephrine. No. That wasn't it.

She picked up the first bottle and slid the needle into the rubber seal.

Elliot wasn't even looking at her. He knew she was capable. He was focused solely on Grace.

Fifteen naloxone. She pulled it into the barrel and dragged the needle free, feeling a droplet hit her knuckle.

Jamie exhaled, feeling her hands shaking, her heart hammering against the inside of her ribs.

She put the naloxone down a little quickly and snatched up the epinephrine, fumbling it.

She could barely see in the harsh torchlight and the dust was swirling around them in a vortex.

'Jamie.' It was Elliot, his voice even. 'I need the dose. Grace needs it.'

She didn't bother mumbling. She just needed to get it done.

She focused, exhaled around the sides of the torch, and got her fingers around the bottle, twisting it so the rubber top was facing the needle.

She angled them away from each other so she didn't stab herself in the fingers, and twisted it in, drawing the liquid into the barrel, holding the needle vertical and pulling down on the plunger until she hit twenty-five millimetres.

She flicked the bubbles until those rose to the top and pushed out a droplet as instructed, feeling her throat tighten. She didn't know if she could do this for a living. Police work was one thing, but being a doctor?

'Elliot,' she said, taking the torch from her mouth, her voice small. She proffered the syringe.

He glanced over, nodded, kept his count, and then finished his compressions, taking it off her with no seeming care to its sharpness, but without any hint that he was about to prick himself.

His fingers angled so that they took it out of her hand cleanly, and then he rotated it, turning Grace's head at the same time, his hand over her throat, thumb against her carotid artery.

He applied an expert amount of pressure, waiting for the artery to bulge, and then pressed the needle flat against the skin and pushed it through.

Elliot kept his hand there, emptied half the barrel into her neck and then slid the needle out, moving his thumb over the injection site to stem the bleeding.

'Jamie,' he said, moving towards her arm with the needle in his hand, his arms crossing as he leaned over. 'Take this.'

He turned the syringe over and handed her the safe end.

She took it and he swapped hands, a droplet of blood running down Grace's neck as he did.

Grace's back arched and she began to wheeze, breathing quickly as the adrenaline entered her system.

'Support her head,' he ordered, taking the needle back.

Jamie obliged, leaning across Grace's body to cradle it in her hands, dropping the torch as she did.

He moved around her quickly, the light flashing on the wall as he moved past it.

A second later he was next to Jamie, pushing her sideways towards Grace's head with his hip as he took hold of her tracked-out arm.

Elliot squeezed again until the veins began to protrude and found a suitable one, slipping the needle into the skin before Jamie even blinked.

Grace began to groan, her eyelids fluttering, her breathing fast.

Elliot had her wrist now, feeling her pulse. 'Damn it,' he muttered, narrowing his eyes at her, willing her to wake up. 'Hypoxic,' he decided, pushing his fingers into her skin to watch the blood response. 'Hypothermic. The heroin slowed her heart rate and she lost body-heat quickly, slipped into unconsciousness.'

He was talking to himself as much as Jamie.

'We need to get her to a hospital,' he said finally, something like disappointment in his voice over urgency.

Hospitals meant questions. Questions weren't always good. She was suspended and who knew what repercussions he faced, what protocols he'd broken. And that would only be compounded by the police report that would need to be filled in for a drug overdose, which couldn't contain their trespassing, breaking and entering, and destruction of property, which meant omitting details from an official report. Which was a crime.

But it didn't matter. None of that mattered. A girl's life was hanging in the balance.

'Right,' she said. 'What do you need?'

He put the syringe back in his case, replaced the bottles and latched it all in the time it took Jamie to ask. His keys flashed in the torchlight and she caught them. 'Bring the car to this side of the cemetery. Use the floor-mats to cover the spikes on the fence — we'll need to pass Grace over.'

Jamie looked at his face, like a statue in the half-light, shadowed and grave.

'Go.'

She felt her legs twist up underneath her as she rose to her feet, the look in his eyes telling her that it wasn't a negotiation. She was in this now.

They couldn't call an ambulance there — they were breaking the law, and it would cost her her job. And probably him his. They had to get out, and they had to take Grace with them. And fast. If they hadn't attracted attention already, they would be passing Grace over the fence, and neither of them could afford to have uniformed officers show up.

'Okay,' Jamie said, sucking in a deep breath.

She took off at a run, the cold air outside blasting her in the face as she plunged into the cemetery once more, her lungs like bellows in the clean air. She drank it in hungrily, cutting back between the tombstones as quickly as she dared, the torch in her hand flashing on the granite and marble.

She stumbled a couple of times, breathing hard, her eyes covering the windows in the houses around, more of them lit than she would have liked.

Jamie ignored them and pressed on, trying to remember where the car was parked.

She paused, panting, and turned around — disoriented in the dark with no lights to guide her.

'Shit,' she growled, lifting Elliot's keys up and blipping them.

Yellow lights flashed to her right and she made a beeline there, taking the fence with near-reckless abandon, tweaking her ears continually for the sound of sirens.

Her skin was hot with eyes.

Jamie's heels hit the ground, the flakes of ancient paint from the fence still lodged in the skin on her palms.

Sweat and grime covered her totally.

Everything was itching.

Jamie slotted down into the driver's seat and pulled it forward, cranking the key in the ignition and pushing it into gear all at once.

She shoved it into reverse and turned the wheel, the car lurching backwards and mounting the kerb with its passenger wheel. Jamie swore and straightened out, thudding down into the street again.

She manhandled the car straight and zoomed backwards, the gearbox whining as she accelerated as quickly as she dared.

The mausoleums were at the other end of the cemetery, behind the stone wall, but she could pull up to where the fence started.

She just hoped it would be close enough.

Her heart was still beating hard, her hands sweaty on the wheel, the angst clawing at the skin on the back of her head getting more intense.

They were on borrowed time now. If someone hadn't already called in their trespassing and given Elliot's number plate, they would soon. There was no getting away from doing this out in the open. They just had to endure it, regardless of the consequences.

Jamie stood on the brake and the car jolted to a halt just where the stone wall halved itself and turned into fencing.

She was ripping up the floor-mats from under her feet — stiff, hardwearing, plastic-backed — before her heels had even come off the pedals.

The driver's door opened and started beeping because of the running engine, but it didn't matter.

Jamie circled the car, pulled open the passenger-side door, and ripped the second mat free. It popped from its mounting and she turned, one in each hand, to see a figure emerge from the mausoleum. It tottered sideways through the door, a prostrate body slung over its shoulder, a hard-case swinging from its other hand.

The glare of the headlights bounced off the cars in front and threw a shadowy light over the surroundings.

Jamie swallowed and checked around, seeing more and more lights come to life in the windows with every passing second.

Elliot approached as quickly as he could, panting with each step. Grace weighed no more than eight stone, but a dead-weight was dead-weight. Difficult to carry.

The case banged on passing headstones and the noise echoed around.

Jamie came forward and stepped onto the half wall, slinging the floor mats over the spikes one by one, pressing them down and creasing them over the points so they stayed in place. She didn't like it, but they didn't really have any other choice.

Elliot stepped between the last two headstones and swung the case backwards, and then launched it upwards over the fence without a word.

It glinted in the glow of the distant streetlights and Jamie back-pedalled, surprised by it. 'Shit,' she grunted, hitting the side of Elliot's car with her hip, catching the case as it careened down at her.

The corner thumped into his window and her ribs and she made a strange grunting sound, managing to wrestle the case into submission before it hit the ground.

Her hair flipped down and stuck to her cheeks as she turned and opened the back door, shoving it through the gap, being hurried by Elliot all the while.

'Jamie,' he said breathlessly. 'Here.' And with the same haste as he'd tossed the case he trusted the integrity of the floor-mats and heaved Grace off his shoulder, spinning her around and throwing her up onto the fence so that her stomach hit the spikes and her arms and upper body flopped over.

Jamie ran forwards to catch her, not sure what the hell she was supposed to do.

'Brace her weight,' Elliot said, stepping up after her, Grace's knees on his shoulder.

He locked his arm around her calves and hoisted her clear of the spikes, lifting her legs over, dropping her weight onto Jamie, who had her around the ribs, Grace's chin resting limply on her shoulder.

She stepped back again, feeling Grace's heels flying somewhere above her, the girl's greasy hair thick in her face.

And then she was limp and swinging downwards.

Her feet hit the ground and dragged and Jamie started to topple, the momentum pushing her off balance. She wasn't much heavier than Grace herself.

Elliot landed cleanly and snatched them both from the point of falling, taking Grace around the waist and holding her upright with one arm, his other around Jamie, his hand in the small of her back.

Jamie and Grace were face to face for a second, her pale visage like a ghost of itself.

The girl had broken out in a cold sweat, her breathing fast and shallow, skin blotchy as the adrenaline fought the hypothermia.

'You drive,' Elliot said over her head, releasing her and pulling Grace into his arms again. 'St. Mary's.'

Jamie nodded and ran for the driver's door.

'The mats,' Elliot added, his voice still dripping calm. 'We can't leave anything behind.'

She circled back and grabbed them as Elliot forced Grace down through the back door and into the back seat, laying her across his lap, where he immediately continued with CPR.

Jamie didn't think she'd ever been so nerve-wracked.

Her heart was pounding.

She threw the mats into the passenger footwell and lurched down into the driver's seat, cracking the side of her head on the roof of the car as she did.

Jamie clenched her teeth, ignored the pain above her left ear, and pulled the door shut.

She stole a glance over her shoulder at Elliot, face streaked with grime and dust, cradling Grace and saving her life at the same time, heels of his hands pumping on her chest, and swallowed hard.

He looked up as the first sounds of sirens punctuated the still night air. 'Drive,' he said, and without another moment of doubt, she did.

33

J amie dreamt of blue lights.

As they'd pulled away from the kerb and hurtled towards the corner, she'd imagined patrol cars skidding to a halt to block their way. She'd imagined having handcuffs snap around her wrists and being shoved down into the backseat of a police car.

She'd hung a left and bolted straight down the road in front of the church, pushing it up to about sixty on the narrow street, her hands tight and sweaty on the wheel.

She wanted to be as far away from there as she could. And fast.

The junction loomed and she stomped on the brake as late as she dared, feeling the German saloon snake to a stop under her feet.

In the distance behind, the first flashing blue lights appeared around a corner, no more than a pinprick in the night. No doubt responding to a call about their doings at the cemetery.

Jamie eased into traffic and oozed forward, feeling all at once safer and trapped. She was camouflaged now among the other cars, but at low speeds, they'd be easier to catch. She just hoped that no one had caught their number plate. Though she didn't know how much she would have bet on that.

Every five seconds she checked the rearview, staring past Elliot, who knew not to hurry her or say anything. All he could do we focus on Grace. The only thing he had asked was for Jamie to crank the heating up, and she did.

They'd swam through a sea of lights and horns and Jamie's eyes grew tired in the warmth.

'Here.'

Jamie inhaled sharply and sat up, the plastic covering on the hospital chair next to Grace's bed groaning under her.

Elliot was standing there with a cup of coffee held out for her.

'I must have drifted off,' she said, her voice hoarse, and accepted the coffee. She'd been reliving the drive over on repeat in different ways. Sometimes they crashed. Other times they were headed off by patrol cars. Once, Elliot leapt forward from the back seat and wrapped his arms around her face, digging his fingers into her cheeks, her mouth, scraping at her arms and her throat, pinning her against the seat. And she couldn't move, her hands glued to the wheel as he choked the life out of her.

And now here he was offering her coffee. She looked up at him, feeling a sense of guilt ride up in her guts. She couldn't blame him for the events of tonight. It wasn't his fault that she broke the law. She could have called it in at any time.

But she was glad she didn't.

Grace's heart monitor beeped softly, steadily in the background She was unconscious, but they'd pushed fluids and covered her with heated blankets. All they could do now was monitor her. They wouldn't be able to assess any brain damage or after-effects from the hypoxia until she woke up, and with the sedative they've given her to counteract the epinephrine, that wouldn't be until morning.

It was now after midnight.

Jamie didn't really want coffee, but accepted it anyway.

'You did a good thing,' Elliot said softly, pulling a chair from the other side of the bed a little closer and sitting down.

'Mmm,' Jamie said, not sure what else she could say.

The door to the hallway was open just a crack, loud enough to hear the muted bustle of the nurses outside.

The ward was in darkness for the most part, except for the lights burning over the nurses' station.

Jamie wanted nothing more than to go home, but she didn't have her wallet and Elliot's car was the only one in the car park downstairs. She didn't feel right asking him to pay for a taxi, and didn't think he'd stay all night anyway.

He wanted to stay for a little while, though, so Jamie just had to endure it.

She didn't remember falling asleep.

Elliot watched Grace with a softness in his eyes. Like a father would.

Jamie exhaled and held onto the coffee, letting it warm her fingers. 'She'll be okay.'

'Maybe,' Elliot said, looking at her. 'It all depends how long she was there before we arrived, how long she was hypoxic, how—'

He cut off as Jamie leaned forward and put her hand on his knee. She smiled and looked into his eyes. 'She'll be okay.'

He exhaled slowly and leaned back, moving his chin back and forth across his hand, his knuckle pressing into his lips. 'Until she gets out,' he muttered. 'Then what? What kind of life does she have ahead of her?' He was asking himself as much as Jamie.

'At least... at least Paxton is dead,' Jamie said softly, not sure if it made her cold, cruel, or both to say that.

He looked at her, narrowed his eyes a little, and then his expression softened. 'How are you feeling?'

She knew he meant about what happened on the platform. She let out a long breath. 'I'm dealing with it. As best I can, at least.' She swallowed and looked away.

'It wasn't your fault. You know that, don't you?'

Jamie's jaw flexed. 'We backed him into a corner. He cut his wrists.' She felt herself staring into space as she pictured it. 'If we'd have handled it differently, he'd still be alive.'

'You couldn't have known it would end like that.'

'If I'd just taken a second to think—'

'You can't blame yourself for his death. Paxton was unstable.

Dangerous. You did what you had to.' He reached out and laid a hand on her knee for a second.

She stared at it and he let it fall away.

'Dangerous is right.' She shook her head. 'There was so much blood. It got all over me. The platform...' She looked down at her hands in her lap. 'Jesus, how could I be so stupid? He was HIV positive. Or so he said.' She looked at Grace, sadly. They'd been having sex. 'She should get checked.'

Elliot looked at Grace and then back at Jamie. 'How much blood?'

'A lot. Pints? All of it.'

'Any open wounds? Did any get in your eyes? Your mouth?'

She shook her head.

'Your chances of contracting the virus are very low,' he said pragmatically. 'And as for Grace...' He turned back to her. 'She may be reckless, but she's not stupid. She knows that contracting something at this point is a death sentence. She doesn't *want* to be here. Like this. She's just...'

Addiction. Jamie knew what he meant. It took hold and it sunk its claws in deep.

She thought back to the mattress in Sippy's den. There'd been condoms on the floor. Maybe she had been smart. That would be something at least. If she was sleeping with him — whatever the reason — there were ways to minimise the risk. She hoped for her sake, strung out or not, that she'd tried.

Elliot was watching her, his expression conflicted. Disappointment more than anything else swimming behind his eyes.

Who was she to him? Why did she matter so much?

Before she could stop herself, she was speaking. 'Why her?' Jamie asked.

'Hmm?' Elliot looked up.

'Why Grace? When there are so many others. Why her?'

Elliot bit his lip, looking hard at Jamie. Maybe he was trying to decide whether or not to open up. Maybe he was working up the nerve to. 'My sister,' he said quietly, after a long time.

'Tell me about her.'

Elliot swallowed, filled his lungs, and then leaned forwards, rubbing his hands together slowly. 'She was seventeen when she went missing.'

Jamie knew not to interrupt. When a story started like that, it was never good to press the person telling it.

'I wasn't there. My father put us both in boarding school — separately. We weren't at home much, and when we were…' Elliot sat back and looked over his shoulder into the hallway.

Jamie could tell he wasn't comfortable talking about it. But she wanted to know him.

She said nothing when changing the subject would have been the easiest thing to do.

Eventually he went on. 'My father and her had a troubled relationship. *Difficult* my mother called it.'

'What was her name?'

'Victoria.'

That hung in the air for a few seconds.

'She was expelled from boarding school, I found out afterwards. At the time, I didn't know anything about it.'

'How old were you?'

'Eleven. Too young to understand, to do anything about it.'

Jamie nodded. She knew that feeling.

'She had, uh,' he said, smiling, his eyes sad, as though it were all funny in some cruel way. 'She snuck a boy into the school, and she was caught. Of course, if that was the end of it, it wouldn't have been a problem. Not really. That sort of thing happens a lot. And a sizeable donation from a parent will make that sort of thing go away.' He shook his head, as if resentful of his upbringing. Private boarding school, parental donations. She was picturing the manor house that he grew up in.

There was so much she wanted to know, but she didn't dare interrupt.

'She got pregnant.'

Jamie drew in a breath, looking at him.

He nodded. 'I never knew. But that was why they expelled her, said she couldn't be there, around the other girls... and when she came home, she refused to tell my father who the boy was.' Elliot's fist curled and he knocked it on his thigh. 'I don't blame her. He could be...'

Elliot trailed off, but Jamie knew the word he was reaching for was *violent.*

'He told her that she had to get rid of the baby. He scheduled for a doctor to come to the house.' Elliot smiled again, almost laughing, his eyes glazing over. 'She refused of course — as stubborn and strong-willed as he was.'

'He gave her an ultimatum. Either she got rid of the baby, or she left the house.' Elliot did laugh now. 'A stupid thing to do, really. But neither of them would back down.'

'So she left?'

'I didn't come home for Easter that year — so it was July by the time I got home. She'd been gone for nearly four months by that point.'

'Jesus. Where did she go?'

Elliot shrugged and then sighed. 'I don't know. My father, in his infinite wisdom, called her friends' parents, told them not to offer her a place to stay. They all knew each other of course, and they wouldn't cross him. No one would.'

'Did she come back?' Jamie asked, knowing the answer.

'No.' Elliot laced his hands together and started cracking his knuckles. 'She contacted my mother about six weeks after she left — said that she'd sold all of her jewellery, everything she had, and had run out of money.'

'What did she say?'

'She was as scared of my father as I was. She told her to come home, to get rid of the baby, to go back to school. But she wouldn't.'

'What about the father?'

'Of the baby? I don't know. She never told us who he was. And I think she was too afraid to go to him in case my father found out. He had reach. Influence. And we all knew what he would have done to him if he knew who he was.'

Jamie swallowed. Elliot's father sounded like a real piece of work.

'What happened then?'

Elliot was silent for a few seconds. 'And then, nothing. We never heard from her again. We never found out who the father was. She disappeared.'

'Jesus.'

Elliot nodded, looking grave.

'So she could still be out there? With the father maybe—'

'She'd dead,' he said coldly. 'Her body was found less than a year later. Heroin overdose.'

'What about—'

'It looked like she miscarried because of the drugs. Late. The report said that she had overdosed almost immediately after.' He said it with the sort of detached coolness that doctors and detectives both had to develop in order to do what they did. To tell people what they had to tell them.

'They said,' he went on, 'that she had been prostituting herself.' Elliot stopped talking and looked at Grace.

She was peaceful.

Jamie leaned back, sipped her coffee. 'I understand.'

Elliot nodded. 'I never knew any of it. Until my mother told me, two years later.'

Jamie knew now why Grace. She was about the same age as Elliot's sister would have been. Maybe they looked alike. But either way, she understood. And she liked him all the more for it.

'If I'd have known…' Elliot started.

'Don't do that to yourself,' Jamie said, her voice small in her head. 'We were—' she caught herself, cleared her throat, and then started again. 'You were a kid. You *couldn't* have known. Couldn't have helped. Your parents chose to protect you from it. And that's not your fault.' Jamie had been through this herself. She knew the sting of finding out your parents had sheltered you, lied to you about something so important it made your heart ache to think about it.

Elliot didn't respond. He just kept looking at Grace. Reluctant to leave in case she woke up and ran away again. How many times could he save her before it was too late?

She felt like the answer was simply as many times as he could.

'I do what I can,' Elliot said, not looking away. 'For the people who need it. Some throw their lives away. Some can't be saved. But some can.' He looked at her now, his eyes intense. 'You understand that, don't you? Some lives can be saved. And some should?'

She forced a smile onto her lips. 'Yeah, Elliot. Some people can be saved. Others… can't. No matter how hard you try, or how much you want to. You understand that, don't you?' She felt more patronising than compassionate saying that to a doctor. But he was too close to this. He needed the perspective.

'But we should still try.'

'We all have the power to try. And sometimes, that's all you can do.'

Elliot nodded, processing. 'I'm glad you were there tonight, Jamie.'

'Me too.'

They smiled at each other, a moment hanging in the air.

He looked like he wanted to say something else, but Jamie didn't know what. It was like he was holding something back. But he didn't say another word, and instead just looked at Grace again, his eyes unmoving.

She could tell he was going to sit there for a long time.

Jamie had a pang of longing for bed, but the thought of travelling all the way there was too much. Here, with Elliot… That was okay. She'd stay.

If anything, she was happy to be there.

She'd done a good thing.

They both had.

They'd saved Grace's life, and when she woke up in the morning, she'd see both of them, and they could talk about it. About getting her help.

Elliot was right, and so was she.

You couldn't save all of them, but maybe you could save some.

And if you couldn't save some, then maybe you could save one.

And as far as she was concerned, one was a thousand times better than none.

And it was worth fighting for.

She laid her head back, her eyes settling on Elliot's pensive stare and let her eyelids grow heavy.

She was tired, and she needed to sleep.

It had been a long day, and despite the discomfort of the chair and the strange angle she was sitting at, sleep came quickly, creeping up over her shoes and shins, snaking its way over her thighs and climbing up her stomach and over her chest.

It curled its tendrils around her neck and pushed them into her ears, drowning out the sounds of the heart monitor and the squeak of the gurney wheels as the night porters moved through the hallways. They wrapped themselves around her eyes and blotted out the dim glow of the emergency lighting over the door, and threaded themselves up her nostrils, blocking the smell of bleach and rubber mattresses.

Sleep came awkwardly and uncomfortably, but it came all the same.

And dragged her down into the darkness.

The last thing she saw was Elliot.

And then there was nothing.

I t was eleven minutes past four in the morning when her phone
started to buzz.

She sat upright in the chair, disoriented, and looked around.

Elliot was right where she'd left him, arms folded across his chest,
chin leaning on his collarbone.

She pulled her phone from her pocket, rubbing her sore neck, and
stood, slipping out into the hallway before she answered.

Her eyes stung in the glow of the halogens and she squinted at her
screen. It was DCI Smith.

She answered quickly. 'Hello?'

'Johansson.' She could tell by the tone of his voice he hadn't been
sleeping before he called. He'd been awake for a while. Maybe all
night.

'Sir.'

'Something's come up. Can you head in?'

She looked around the empty hallway, feeling the grime on her skin
from the night before. 'Uh, sure? What's going on?'

'It's Donnie Bats.' She could hear him slurp on some coffee
between the words. 'It seems your little stunt with Paxton shook some
branches if nothing else. Thompson brought in another of his dealers,

managed to flip him. The warrant for Bats' arrest just came in. We're moving on him.'

'Now?' Jamie looked around again, trying to figure out how the hell she was going to get there.

'Now, Johansson. How long before you can get here?'

'Uh — that might be a problem. Can you send a car for me?'

'A car? Where are you?'

'St. Mary's.'

'The hospital? Why?'

She looked at the door to Grace's room. 'Visiting family. I must have fallen asleep.'

It was a weak excuse and Smith knew it, but he didn't care enough to interrogate her over it. 'Sure. I'll make the call. Be ready.'

He hung up before she could say anything and she sighed, looking at her screen. Damn it was early. She was beginning to forget what a full night's sleep looked like.

Jamie turned back to Grace's door and she looked at it, deciding whether to just leave or not. She could always text Elliot...

No, that didn't feel right.

She headed back inside and kneeled next to his chair, putting her hand on his arm.

He drew in a breath and lifted his head, blinking himself clear.

She felt the muscles in his forearm roll as he gripped the end of the chair, reacclimating to his surroundings. 'What's wrong?' he asked, looking at the bed. 'Grace?'

'Nothing's wrong,' she whispered, not sure whether Grace was sleeping or still sedated. She held up her phone. 'I've got to go, I'm sorry.'

He looked at her, nodded, and then started to get up. 'Okay, I'll drive you—'

'They're sending a car,' she said, squeezing a little tighter on his arm. 'You stay. Honestly.'

He sat back down, letting his mouth grow into a smile. 'You're beautiful,' he said suddenly, inspecting her face, his blue eyes moving quickly over her features. 'Do you know that?'

She tried to stop her cheeks from flushing. 'I'll call you, okay?'

He put his hand over hers on his arm. 'Be careful, Jamie.'

She stood up and he released her, and then she was gone at a brisk walk, feeling the blood hot in her cheeks.

Jamie passed the elevators on her right and dipped into the stairs, smirking as she did it on autopilot.

Old habits, she thought.

A minute later she was on the ground floor and heading for the main exit.

Two minutes after that, a patrol car pulled up at the kerb and she got in, headed for home.

They waited while she went in, showered, changed into something clean — jeans and some functional black boots. They weren't her hiking boots by any stretch, but they were tough leather and she could run in them if it came to it.

She walked back out into the early-morning air, plaiting her hair on autopilot as she did.

The officer waiting in the patrol car said nothing as she got in. No one liked night-shifts, especially not when they had to play taxi.

It didn't bother Jamie. She was settling into a deep focus. If Smith was asking her back then it meant her suspension was most likely being lifted. And though Donnie Bats was wanted on drug charges, having another investigation overlapping meant that there were two opportunities to nail him. If they closed in and they couldn't pin any drug-related crimes on him, then having him on kidnapping, extortion, and manslaughter was a great backup. And with Paxton's testimony — flimsy as it was — along with the guy Thompson had flipped, all they had to do now was get him in chains, and there was a great chance that he'd be going away for a long time.

She found herself grinning as the patrol car sped back towards HQ. If that news wasn't good enough to help keep Grace on the wagon, then she didn't know what would be.

There was nothing that would bring Oliver back, but knowing that the person responsible for his death was behind bars was as good as they could hope for.

.   .   .

They pulled up outside HQ a little after five in the morning.

A thin drizzle was falling and the air was cold.

Jamie was wearing a leather jacket and the rain beaded on the black hide like jewels in the streetlights.

She gave a quick nod to the officer who'd dropped her off and she peeled away from the kerb and disappeared into the early morning darkness.

Jamie's skin was prickling with anticipation.

She'd quickly come to accept the suspension — she was even looking forward to a little time to herself. To collect her thoughts and reflect on the past events. But now that there was an opportunity to get back to it, she couldn't wait.

There was blood in the water and her predator drive was kicking in.

Donnie Bats would go down before the sun rose, and he'd be back behind bars.

And then maybe Grace could start rebuilding her life.

With Elliot's help — and hers, she had decided — she could turn it around.

Jamie took the steps two at a time and then practically ran up the stairs, her muscles well-oiled and oxygenated. The strains of her work-out with Cake seemed to have faded to nothing. If anything, she felt sharp. As if the refresher had burnt off all the excess stress and anger she'd accumulated and now she was left with a clear and focused mind.

She exited the stairwell on her floor and entered into a maelstrom.

The rest of HQ was on night-mode. Zombies shuffling around the corridors waiting for their shifts to end. But on her floor, it could have been the middle of the day.

Bodies thronged. Some in uniform, some in plain clothes, some in tactical gear.

Jamie could see Smith in his office through the glass wall. He was looking at something on his desk — a large piece of paper. Blueprint maybe, or at least a plan of Donnie's building. On his right Thompson was pointing to things and talking. And on his left a big guy — six feet or so, dark hair, built like a bison — dressed in dark grey fatigues and a flak-jacket, was nodding. He was a senior officer in the armed response unit. Donnie wouldn't go down without a fight. Especially not if they backed him into a corner.

She looked over to her desk and saw Roper there, leafing through a file. He was leaning against it, a cup of coffee steaming next to him.

Jamie went over, seeing his pensive, sober eyes fixed on the words he was reading.

'Hey,' she said.

He looked up, totally dry. 'Hey yourself.'

She was glad to see him sober. Maybe Smith's talk had gotten through to him. Maybe he'd just taken a day off. She didn't say anything about it. 'What's going on?'

He shrugged. 'Dunno, got a call. Guess we're moving on Bats.'

'What's that?' She nodded to the file.

'Hammond's autopsy report. Came in last night. Found it on my desk this morning.'

'Anything interesting in there?'

He closed it and proffered it to her. 'See for yourself.'

She reached out, taking the file.

Roper slurped his coffee as she opened it, seeing a photo of Ollie on the front page.

'Roper. Johansson.' Their names echoed across the room over the din of officers and detectives.

Jamie looked up from the file. Smith was standing in the doorway of his office.

They looked at each other and then headed over.

When they got in, Smith let the door close behind them.

Thompson nodded to Roper and he nodded back.

Jamie wondered if he had anything to do with them being called in, or with Roper's sobriety.

Smith moved back around to the other side of the desk, between Thompson and the senior armed response officer, and planted his hands on his glass desk. Roper and Jamie stared across at him.

'Right,' he said, pressing his lips together. 'Effective immediately, your suspensions are lifted.' He reached down to the little filing cabinet under his desk and pulled their badges out of the top draw, slapping them down above the plan on his desk — which looked to be an architectural plan of the apartment building that Donnie lived in.

Jamie and Roper both took their badges without a word, as if saying anything might make him reconsider.

'It doesn't mean you're off the hook,' Smith said, looking from one to the other. 'That stunt with Paxton has been a perpetual headache for me. The PR team want your heads on pikes. An addict slitting his wrists on a public tube platform? I don't think I could imagine a worse scenario.' He hung his head a little and shook it. 'But in terms of a statement, well, it's not all bad. Thompson managed to shake some trees in the aftermath, got one of Donnie's street-level pushers to flip.' He paused for a few seconds. 'A kid. Sixteen. We can try him as a minor, protect his identity in court, disguise his testimony. We've got the warrant for Donnie's arrest based on what the kid's told us so far. Because—' he looked at Jamie ' — despite what Paxton said being a deathbed-confession, I'm guessing it's not actually worth shit, is it?'

Jamie clenched her jaw and shook her head quickly.

'Right. But the kid doesn't know that, so we got *something* out of it at least.' He drew in a slow breath. 'Maybe more than if we brought Paxton in alive. I'm not saying it's a good thing he's dead, but…'

Thompson was willing to. 'One less shit-bag H-slinger on the streets is never a bad thing.'

Smith ignored it. 'We need you there for Bats to see. So when we walk him out in handcuffs, he sees Thompson, and you two. So he knows that we're going to nail him on *something*. He might think he's smart, but with priors, and everything we have, any jury worth their salt is going to want this asshole off the street.'

Jamie and Roper nodded.

'I want you two in vests, outside the front door, alright? You're not going in. Is that clear?'

Jamie and Roper both glanced at each other. While they wanted to be the ones to put Bats in chains, they didn't want to push it.

'We're meeting in the operations room to go over the plan in five minutes.'

That was their invitation to leave.

And they both did so without being asked.

Outside, Roper did something Jamie rarely saw him do. Smile.

'You're happy,' Jamie said.

'It's 'cause I'm not hungover,' he joked.

She knew it was because he'd been reinstated. As much as he liked to sport that *I don't give a shit* attitude, she knew that he cared about his job.

They got back to her desk and he picked up his coffee.

Jamie reached for the autopsy file again.

'Euch, cold,' Roper said, staring into the cup. 'You want one?'

Jamie looked up, only getting as far as the diagram of Ollie's body and the marks logged. 'Hmm? Sure.'

'Great,' he said. 'Black, two sugars. I'm going for a cigarette.' He pushed his cup into her hands, grinning.

She dropped the file and took it. 'Funny.'

'I thought so.'

'You know, I like you better when you're hungover.'

He held onto his grin all the way to the elevator.

Jamie stared at the file and then at Roper's cup. It wasn't going to tell them anything useful. They were about to nail Donnie anyway, and she needed coffee. She was already cutting it fine to grab a cup before the meeting.

She chose caffeine and headed for the kitchen, setting up a new pot.

Jamie leaned against the counter and folded her arms, closing her eyes against the sting of the halogens.

After a few minutes, she heard footsteps pattering towards the operations room.

The pot had enough in it for one decent cup.

She stared down at Roper's, still half full and cold. He'd not notice, his taste dulled by the cigarette.

She filled one for herself and put his in the microwave instead.

Jamie watched it turn as she sipped on the fresh coffee.

Everyone piled into the operations room and Smith brought up the rear, pausing at the doorway to the kitchen. 'Johansson,' he said. 'You ready?'

She hit the door release and pulled Roper's cup out, feeling herself smirk. 'Yeah,' she replied, heading out. 'I'm ready.'

35

R oper slipped into the operations room, a fresh shroud of
cigarette stink following him, and sat next to Jamie.

She'd chosen a seat at the back, so that he could. She handed him
his coffee and he lifted it to his bristled lips and drank deeply. 'You put
sugar in this?' he asked.

She'd actually just tipped a little of the fresh coffee in on top before
she'd put it in the microwave.

'Yeah,' she lied. 'Of course. Two, you said.'

'Hmm.' He shrugged. 'Tastes weird.'

'Uh, maybe it's a different brand,' she hedged. 'Or decaf?' She
looked at him, and shrugged.

He was grimacing at the cup. 'Hope not.'

It struck her as ironic that he was a good enough to detective to
catch killers, but couldn't tell when coffee had been microwaved.

She retrained a smile and faced front as Smith took to the lectern
and turned to face the screen at the back of the room.

A projector had been fired up and was beaming a huge version of
the floor-plan of Donnie Bats' building up on the wall.

The room was filled with half a dozen uniformed officers, eight
armed response officers, as well as the senior officer at the front next to

Smith. Otherwise, it was Thompson, Roper, Jamie, and three other detectives that Jamie assumed were working the Bats case with Thompson.

'Okay,' Smith said, rubbing his eyes. He definitely hadn't slept. 'This is the top floor of Donnie Bats' apartment building. Thompson has informed us from his first-hand experience that we can take the lift to the nineteenth floor, and that we access the twentieth through this stairwell.' He had an extendable pointer that he used to tap the stairs that they'd used to get up to Donnie's floor when they'd gone in there a few days before. 'We're told that Bats is occupying this apartment here —' he tapped again '—at the end of the corridor. As we understand it, he's knocked these two apartments into one, so we'll be breaching simultaneously. I don't want him slipping out before we can get our hands on him.'

Thompson, who was also at the front, stepped forward now. 'He'll have lookouts posted. We know he'll have one at the top of the main stairwell. And we assume others, too. Jones, MacGinley—' he was addressing two of the other detectives '—you'll go in first, clear out the lookouts on the ground floor if you can, check the area for anyone else. I don't want Donnie to know we're there until we're through the front door.'

A guy and a woman in the front row nodded.

'Cameron,' he said, addressing the third. 'You're with me. We're going in with armed to make the collar. We're at the head — we put the lookout at the top of the stairs down, pass him over to uniformed, and then we prep for breach. Clear?'

He nodded.

Smith stepped back in. 'There's another stairwell here,' he said, pointing to the far side of the diagram. 'That runs down to the ground floor and lets out at the rear of the building. We'll have two officers posted at the exit just in case. But if he wanted to get to it, he's going to have to go through eight of our guys.'

The armed response officers, all clad in their tactical gear and flak jackets, laughed. Jamie wouldn't have wanted to tangle with them.

They were all tough as hell in their own right, and with guns in their hands they were lethal.

Though that was sort of the point.

'Captain Hassan,' Smith went on, turning to the burly armed response officer behind him. 'Over to you.'

'Alright, lads,' Captain Hassan said in a gruff south London accent. 'Business as usual. Thompson's on point here — once he's set up, we breach, four on each door, alright? Coordinated. We go in hard, sweep. We don't know about weapons. But if you make a positive ID, shoot don't get shot. You know the drill. We all come home tonight. I don't want to be calling anyone's wife, alright?'

Everyone nodded.

'Once the room is clear and the threats are down, Thompson and Cameron will come in and make the arrest. Got it?'

Everyone nodded again.

'Good.' He checked his watch. 'Let's move out. I want to be breaching at seven. Which means I want to be in place by six-thirty.'

Smith came from around the lectern and shook the captain's hand. 'Good luck, Captain. Thompson?'

Thompson looked at Smith.

'It's your show.'

Thompson nodded.

'Go get him.'

Smith stepped from the front and walked down the length of the room, heading for the door. He glanced at Jamie and Roper and then moved through the door behind them.

Thompson didn't say anything else. Which meant that Jamie and Roper wouldn't have anything to do in the raid. They'd hang back with the other uniforms. Just there to be seen when Bats came out.

Window dressing.

Though Jamie didn't mind all that much. Bats was a hell of a collar for the department, and catching a piece of shit like him was its own reward. Whether her name was on the arrest form or not.

Thompson's detectives got up and followed him out.

The armed response officers followed quickly.

Everyone was tense. She wasn't surprised.

Bats was a notorious criminal. No one knew what was waiting for them in there.

If one of his dealers had been picked up and Paxton was dead, he'd be on the defensive. The place would be fortified. He wouldn't go down without a fight.

Jamie and Roper waited for the room to clear out and then got up.

'I'll drive,' Roper said.

Jamie opened her mouth to argue, and then realised that her car was still outside Elliot's. She didn't want to invite a line of questioning, so she stayed quiet.

'Don't worry,' he said, reading the unhappy look on her face. 'I just had it cleaned.'

'Really?'

'No,' he laughed.

Jamie sighed. 'I definitely like you better when you're hungover.'

Roper's car was just as dirty and smelly as it had always been. But somehow, she didn't mind. Maybe it was being reinstated, or maybe it was knowing that after they got Bats it would all be over and she could actually see whether there was anything real between her and Elliot.

'You do much last night?' Roper asked casually as they drove.

'What? No. Why?' Jamie answered snapping out of her thoughts, trying not to sound sheepish.

Roper gave her a sideways look. 'No reason. Just making conversation.'

In fact, she'd done a lot the night before. Breaking and entering. Criminal damage. Trespassing. The list went on. 'I watched TV,' Jamie said, looking out the window. 'What about you?'

He exhaled slowly, watching the road as they drove towards Donnie's. The armed response van trundled forward in front of them, lights and sirens silent. 'I went to AA.'

'AA?' Jamie's head turned around and she looked at Roper to see if he was joking. 'As in alcoholics anonymous?'

He nodded. 'Yeah. I mean, I'm not an alcoholic, but…' He glanced at her. 'You know, I was speaking to someone and they told me to stick my head in, listen to some of the people there… Listen to the stories. Easier to stop before you get there than to come back.' He sounded wistful, sad.

She didn't know who the *someone* was — Roper was divorced, so it wasn't his wife. He didn't have any kids or a girlfriend, and his circle of friends consisted of the regular boozers at his local pub. Could it have been Thompson? Smith? She didn't want to ask. He was forthcoming with the other information, so she didn't want to pry.

'What did you think?' Jamie asked as if she was only cursorily interested. She wasn't. She cared about Roper. But she didn't want to make it seem like a big deal.

'I think that a lot of people got it worse than I have. The shit they were saying…' He shook his head. 'I don't want to get like that.'

'Mmm.' Jamie leaned her head back. She didn't want him to get like that either.

'I'm going to be better,' he said finally. 'Okay?' He looked at her and she looked back at him, forcing a smile onto her face.

'Okay,' she said. There was nothing else to say. Drinkers always made promises. The proof would come with Roper's actions. She knew that asking if he was stopping drinking wouldn't help, because it would make him admit that either he didn't want to stop, or it would make him lie and say he would. And then he wouldn't. She said all she could.

He'd prepared a speech by the look of it. About how he was going to be better. But she didn't really care. She liked Roper, but words meant nothing. She'd grown up with words and promises. All that mattered was what you did every day. Whether you drank or not, and whether the fallout engulfed those around you.

She'd wait and see. But she didn't have high hopes. And that made her feel numb inside.

All she could do was endure it with a little bit of cold indifference and wait for the next slip up.

Allowing yourself to hope set you up for a fall. She didn't know if that made her a cynic or just protected her.

She'd have to wait and see.

They pulled up at the rear of the apartment block next to Donnie's, out of view of his apartment.

The lamps in the corners of the car park were haloed in the drizzle, the orange glow bleeding outwards into the dark.

The patrol cars moved in first and parked at the sides, so that the armed response officers' van could slot into the middle.

Thompson pulled up in his old BMW and either MacGinley or Jones — Jamie didn't know which was which — pulled in behind him in a hatchback. Roper pulled in last and slotted into a space next to them.

The six detectives all disembarked and moved towards the back of the police van while the uniformed officers got out and began to walk in a perimeter. Things were going to move fast now.

Jamie could feel it in the air, like a storm. Things were still, silent. But they wouldn't be for much longer.

The rear doors of the police van opened and nine guys in tac-gear all came into view, strapping themselves up with body armour and checking their weapons. Each had a body-cam on their ballistic vests. The footage from these sorts of raids was often poured over by ethics and conduct committees. The captain stepped through the middle of the seated men and dropped heavily to the ground. He must have been sixteen stone of solid muscle. Probably more.

He was around six feet, but despite not being *that* tall, he still seemed big. The boots, the vest, the wide shoulders, the SIG516 carbine rifle cradled in his arms. It all contributed. Though it was still before dawn, Jamie could make out his strong features, his dark skin, short, curly hair that had been pulled back with industrial strength product so that it was pressed to his head.

She could see the name 'Hassan' embroidered on the name-badge Velcroed to his tactical vest.

He nodded to Thompson and started inspecting his weapon. On his belt he was carrying a Glock 17. Though Jamie wasn't a part of armed response, she took an interest in it — and had thought about applying a few times. She knew what it entailed, what they were equipped with. She'd even done her firearms training, sailed through the tests.

Though what scared her the most was that they *needed* that firepower and protection.

She was good with a few more years of detective work.

Captain Hassan reached back into the van and pulled spare Kevlar vests from under the near bench. Four in total. He handed one to Thompson, and then to the other detectives. Jamie and Roper didn't get one.

But then again, they wouldn't be going in.

Hassan accepted a pair of walkie-talkies handed to him and gave one to Jones — or MacGinley — and one to Thompson. He then took a third from the guy on the end of the bench in the van and handed it to Roper. He took it and hooked it on his belt.

Thompson hung his on the front of the vest he'd slipped over his head and turned to the detectives under his command — Jones, MacGinley, Cameron — as Hassan and his squad finished their final checks.

'You two,' Thompson said, speaking to Jones and MacGinley. 'Know your orders? Move in, subdue any lookouts on the ground floor. Uniforms will come in behind you and secure the entrance. Armed Response will follow you up in the elevator. You take the lookout down quietly, and then Cameron and I will move in with AR for the breach. Alright? You cover the hallway then in case anyone tries to come up or out of the other rooms. Our intel says that it's just the two apartments, that the rest are normal occupants.' He looked at them, strapping himself up. 'I want to be in and out before they know what's happening. Got it?'

MacGinley and Jones nodded, looking nervous.

Hell, Jamie felt nervous and she wasn't even going in.

Thompson sighed, wiped the thin sheen of drizzle off his forehead. 'Captain, your men ready?'

Hassan nodded, his rifle tucked against his ribs, pointed down, his finger against the stock.

'Alright,' Thompson said, looking at everyone in turn. 'Let's go.'

36

The uniforms were called back over, and then everyone was moving.

Captain Hassan was at the front, strafing quickly, nose of his rifle pointed downwards as he moved across the open space between the two apartment blocks.

Thompson was right on his shoulder, with Cameron behind. Then there were two more armed officers, each facing outwards, covering the flanks, Jones and MacGinley behind, then another four armed officers, Jamie, Roper, two of the uniforms, and the final two armed officers at the rear, covering them.

Jamie moved lightly, keeping pace, half-crouching, though there was no need.

The armed officers moved like robots, their faces covered, helmets low on their heads. She couldn't tell any of them apart — their movements were identical. Honed and practised.

Roper was wheezing to her right, his breath seemingly louder than everyone's footsteps combined.

They came up on the apartment block fast and slowed down.

Hassan motioned MacGinley and Jones forward and they both zipped up coats to cover their vests.

The one that Jamie thought was Jones was breathing hard, her hands shaking.

MacGinley put his hand on her shoulder. 'You good?' he whispered.

She nodded.

'Stay on me, okay?'

She nodded again, faster this time.

'MacGinley,' Thompson hissed, tapping his watch.

MacGinley took a breath, and then stepped out of line and walked into the doorway of the apartment block. The foyer was lit, the light spilling out through the glass doors.

Jones stayed on his shoulder, as instructed, and they walked inside as everyone pressed themselves against the wall.

After a few seconds, the walkie that Thompson had hooked onto the front of his vest crackled quietly. 'Clear,' came MacGinley's voice.

Hassan turned and gave a signal to his men, and they all stepped out from the wall and filed in through the doorway along with Thompson and Cameron. Two uniforms brought up the rear, and then suddenly, Jamie and Roper were alone.

She checked over her shoulder and spotted the two other uniformed officers in the distance, patrolling the space between the two apartment buildings.

Jamie exhaled and relaxed, feeling her heart slow. 'Now we wait,' she muttered.

'Mmm,' Roper hummed, stepping out from the wall and peering in through the apartment door. Jamie stepped carefully away from the concrete, catching a glimpse of the first lot of armed officers bundling into the lift. They'd go up in two batches, ready for the breach.

'Crazy stuff,' Roper said, pushing a cigarette into his mouth. He squinted upwards in the rain, lighting it. 'Better them than me.'

Jamie swallowed, feeling her throat tight. 'Never appealed to you?' she asked, feeling like she needed to keep her voice low.

He shrugged. 'Enough chance of getting shot or stabbed as it is without putting yourself in more danger. I can see why people do it though.'

She thought about her father. He'd always carried a gun. Always liked having it.

Jamie didn't know if that was inviting violence or just being prepared. Probably a little of both.

'Disembarking on nineteen,' came Captain Hassan's voice from Roper's belt. He kept sucking on the cigarette like nothing was happening. 'Clear.'

'What about you?'

'What about me?' Jamie asked.

'You want to be up there, or you happy being down on the sidelines?'

'I can't say I wouldn't want to be the one putting my boot in Donnie's back, but...' She could see Roper eyeing her. 'I think we've had enough excitement for one week, don't you?'

'Nineteen, clear, lift coming back down,' came Hassan's even voice.

Jamie and Roper watched in silence as the second batch of armed officers piled into the box and it sailed smoothly upwards.

'That we have,' Roper said, carrying on the conversation seamlessly. 'How are you, by the way?'

Jamie arched an eyebrow. 'After Paxton?'

He nodded. 'And the suspension.'

She sighed, reliving it. She didn't know if she'd ever forget it. In fact, she knew she wouldn't. 'I'm okay,' she said after a few seconds.

'Smith'll still put you in for psych, no doubt. Wellness, and all that.' Roper had the same old-hat dismissive attitude of mental health as a lot of people. Depressed? Buck up. Anxious? Don't be. Stressed? What have you got to be stressed about?

She kept her mind straight, but talking helped, and the Met was getting a lot better at dealing with the fallout from incidents like that. She was half surprised that he hadn't put her in for counselling already.

She knew he would the second the investigation was over.

Hassan's voice came over again. 'Moving up to twenty.'

'You get used to it,' Roper said, dropping the cigarette and grinding it out under his toe. 'I've seen so much shit in my years… this sort of thing doesn't really affect you after a while.'

Jamie resisted saying, *no wonder it didn't affect you. You ran away before the blood started pouring*. Instead she said, 'I bet.'

'Counselling? We never had that. Not when we needed it. Not when we didn't. We just got on with things.'

Jamie could name ten detectives who'd retired early due to stress and PTSD. The job took its toll. She was glad now that people were recognising that.

'Moving in,' came MacGinley's voice. 'One suspect, top of the stairs.' He was whispering, his voice muffled as he rested his chin on his chest to speak into the walkie.

She could picture them moving up the stairs towards the doorway, towards the kid there on the chair.

MacGinley must have toggled the switch. They could hear breathing and shuffling steps as they got to the top of the steps.

'Ready?' he whispered to Jones.

Jamie and Roper both held their breath, staring up into the darkness.

'Go.'

The door whined on the hinge and there was a shout — Jamie couldn't tell what. Something banged and clattered and then there was a loud grunt, a hiss.

'Knife!' It was Jones.

Someone yelled.

'Move! Move!' Hassan was yelling now.

Footsteps on the stairs.

Someone groaning.

Someone shouting.

It was a mess.

'Stay down! Stay down!' Thompson was yelling now.

'Gerroff! Bats! Baaaats!' The kid was screaming his lungs out, no doubt subdued.

'Shut up!'

'MacGinley!' It was Jones again. 'Jesus! We need an ambulance.

MacGinley!'

The uniformed officers who had hung back now rushed towards their patrol car to call it in.

Hassan's voice echoed through the melee and Roper and Jamie squinted upwards, both on edge. 'Form up. On three — one, two — breach!'

A huge crash resounded down the airwaves as the armed officers rammed the door down, drowning out MacGinley's mewling cries.

'Keep pressure — Jones! Keep pressure on it!' Thompson got to his feet and pounded down the hallway now, presumably towards Donnie's door. MacGinley was down, the kid subdued — but only after he'd managed to stab MacGinley by the sounds of it.

Jamie's throat was tight, her heart beating against the inside of her chest.

Roper was stoic, his lips turned down into an ugly grimace.

A thunderous bang rang out, and then another, coming through as barely more than static. Flashbangs.

'Living room — clear!'

'Bedroom — clear!'

The officers checked off the rooms.

'Bathroom — one target.'

There was yelling.

'It's not Bats. Shit.'

'Bathroom — clear.'

'Second apartment?'

'Two suspects — subdued.'

'Bats?' It was Thompson.

'He's not here.'

'What?'

'He's not here!'

'Bedroom door — locked.'

'Form up. Michaels, Shaughnessy.' Hassan again. 'One, two — breach!'

Another crash.

'Room clear! Wait—'

'What is it?' Thompson was running, panting.

'What the hell is this?' One of the armed officers.

'Jesus Christ, he—'

'Move, move! Get down to nineteen. The goddamn asshole's — shit, move, get out of the way — he's cut through the floor!' Hassan was yelling.

'What?'

MacGinley was still moaning.

'Move, move!'

Jamie and Roper both froze.

'Goddammit! Where is he? Anyone got a visual?' Thompson's voice was frantic.

'Negative. Proceeding to nineteen.'

Jamie and Roper both came forward instinctively, neither breathing.

'Stairwell, clear! Moving to eighteen!' Hassan.

'Check the goddamn lift!' Thompson.

'It's — it's moving! I can't — it won't stop.' That was Cameron.

'Eighteen — clear.' Hassan again, breathing hard, feet churning on the steps. 'Moving to seventeen. No sign of the suspect.'

'Jesus Christ — this is a shit show! Roper, Johansson — come back.' Thompson was breathless, running. Pounding down the stairs as well.

Jamie and Roper both looked at each other.

The lift was coming down, and Donnie was in it.

Jamie looked over her shoulder. The uniforms were gone, back to the car to call for an ambulance. It was just them. The last line of defence. If Donnie was going to be stopped, it was then and there.

Roper let out a long breath and cracked his neck. 'Looks like I picked hell of a day to quit drinking.'

Jamie set her teeth and curled her fists, stepping back from the door to give herself room. Donnie was coming out of there like a freight train. They had to be ready.

Roper looked at her. 'Stand back,' he said, trying to sound confident. 'I'll take him.'

Jamie glanced at Roper — a little shy of six feet and wiry. Bats was stacked muscle and fat. Roper would never be able to take him down.

And now that it was coming down to it, could she? Cake and his pads were one thing, but this was a guy who was going to kill before he was captured.

She gave Roper space. Maybe he *would* take him down. Be the hero.

That would be something.

And as much as she wanted it to be the truth, as the lift bottomed out, she knew deep down that it wasn't the case.

Bats was going to go through him like he was made of paper, and then it would just be her.

And she didn't think she'd ever been more terrified.

Roper squared up to the doors and Jamie gave him space until her heels squelched in the soft mud separating the entrance from the green in front of the building.

She could see his shoulders rising and falling quickly as he reached for the walkie on his belt, pulling it to his mouth. 'This is Roper,' he said, almost absently. He didn't sound like himself. 'Bats is here. He's on the ground.' He dropped it behind him and sank into his knees a little, readying himself.

The elevator bottomed out and dinged beyond the door, the light above it illuminating.

Time seemed to stand still as the doors slid open.

There was a moment of nothing, and then a shape flew from it.

Bats was big, maybe an inch over six feet, and wide-set. His round shoulders made him look like a bread-roll, but considering the extra weight he was carrying, he moved fast.

His close shaven head and thick stubble tracked down his neck and joined with the knots of chest hair sticking out of the top of his white vest. But it wasn't the unshaved beard or bearish body hair that Jamie and Roper homed in on.

It was the baseball bat he was carrying.

Donnie Bats looked up as he hung a right and sprinted for the door.

He didn't know if Roper was carrying a weapon or not, so his only priority was closing down the gap as quickly as he could so as not to get shot.

Roper froze, fists half raised as Donnie kicked the door open with the heel of his tan work-boots and lunged forward.

Roper tried to react, cocking his fist a half second too late.

Jamie didn't see what happened, the view obscured by Roper's back, but he doubled forward, his knees rising to his chest, and then collapsed over Donnie's arm.

Bats rolled sideways around him, ripping the hilt of the bat from Roper's guts — he'd slammed the thing lengthwise into his stomach and blown all the wind out of him.

Roper twisted onto one hand and a knee, expelling all the air he had in his crippled lungs with a high-pitched whine, and slumped to the floor clutching at his midriff.

Bats regained himself, face sculpted into an ugly snarl, and locked onto Jamie.

His best bet of escape would be to disappear across the green, into the darkness, and then into the depths of the city.

And the only thing that stood in his way was Jamie.

She stayed loose, pushed all the air out of her lungs, and tensed her body as Donnie took three big steps forward, slid his hands to the handle of the bat, and wound up like a pro-league slugger.

He was right-handed, pressing into his right foot.

It hit the ground, took his weight as he twisted back, hoping the threat of the swing would be enough to make her dive for cover.

It took a long time to break the mind out of wanting to run when outclassed. But eventually, with enough practice, facing down a bigger opponent turned into a problem of angles and timing, not of weight and power.

Jamie danced to her left foot, putting it close to Donnie, and then skipped right as he cocked the bat behind his head.

The balls of her right foot hit the ground somewhere outside Donnie's left heel and she leaned into it, flexing her leg, her left knee rising towards her chest.

She filled her lungs quickly as Donnie froze, following her around to his off-side, recalculating his swing to deal with her new position.

Jamie lashed out as he began to spin, throwing her left heel into the side of his left knee.

It popped, the impact reverberating back into her own hip.

Donnie buckled, the bat now unwinding with a sinister hiss.

He cried out, the bat flying wildly in a wide arc.

Jamie was already on her left again now, planting it in front of her right, Donnie almost completely behind her.

She couldn't think about the bat — didn't have time. She was sacrificing her defence for a strike, ignoring every fibre of her instinct telling her to get the hell out of the way.

But she wasn't going to. Because if she did, if she dove forward under its path, he'd be on top of her and there'd be no stopping him. He'd kill her in a second.

No, this was it. Her foot, his bat.

Her right leg lifted, arcing upwards at a steep angle, her left knee straining under the motion as she twisted into it, showing her back to Donnie, using the weight of her foot to swing up and around.

In the last instant she clenched her fists, dropping her right arm into the path of the bat to protect her ribs.

It connected with a dull crack and pain ripped through her arm.

But what was happening in her heel was separate. It was muscle memory.

At the same moment the bat connected, her knee hinged and the muscles in her back and hip brought it in tight, behind Donnie's swing, and slingshotted her heel square into his nose.

It exploded under the crescent-hook and Donnie reeled backwards, a thick blood mist punctuating the air.

Jamie was flying before she knew what had happened.

She hit the ground with a dull thud and the pain rippled through her arm in waves, threatening to push her into unconsciousness.

She was screaming before she even registered that she was, fire ripping through her fingers.

She could feel the pavement cold under her cheek, hear nothing but a ringing in her ears.

Instinctively she tried to crawl — if Donnie could stand, he'd bludgeon her. He'd crush her skull. He'd kill her.

She had to move.

Her left hand moved out ahead and scrabbled on the tarmac, her nails straining against the beds as she tried to move.

It was no good, she was lame, her right arm folded underneath her, throbbing and smarting all at once.

There were tears in her eyes, her vision blurry and pulsing black.

Footsteps behind her.

No.

Hands on her collar.

No!

She was rolled roughly onto her back and kicked out with her legs, scissoring as hard as she could.

They connected with something solid and she flipped herself onto her right side, wailing as the pain bolted into her shoulder and chest.

More hands, on her lapels this time.

Everything above her was blurry with tears.

'Get off!' she roared, trying to kick again, feeling her laces connect with a solid mass.

Someone's ribs.

An arm locked around her foot and pinned it in place.

'Get off!'

'Hey!' came a rough voice. Bats! He had her.

She pulled her left arm up to protect her face and threw her right heel out, aiming for the general vicinity of the crotch, and hit home.

Bats grunted and let go.

'Jesus, stop!' came the voice again.

Her brain stuttered — it didn't sound like Bats.

She kicked herself backwards, trying for space, and blinked quickly, trying to restore her vision, her heart thundering in her ears.

A shape swam into view. But it wasn't a shaved head and round shoulders — it was the black dome of a helmet, the sharp angles of shoulder pads and body armour.

Hassan, clutching at his groin, stared at her from under the brim of his helmet. 'Johansson!' he wheezed, holding out a hand, willing her to stop. 'It's me, you're okay — Jesus —' He coughed and spat on the ground. She'd caught him good. 'It's me...' He went to a knee, raking in deep breaths. 'You... that's... a hell of a kick.' He retched a few times, jamming his fist into his stomach.

She looked past him towards the scene behind, cradling her right arm. She could see three figures on their feet — what looked like two armed response officers and Cameron, all panting like they'd just run a marathon. Thompson was crouched, one knee in the middle of Donnie Bat's back, snatching at the Right to Silence between ragged breaths as he fumbled for a pair of cuffs.

Bats was face down on the floor, his face tilted towards her. His eyes were closed, his nose a pulpy purple mess, the side of his face soaked with his blood.

She'd kicked him unconscious.

A strange, single-noted laugh escaped her lips and she laid her head back, descending into a sobbing cry as her grip tightened around her right elbow, the pain not like anything she'd ever experienced.

Her mind remembered the crack that had rung out when Donnie's bat had connected.

It was broken.

There wasn't a doubt in her. Her elbow — or her arm — her ulna, her radius, her humerus — all three. She didn't know. But something was broken.

Hassan heaved himself to his feet and came over to her, kneeling down at her side, leaning over her.

She could hear Roper coughing and swearing somewhere out of view, could hear Thompson snapping cuffs around Bats's wrists.

They must have hammered it down the eighteen flights the second they realised Bats was in the elevator.

But without Jamie, he would have gotten away.

'Johansson,' Hassan said, grabbing her by the shoulders. 'Are you okay?'

She didn't know if she was laughing or crying — it felt like both. All she could feel was pain.

'Speak to me,' he urged her. 'Are you okay?'

'No,' she wheezed, cradling her elbow. She looked up at him, at the concern in his eyes.

'What's wrong?' he asked desperately, squeezing at the top of her arms with his big hands.

She gritted her teeth against the pain, feeling tears streaming down her cheeks. 'My goddamn arm's broken… And you're leaning on it!'

37

Her ulna was fractured and chipped.

The x-ray revealed that the bat had impacted just below the tip and resulted in a pair of lengthways running fractures, as well as chip being separated from the head of the bone. On top of that the bone bruising was severe, nerve damage was possible, and her skin had swollen up like a plum. In both colour and shape. The welt was darker than she ever thought it possible for human skin to turn.

All in all, it hurt like holy hell.

They set it and got her into a hard cast which she'd need for three to six weeks, followed by a flexi-cast. Depending on how quickly the chip fused.

Despite the break, though, she was back at HQ by one that afternoon.

They'd brought Bats in and after getting his nose set, put him into an interrogation room.

Word had spread quickly of what she'd done, and despite the cast, people had still wanted to give her high-fives and back-pats. She couldn't believe how tough it was to coordinate a high-five with her left hand.

Jamie treated herself to the elevator, her brain a little fuzzy from the painkiller they'd given her, and stepped out on her floor.

Things seemed subdued. Some of the team were missing — Thompson, Cameron, Jones, MacGinley.

MacGinley was at the hospital, the stabbing described as *superficial*. Jones was with him. Cameron and Thompson were interrogating Bats, and the others who weren't on the floor… Jamie didn't know where they were. But the place seemed empty.

She was glad of that. She didn't think she could handle any more excitement.

Smith was standing in the doorway of his own office. He folded his arms as their eyes met, and then gave her a single nod of approval, twisting his face into something resembling a smile.

That was all she needed.

She returned it and headed for her desk, sitting at it with a satisfied sigh.

He'd told her she could have the day off to recover, but she wanted to be there for Donnie's interrogation, and get a jump on her paperwork. It had a way of mounting up fast when you were away from your desk.

Roper appeared with a cup of coffee in his hand as usual. 'Hey,' he said.

'Hey yourself. How's the stomach?'

'I think my pride is more bruised. Coffee?'

She curled a smile. 'I'm not falling for that again.'

He laughed a little. 'No, look — coffee.' He put the cup down in front of her. It was still steaming.

She picked it up with her left hand and tried not to spill any. 'Thanks,' she said.

'You earned it.'

'Gee, if I knew that getting my arm broken by a madman was all it took to get you to make me a cup of coffee, I would have done it years ago.'

He chuckled. 'Well, don't get used to it.'

'I've still got another arm.'

'And two legs. If you get them all broken at the same time you get a hot-chocolate instead.'

'I'll bear that in mind.' She laughed and took a sip. It was good. 'Bats crack yet?'

Roper shrugged. 'Don't think so. Thompson's sweating him. But if nothing else, we've got him on assaulting two officers.' He clicked his tongue and pointed to himself and then her. 'Which is enough to get him convicted, if only for a little while.'

'Every cloud, I guess.'

'Yeah,' he laughed.

'Hey, how's MacGinley doing?'

'Stable, but he'll be off his feet for a week or so by the sounds of it.'

'Good. Was a close one.'

'Yup.'

'I'm just glad Donnie's off the streets.'

'Mm,' Roper hummed. 'Not sure whether or not we'll be able to nail him on Hammond's murder, though.'

'Why not?'

'If he doesn't confess, we've only got circumstantial at best. The kid Thompson flipped didn't know anything about it and when they tossed his apartment they found nothing that would put Hammond there.' Roper looked over her head, inspected the room, then came back to her. 'Must have been keeping him somewhere else. And if he's not talking…'

Jamie sighed. 'Damn. Still, he's going down. And that's the important thing.'

'Yeah,' Roper said. 'Still, would have been nice to have our names on the case.'

'It's all for the greater good, right?'

He scoffed. 'Sure. Because detectives get promoted off the back of the *greater good.*'

'We'll get there,' Jamie said, smiling up at him. The painkillers were wearing off, her arm throbbing again. 'We just gotta keep putting bad guys away.'

'Haven't we just.' He clapped his hands. 'Right, I'm going to go and fill in my reports before they all fall down and crush me.'

Jamie exhaled, looking at her computer screen. 'Yeah, better get to mine, too.' The thought of doing them all with one hand — and her left at that — was almost as bad as facing down Bats.

Roper gave her a faux salute and strode away, leaving Jamie alone at her desk.

She looked at the screen again, wondering whether she could face even starting.

After a few seconds she reached for her phone instead, pulling it awkwardly out of her opposite pocket. She thumbed it open with her left hand and found Elliot's number. They'd taken her to Charring Cross, not St. Mary's, for the x-ray and cast, so she hadn't been able to check in on Grace. She'd tried Elliot when she was there, but it had gone straight to voicemail. She'd not left a message.

But when she'd called the hospital and given Grace's name, they said she hadn't checked out and was still in recovery.

That was something at least.

They didn't know about Elliot, but he'd said that he was working a nightshift the day after, so maybe he was just sleeping.

She clicked his name and listened as the call connected and then rang. After a few rings, Elliot answered. 'Hey,' he said brightly.

'Hi,' Jamie replied, grinning to herself. She leaned back on her chair and looked up. 'How're you doing?'

'I'm okay — sore neck. But sleeping in a chair'll do that to you.'

'I tried to call earlier.'

'Yeah, sorry. My phone died. I've not long got home.'

'How's Grace?'

'Doing a little better. She came to, but she needs to detox. It's going to be a rough withdrawal period — hopefully rough enough to keep her hospitalised.' He took a breath. 'I don't mean—'

'I know what you mean. The hospital is the best place for her.'

'I can check in on her during my shift — ask the nurses to let me know if she gets nervous, tries to leave.'

'That's good.'

'What's wrong?' Elliot asked, perceptive as always. He was reading the tentativeness in her voice.

'Nothing,' she almost croaked. She was nervous, all of a sudden.

'Is everything okay?'

'Yeah, it's just… We got the guy.'

'What guy?'

'The guy who killed Oliver. Really mean son-of-a-bitch. Nearly slipped away.' She could feel herself grinning again and she looked at her broken arm. 'But we got him.'

Elliot was silent for a second. 'That's… That's really great.' He sighed with relief. 'Grace will be happy. With Paxton gone as well, she'll be able to breathe easier.'

'Hopefully start putting her life back together.'

'I really hope so too.'

There was silence for a few more seconds and Jamie could hear her heart in her ears, nervous again. 'You know, now that we've got him…'

Elliot waited patiently. She thought he knew what she was going to say. 'Yes?'

'The investigation is as good as over.'

He kept waiting.

'Which means you're no longer a witness.'

He was punishing her. She knew it.

'Which means there's no longer a conflict of interest…'

He was definitely punishing her.

'If we wanted to, you know…'

'You know *what?*'

She growled a little. 'You're going to make me say it?'

He chuckled a little and she had the same prickle in the back of her head she had when they'd first met.

'Do you want to have dinner with me?'

He exhaled slowly, drawing it out.

'Jeez, come on!' She laughed. 'Before we're old.'

He laughed. 'Sure. I'd love to. When?'

'Tonight? Before work?'

He sucked air in through his teeth. 'I can't — I'm heading in early, in a few hours. Won't be done until the morning. What about tomorrow, though?'

'That sounds great.' She looked around the room. No one seemed to care that she was on the phone.

'Okay. I'll call you.'

'I'm looking forward to it.'

'Me too.' He hung up and she put the phone on her desk, still grinning.

After a few seconds, she fired up her computer screen and cracked her neck. No point procrastinating anymore. The quicker she got started, the quicker she'd be done.

Two hours later, she was reminded of how painfully slow her progress was.

Roper sidled over, shuffling freshly printed pages from the printer into a case file.

He dropped it on Jamie's desk with a dull clap and then leaned against it.

'I think this is the first time I've ever finished my reports before you.'

'I am lame,' Jamie said, shaking her broken arm. She instantly regretted it and winced.

'Maybe you're just losing your edge.' He shrugged. 'Or maybe I'm just becoming a beacon of efficiency.'

'Neither of those statements are true,' she said, running her hand through her hair, pushing the errant strands off her forehead.

'Well, take a look for yourself. Tell me if it's up to standard.' He pushed it towards her. 'Some of my best work, I think.'

She laughed a little. 'If you say so.'

Jamie pulled it in front of her and flipped the page. 'What, no clip-art?'

'Just read the damn thing,' he chuckled.

Jamie scanned the document. It looked okay. Excellent for Roper.

Though he was usually stinking of a hangover when he did his paper-work, so there was something to be said there. Jamie would have bet there was a direct correlation between the quality of his reporting and the volume of alcohol imbibed the night before.

But she didn't say anything.

'Oliver Hammond,' she muttered, reading his notes. 'Yup, we were on scene originally… Times look good. Initial assessment…' She nodded, checking things off in her head as she went. 'Seems accurate to me. Coroner's report?' She looked up.

'Next page.'

She found it and kept reading. 'Coroner's notes included — right. Ligature marks on the wrists. Fingernails torn off — suspected self-inflicted. Wood particles found in the nail beds.' Jamie stuck out her bottom lip, skimming quickly. 'Lacerations to the soles of the feet congruent with a short run over paved surfaces. Particulates extracted confirm running on a roadway. Evidence of a cannula.' She paused. 'Cannula?'

Roper was chewing his lip. She could see he was dying for a cigarette. 'Yeah,' he said, holding his hands up. 'Looks like that's how they were administering the drug to keep him sedated.'

She leaned back and sucked on her cheek, thinking about it.

'Him and Bats might have agreed on the whole ransom thing, but it seems like he wasn't taking any chances.' Roper added.

'No?'

'The report says that he was in good health, otherwise.'

'Does it?' Jamie's chair creaked as she rocked back and forth on it.

'Yeah — no signs of dehydration. Emaciation was limited, all things considered.'

'Huh.'

'Yeah. Maybe he really was getting back on the straight and narrow. Making a real go of getting off the heroin, like Grace said.'

'What do you mean?' Jamie cocked her head.

'The kid was clean. Not a trace of heroin in his system, and there were no signs of withdrawal, either.'

'But they were keeping him dosed, right? So he didn't make a break for it?'

'Not with heroin.'

'With what, then?'

'Er...' Roper scratched his head. 'Tri... Something. Trimoxi... Triazapam? Tri—'

'Triazolam,' Jamie said, reading it on the overleaf. 'Trace amounts.' She sank her teeth into her bottom lip. 'Why does that sound familiar to me?'

'I dunno,' Roper said, shrugging. 'But it looks like it wore off. There was barely anything in his system when they pushed him in the river.'

'That makes no sense.' Jamie drew a slow breath.

'What doesn't?'

'Why they'd push him in the river if the drug had worn off — hell, if he'd run there, throwing him in the river wouldn't guarantee his death. He could have swum for it?'

Roper arched an eyebrow. 'It's November, Jamie. Kid would have frozen whether he was dosed or not.'

'It still doesn't make sense. Why they wouldn't just grab him?'

'So he jumped. Tried to get away. What does it matter? Donnie's in custody, and he's going down. Paxton told you he did it. Five minutes ago, there wasn't a doubt in your mind that Bats was the guy.'

Jamie exhaled. 'Yeah, I know. Guess we'll never get the full story.'

Roper shrugged again. 'We did a good thing, Jamie. You did an amazing thing. Taking down Bats? You should get a medal, or whatever they give out for doing something like that.'

She laughed. 'A commendation, you mean?'

'How the hell should I know? I've never had one.'

They both laughed.

'Right, I'm going for a smoke.'

'See you.'

Roper headed for the lift, leaving the file with Jamie.

She kept turning the pages.

Triazolam. Where did she know that from? She leaned forward and pulled up a search engine on screen, typing it in.

It was in the benzodiazepine family — used for anaesthetic. From a biological standpoint it made sense to use that if they wanted to keep Oliver in place until the ransom came through. It was stable. Had all the right properties. Though she didn't know where the hell Bats would have got something like that and why he wouldn't just use heroin instead. But then again, he was a man of means and dealt drugs for a living. It wouldn't be that hard for him to get hold of something like that. She was sure he probably knew someone who could get their hands on it.

She sighed and flipped the next page. There was a photo of the gold watch they'd found at Grace's tent. It was in a plastic evidence bag.

Jamie stared at the picture. She could picture Bats wearing it. Or Paxton. Or maybe Grace stole it from someone else entirely. Or Oliver did. Maybe it was Oliver's dad's.

She rubbed her eyes, the pain in her arm bordering on searing.

It was all too much.

She picked up her phone and rang down to holding, asked if she could speak to Thompson or Cameron.

Thompson was in with Bats but Cameron was on the other side of the glass. She got connected to him.

'Yeah?' he said stiffly. Just from the tone Jamie could tell that the interrogation wasn't going as well as they'd hoped.

'It's Johansson.'

'Humph,' he said. 'How's the arm?'

'Been better. How's it going?'

He sighed emphatically. 'What d'you want? You and Roper better not be asking to get in on this.'

'No,' Jamie said. 'It's your show. It's just...'

'Yeah?'

'I've got a loose piece of evidence that I can't tie to anyone. If you run out of questions, you want to ask Bats if he's missing a watch?'

'A watch?'

'Yeah, gold thing. Kind of classy. Expensive.'

'Sort of thing a drug dealer wears.'

'I guess,' she said with a little laugh. 'I can't say I know any to comment.'

'Humph.' It was almost a chuckle. But just one syllable of one. 'I'll keep it in mind. Though if nailing this son-of-a-bitch comes down to asking about a gold watch, I think we've got bigger problems.'

'Just a thought.'

'Sure. And hey, you did good this morning.'

'Thanks.'

He hung up without another word and Jamie replaced the phone.

It was still niggling at her.

But her head was all over the place. The pain, combined with the painkillers and the lack of sleep was making everything murky.

Her progress on the reports was as good as non-existent, too. She could do with taking some time to gather her thoughts.

Some fresh air, maybe.

There was a spark of something fizzling in the back of her mind.

But she just couldn't put her finger on it.

She was out of her chair before she realised, heading for the door.

If she couldn't think her way through this, she'd have to rely on her gut.

And right now, it was telling her that she was missing something.

And before the case was closed, she was damn sure going to find out what.

38

J amie got outside and found Roper just pulling the last smoke out of his cigarette.

'Coming over to the dark side? Want to be one of the cool kids, eh?' he said with a grin, offering her the smoking butt of his cigarette.

She held her good hand up. 'No thanks.'

'Oh no,' he said with a sigh reading the expression on her face. 'I know that look.'

'Come on,' Jamie said. 'We're going.'

He flicked his butt into the ashtray on top of the bin next to the door and put his hands on his hips. 'Jamie, come on. Think about this.'

'Think about what?'

'Don't you see it? We can't nail Bats for the murder, so you're reaching for something else. Your creating these holes in the case, looking for another killer because you don't feel like we got him.' He smiled warmly at her. 'But we did. And though our names aren't on the arrest sheet, that—' he pointed to her cast '—is proof that you took this piece of shit down.'

'But—'

'No buts, Jamie. The investigation is over. Now I'm heading back inside.' He started for the door. 'Going to put this thing to rest, and then… And then it's onto the next one.'

He stared at her for a few seconds and she stared back, trying not to glare. She needed him on this one.

He sighed. 'I'll see you upstairs, okay?'

She nodded slowly and he went inside.

Jamie waited until she was sure he wasn't coming back, and then turned and walked the other way around the building towards the city.

She grabbed a taxi off the street and headed to Elliot's, picked her car up, and then headed north.

While she sat in traffic, she rolled everything over in her mind.

It was getting late in the afternoon now and people were beginning to head home for the day.

Driving with one good arm was tough and the fingertips on her right hand were tingling, her whole arm trapped somewhere between numb and on fire.

She didn't want to take any more of the pills they'd given her, though. She needed to think. She needed to be clear.

There were puzzle pieces laid down in front of her, but she couldn't figure out how they all fit together.

The start. She had to go back to the start. Retrace her steps.

The river. The Lea.

She headed there as the light began to fade and parked in nearly the same spot that she had when it had all started.

At this time of day things seemed different. The light was flatter, waning with every second.

The sky looked as beaten up as she felt, full with rain but not bursting just yet.

The clouds hung over the city, brooding and still.

Jamie walked across the street towards the riverbank where they'd first seen Oliver's body.

The grate that spanned the bridge was full with sticks and leaves washed down from further upriver, but the current was fairly slow-moving. Still, the water would be cold and fully clothed she wouldn't want to take her chances coming out of a stupor in the middle of the night.

She crouched and touched the cold earth where his body had been.

There was no sign there'd ever been anything there.

Jamie exhaled and stood up, looking around.

The medical examiner's report had said that the damage to Oliver's feet wasn't that extensive. But was congruent with a relatively short run.

Donnie's apartment block was miles from the River. Though the report from it had said there was no sign that Oliver had been kept there.

Where would he have been kept? Somewhere quiet that he couldn't be found, or wouldn't be heard if he came around and started screaming. Somewhere private.

Hell, where was private in London?

She didn't know.

Jamie headed back to her car. Nothing was presenting itself just yet.

The air was thick and cool, ready to tear itself apart, pressing her clothes into her skin, making them damp.

She shivered as she pulled out from the corner and traced a path towards the homeless shelter.

It was after five when she arrived and the sun had blotted itself out behind the buildings to the west, throwing deep shadows across the city.

Street lamps hummed to life around her, drowning everything in an orange bath.

Jamie closed the car door with a dull thunk and zipped up a hooded jumper — the only thing she'd had in work that was stretchy enough to fit over her cast.

Mary Cartwright was just locking up as she crossed the street, turning an inordinately large set of keys in the door with an audible jangle.

'Mrs Cartwright,' Jamie called, jogging a little. The motion made her arm ache and she winced as she got up onto the kerb.

'Oh,' Mary said, startled. 'Detective Johansson — this is a surprise.'

'Sorry to bother you like this.'

'No, no, it's fine. What can I do for you?' Mary was her usual bright self.

Other than the two of them, the street was completely empty.

'I was hoping to take another look around the shelter, if that would be possible?'

Mary bit her lip, sucked in a long breath, and then checked her watch. 'I would... But I've got dinner plans, and I'm probably not going to have enough time as it is.' She shifted from foot to foot.

'I can come back,' Jamie said politely, though she didn't really want to. It would be gridlock traffic at this time, and she didn't really know where else she was going to go. She hoped that the shelter would give her something.

Mary sighed. 'You know what? This door latches — just set the lock and pull it after you.' She smiled warmly. 'I'd hate to disrupt your investigation, and who are we kidding, there's nothing worth stealing in there anyway!' She laughed and Jamie joined her for the sake of her entry into the building.

'Thank you,' Jamie said. 'I'll make sure it's locked when I leave.'

'I'm sure. If you can't trust the police, who can you trust?' She laughed again, almost madly. Jamie didn't know if she was in high spirits because of her dinner plans, or if working here was making her lose her mind. Either way, she thanked Mary again and waited for her to unlock the door.

She pushed it inwards and Jamie stepped over the threshold.

'If you need anything or you get trouble with the door, just give me a call. You have my number, don't you?'

'It's on file,' Jamie assured her, holding the door open.

'Great. Well, I hope you find what you're looking for. I have to dash.'

'Enjoy your dinner.'

'Ha! I'll try.' She shook her head and walked away.

Jamie didn't know what that meant, and on her list of things to figure out, it didn't place very highly.

She closed the door behind her and watched as the latch snapped shut.

It couldn't be opened from the other side without a key, and all Mary was doing was setting the deadbolt underneath.

Jamie wouldn't be interrupted. Which was what she wanted.

Peace. Silence. Solitude. Time.

She stepped forward and flicked the lights on.

They hissed and sputtered to life, illuminating the room and low-slung stage.

The scent of oxtail soup and sweat hung in the air.

Jamie exhaled and looked around, not knowing exactly where to start, but hoping that somewhere in this room there was something that would point her in the right direction. Either towards the conclusions already drawn, or in another direction.

She wasn't sure which she hoped it was.

After thirty minutes of searching, she'd found nothing except a soiled sock and evidence that there were ants living under the stage. Otherwise, there was nothing of interest out front.

Jamie slumped backwards and let the curtain that separated the underside of the stage from the audience fall back into place.

A plume of dust rose up in the light. Her eyes were beginning to ache and her arm was throbbing. She'd caught it a few times.

All in all, she was getting tired and disheartened.

Jamie looked around, wondering whether it was time to call it a day.

She sighed and pushed herself to her feet. They hadn't looked in the bathroom when they'd first come in, but after a quick inspection, Jamie decided there was nothing of use in there. At least not for the investigation.

The homeless people using the shelter were using it heavily by the looks of things. Everything was filthy, but other than the urine sprayed around the toilets and the grime in the sinks, there was nothing else to find.

Feeling a little bit queasy — partially because of the pain in her arm and partially due to the faeces spattered on one of the toilet bowls — she headed back into the main room.

'Two down,' she said, staring at the back office. 'One to go. And then... I can move on.' She rarely talked to herself, but it seemed appropriate now. Maybe Roper was right and she was just reaching for something.

Jamie looked up, seeing her father leaning against the stage, arms folded. He was looking at her intensely.

'What?' Jamie growled, heading for the office.

'Nothing,' he said, smiling like he always did. Like he was in on a joke no one else was.

'Want to let me in on what you're thinking?'

He lifted his shoulders slowly, never looking away.

'Helpful as always.'

He laughed a little and then looked at the office door.

'Yeah, yeah,' she muttered, heading for it.

It wasn't locked and creaked open.

The door moved slowly, banging on the jamb.

Jamie shivered, staring into the darkness.

Everything was silent.

She reached inside the frame and looked for the light switch, feeling on the wall for it.

Her fingers touched the smooth plastic and the tension in her shoulders eased.

The light flickered to life overhead and threw a pale, clinical brilliance over the room. The same examination bench in the corner. The same sink and hand towel dispenser.

Nothing of interest.

Jamie moved in and looked around. Where didn't she look last time?

She remembered her father's advice. Make it a process. Map a route. Check things off one at a time. Search methodically.

She exhaled and turned, facing the corner. She'd work in a clockwise direction, turn every stone.

It just so happened there was no stone to turn in the corner, but there were the steps up to the stage door.

She pressed her foot into the bottom one, felt it give a little.

What was she even looking for?

The steps must have been put in when the building was built. The sixties some time. Steps back then were different. Fashion was different. They were missing the upright panels, the backs. They were just slats between two pieces of wood.

Jamie squinted through the gap into the darkness underneath.

She didn't look there before.

The room smelled like ethanol sanitiser as she moved through it.

At the side of the steps, a blue curtain had been stapled in place, roughly hacked straight so that its hem fell to the floor.

Jamie lifted it and reached underneath, pulling out an old cardboard box.

The material felt soft and musty under her fingers.

Inside, she found a few old paint cans. She pulled up the handles and shook them. Of the three, two were solid, the paint inside long-since dried. But the third still held liquid.

When she checked the labels, she found that it looked a lot newer than the others.

'Huh,' she muttered, looking around the room. The paints matched. New and old. But the same colour.

If this place hadn't been decorated since the sixties, then maybe Elliot had given it a fresh lick of paint. To cover mould, maybe. He'd gone as far as putting up a towel and sanitiser dispenser. It wasn't out of the question for him to have thrown up a fresh coat of paint. Even if it was the colour of baby-shit.

She never got the British obsession with magnolia. She always preferred white. But maybe that was just the Scandinavian in her.

Jamie pushed the box back in and got up, turning back to the room.

A dull thud rang out and she screwed up her face. 'Goddammit!' she practically yelled, holding her right arm. Pain shot up through her bicep and into her shoulder, the broken bone ringing like a bell. She'd knocked her cast on the steps as she'd turned.

She hissed, feeling like electricity was running through her fingers.

What the hell was she doing? She should be at home, recovering. She should have taken the day off. And now, not only was she *not* taking the day off, she was looking for a killer they'd already caught in a place he'd never been.

It seemed like all the blanks had been filled in except those surrounding the victim himself.

She didn't know Oliver.

Part of her thought that he was just a wayward kid, in love with a girl, trying to save her…

And part of her thought there was more to him. That he was caught up in more than they knew. That what had happened between him and Paxton and Bats would never come to light. That she'd never find out the truth. And with only one of them left, Bats could peddle whatever story he wanted with no one to dispute it.

She knew that Oliver wanted to ransom himself back to his parents to pay off his and Grace's drug debt, but Bats holding up his end of the deal made no sense. He'd be losing two lifetime customers, Paxton would be losing Grace as his… whatever she was to him… And if Bats could extort money from Oliver's well-off parents, then he'd want to get as much as he could. Maybe more than Oliver wanted to ask for.

It made sense. It all fit.

Oliver goes to Bats to make the ransom happen, to be there for the phone call, the crucial *proof of life* that would make it happen. But Bats changes the amount, Oliver gets cold feet, Bats restrains him, drugs him. Then the dose wears off, Oliver makes a run for it… And she knew the rest.

But Jamie needed closure. Or at least to exhaust every other option.

With her arm still throbbing she pressed on. There was little else to inspect in the room. Only the filing cabinets, and she'd already gone through both Oliver's and Grace's files. Elliot hadn't seen either of them since she checked last time, and most of the other drawers were empty.

She sighed and walked towards the examination table.

It looked the same as it did before. Dated. Yellowed sponge sticking through the faux-leather veneer.

She inspected it for the sake of thoroughness, but found nothing. Just rusty screws holding it together and chewing gum stuck under it from a by-gone decade.

Her eyes were growing heavy. Time was wearing on. She'd been in there for over an hour in total, and had found exactly nothing.

It was just the cupboard door next.

She stood up, minding her arm, and stepped towards it.

It was painted shut, like before. Probably had a gas-meter in it. Or black mould. Or asbestos. Painting over it was easier than cleaning it out and dealing with the problem.

Jamie leaned in, inspecting the paint. It looked fresh, like everything else.

There was no handle. It looked like it had been removed. All that remained of it was a lock set flush to the wood. But that looked like it had been painted over too.

Jamie knelt down. She'd not seen it before when she looked.

With her nail she scratched at it and felt it come away under her fingers.

She massaged it between the pads, feeling it flake, and held it to her nose. It still smelled like paint. Which meant it couldn't have been on there long.

In the light, the brass underneath shone, too. The lock looked like it had been replaced recently.

Looking around the room, she wondered when it was painted last. How recently Elliot had gone over the whole place.

Jamie let out a long sigh and stood up.

The floor under her heels creaked and she froze.

Her brow furrowed and she looked down, bouncing on the balls of her feet. It flexed under her and creaked again. The pale wooden laminate — something reminiscent of beech — moved under her weight.

A few steps away from the door there was no movement.

She stomped her heel a few times and felt solid concrete.

But in front of the cupboard door it was floorboards. It was hollow underneath.

Instinctively, she pulled out her phone and opened the case file, looking for Mary's number. She dialled before she could second guess herself, and on the fourth ring, Mary answered.

'Hello?' she said breathlessly. She was walking. Jamie could hear her heels clicking in the background.

'Hi, Mrs. Cartwright — Detective Johansson.'

'Oh, hello,' she said, bright and struggling to keep her breath. 'Is everything okay?'

'Yeah, I just wanted to check something. In the back office—'

'Yes?'

'The cupboard.'

'Cupboard?'

'Yeah.'

'There's no cupboard in the back office.'

'I'm standing right in front of it. The door?'

'Ah, yes. I know where you are. Go on.'

'Wait, if it's not a cupboard, what is it?'

'It's the door to the storeroom.'

'Storeroom?' Jamie looked down, bounced on the floorboards again. 'Is it a basement?'

'Yes. It goes under the main room and the office. Huge space. Nasty, though.'

'Nasty? What do you mean?'

In the background she could hear a man's voice, and then Mary's, muffled as she cupped her hand over the phone. '—yes, yes, I know,' she said. 'I'll just be a second.' Her voice was clear again then. 'Oh, uh — Doctor Day checked it out when he first started using the room. We don't go down there.'

'Why not?'

'—I know, yes. I know — sorry —' She was talking to the man she was with, her husband maybe. He didn't sound very pleased. Jamie was obviously interfering with their plans. 'Detective?'

'I'm here.'

'What were you—'

'Why don't you go down there?'

'Rats.' She sounded hurried now.

'Rats?'

'Yes — Doctor Day said they were everywhere. He put poison down to kill them. I hate the things. Good riddance! But the poison, you know. So we just locked the door and don't go down there. Damp, filthy place. Anything you stored down there would be soaked if it wasn't eaten, anyway.'

'Right.' Jamie looked at the door. 'Is that why he removed the handle?'

'Did he? Oh, I don't — yes. Yes. I know.' She turned from the phone. 'Yes, dear,' she said sharply. 'Okay.'

'I'm keeping you,' Jamie said. 'Sorry.'

'It's fine. My husband,' Mary said. 'Hates to be late. You know how men are.'

'Of course,' Jamie said with a polite laugh. She really didn't.

'I'll be in first thing if you want to come down and take a look. I can open it up for you then.'

'That would be great.'

'Though I don't know what you expect to find.'

Jamie sighed. 'Nothing. I don't expect to find anything, but you know.'

'Is there anything else?'

'No,' Jamie said, still staring at the door. 'That's all.'

'Have a good evening.'

Jamie sank her teeth into her bottom lip, still looking at it. 'Yeah,' she said. 'You too.'

39

J amie was in a box.

Everything was dark and silent.

Her breath felt close, reverberating in her ears.

When she moved her arms, she could feel the sides against the outside of her little fingers.

Her legs were bent upwards, her heels against the bottom.

The crown of her head was touching the top. She could hear her hair rustling on the wood.

'Hello?' she called out, listening as the sound died, muted by the wood.

She lifted her hands and ran them over her body.

She was naked.

Jamie gasped, then shivered, feeling the cold touch of metal against her exposed flank.

With her right hand she reached over and touched her lift wrist, felt the hard, sharp edges of a watch.

She could hear it ticking.

Tick.

Tick.

Tick.

She knew which watch it was.

But she didn't know who it belonged to.

The latch was sealed shut. She couldn't get it off, couldn't slide it over her hand.

She grunted, then cried out, feeling the metal cut into her skin.

Jamie crooked her elbow and felt something pinch sharply.

She reached up with her left hand and touched at the tube taped to her bicep, ran her fingers over the ridge of the needle in her skin, inserted into her vein.

The tube disappeared over her shoulder and through a tiny hole in the side of the box.

Her heart beat harder and she slammed her hands against the lid no more than sixteen inches above her face.

It was solid.

There was no light and no hope of escape.

She was completely alone.

She was trapped.

And there was no one coming for her.

All she could do was scream and beat at the wood.

She wouldn't give up until she was dead.

Jamie's eyes opened slowly and she stared at the blank, white ceiling over her bed.

Her throat was tight and she could feel the sweat beaded on her skin.

A deep, throbbing pain ran through her right arm and she lifted it, squinting in the darkness at the cast. They had forced it into a right-angle to let the bone heal.

The bed covers were tangled around her legs and her heart was beating hard. She'd woken herself up, but hadn't felt panicked. Just sick.

It was as if she knew it was a dream before she opened her eyes. But the feeling of claustrophobia didn't abate.

And yet there was no fear with it, just a weight that seemed to be pressing her in place, like the drug running through the cannula wasn't in effect in the dream, but it was out here.

She lay perfectly still in the darkness and felt something she'd been searching for all night.

Clarity.

Jamie rolled over and picked up her phone. It was just after five in the morning.

She unlocked it and found Elliot's number, pulling up a new message. She simply typed, 'Need to talk to you. Call me if you can.'

She put it back down and swung her legs off the bed, hoping against all odds that she was wrong. That for once her mind was betraying her and that the next few hours weren't going to unfold in the way she was dreading.

Jamie showered, keeping her phone nearby and on loud, her arm covered in an elasticated plastic bag they'd sent her home from the hospital with.

At nearly five-thirty, it began to ring.

Fully dressed, she reached for it with a shaking left hand and pulled it to her ear. 'Hey,' she said, trying to balance her voice. Calmness was what she was aiming for.

'Hi,' Elliot said, sounding tired. 'Everything okay?'

'Yeah,' she said. 'Just couldn't sleep. Bad dream. Just felt like talking to someone. Hope you don't mind?'

'Of course not. Best thing that's happened to me all night.'

'You still in work?'

'Finishing at eight. What was the dream about?'

'Not long then,' she said, dodging the question.

'No,' he said warmly. 'Just one more appendectomy, and then I'm all done.'

'You sound relieved.'

'It's been a long shift.'

'It's been a long week,' she said with a laugh.

'Tell me about it.'

'Pretty much finished now that we got the guy.'

'I called in to see Grace. She was really happy about that,' Elliot said warmly.

'I'm glad.'

'Me too.'

Jamie bit her lip, sat on the sofa with her legs folded up under her. 'So I was just finishing up some paperwork yesterday, and turned out I had to call back to the shelter.'

'Oh?'

'Yeah. Just had to take some photos, you know, get some information of Mary. Cross the Ts and dot the Is. Boring stuff, you know?'

'No, I don't. Doctors don't have to do any paperwork.' He laughed a little and she did her best to join in.

'On my travels, I found something.'

'Oh yeah? And what's that?'

'Guess.' Jamie said, trying to sound humorous.

'Hah, uh… Oh… I don't know? You want to give me a clue?'

'What have you lost?'

'Nothing, as far as I'm aware?' He inflected it like a question, not sure where she was going with it.

'A gold watch? I'm looking at it right now. It's here on my nightstand.'

'Really?' He sounded surprised. 'Where'd you find it?'

'At the shelter. Under the desk. Is it yours?'

There was a pause and Jamie felt her throat tighten.

'Yeah,' he said after a few seconds. 'It's mine.'

'I'll bring it to dinner for you. Are we still on for tonight?'

'Of course,' he said evenly. 'I wouldn't miss it.'

'I'll see you then.'

'I've got to go,' he said. 'They're calling me.'

She didn't hear the tannoy in the background this time. 'Okay.'

'Goodbye, Jamie.'

'Bye.'

He hung up and she felt her grip tighten around her phone.

She exhaled hard and tapped the corner of it against her forehead, filling her lungs as she did. She needed to settle herself. What happened next would decide everything.

Exactly four and a half minutes later she was stepping through her front door and getting into her car.

She'd made three phone calls in that time, woken three people up, and set in motion a series of events that she knew there was no coming back from.

40

J amie was sitting outside the shelter with Roper in her passenger seat, drumming on the steering wheel.

'Come on,' she muttered to herself. 'Where are you?'

'Relax,' Roper said in a quiet voice. He looked tired, but she couldn't smell booze on him.

They were bathed in the orange glow of a streetlight overhead but the sky was still dark and moody. It was going to rain later.

Roper's car was parked behind hers. He'd gotten there surprisingly quickly and after she'd filled him in on her suspicions, he'd been swayed.

She'd also contacted Smith, and he'd put officers on standby, ready to move if she made the call.

He was a hard-ass at times, but he knew Jamie was smart, and when she brought the sort of evidence that she had to him, he'd shaken off the anger at being woken up before six in the morning and snapped to attention.

She appreciated that.

Mary, though, wasn't quite as enthusiastic, or hurried.

It was after six now, and they were still waiting on her to arrive at the shelter.

She'd been more difficult to wake up, and even more difficult to persuade to come down before the usual opening time. Jamie didn't like throwing the weight of the Met around, but sometimes she had to.

And now was one of those occasions.

'Finally,' Jamie said, watching Mary's estate car sidle around the corner and pull up in front of the shelter. She and Roper got out in unison and walked purposefully across the road.

She checked the street instinctively, but it was empty and quiet.

'Mrs Cartwright,' Jamie said, jogging over, ignoring the pain in her elbow.

'Detective,' Mary replied, seemingly devoid of the perpetual happiness she'd carried thus far. It didn't seem like she was a morning person. 'I hope this is worth whatever it is you're looking for.'

Jamie kept her lips pressed together. If she said, 'Me too,' it would have been a lie. She desperately wanted it to be pointless. She'd be much happier if it was.

Mary opened the front door and it swung inwards.

Jamie stared into the darkness and shivered again, feeling about as claustrophobic as she had done in the box.

Mary sighed and walked in, mumbling about how she didn't see why this couldn't wait until nine.

She clicked the lights on without looking and moved forward, fumbling through the big bunch of keys she had. There were at least twenty on it, and Jamie couldn't possibly imagine what they were all for.

She didn't ask as Mary moved towards Elliot's office, finding the basement door key as she did.

'Ah,' Mary said, pulling it out and holding it up. 'Here we go.'

Jamie resisted the urge to tell her to hurry up.

Roper was right on her shoulder, the both of them shuffling behind Mary, willing her to move faster.

She approached the door slowly, unhurriedly, and bent forward a little, inspecting the handle.

'Oh, he has taken the handle off, hasn't he?' she remarked.

'Yes,' Jamie said through gritted teeth.

'I wonder why he'd do that?'

Jamie felt like yelling, *open the door and we'll find out!* But she didn't. She just shrugged. 'Who knows.'

'And he's painted it shut.' Mary ran her nail up the seam and it flaked off over her finger in a kinked tape of paint. 'How strange.'

'It's meant to look sealed,' Jamie said, hoping that an explanation would be enough to press her into action. 'Unused.'

'That makes sense,' Mary said, going back to the lock. 'Don't want anyone going down there.'

Jamie narrowed her eyes at Mary.

'On account of the rat poison.'

'Right,' Jamie said, sighing. 'If you wouldn't mind, can you...' She nodded to the lock.

'Someone's in a hurry.'

'Just a bit.'

Mary raised her eyebrows and turned back to the lock, pressing the key into it. It slid in with a grating noise and hit a stop about three-quarters of the way up the key.

She made a, 'Huh,' sound and jiggled it, pulling it out and pushing it back again. Same thing. It didn't fit. 'I thought this was the right key,' Mary said. 'I was sure of it. Look.' She held it up to Jamie. On the bottom of it someone had written a small 'C' in permanent marker. 'C for cellar,' Mary said.

Jamie only needed to take one look at it to know that it used to be the right key, but wasn't any more. 'Move out of the way,' Jamie commanded.

'Sorry?'

'Move,' she snapped this time and Mary did, stepping sideways like the floor was falling out from under her.

'Roper?' she said, turning to him.

'Yeah?'

'Put it through.'

'What?' He looked surprised.

'Break the door down.'

'Jamie, I don't know if—'

'Now, Roper!' She practically yelled it. Her blood was running cold, her heart beating fast and quiet.

He swallowed, seeing the seriousness in her face, and drew a deep breath.

Without another word, he took one step, leaned into his left foot, and slammed his right heel into the wood next to the lock.

'Oh!' Mary cried in shock. 'What are you—'

'Again!' ordered Jamie.

Roper wound up and lashed out with a grunt.

The wood splintered.

Mary was flapping her hands. 'You can't just—'

'Again!'

He kicked.

'Again!'

A crack ran diagonally through the door.

'Again!'

Mary was wailing about her rental deposit.

'Again!'

Roper was sweating already.

Jamie would have done it herself if it wouldn't have destroyed her arm.

He was making do though.

Roper panted, stepped back, and put his hands on his hips.

'Roper,' Jamie said, focused on the door. 'Again.'

He took a final breath, stepped in, lifted his knee, and threw his weight into the wood.

The frame cracked and it flew inwards, sending splinters flying into the darkness behind.

Jamie's left hand shot out and she grabbed Roper's arm before he fell after it.

'Jesus,' he said, looking down into the hole.

Jamie was silent.

A cold stream of air curled from the basement, the smell of bleach hanging thick in it.

Jamie released Roper's arm, her fists closing, and she moved past him, taking the first step.

He followed behind her as they traced their way down, their breath ringing around them.

Above, Mary was walking in circles, throwing her hands in the air, jabbering away to them about kicking the door through.

Jamie tuned it out, getting to the bottom.

There was another door there pulled to against the frame.

It wasn't locked or even bolted. It was just a piece of plywood suspended on shiny hinges with what looked like heavy woollen blankets nailed to it.

Jamie rested her hand on the damp material and pushed.

It creaked open and something clicked above her. She froze and looked up, seeing a magnetic sensor sticking out just a centimetre above where the top of the door had been.

The room beyond was shadowed by a dim red light, its brilliance failing to do more than vaguely outline what it contained.

Jamie stepped cautiously forward and craned her neck to get a look at what had made the noise.

There was a little white box hooked up to it, a red light glowing from its centre.

They'd definitely tripped something.

She drew a sharp, chemical-laced breath and took another step, letting Roper down into the room next to her.

'What the hell?' Roper mumbled, squinting around.

The room was huge, but they could barely see six feet in.

Something was in front of them — it looked like a wall, but they couldn't make it out.

Jamie was practically holding her breath.

She reached into her pocket and pulled out her multi-tool, flicking the torch on.

The thin, white beam lanced into the darkness and fell on the wall.

Except it wasn't a wall at all.

Translucent plastic sheeting glimmered in the light, suspended from the ceiling.

'Roper,' Jamie whispered, turning to see his features grave in the darkness. 'Look for a light switch.'

He nodded, fishing in his coat pocket for a pair of latex gloves.

Jamie shone the torch at her feet, seeing that she was standing on bare earth, and pushed the end of the torch into her mouth, reaching into her own pocket for gloves.

She managed to pull one on to her left hand with difficulty, and left her right free to hold the torch, the cast stopping at her knuckles.

Roper shuffled around behind her, and then a buzz of electricity surging through ancient wires filled the darkness.

Overhead, strip lights chugged to life, strobing before they lit the space.

Jamie and Roper both froze, staring at the construction in front of them.

The polythene had been hooked up to what looked like a steel frame.

Four long struts rose vertically until they reached the concrete ceiling overhead, and then shot off at right angles, forming a steel cube.

Sheets had been affixed on all sides, sealing it in as a self-contained space.

The lighting in the rest of the basement was reasonably dim, but inside the cube, it was blinding.

It filled their entire field of vision.

Jamie had to squint.

She swallowed, stepping forward.

In front of it a piece of carpet had been laid down, and on top of it was a box of shoe-covers and a plastic tray filled with a shallow pool of what smelled like disinfectant.

Roper came up behind her and stared at it.

He didn't know what he was looking at, but Jamie's dread was growing with every passing second.

She approached the carpet and reached out for a split in the plastic, pulling back the one sheet that didn't seem to be fixed to the floor.

All the others were.

She pulled sideways, her fingers shaking, and stared into the bright interior, her heart seizing in her chest.

The floor had been raised up on the steel frame, clear of the dirt floor, and non-slip plastic panels had been laid down.

The space was about twelve feet by twelve feet, drowned in a harsh light. An articulated lamp hung from a hinged arm.

And in the centre of it all was something that made her blood turn to ice.

A steel table.

All around it was a blood-trough.

'What the…' Roper breathed, pulling the sheet from her grip and stepping inside next to her.

'It's an operating theatre,' Jamie said, her voice alien to her.

Everything was surgically clean.

At the far side, there was a steel desk set up, a tray of surgical tools — scalpels, clamps, saws — covered in a sealed plastic sheet. Next to it was a glass-fronted fridge. A faint blue light was emanating from inside.

She didn't need to go over to see what was in there.

Blood bags.

Lots of them.

There were IV stands and a heart monitor too, and through the sheeting opposite Jamie could make out the blurred line of a cable that ran vertically up the outside of the theatre, providing power to the fridge and the lamps.

'What do—'

'Let's keep looking,' Jamie said, cutting him off. She didn't want to say anything or even think about it until they'd seen it all.

She started backing up, the stench of bleach making her feel sick to her stomach.

Except she knew it wasn't the bleach making her feel ill at all.

The sheeting brushed across her shoulders and then she was back in the dankness of the basement, swimming in the thick, wet air.

Roper came after her as she tiptoed towards the corner of the frame. There was still a lot of basement beyond, and she didn't know what there was to find.

Jamie got to the corner and stopped, her heart sinking.

All of her fears were confirmed.

A lot of junk had been dragged to the walls and piled up, but the wooden box sitting in the middle of the space in the middle was unmistakable.

The lid had been pushed off and was lying against the crate.

The scores in it shone black in the half-light, smears of blood trailing from the bottom of them.

Fingernail marks.

Oliver's fingernail marks.

The shelter was no more than about a kilometre and a half from the river.

He had run there from here.

Jamie swallowed hard.

Roper was silent next to her.

They both moved forward slowly, neither able to muster the strength, or courage to move quickly.

As she got closer she could see the bent nails sticking out of the lid, could see the blood caked around the edges where he'd heaved himself out with bloodied hands.

He was never meant to escape.

Jamie approached it, holding down the bile rising in her throat.

Roper walked to her left, circling the theatre.

She stared into the box, remembering her dream. Remembering how horrible it had been.

She couldn't imagine what it would have been like to wake up in one in reality.

'Jamie.' It was Roper.

She turned to look at him, feeling her jaw shudder, her teeth chatter. She had come out in gooseflesh. 'What is it?' she asked, barely able to squeeze the words out.

Roper was next to a wooden shipping, holding the lid open with one hand. He reached inside and took hold of something, pulling it out and holding it up.

The box was red, with a white handle.

Jamie stared at it in disbelief, the puzzle pieces snapping altogether at once in front of her eyes.

'It's a transplant box,' Roper said, his voice like gravel.

'He's harvesting them,' Jamie muttered, the words barely forming on her tongue.

She'd said *them*. She only knew of Oliver. But she thought back to all the other missing persons reports she'd read over. Thousands every year.

How many had he cut into? And why?

Vomit rose in her throat and choked her.

'Jamie,' Roper said, putting it back, his eyes fixed on something behind her.

She knew from his tone that things were about to get worse.

'Look.' He lifted a hand and pointed past her. Past the box that Elliot had been keeping Oliver in.

Jamie turned, feeling her heels grind in the soft earth, and followed his finger.

Beyond the crate, in a neat row, she could see ridges in the dirt.

Mounds.

They caught the light like waves, rolling gently towards the wall.

One, two, three, four, five, she could make out, just from the first glance.

Her cheeks burned hot, her throat closing up altogether.

There wasn't a doubt in her mind.

Tears formed in the corners of her eyes as she looked at them, knowing what they were.

Graves.

Lots of them.

41

It was a sea of flashing blue lights.

Jamie was standing on the kerb, floating in it.

A door slammed in her peripheral vision and a figure strode towards her.

It was DCI Smith, and he didn't look happy.

'Johansson,' he called, making a beeline for her.

The sun was still lurking beyond the buildings, but the street was lit up by dozens of headlights and spinning blues. Four patrol cars, two ambulances, canine units, medical examiner's vans, SOCOs in white plastic jumpsuits — you name it, they were there.

The entire street had been cordoned off.

Jamie looked around, seeing Smith approach. 'Sir,' she said, her voice catching in her throat.

'What a mess,' he said as he got close, dropping his own so no one else would hear.

Though the street was abuzz with activity, an eerie silence had settled over the area. All the lights flashed, but no sound rang from them.

Everything was quiet.

As a graveyard.

Jamie grimaced at the thought.

'What's the latest update?' Smith asked, folding his arms.

'Uh, three confirmed—'

'Five,' Roper said, stepping down out of the shelter behind her. He pulled off a pair of latex gloves and ran his hand through his hair. 'Five bodies confirmed. But they think some of them may be stacked.'

'Jesus,' Smith muttered. 'And what about Day?'

Jamie cleared her throat. 'Uniformed officers have been dispatched to St. Mary's. He was on shift until eight and when I spoke to him at five he was heading into surgery. I'm hoping we can pick him up as he comes out.'

Smith narrowed his eyes at her. The fact that she was making social calls to what could only be described as a serial killer wasn't something Smith was happy about, but an hour ago, everyone else in the Met except Jamie was sure that Donnie Bats had killed Oliver.

He said nothing.

No one could have known.

Smith sighed. 'Keep me updated. I want to know the second they have this bastard in custody.'

Jamie nodded. 'Of course...' She paused for a second and then opened her mouth again. 'Look, sir, I—'

'Save it, Johansson. From what I understand, people thought he was a saint. You couldn't have known.'

I could have, Jamie thought. *I should have.*

'The important thing now is that we get him. Alright? Focus on that. And keep me—'

He trailed off as Jamie's phone started ringing.

She dug it out of her pocket and glanced up at Smith. It was the uniformed officers.

'Yes?' she said, answering quickly.

Smith leaned in.

'Detective Johansson,' a voice said on the other end. 'He's... Uh... He's not here.'

Jamie's hand tightened around the phone, her jaw flexing. 'What do you mean he's not there?'

Smith pinched the bridge of his nose and shook his head.

'He's, uh — they're saying that he was scheduled for a six a.m. surgery, but missed it. No one's seen him, and his car was clocked leaving the car park, too. What do you want us to do here?'

Jamie exhaled, forcing down the urge to scream and launch her phone into the shelter wall. 'Grace Melver,' she said through gritted teeth.

'Who?'

'Grace Melver — she's a patient there. See if she's been checked out. And get the security footage from the car park.'

Smith was already on his phone, barking orders at the operator. 'I want officers at his home, now. Freeze his bank accounts, put out a bulletin on his car. Alert Interpol, border patrol, traffic, everyone. I want to shut this guy down before he can even think about which way to run.'

'She's gone too,' the officer on the other end of Jamie's line said. She could hear the voice of someone she guessed was an administrator in the background. 'Checked out six minutes before Day left the car park.'

'They're together,' Jamie muttered to herself.

'What was that?'

'Nothing. Just get the footage.' She hung up before the officer could say anything else, and turned to see Smith red with rage.

'Do it now,' he half-shouted into the phone. 'He does not get out of the city.' He hung up and shoved his phone back into his coat, heading for his car.

'Sir,' Jamie called after him.

'Don't,' he snapped, turning back to her. He lifted his finger at her. 'Just don't...' He was seething. 'If I find out that your phone call tipped him off...' He shook his head. 'Find him, Johansson. If you value your job, you'll find this son of a bitch.'

'But—'

'Just find him!' Smith stormed towards his car, slid into the driver's seat, and peeled away with a long note of tire-squeal.

Jamie turned to Roper, who could have been a statue. He turned his head to her slowly. 'Now what?' he asked.

Jamie sucked in a deep breath and stared at her phone. 'I… I just don't know.'

42

Jamie pulled up outside Elliot's apartment to find two patrol cars and an armed response van stationed at the kerb.

The armed officers were trudging back down the front steps defeatedly while the uniformed officers cordoned off the area and held back the morning commuters, diverting them around.

A crowd was beginning to gather at the tape and the sun had risen.

Jamie walked across the road with Roper at her elbow and caught the attention of the captain leading his men back towards the van. Jamie didn't recognise him. It wasn't Hassan.

She and Roper flashed their badges and he stopped.

'What happened?' Jamie asked, knowing the answer.

'No sign of him,' the captain said, a tall guy with buzz cut, the nose of his rifle pointed at the ground, his right elbow crooked, hand on the grip, index finger flat against the stock. 'We breached, swept the apartment, but there was no sign that he'd been there in at least twelve hours. No clothes missing, nothing to suggest that he'd been home. Though the fridge was stocked and the bins were full.' He sighed. 'Looks like he made a clean break for it.'

Jamie ground her teeth as the captain nodded to them and turned away.

This was getting worse by the minute.

The security footage from the hospital showed that the second he'd hung up the phone, he headed straight for Grace's room, checked her out, and then left the hospital without missing a beat.

They were still trying to requisition the security footage from surrounding buildings, and were yet to track his route more than a few hundred metres from the car park.

London was one of the most heavily surveilled cities in the world, but Elliot was thoroughly prepared for this eventuality. He'd taken streets that no one would have normally, just because they were blind spots in the city's vision.

And now he was out there somewhere, loose, and he knew that Jamie was coming for him.

'What did you say to him?' Roper asked, barely above a whisper.

She knew he meant Elliot. He'd asked the question four times already. She didn't know how long she could just ignore it.

'Nothing,' she said. 'I didn't say anything that would tip him off.'

'Well, you and I both know that's a lie,' Roper said, turning his back to the armed officers.

Jamie stayed quiet.

'You wouldn't say anything intentionally. I know that.'

She fired him a look. As if he had to question it.

'But you obviously said something that alerted him to the fact that you were on the trail, at least. That you had a suspicion.' He hung his head and kicked at a bit of grass poking through the kerb. 'I'm not qualified to give advice — and certainly not about work, but... There'll be an inquiry into this, Jamie.' He looked at her. He was being sincere. 'And I don't want one mistake to cost you everything, okay?'

She nodded, unable to find any words to say.

'Just... Just think about what you're going to say. The only story they'll have is yours.' He sighed. 'We'd have still been trying to pin it on Bats if it wasn't for you, but that doesn't mean they'll give you a pass on this. I just... I just don't want to see you go.' He reached out and put a hand on her shoulder. 'But I can't help you. You're on your own.'

She nodded again. She knew that. Roper was on thin ice as it was. He couldn't be involved, and trying would only cause more harm.

He was right. She'd have to come up with an alternative to the truth, and she'd have to stick to it.

They'd gone to Elliot's work, and they'd gone to his home, but he wasn't in either.

Now they were scouring the city for him.

But there was one thing that they hadn't tried. It was almost too obvious to even bother with, but Jamie was out of options and verging on another suspension for misconduct.

If there was ever a time to go for a long shot. It was now.

She thumbed open the case-file on her phone and opened a new audio recording.

Jamie set it to run in the background and then closed the file, pulling up Elliot's number instead.

She took a deep breath, checked the street on autopilot, and then dialled.

There was a crackling sound for a few seconds and she thought it was just going to go straight to voicemail.

And then it didn't.

It rang once and she felt her heart hammer in her chest.

Her palms began to sweat, her throat tight.

It rang again.

And again.

He wasn't going to pick up.

Why would he?

If he had any sense he would have hurled his phone into the Thames or thrown it onto a train heading in the opposite direction. If he was smart enough to dodge cameras then he'd be smart enough to—'

'Jamie?'

Elliot's voice rang in her head like someone had shoved an ice-pick in her ear.

She wasn't sure if she imagined it, or he'd really just picked up.

'Elliot?' she croaked.

'It's good to hear your voice,' he said calmly.

Jamie strained to hear every word, to see if there was anything she could pick out to place him. 'You too,' she said automatically. As much as she hated it, she was glad to hear it.

There was still a lingering, waning hope that he'd say, *I can explain! It's all a misunderstanding and it's not me at all...* But she knew he couldn't. And he wouldn't.

'How is your morning going?' he asked as though nothing was wrong.

'Oh, you know,' she said, looking at the flashing blue lights around her. 'The usual... Quiet.'

He chuckled softly.

Prickles again.

'How did your surgery go?'

'Routine,' he said.

'You still at work?' She was struggling to keep her voice even, her heart plunging in and out in her chest. She could feel the blood rushing in her neck, her jaw, at the back of her eyes, in her ears.

'Just popped out.'

'Where to?'

'I just had to run a quick errand.'

'Oh, is everything okay?' It was almost easy to forget reality when they were talking like this. Almost. It made it all feel like a dream.

'Yeah, of course.'

She exhaled slowly, feeling her hand shaking around the phone. 'Are we, uh...' She cleared her throat. 'Are we still on for dinner tonight?'

He paused for a second and she thought he was about to hang up. She wasn't tracing the call. There was no point. His position could be triangulated through the GPS on his phone, or pinged off the nearest antenna towers if he'd turned it off. If his phone was on, they'd know where he was.

But she thought he was too smart for that. The crackling at the start

— she guessed some sort of forwarding device, maybe. That his phone was somewhere far, far away from where he was, and that the call was being routed to him.

He'd been planning an escape like this for who knows how long.

Smart enough to not get caught.

Smart enough to plan for that eventuality anyway.

'Yeah,' he said, a tone of sadness in his voice. 'We're still on for dinner.'

'You know,' she said, looking up, feeling her eyes burn in the cool morning air. 'I'd really like to see you. Do you want to get breakfast instead? Just, uh, tell me where you are, and I can—'

'Jamie,' he whispered, his voice soft.

She stopped talking.

He sighed slowly on the other end of the phone. 'I really am sorry.'

'For what?' She feigned ignorance.

'Jamie.'

She swallowed. 'Where are you, Elliot? This can only end one way.'

'Rain-check on dinner, I guess.'

'Tell me where you are. Make this easy on yourself.'

'You know I can't do that.'

'At least let Grace go. Just drop her off and—'

'Grace is here because she wants to be. I'm not holding her against her will.'

'Goddammit, Elliot.' Jamie pulled the phone from her ear, feeling anger rising in her chest. She pushed it back against her cheek. 'Don't do this. Turn yourself in and we can talk about this. We can figure it out, and…'

'There's nothing to figure out, Jamie.'

'Then just… Then just tell me why. Why? How? How could you…' Her voice was cracking, rising, becoming strange in her ears.

'Do you remember what I said to you? That some people are worth saving?'

'Grace.'

'Grace, and others.' He collected his words for a second. 'Not all lives are equal. And life isn't fair. Children die of heart defects every day. Of leukaemia. Of kidney failure, of a thousand different things. Parents lose children, children lose parents. Lovers lose partners, and brothers lose sisters.' He sighed. 'Do you know how many people die every year waiting for organ transplants that aren't coming? Bone marrow has to be donated willingly. Humans can survive with one kidney, half a liver. They can give away a lobe of their lung. But they don't. They hold onto them. Destroy them with cigarettes. They poison their livers and kidneys with alcohol, destroy their hearts and bodies with drugs... They squander what they have. They hate themselves, their lives. They don't want to live, to survive. They want to die. And they want to waste everything they have. While good people die waiting for a day that's never coming.'

'And you're the one righting that wrong, are you?' She couldn't keep the cold scorn from her voice.

'I'm allowing people who deserve to live another chance to do so. I'm saving lives.'

'You're harvesting innocent people. Like animals. You're killing them.'

'I'm making their lives worth something.'

'You're a monster.'

'They're monsters. None of them innocent. All of them selfish, addicted, weak—'

'Oliver was innocent.'

'No he wasn't.'

'He was just a kid!' Jamie was nearly yelling.

Roper came back towards her, a questioning look in his eyes.

'He was as bad as the rest of them. And he was the biggest waste of all. A girl was waiting for his heart. A boy for his kidneys. And now they'll die. And his death is on them.'

'No, it's not!' She shook her head and flung tears onto the cold, damp tarmac.

Roper was hovering, leaning in, listening.

'He was a heroin addict. He was a thief. He was nothing worth saving.' Elliot drew a deep breath. 'He came to me. Told me what he wanted to do — to broker a deal with Paxton, with Bats, to ransom himself back to his parents. To extort them, to take everything from them.'

'For him and Grace. So they could get away from it all.'

'He wasn't going to get clean. He couldn't. He tried. He failed.' Elliot paused, settled himself a little until his voice was dripping calm again. 'He would have wasted it all. Killed himself and Grace. Shot it all into their arms and died. And for what? Two more meaningless deaths.'

'You don't get to decide.'

'I know you don't understand.'

'It's you who doesn't understand, Elliot.'

'He came to me. Asked me to help him with it. To look after Grace while he was gone. But I couldn't do that. I couldn't let him do it. So I took him.'

'You *took* him?' Her voice was incredulous.

'Yes. It wasn't planned. Not him, at least. But it wasn't difficult to find people in need.'

'So you shoved him in a goddamn box? Pumped him full of drugs, put him through detox, fattened him up ready for harvest? Is that it? Just like that? Like an animal?'

'Humans do it to animals all the time. Pigs. Cows. Chickens. Kept in cages so small they can't even turn around. And I'd say that an animal is far more innocent than Oliver Hammond was. And yet we slaughter them by the thousands. Cast their carcasses into the fire like they're worthless. And that's the difference, Jamie. Oliver, the others, they weren't innocent. And I made their lives worth something.'

'You're sick.' She was shaking, ready to empty her stomach all over the street. 'You're sick, Elliot, and you need help. Tell me where you are, and I'll—'

'No, Jamie.' She couldn't hear any remorse in his voice. 'Putting me behind bars will solve nothing. The world will keep turning, keep darkening. There are people out there who deserve to live, and those that don't.'

'You don't get to be the one to make that call.'

'I already am.'

She grit her teeth so hard she thought they'd crack. 'Are you going to kill Grace?' She had to ask it. She couldn't not know. After everything they'd done to save her. Was he just going to use her for parts, too?

'Grace is finally getting her new start. I'm not a psychopath, Jamie. I don't have a need to kill, a bloodlust to satiate.'

'Just a god-complex,' she growled, bile rising in her throat.

There was silence on the line for a long time.

Jamie listened to him breathe, quiet and steady in the ether. 'This is your last chance, Elliot. Give up. Turn yourself in. It will be better.'

'Goodbye, Jamie.'

'Elliot—'

'I'll see you soon.'

'Not if I see you first.'

He chuckled softly and a cold hand ran itself up her back.

'I'm looking forward to it.'

The line went dead and a surge of fury rippled up from her heels and seized her body. A strangulated, guttural noise rose in her throat and she twisted, slinging the phone into the wall of Elliot's building with everything she had.

It impacted and shattered, splintering into the morning twilight.

Jamie swayed, and then fell forwards, landing on her knees right there in the street.

Tears ran hot down her cheeks.

Her eyes closed against the sea of flashing blues.

After a few seconds, she felt Roper's hands on her shoulders, pulling her up to her feet.

She let him lead her away towards her car, and towards whatever lay ahead.

The only thing that she could think of was Elliot.

That he was out there somewhere, scalpel in hand, leaving a trail of blood and bodies in his wake.

He said he wasn't going to stop. So whatever happened — whether she had a badge on her hip or not — she couldn't either.

Not until he was behind bars, or dead. Whichever came first. She didn't care.

Roper stood her next to the passenger door and let go of her shoulders, seeing if she'd stand on her own.

He circled, going for the driver's side.

But Jamie wasn't looking at him.

Her father was standing next to her, leaning against the car, drawing hard on a cigarette. He looked at her with her own blue eyes.

She stared back.

He blew out a long stream of smoke and it curled upwards into the night. 'Shit-pie, this one,' he said, his voice low and dark.

Jamie set her jaw.

'Well?' he asked.

'Well what?' she growled.

'You just going to roll over, get fired? Let him get away?'

She turned her back on him and stared into the dawn-riddled sky.

It was the colour of blood.

'Don't look away, Jamie,' he said.

She filled her lungs.

'There's work to do.'

She swallowed hard, clenched her shaking hand into a fist. 'I know.'

Roper poked his head out of the door and looked across the roof at her. 'Who are you talking to?'

'No one,' she said.

He nodded slowly. 'What do you want to do now?'

Jamie took hold of the handle and pulled the door open. 'Now? Now I want to catch this son of a bitch.'

Roper grinned. 'Well okay then. Let's go.'

She slotted down into the passenger's seat and leaned her head back.

Roper got into the driver's side and she handed him the keys.

He cranked them in the ignition and adjusted the seat.

Jamie looked in the rearview, saw her dad sitting in the back. He smiled. Proud, almost. 'Go get him, Jamie.'

'I will.'

'What was that?' Roper asked.

'Nothing,' Jamie said with a sigh, staring out at the glowing skyline, soaked red in the rising sun. 'Just drive.'

AUTHOR'S NOTE

Bare Skin was a novel that I had been thinking about for a while.

I love and have loved hard-boiled detective novels since I can remember. There's nothing quite like a lone wolf taking on a big, dark, twisting case, and coming out of the other end bloodied and broken. But on top.

I knew what I wanted to create, but it took a while to choose the right story.

I wanted to do something modern, but something distinctly real. To start with a character like Jamie, at the beginning of her detective career, and to take her on the journey that so many detectives have already lived by the time we read their books.

Scandi-noir novels that feature characters like Jamie's father have always been something that I wanted to write, and I planned to write one of those first. But while in London a few years ago, I saw a place not unlike the bridge described in the book. A collection of tents and tarps. People huddled together in the mud and the dirt. The people who fell through the cracks of society. That others walked past, and just didn't see.

And my mind began working then.

I wanted a villain that would plague Jamie. That would get under her skin, and stay there, for books to come.

I talked to the father of a friend, who worked as a detective and police officer for many years, both in and outside the city. And we spoke at length about the homelessness crisis, about the drugs, the prostitution that goes on. About how impenetrable that world is for the law — as often the people who need the most help are, in effect, criminals themselves. They're in possession of drugs that they need to face their lives, they're in possession of weapons that they need to protect themselves, and they're in possession of stolen goods that they've taken just to make ends meet.

This is an imperfect world, and it is one that works against them.

And when we got onto the topic of how many go missing each year, seemingly disappearing into nothingness, an idea began to form.

When it came to the modern aspects of the book, I was torn. Unsure whether readers would be interested in the more procedural side of the story. And even whether that was something I wanted to write.

I felt a certain push towards wanting to include some realism, in having Jamie and Roper being the kind of detectives doing the sort of police work that really happens. Talking to witnesses, calling parents. Paperwork.

But striking that balance was always key for me, and I hope that I made the right calls.

It was always at the forefront of my mind that Jamie be believable, too. That, as a woman, the book faced head-on the challenges she would face. The difficulty her smaller physical stature might pose. But in giving her the tools to defend herself, I was conscious of introducing the violence she was capable of in a measured way. I wanted to use her father as a way to do that. As a mirror that she holds up to herself. And in doing so, I hope I drew a line between this novel and those hard-boiled detective stories we all know.

This novel never sought to tear them down, but simply to pay homage in a certain way. But then to build upon as well. The world is changing, and while those novels will forever be written, I hope that there is enough space for a novel like this, too.

One where the main character isn't kicking down doors, shoving their gun in someone's face, or getting into fights at every turn.

And in this, there is space. That as Jamie grows into the detective I know she can be, that she can be forced to confront the necessity of violence. That she can be placed into situations were she must do the things she strives to resist. And in that, I hope that those scenes, those stories, are more rewarding.

In reality, I am not a detective myself. And I have not read every detective novel ever. But I am a fan of the genre, a reader, like you, and I am someone who just wants to create a stories that feel rich, and dynamic. That have layers to them, and that feel real.

The second novel in this series is completed, and will be launching soon. The third is being written, the fourth is spread across my wall in post-it notes and scribbled in notebooks, waiting to be assembled.

This is a labour of love, and if you enjoyed this novel, then you might be glad to know that there is a lot of life left for Jamie to live, and a lot more cases to solve. The question is, what toll will it take on her, and by the end, who will she be?

Jamie will change and grow with each book, and if nothing else, her journey will be a story to remember.

Read on to discover more about *Fresh Meat*, the follow-up to *Bare Skin*.

FRESH MEAT

Book 2 in the DS Jamie Johansson Prequel Trilogy

Unable to escape the bloody grip of Elliot Day, Jamie's life will never be the same again.

With a capture attempt gone wrong and the murder of an Interpol agent weighing on her shoulders, Elliot reaches out, and in recompense for his actions, offers Jamie a deal. Information for freedom.

Names begin to arrive in Jamie's letterbox — names of criminals about to strike.

She ignores the first, but quickly realises that Elliot isn't playing games. He's well connected, and he's not bluffing. These people are dangerous, and need to be stopped.

Then, when a message arrives detailing the ruthless murder of an unknown pregnant woman, whose investigation is dead in the water, a series of events is set in motion that could cost Jamie her job, and even her life.

Men far worse than Elliot Day lurk in the darkest parts of the city. And Jamie may have just shined a light on the wrong ones.

Hot on the trail of a human trafficking ring that has ties to criminals all over the city, Jamie finds that guys of this calibre don't play by the rules and aren't afraid to get their hands dirty. One wrong step could mean the end for her.

But if there's one thing that Jamie's father taught her, it's that what's right and justice aren't always the same thing.

Sometimes, you have to talk the law into your own hands to get things done.

And Detective Sergeant Jamie Johansson is about to learn that the hard way.

———

Fresh Meat, the thrilling followup to Bare Skin is out now!

Printed in Great Britain
by Amazon